W9-BDY-688

RITUAL MURDER

The mnoerri moved across the meadow, forming a rough circle where they sank down to sit or lie on the ground, casting their spears and pouches behind them in the tall grass. The circle grew tighter, mnoerri touching mnoerri, wing-flaps outstretched and rustling.

Out from the shelter of the trees bounded ten or twelve kelg, moonlight gleaming on their fangs and unsheathed claws. The leader gave a gargling cry of triumph and leaped upon the nearest of the mnoerri, razor claws shearing through the soft flesh. Not a mnoerri moved to rise or defend itself.

The attack was no meal; it was a massacre.

WALK
THE
MOONS
ROAD

Jim Aikin

A Del Rey Book

BALLANTINE BOOKS • NEW YORK

A Del Rey Book
Published by Ballantine Books

Copyright © 1985 by Jim Aikin

All rights reserved under International and Pan-American Copyright
Conventions. Published in the United States by Ballantine Books,
a division of Random House, Inc., New York, and simultaneously
in Canada by Random House of Canada Limited, Toronto.

Library of Congress Catalog Card Number: 84-91808

ISBN 0-345-32169-3

Manufactured in the United States of America

First Edition: June 1985

Cover art by Ralph McQuarrie

for Marie

Moons Road: the luminous band visible in the west after sunset and in the east before sunrise, believed to be a ring of unknown composition encircling the world.

to walk the Moons Road (idiom, original Falneresc): to wander, especially along tide-washed shoreline; to talk at length and without point; to be visible at all times; to serve as an example to others; to be an adherent of an esoteric doctrine; to retire to an inaccessible place; to act in a disturbing or inexplicable manner; to speak in error or act inappropriately, usually through ignorance rather than guile; to act without thought of consequences; to engage in a difficult enterprise, one whose outcome is uncertain; to be in love; to die

—Martella Berimbba Quoi
The Great Dictionary of Olmalinu

Chapter 1

*T*he last gray glow of sunset hung low in the west, a landfall of daylight draining silently away before a foaming sea of stars. Across the dark reef of hills the yellow lanterns of Falnerescu were a net of jewels. Below, the placid swell of the bay threw back bright scraps of city and sky; above stood the Moons Road, a ribbon arcing silver upward to where it reddened and was lost in shadow, half an unwavering metal rainbow at whose foot was strewn the gold of the approaching city. Three moons rode the sky tonight: yellow-brown Cheth, a crescent in the west, a fingersbreadth to starboard of the Moons Road; Aptar the swift, a blue-white pebble gleaming in the east; and green Nardis, plump and gibbous at the zenith, Nardis who was said to watch over childbirth and the fecundity of crops. Long after midnight the fourth moon—gray Gavril with its enigmatic dark streaks, the scholar's moon—would rise, and the Moons Road, radiant, would follow it up the eastern sky, drawing the day forth out of the sea.

Leaning out at the bow rail, the lilith let the cooling breeze stroke her cheeks and brow, and tasted the salty-sour smell of land. Below and behind her the oars of the galley dipped in rhythmic unison, leaving faint swirls of foam in the glassy water, and the boards beneath her slippers throbbed with the deep slow strokes of the drum, the ship's heartbeat, that she had heard so many days now, waking and sleeping, that it was in her blood and she heard it no more. Her gauzy cloak, the tawny cream of tree-milk spiced with herbs, fluttered gently along the contours of her body, hinting at what it concealed. She had drawn the veil away and let the hood fall back onto her shoulders; she wanted to *see* Falnerescu if she was to visit it, not be carried in and out again in a box. Her long dark hair was caught at her neck with a silver clasp. She lifted one hand from the rail to snatch the clasp away so her hair could blow free, but stopped, hand raised, to look out of the corner of her eye at the tall man standing beside her. She had better not. Qob Qobba was kind, but he could not be expected to approve, not with the harbor pilot aboard. The pilot's cutter had intercepted them late in the afternoon in the deep waters offshore, and the pilot stood now on the afterdeck, helmsman at one elbow and Captain Bolya at the other. And of course the pilot was not Vli. Even among the Vli a lilith's hair was a thing to be hidden, a secret glory that one might unveil and touch, tenderly, lingeringly, in the intimacy of the Nest, but hardly something that might be let blow in the wind. To have thrown back the hood, here under the waking stars, was daring enough.

"My lilith, it is unseemly to stand so exposed," Qob Qobba said as if echoing her thought. "Will you not cover yourself?"

"I only wanted to see. It's so beautiful." The city spread out its winking net, and up from it the Moons Road arched, reddening. "Would you deny me beauty?"

"My lilith knows I can deny her nothing. But if the people see that you have appeared unhooded within view of the harbor pilot, they will be greatly disturbed. I myself might be inclined to ignore so minor a dereliction, at least at such a distance and in such poor light. But all those aboard are not as broad-minded as I." He looked at her meaningfully. Qob Qobba was tall and bone-lean, with a thick mop of tightly curled red hair that stood up startlingly above his balding dome of brow. Thin lines incised around his wide, nearly lipless mouth said he was no longer young, and his air was as somber as his dark vest, trousers, and high boots. "Will you not at least pull up the hood?" he went on. "The veil you can easily hold aside, if you would see. Then you may look at the city, and I may look at you—and which of us shall see the greater beauty?"

"Flatterer." She fingered the edge of the hood, but did not yet draw it forward. "Oh, listen!" From port and starboard across the water a brass antiphony, deep-throated and sonorous, clanged. "You said our coming would be secret," she said with a pout. "Why are they ringing bells?"

Qob Qobba looked into the dark pools of the lilith's eyes. He was never sure when Zhenuvnili was being truly naive, and when she was teasing him. Her innocence welled up from depths he could not fathom. "Those are bell buoys," he explained. "They mark the channel. Without them the pilot might run us aground."

"I never heard anything like them at home."

"At home the harbor is deep, because the land is rocky. Falnerescu stands at the mouth of a river that flows from the interior of the island. The river alone would silt up the harbor, to say nothing of the tides, if a channel weren't kept dredged. They use barges with weighted buckets on ropes, you see, suspended from long arms that swing out over the water, and a diver goes down—" Arms bent out in a gawky imitation of a dredge, Qob Qobba stopped and ran bony fingers self-consciously through his hair. "Forgive me, my lilith. After a hundred fifty chetnes in the diplomatic service, I still talk like an engineer." A chetne was the period from full to full of yellow-brown Cheth, usually reckoned at forty days. The procession of the stars informed scholars and navigators of a longer 437-day cycle, but in the absence of seasonal weather fluctuations, time was universally measured in 11-day aptarnes or 40-day chetnes.

"I don't mean to bore you," Qobba said, "talking about how foreigners dig in the mud."

"Oh, nothing bores me, Qob. I want to know everything, see everything! There's so much, I hardly know how to take it all in."

"'The world's a soup of strange delights,'" a voice croaked at her elbow, "'of bitter thrills, and greasy frights.'" A stout man, not short but so broad he seemed short, had come up between them. Like the tall man, the newcomer was soberly dressed, with a double chain of silver links doing its best to bring the halves of his vest together over his stomach. His head was an oblong block, the once-red, iron-gray hair cropped close to the scalp. He eyed Zhenuvnili's bare head with something akin to distaste, and breathed out audibly through his nose. "Be so good as to cover yourself," he snapped. "We're charged to keep you safe, and I mean to do it, even if you're determined to shame yourself before these foreign grubblers."

The lilith drew the hood forward over her ears, but peeked out coquettishly at the stout man. "I was only enjoying the night, Ranga," she said. "I do believe you'd prefer it if I entirely lost the capacity to enjoy things."

Ranga Strell flushed in embarrassment, but stood his ground, scowling sourly. "There are enjoyments that are proper," he declared, "and those that are improper. As my lilith well knows."

"I've heard it said that the improper joys are the sweetest, dear Ranga. But surely there's nothing improper about looking at the city! Isn't it beautiful?" She held out a slim hand toward the irregular array of lights.

"It's a nest of filthy foreign grubblers. The sooner we're quit of it and bending oar for home, the better." He seemed about to say more, but closed his mouth and pressed his lips together.

"I know you're right," Zhenuvnili said diplomatically. "Their ways are not our ways, and we mustn't let ourselves become contaminated. I know it's only your concern for me, dear Ranga, and for all our people, that makes you so grumpy. But think what an adventure this is! Qob Qobba here has been voyaging the Island Sea most of his life, so it's little enough to him. And even you have been quite a traveler, riding your coach up and down the provinces. But no lilith has *ever* been so far from Vli Holm!"

"With good reason. One way and another, the whole thing's a mistake. I'm not convinced we should ever have come—and certainly we should never have been persuaded to let *you* come."

Qob Qobba had heard all this before, and knew that arguing with Strell was useless. "Like it or not," he said, "we're here.

Or nearly here." The city was so close that they could make out the tall pilings of the docks standing like the stilt legs of a close-packed herd of marsh-walkers in the distance. "The course ahead is treacherous enough with hidden shoals. Best we pull together. We've all got the same interest at heart."

"Do we?" Ranga Strell said in an ugly tone. "You've lived so long among foreigners, I think you're half a foreigner yourself."

"Ranga, do be reasonable," the lilith said, taking his arm.

"Reason. That's your specialty, isn't it, Qobba? Reason. Compromise. 'Practical' solutions. If we're betrayed, it'll be by reason."

Zhenuvnili lowered her head so the hood and veil fell forward over her face. It pained her when Strell chose to be obstinately bad-tempered, as he had been more and more often the longer the long voyage wore on. But it was not the way of a lilith to argue with a man or woman who was being difficult, to challenge them to change. Change, it was taught, was not brought about by force. Force led only to resistance. Change was born and nurtured in love. Knowing that they were loved, one's lovers were free to love themselves, and loving themselves would naturally love most that which in them was best, and thus would become better. When one could not quite love them, it was better to withdraw; for if ever they felt unloved they would grow fearful, and growing fearful they would cling to whatever was strong and near at hand, which usually meant to whatever anger or fear or pettiness had started the disturbance. This clinging, in turn, would draw them further from the love of the lilith, which was the love of the Goddess Li Herself. To drive anybody away from Li was a terrible sin.

Behind the veil Zhenuvnili could scarcely feel the breeze. She felt stifled, and vaguely grumpy, which was annoying because it was not the way she wanted to feel at the moment she landed in Falnerescu. She needed the nalas to cheer her up. Her first impulse was to send Strell for them, just to have him out of the way for a minute. But that was unworthy of her. Besides, in his present mood he would likely balk. "Qob," she said sweetly, not relinquishing her gentle hold on Strell's elbow, "would you go fetch the nalas? They won't want to miss the landing."

"Certainly, my lilith." With a little bow, Qob Qobba strode away across the foredeck. Why did she prefer that fool Strell's company to his? But no, that was absurd. A lilith loved everybody equally. Zhenuvnili had only been taking the opportunity to soothe Strell by giving him a little attention. She had the wit to see what needed doing. It was getting to them all, though, having her aboard, never more than a few steps away. Having no lilith on a voyage, Qobba decided, was preferable to having a single lilith, in spite of the obvious advantages. Before long they might actually start to compete for her affection—a sacrilege and an obscenity both. Also a decided impediment to the orderly progress of a diplomatic mission, which was, after all, his first priority. The fate of a single lilith, or for that matter of a single fat intractable senator, was nothing beside the fate of their race. And that was what was at stake here, one way or another. Whatever must be done to safeguard the interests of the Vli, Qob Qobba would do it, and add up the cost afterward.

He rapped on the door of the forecabin. After a moment it swung open, and lantern light within traced the yellow outline of a slightly built figure whose long, dull gray robe was hooded and veiled like the lilith's. "Yes?" the figure said in a flat, colorless voice.

"Zhenuvnili sent me to bid you come up on deck, both of you, to see the landing."

"Karanli is not feeling well." The tone might have been faintly disapproving.

"Who is it, Ehli?" said a voice inside the cabin, bobbing uncertainly from word to word.

"Zheni wants us on deck."

"No! I won't go. I'm not going anywhere. I'm staying right here."

The figure at the door nodded politely to Qob Qobba. "You will excuse us. Tell the lilith we will be with her shortly." The door swung closed, leaving Qob Qobba blinking in the darkness on the deck.

Inside, Ehlanli had thrown back her hood and stood, fists on hips, glaring at Karanli. The younger nala was sitting on the narrow starboard bunk, shoulders slumped dejectedly, hugging her knees with both arms and rocking forward and back. Like Ehlanli, she was wearing the gray traveling robe of a nala with its hood back, but where Ehlanli was round-faced and ruddy-cheeked, with a luxuriant mane of golden curls, Karanli's features were ethereal, the skin nearly translucent, chin and nose narrow, cheeks hollow, ears finely chiseled, rust-brown hair drawn back flat against her skull. Around them the cabin was an obstacle course of packing-chests whose lids gaped, revealing tumbles of bright fabric and beveled bottles of perfume. "So," Ehlanli said. "You're going to make trouble again. I don't know why Li Ranli picked you."

Karanli looked around at the bare wood walls of the cabin. "I wish they hadn't taken the hangings down," she said miserably. "I was starting to like it here."

"Like it? That's a new one. You're the one couldn't leave off complaining about how crowded it was, and how the waves made your tummy all queasy."

"Oh, Ehli," Karanli wailed. "Do we *have* to go ashore? Can't we just all stay on the ship till they sign the treaty, and then go straight home again?"

"You can stay if you like," the blond nala said scornfully. "You can spend the rest of your life on a boat if you like, and be the lilith of the waves, and never go ashore again. But that wasn't what Li Ranli sent us to do, was it? She told us to take care of Zheni." Li Ranli, radiantly beautiful, had rested a palm on each nala's forehead, and made them promise to follow Zhenuvnili wherever she went, and obey her wishes, and see that she was comfortable and provided with whatever she might need. "Your trouble," Ehlanli said, "is that you're always thinking of yourself, not how to love others."

"That's not true. I'm thinking of Zheni as much as myself. She could stay here with us, where it's safe."

"It won't be safe here, not when all the oar go ashore. If you want to be safe, you've got to come with us. They've set up a nice Nest for us in some rich merchant's house, with a great big wall around it, and a guard. And we'll be able to take a real bath again! Doesn't that interest you at all?"

"But we'll be surrounded by foreigners!"

"Not in the Nest. We'll never even have to see a foreigner if we don't want to."

"But what if something horrible happens?" the pale nala persisted. "What if something goes wrong, and all the guards are killed, and we can't ever go home again, and we have to spend the rest of our lives living among foreigners, with them always l-l-looking at us?" She drew the robe tighter around her shoulders and clutched the fabric in both fists. Her fingernails were gnawed to nubs.

"Nothing will go wrong," Ehlanli said patiently. "Don't you have any faith in Li? Would She have brought us all this way if She didn't intend to take care of us? We'll be as safe as we would in a Nest at home. I promise. Now, come on. Zheni is waiting."

Karanli untensed her fists slowly, and took deep breaths. "Li," she repeated. "Li will protect us. We are in the heart of Li."

"We are in the heart of Li."

Both nalas made the ritual gesture, touching with the left middle finger first forehead, then breastbone, then groin.

"Come *on*," Ehlanli said, savagely snapping her hood for ward. "Zheni will think we've fallen overboard."

Karanli stretched out her legs and got slowly up from the bunk. After another tense breath, she covered her head and followed the elder nala out the cabin door.

The pilings loomed close now, and the great sonorous beat of the drum had slowed so that the ship was barely gliding forward. The nalas climbed the ladder to the foredeck, where Zhenuvnili and the two men were waiting, looking out across the water. At one of the piers a lantern was being swung back and forth. Zhenuvnili put an arm around each of the nalas. "Look," she said. "That's where we're to land. They're signaling."

The pilot shouted an order, which was swiftly relayed below-decks, and the port oars lifted clear of the sea. After two more

pulls, which brought the galley around to port, the starboard
oars were lifted as well, and the galley slid, slowing, toward
the berth beside the dock. At another shout the oars were
brought inboard, with thunderous clatter. The sea, because the
moons were scattered, was far below tide-crest, and the pitch-
smeared logs sliding in beside them stood as high as the galley's
mast. A narrow stair zigzagged up to the dock platform high
above.

Men and women boiled from the hatches and took up padded
fending poles, leaning into them with their shoulders and being
pushed backward along the deck, grunting, bare feet slapping
on wood. At the bow and stern, others uncoiled and tossed
loops of heavy line at exposed mooring posts. The rope snapped
taut on the cleats and thrummed. The ship drifted sideways,
thumped against the dock, and was still.

The lilith's eyes flooded with happy tears. "We're here,"
she said. Motionlessness, after such an endlessness of motion,
made her head feel light and fuzzy. The ship creaked softly
against the pier. Around her the tall pilings were dark and
deserted, a brooding presence that seemed faintly menacing.
She wished for musicians and fireworks, but of course there
would be none.

Ranga Strell squinted up at the dock platform. "I shall see
that a lift chair is provided for my lilith," he said.

"Ranga," she chided. "I appreciate your concern, but I *am*
capable of climbing a flight of stairs."

"Who's that coming?" Karanli said apprehensively. Three
figures bearing lanterns were descending the stairs.

"Can you make them out, Qobba?" Strell demanded. "Which
one is Metterner?"

"The one in the middle, I think. The one with the beard."
The lantern bearers reached the small platform that was not
much above the height of the deck and stood waiting while the
crew unclamped the gangplank and extended it out through the
hinged opening in the rail. The lilith's heart raced. She felt as
excited as if she were about to set foot on the Moons Road
itself. The gangplank reached the platform, and the newcomers
sprang up on it and clomped across to the deck. She could see

that they were Vli, her people. Behind the veil she smiled at them, opening her heart in love. They crossed the deck to the foot of the mast, where they bowed their heads and touched forehead, heart, and groin before the carven statue of Li that held the soul of the ship.

She had to turn her back on them to come down the foredeck ladder, and when she stood before them she saw that their eyes were alight with joy. The bearded one was younger than she had expected for a successful merchant. His close-cropped beard and hair ringed a slightly pudgy face that was the more moon-round because he kept his upper lip shaven. He touched himself thrice again, and bowed. "Welcome, lilith. Welcome," he said thickly.

"Thank you, Habil Metterner." She brushed his cheek with her fingers. "We understand you are to be the master of our Nest while we are here. Your lilith thanks you for extending such hospitality."

He closed his eyes a moment, and tucked his lower lip between his teeth. "My lilith," he said in acknowledgment. To address a lilith thus meant that one had been, or would soon be, intimate with her. He would not have used the phrase unless she had guided him to it.

She turned to the companions who flanked him, both of them broad-shouldered and muscular, with swords sheathed at their belts. "I am Zhenuvnili," she said, turning her head from side to side to include them both. "You are—"

"Malka Durin," the woman said, lowering her eyes to where she clutched the lantern handle in both hands.

"Malka. Your lilith thanks you for coming to make her welcome."

"My lilith," the woman whispered.

"And you?"

"Gorin Metterner. In the service of my uncle." He was little more than an adolescent, with a pouting mouth and dark hair that hung forward, badly trimmed, over his ears.

"Your lilith thanks you for coming to greet her."

"Thank *you* for coming to *us*," the boy bubbled. "Oh, my

lilith, how I've dreamed—I mean, we all have—I mean, it's so wonderful—"

"Yes. Dreams can come true, you see."

"Malka and Gorin are to be your bodyguard," Habil Metterner explained.

"Bodyguard? So, I am to have a bodyguard." The lilith regarded that bit of information gravely.

"If my lilith will forgive my lecturing her," Metterner said, "things here are not as they are in Vli Holm. Our people are but a tiny minority—and not, it shames me to say, well liked."

"How strange," Zhenuvnili mused. "Li creates us all, and yet we find reasons to quarrel."

"It is not we who choose the quarrel, my lilith," Metterner pointed out. "They call us names, names I would not repeat to you. Because we keep to ourselves they say we despise them. And they accuse us of dishonest business practices, simply because we know the value of an olmin and aren't afraid of a little hard work."

"You misunderstand," Zhenuvnili said gently. "When I say Li creates us all, I mean everybody, Vli and foreigner alike."

Ranga Strell muttered something that sounded like "Sacrilege."

Ignoring him, she went on. "Yet we quarrel. It is said that if you would have another open her heart, you must first open yours. How simple it is! Yet how many of us practice it?"

"It's not our hearts I'm worried about us opening," Strell said. "It's our harbors." His face was blotched an ugly red.

"At home we wouldn't need a bodyguard," Karanli blurted. "At home we'd be safe."

Zhenuvnili put an arm around the nala. "Hush, little one. We'll be safe here. As safe as we would be at home." But would they be?

Arrangements were made to have the party's luggage carried up to the dock and transported to Metterner's mansion. The nalas ducked into the forecabin to retrieve a few personal things, and Qob Qobba went aft with Captain Bolya to get the valise of papers he had locked in a cupboard in her cabin. The captain was a lean, wind-bronzed old Vli woman who went barefoot, like her crew, in all weather. For the occasion of their arrival in Falnerescu she had donned her good dark-green tunic and combed her tangled mat of gray hair into a semblance of order. Jingling the brass key ring, she selected a key and unlocked the cupboard. "It's been a fair voyage," she said. "We'll all be praying it continues so, for you and for her."

"You and your crew have been most hospitable," Qobba assured her. "If we meet no worse in Falnerescu, we'll be back aboard in an aptarne, and bound for home."

"There are worse in Falnerescu," Captain Bolya said darkly. "Aye, there are worse. I pray Li you do not tangle in their nets." She shut the cupboard firmly, locked it, and followed him back out on deck.

Ranga Strell stared around at the night-shrouded waterfront and fidgeted. It was folly to stand like this on the well-lighted deck, where the lilith could be spied on by anybody. Until she was safely indoors, he would be unable to relax. When the nalas reappeared, and a moment later Qob Qobba and the captain, and still the party stood milling at the mast, Strell's impatience goaded him beyond ignoring. He bounded up on the gangplank, where he stood glaring back at the others, willing them silently to hurry.

Captain Bolya's voice rang out, high and harsh. "Ranga Strell! You forget yourself! Dare you leave the ship so discourteously, when it has carried you safe across the sea?"

Strell flushed in embarrassment. A landlubber, he had omitted one of the most basic rituals of seafaring. One did not leave a ship, unless it was sinking, without taking leave of the idol that housed its soul. With ill grace he stepped back on deck, strode to the carven figure that smiled seraphically down, and touched himself thrice.

The lilith did likewise, lingeringly, for the idol was an image of Li. The gentle eyes, painted in loving detail, beamed down upon her. *While I am here you will be always in my heart.*

Ranga Strell went toward the gangplank again—but then, realizing that the others were not close at his heels, he paused, still standing on the deck, and turned back to see what was causing the delay.

Captain Bolya heard a crewman gasp in disbelief, then turned swiftly and saw. Her heart sank. For the entire voyage Strell had been nothing but trouble, complaining about the accommodations, the food, the crew's language. She had borne it with a shrug. But now he had done something truly appalling. As every seaman and seawoman knew—and on the Island Sea there were few who were not seafolk or the sons and daughters of seafolk—when one had taken leave of the idol one went straight to the gangplank and disembarked. Those who wished to wait for their companions might wait on the plank itself, or on the dock, but never, *never* on deck. To bid farewell to the soul of the ship and then fail to leave her was the worst sort of bad luck. In effect, anybody who did so was leaving himself at sea unprotected by the soul of the ship, as surely as if he had fallen overboard. What punishment the Goddess would exact for this breach of conduct could only be guessed at, but a punishment there would certainly be. At a stroke, Strell's carelessness had put the whole mission at jeopardy.

The harbor pilot, standing beside the captain, had seen what happened. The only foreigner on the ship, he had been tolerated for the last few hours out of necessity. He had accepted courteously the personal reserve of the Vli, and Captain Bolya found that she liked the stoop-shouldered, keen-eyed old man well enough.

The pilot shook his head. "You'll be glad to see the back of him, I'll wager."

"Till the voyage home," the captain agreed. "Then he'll be underfoot again for three chetnes straight."

"That's making good time. I would have said four."

"We barely stopped to take on fresh water. We'll home the same way."

"Ah," the pilot said. "Only makes sense, I suppose, considering the nature of your passengers."

The captain looked sharply at him. "As to that," she said guardedly, "you've seen nothing. Nobody was on this ship, save a couple of noblemen. I'm sure a harbor pilot knows how to hold his tongue."

"Oh, aye, when he chooses. I've seen cargos would curl

your hair to hear the tale, and singe your tongue in the telling of it. Speakin' of tongues, now, mine's a mite dry, if you catch my meanin'. You wouldn't be wantin' to treat me to a mug, would you?"

He meant only that he could be persuaded to be silent for the price of a mug or two of ale. But Captain Bolya, a Vli woman both pious and well adjusted to her race's sexual customs, mistook him to mean that they might hoist a few together— and she did not like to think where such conviviality might lead. Offended, she turned her head away. "Be off with you," she ordered curtly. "I thank you for guiding us safe to harbor. Now leave my ship, and leave it proper."

"As you'll have it, then," the pilot said with a shrug. He wasn't surprised; everybody knew the Vli were a stiff-necked, penny-pinching lot. Let her keep her own secrets, then. He wouldn't be bothered.

On another dock twenty tadigs away—a tadig being the height of a man, or six feet—two unshaven rag-clad figures crouched in the dark and watched the lilith and her retinue climb the zigzag stairs. "Vli, by the look of her," the taller of the two said, referring to the ship. A ragged scar descending from his left eye like the crooked track of a tear gleamed silver in the moonlight.

"Aye," the shorter said, scratching himself absently and squinting at the halo of lantern light across the water. "And no ordinary cargo. Robed like a priestess, look you—and arrivin' in the dead o' night, and greeted by Vli guards bearin' swords. Most interestin', I'd say."

"You wouldn't be thinkin' what I'm thinkin', now would you?" the tall man said.

"I'm thinkin'," his companion said, "that there may be certain parties who'll be curious to hear about this arrival. Maybe even curious enough to pay for the information. Wouldn't you think?" The short man cackled softly and nudged the tall man in the ribs. The tall man nodded slowly, greedily, and the two slipped away into the shadows.

Chapter 2

"*So this is how the common oar takes his ease,*" Vod
Penna Osher said, gazing around at the crowded, ill-
lit room. "I can't say I'm surprised."

"What?" Salas Tarag's teeth flashed in a grin. "You mean
it's no dirtier or noisier than your imagination painted it?"

"Dirtier, no. Noisier, yes." Osher raised his voice a little to
cut through a shouting match that had erupted at the next table.

"Call this noisy? Wait till later, when they start singing!"

The tavern was called the Brass Paum, because of the por-
trait of that stolid draught animal hammered in metal and nailed
to a board hanging outside the door. There was little to distin-
guish it from a dozen such establishments dotting the Falneresc
waterfront, save perhaps the quality of the music. On a raised
platform at one side of the room five players were exploring
the contrapuntal ramifications of a well-known bawdy song;
but the arrangement was languorous, almost melancholy, and
none of the revelers had the temerity to try to sing along—if
indeed they recognized the tune at this tempo. Above the noise
the instruments were nearly inaudible. That night several ships
were lately in, and the benches between the long tables were
a press of bodies, the air thick with smoke and loud laughter.
Serving-men and -women rushed back and forth with trays
heaped with brown bread, roast meat, and pitchers of ale. The

15

bare boards of the tables were scarred from rough use, and ages of candle smoke had blackened the rafters.

"Do you come here often?" Osher went on. "You're a complicated man, Tarag. I confess I fail to understand how you can be equally at home here and in polite society."

"An oar has no home." Tarag shrugged. "An oar's home is wherever the wind and current, and the strength of his two arms, carry him."

In spite of this assertion, Salas Tarag was no ordinary oar—nor did he quite appear to be, though he wore an oar's plain tunic and trousers. No taller than average, perhaps even a hair shorter when he stood, he was nonetheless broad in the shoulders, his chest uncommonly deep. Still, this development of bone and muscle, which showed he had benched a galley as a boy, and for long years, did nothing to set him apart in the crowded tavern. Those here who had never pulled oar were but a handful. Two things made Salas Tarag the target of curious glances. One was his air of confidence and calm, the air of a man who would not easily be bested or taken unawares. The other was his coloring. In the racial soup on the Island Sea, hair and skin tone varied widely, but few had the striking combination of white-blond hair and deep bronze skin that had been common in the tiny island principality where Tarag had been born. His hair and beard, neatly trimmed, stood out startlingly against the leather of his face, the former lightened and the latter darkened further by years of sun and wind. Beneath feathery brows his crystal-blue eyes darted, alert and restless.

Tarag's companions were even more remarkable, and might not have been welcome at the long table had they come alone rather than with one who was known. The first was a Potheqi giant, taller by a forearm and more than anybody else in the room, his head a stone block split into thirds by the horizontal lines of brow ridge and wide mouth. The giant's name was Graio, and his race were masters of a mysterious land far to the west and south, beyond the Island Sea. There, it was said, they raised dragons in underground vaults, and worshipped them as gods, and sacrificed to them in gory ceremonies the prisoners taken in battle—a practice concerning which Graio,

living alone among the pygmies who were his people's sometime enemies, maintained a tactful silence. On the bench beside
him sat Vod Penna Osher, whose long narrow head, dead black
hair, and fishbelly-pale complexion made it unmistakable that
he was a Berkender—the only Berkender in the tavern. Even
out of uniform he drew a few scornful glances and muttered
oaths from nearby tables. The Potheqi might or might not be
a bloodthirsty freak, but the Berkender was a known quantity:
he was an oppressor. Caught on the bench between the muscular
slab of Graio on one side and a foul-smelling little seaman
named Zimba on the other, Osher contrived nonetheless to hold
himself a little apart, his unsmiling mouth set, bony fingers
wrapped securely around a mug from which he did not drink.

Osher was regretting having let Tarag, who had a reputation
for mad exploits, talk him into this jaunt. Boredom had betrayed
him. Educated at the finest university in Berkenland, Osher
was the only real intellectual among the officers of the garrison
at Falnerescu, and one of the few whose noble blood was
untainted. He had first encountered Tarag at one of the glittering
parties thrown by Shuma Borando, wife of the commander of
the garrison. Shuma herself, looking especially decorative in
a new gown and rather too much jewelry, had dragged Salas
Tarag toward him by an elbow and said airily, "Penna Osher,
you've got to talk to my sea captain. I know you'll get along
famously; you both read *books*."

And in spite of the differences between them, they did get
along well enough. Tarag had no formal education at all, but
he had a voracious appetite for facts and speculations, and a
keen mind that sorted them out and glued them back together
in unexpected ways. He pumped Osher for everything he had
learned at the university, and Osher, glad of somebody to talk
to about such things, quickly forgot that the man was a dark-
skinned mongrel, spawn of one of the hundreds of inferior
races that swarmed across the Island Sea. In the following
aptarnes Tarag came to his quarters several times, and they
drank sherry and talked science and politics. At the end of one
protracted session during which Osher had tried to make clear
the inherent cultural superiority of the Berkenders and his guest

had politely but firmly scoffed, Tarag said, "It's easy enough to belittle something you're ignorant of. You've no fear of being contradicted by inconvenient facts. When you determine to learn for yourself, though, you'll find yourself developing a new respect for these people. They're unlettered, aye, but that only means they've got to know what they're about. They can't go looking it up in a book. They're good folk. Why not come see for yourself sometime, instead of mouthing dogma you learned in school?" And Osher, who not infrequently harbored grave doubts about the superiority, cultural or otherwise, of his fellow officers, agreed.

And now, here he was. Any inclination he might have had to be swayed by Tarag's argument had vanished in the face of the rowdy incivility of this lot. It was obvious that they were no match for the Berkenders, militarily, morally, or any other way. Osher shook his head. "As to the term 'home,' I'll withdraw it. What I mean is that you're not one of these people. For reasons that I don't pretend to understand, you choose to bury yourself among a lot of smelly rabble."

"'Ere, now, we're not smelly," objected Zimba the seaman, who was clearly oblivious to his own odoriferousness. "And we're not so bad-mannered as to go around insultin' strangers, neither."

"You see?" Tarag said. "The common oar, whom you claim is an unmannered lout, has in fact excellent manners. He's probably more polite than Shuma Borando and her oh-so-tactful friends, because he doesn't know when the stranger on the next bench might be the one to pull him out when he's drowning, or let Bulon have him. And these people know how to enjoy themselves, Osher, which is something the Berkenders have forgot, if you ever knew. I can only take so much of your 'polite society,' and then I have to come down here to clear my head."

"Only you're not happy here either, are you?" Osher persisted. "These people don't satisfy you. You're capable of more, and they're not."

Graio nodded ponderously. "The cap'n's not happy anywhere," he declared in his gravelly contrabass croak. "Hasn't been, all the time I've known him. Always leavin' one port to bend oar for another—meanin' by that both actual ports and things as a poet might call ports, bein' fanciful. Don't know what the cap'n's lookin' for. Don't think he does either."

"Ah." Salas Tarag closed his eyes in a mock swoon. "As usual, our Potheqi friend has put his finger squarely on the meat of it. What is there that's worth living for? Can you tell me that? Knowledge? There is no real knowledge anywhere in this world. We're sunk in an abyss of ignorance. We don't even know how we came to be as we are, much less how to live our lives so as to be happy. And next to those questions, what else matters?"

"There's always duty," Osher said.

"That's an affliction I've never suffered from."

"And women."

"Now you're closer to the mark. But it comes to the same thing in the end. Look you—see that one over there? The drummer." He pointed to the stage, where the musicians had struck up the intricate triple rhythm of a Skavish dance. The woman squatting at the front among the gourd drums slapped and tapped so her brass armbands bounced, long hair flying loose across her tawny shoulders as she frowned in concentration. The other players watched her intently for cues; a Skavish dance was the trickiest kind of piece to play, fitting since Skavish was the trickiest god of them all, a god of pranks and mockery and rude noises. "Her name's Jaima," Tarag went on. "See how she drums? She's lost to the world." Jaima reached up beside her to set a metal rattle spinning, without breaking the beat or even looking to see where the rattle was suspended. Behind her an olive-skinned boy thumped out urgent low notes on a ten-stringed harp whose big bellied soundbox was carved in a design of scallops and curlicues. A thin gray man twanged on a fretted carthina with the metal picks attached to his flying fingers. And two pipers huffed into the mouthpieces of their most piercing pipes, skirling up a shrill, heavily ornamented melody that sliced through the smoky air.

"She's good-looking, for an island wench," Osher admitted.

"A bit coarse, but vital. I can see why you'd be attracted to her."

"I was. This was the last time I was in port here, nearly twenty chetnes ago. What struck me first was the intensity in her when she played—what you're seeing now. But she never made love that way. There was always a part of her that held back, a part I could never touch. I think I would have got closer to her playing music with her. But alas, I'm no musician.

"What I'm saying is that being with her set me thinking. And I saw that I must seem just that way to women, if they've got the wit to notice it. There's something in me that stands apart and watches, that remains unmoved, even during the sweatiest transport of passion. Maybe it's just that I've been with too many women, and the heart's gone out of it. You don't suppose I'm getting old, do you?"

"You're a long ways from old, Cap'n," Graio said. "And even when you're toothless and walk with a cane, I'll wager the wenches won't mind a tumble now and again."

"But that's all it is, isn't it? A tumble. It was different when we were lads. The first lass I bedded I swore was the four moons together, and all the stars thrown into the bargain. Aye, and the second lass, and the third. From head to toe I was aflame with love. Only now, as you say, it's a tumble. When it's done you pull on your pants and bend oar for the next port, and an aptarne later you can't remember her name. Have you ever read Calthurnas, Osher?"

The Berkender shook his head.

"You should. He's an Eloian philosopher, one of their great sages. He says we can't remember passion the way we remember ideas. In a way he's right—an idea returning to the mind is still the same idea, while a passion remembered is but a pale reflection. Still, in another way he's wrong. It's precisely the fact that we *can* remember the passions of our youth that discontents us with our lives as they are now. Or do we paint the memories? Do we conveniently forget the awkwardness and double-mindedness of the past that today blind and cripple us?"

"It's human to think the past was better than the present," Osher said. "Why else should people the world over cling to the myth that we were sent down from a glorious kingdom in the sky?"

"I've got some ideas about that," Tarag stated. "It's a curious myth, when you think on it. We'll have to talk of it sometime. At the moment, I've got some urgent business out back. Graio, flag down a serving-wench and get us a fresh pitcher, while I go relieve myself of my share of the last one."

Standing up, he eased himself sideways between two benches toward the aisle. The music had stopped. At the front of the platform Jaima was conferring with a bearded man, their heads together. As Tarag watched, Jaima nodded and gestured to the man to lead the way. They reached the back door just ahead of Tarag and stepped out into the night. He heard Jaima say, "All right, where is he?" Tarag strained to hear more, but they had gone to the right, and his business was in the small shed to the left.

When he had buttoned his trousers, he didn't immediately go back inside, but stood in the stable yard relishing the cool night air, refreshingly sweet after the oppressive thickness of the tavern. Stars and Nardis hung motionless overhead; the Moons Road would be down by now, and Cheth setting. On impulse he went past the door of the tavern and stepped lightly down the alley into which Jaima and her companion had vanished. Stopping at the corner of a building and peering around it, he saw that they had been joined by two other men—ruffians by the look of them, raggedly dressed and unshaven. The taller of the two had a curious silver mark, perhaps a scar, descending from one eye like the track of a tear; he was whispering hoarsely and making agitated motions with his hands, while Jaima shook her head determinedly. Tarag could make out no words at all. His curiosity was a burning itch, but he could get no nearer without being seen. For a moment he debated going boldly forward and calling out to Jaima, but the discussion was clearly private, and his entrance would bring it to an end. Reluctantly he retraced his steps.

Graio put a fresh mug in his hand. Zimba the seaman was holding forth, telling his own companions and anybody else who cared to listen a long and convoluted tale about an ill-fated voyage he had benched. Tarag sat back to listen. After all, he had brought Osher here to see the ways of island folk; they could discuss the myth of humanity's celestial origin another time. His eye roved the table. The faces were sharp-shadowed in the candlelight and glistening with perspiration. Several of these oar had benched for him on past voyages, and others he knew by sight. There were the Lavorien brothers, Bek and Med, woolly hair sprouting at the necks of their shirts—stout lads who would rather pull than stop to eat. And that scrawny southerner was Omur, a diehard skeptic but loyal as blood. Yes, they were good lads. Before too much longer he'd be shipping out; Graio was right about that. These might be among whom he called on for crew.

". . . and by the time we got to port, every last barrel of it had rotted!" Zimba's punch line drew scattered laughter.

"Now that's a shame," declared a gap-toothed old seaman with a perpetual squint. "Brings me to mind of a time we shipped out from Bellestoru loaded to the rails with naught but dressed logs of weltwood."

"Weltwood?" Omur scoffed. "Nobody ships weltwood. Ain't worth nothin' to nobody."

"Not here in the islands it ain't," the old seaman agreed. "But we was bound for Berkenland, where they'll pay good money for any sort of wood. The captain was a greedy sort. He figured to pick up weltwood cheap and unload it on the Berks for a fat profit. But before many days had passed, we found out *why* nobody ships weltwood, and it ain't because it's too soft to build with.

"We was crossin' the bight of Almenarr when a little cloud appears on the horizon, no bigger than a man's hand. The captain knew what that meant right enough, and we was all piped belowdecks and pulled fair for land. But it warn't no use. The storm smacked into us like it was a paum in rut and we no more than a pickle barrel. There was waves—" The old man craned his neck toward the ceiling. "Well, I reckon you've seen waves."

Tarag had been in storms more than once in the bight of Almenarr. They were a fine thing to tell of afterward, safe back in port with a mug of ale in hand, but they were Bulon's rage itself when a ship was caught in one. It was as if the god of the sea floor had swum up to the surface and was stirring the sea and air with his tail, until they were so churned together a man might drown standing on deck, and never fall overboard.

"Naturally," the gap-toothed man went on, "we shipped oars and battened the oarlocks. But the sea was washin' down across the deck with every wave that broke athwart our bows, and the better part of the weltwood warn't in the hold at all, we were so heavy laden. It was stacked on deck. So we're holdin' on to whatever is handy to keep from bein' swept overboard, when over the howlin' of the wind we hear a creakin' and a groanin' and a tearin', as though Bulon had got the ship in his jaws and was chewin' her up. At first one lad does let out a cry, 'She's breakin' up!' But then we see it ain't the ship. It's the weltwood. The stacks of lumber are swellin' and swellin', till they burst the lines they're secured with. The weltwood was soakin' up the water!"

Conscious that every eye was on him, the man oiled his throat with a long pull of ale and wiped his mouth on the back of his hand before going on. "Never was a ship cursed with such a cargo," he declared. "Every time we pitched in the gale, the logs of weltwood come rollin' and bouncin' across the deck like so many matchsticks. The lads had to leap clear of 'em at every pass, and then grab a hand-hold again afore the next wave swept over. The logs pounded the mast till they snapped it clean off.

"Wellsir. The captain could see he was about to lose his cargo and his precious profit, so he was standin' on the after-deck—out of harm's way, mind you—bellowin' down at us over the gale to grab the logs and secure 'em before they breached the rail and plunged into the sea. Which was nigh impossible, but we was game to try it. So there we are, wrestlin' with these tumblin' logs in a howlin' storm, when what should we notice but that the ship is ridin' lower and lower in the water. Every sea that swamps us we ship a little more of over the rail. The logs, or so it seems, was so heavy with water we was about to be dragged down to Bulon's parlor, ship and all!

"When the captain sees this, he changes his tune quick enough. 'Over the side with 'em!' he cries. 'Over the side!' So we commence to drag these swollen-heavy logs over to the rail. We has to take an ax to the rail, because all of us together warn't strong enough to lift one of them logs *over* the rail, and in that weather we couldn't rig a cargo hoist from the mast, even if we'd still had a mast. We chops the starboard rail away, and shoves the logs on that side into the sea—which leaves us listin' fair to port, so we does the job again on the other side. When we gets the second lot overboard, she rights herself—but she don't spring back up in the water the way she ought. We're still ridin' no higher than Sternvalen Rock at mooncrest.

"So we undog the main hatch and send a lad below, and he calls back that we've been shippin' water through a couple of oarlocks that the captain ought to have seen mended and, bein' a penny-pincher, hadn't. All this time the sea has been pourin' into the hold! Them as was belowdecks finally got the locks watertight, just about the time the storm blows itself out. And damn me if we weren't foundered for fair. There was no more than half a handsbreadth of freeboard left between us and the sea. If we'd been any lower in the water, we'd of been *under* the water. So we goes below with buckets to bail her out. But there warn't no way we was goin' to bail her out, because the sea that had sloshed in had all got soaked up by the weltwood that was stowed in the hold!

"Wellsir." He took more ale. "There we was. We hadn't got no mast, so we couldn't of hoisted sail even in a fair wind. And with the oarlocks under water we sure couldn't row. The auxiliary oarlocks in the rail had gone into the sea when we chopped the rail. And we was smack in the middle of the bight of Almenarr, with the current bearin' us hard southeast, and nary a speck of land nor another ship anywhere to be seen."

The whole table had fallen silent. As if on cue, a youngster with a downy first growth of beard, who had listened to the tale with mouth agape, spoke. "How did you get back to port, then?"

The seaman turned and leered roguishly at the boy. "Back

to port?" he echoed. "Back to port? We didn't. *We're still out there.*"

A roar of laughter greeted this assertion. The boy turned scarlet and tried to shrink down on the bench.

"Now I can't top that story," another oar began, "being no match for Frengur as a storyteller. But I'll wager I've shipped a stranger cargo than any sort of wood."

"Stop him, stop him!" still another voice cried. "He's going to tell the story of the Eloian singing fish again!" After a good deal of outcry, the would-be speaker was dissuaded.

Zimba spoke up. "Lads, I don't know how many of you know it, but Salas Tarag here is a free captain. You may have seen the *Amera Smiles* riding at anchor. She's his—and she's the prettiest little fifteen-oar this side of Olmalinu. He's been up and down the Island Sea in her, and I'll wager that somewhere in his travels he's shipped a stranger cargo than Frengur's weltwood or Klabba's singing fish, either one. What say? Shall we ask him?"

Mugs were pounded on the table. "Tarag!" "Salas Tarag!" Even those he didn't know knew him, it seemed, at least by reputation. Tarag saw he would have to come up with a tale. He took a pull of ale and cleared his throat.

"Well," he began, "there was the time I sailed north from Karsh Holvik to a place called Mirk Menlin with no passengers on board, no freight, and no crew at all save a band of about two hundred mnoerri."

Eyes were turned toward him. "Mnoerri?" Bek Lavorien said, frowning. "Mnoerri don't venture on the sea." A rumble of assent swept the table; everybody knew this was true. The mnoerri were one of the three language-speaking, tool-using species in the world, the other two being the humans and the kelg. The kelg, no more than waist-high to a man, were a viciously combative breed introduced onto the Island Sea by the Berkenders, for whom they served as mercenaries. The mnoerri, by contrast, were peaceful and retiring. Smaller than humans but larger than kelg, the thin-boned, fragile adults were too heavy to fly, though the intricately wrinkled skin-flaps that joined arm to leg betrayed their avian heritage. It was these flaps that Skavish, or his human stand-ins in the holy-day rituals, mocked when he appeared with a cape of leaves and twigs trailing from his arms, leaping and cavorting with a lack of dignity that was distinctly un-mnoerri.

Newborn mnoerri, half the size of human babies, were sometimes seen flying, alone or in flocks, far out at sea. As they grew older and heavier, they chose an island to settle on and stayed there for the balance of their lives. Though they lived surrounded by water, they made no boats, nor were they known to set foot willingly on a human ship.

"These mnoerri did," Tarag replied evenly. "As it happened, I was anchored at Karsh Holvik, at the southern tip of the Blue Islands. Half my crew had jumped ship, because there had been a big copper strike in the hills, and miners were getting top wages. So I was hove to in the harbor, trying to decide whether to trust to the wind to get me back to Salanvelu or whether to stand out in the public square till I took root like a tree, when one day on the street a mnoerri steps out in front of me and says 'Excuse. You are Captain Salas Tarag?'"

"He spoke to you?" Osher asked. Most often a mnoerri, confronted, would slip away without a word. Even those rare few who set foot in a town tended to remain mute when spoken to, averting their large dark eyes and sidling away.

"He not only spoke; he knew who I was. How he found out, I never learned. But somehow he had heard that I was stranded with half my oars dragging. Not that I was the only captain at Karsh Holvik in that fix. Maybe one of the others had turned him down, and sent him in my direction. In any event, it developed that he and his people—or maybe it was she and her people; you can't tell with the mnoerri—needed to get off the island. They were desperate to—again, for reasons I couldn't quite make out. It might have been the copper strike, the miners causing them trouble, but the way this one talked it sounded more like a religious pilgrimage.

"I explained to him that I couldn't take him anywhere because I was short of oar. When I'd got the idea across, he said, 'Very easily. We my people will oar.' And that's just what they did. Four of them on a bench in place of two of you lads, and spelling one another when they got winded, which was often. By that time the whole crew was mnoerri, because when the rest of my lads heard what was in the wind, damn if *they* didn't all jump ship."

"Can't say I blame 'em," Graio rumbled. "Shippin' with mnoerri might be the worst sort o' luck."

"It wasn't bad luck for me, anyhow," Tarag said. "Even though I was blessed with a crew of pipestem-limbed land-lubbers not more than four of whom spoke a word in any of the languages I knew.

"The hardest part was getting them to pull in unison, because there wasn't a one of them strong enough to beat the drum. So for the whole voyage I was running back and forth like a man who's been eating capi berries, beating the drum myself for ten minutes, then rushing up on deck to see that the mnoerri helmsman hadn't steered us off course, then running back below to beat the drum again before the oars had a chance to tangle and leave us dead in the water. They were terrified of being on the water, but they proved a better crew than I'd have guessed, if not near so good as you lads. At any rate, they got us safe to land, and not just to the next island over either, but half a dozen islands up the chain, a fine big island called Mirk Menlin with only the tiniest of fishing villages."

"What did they use to pay you?" somebody asked. Mnoerri were not known to use money.

"We worked out an agreement. I wasn't short of cash that season, only of oar, so I carried them in return for their teaching me a bit of their language and lore. There was a group among them felt they shouldn't part with it, but I made that my price, and in the end they paid it."

"Now hold on, Cap'n Tarag," woolly-haired Med Lavorien objected. "I'm bound to think this is another tall tale, for you've left yourself marooned on an island with no oar at all, only a few odd fishermen. How did you be gettin' home? And don't tell us you're still out there, neither."

"Now that's another tale entirely, and not one with a strange cargo, I'm afraid. I had about determined to run the *Amera Smiles* up on the beach and go live among the mnoerri, having found there was more to be learned of their lore than ever I'd imagined. But that very afternoon a ship happened by, a leaky old tub benched by half a hundred escaped slaves. No sooner did it near shore than it foundered and sank like a stone. They were all for slitting my throat and having off with my ship, but I persuaded 'em I was more use alive then dead, so they benched the *Amera Smiles* up north clear to Olmalinu, where I let 'em off and got myself a proper crew. I was glad to see the last of that bunch, I can tell you—they were a scurvy lot, always fighting and whining and insulting the women, when they weren't having their way with them standing up against the rail. And there's my tale. Another ale. Ale all around."

When the serving-woman had filled their mugs, a stoop-shouldered old man with keen eyes in his little round face spoke up. "Thankee for the ale, Cap'n Tarag. I been wantin' a taste tonight. Now, you lads be talkin' about strange cargos, and I don't know but what you might disqualify me, seein' I'm but a harbor pilot who's never been beyond Sternvalen Rock in me life, not to mention that I've trod the decks of a hundred times the number of ships of any of ye, but I'll wager that this very night I've shipped a stranger cargo than any of ye ever has."

"How much?" someone challenged.

"Ten coppers you can't top Cap'n Tarag's mnoerri," somebody else offered.

"A silver olmin on the pilot."

"Two olmins on Tarag."

"Two olmins, is it? You've not had two olmins to rub together since the last double eclipse."

When the bets were down and order restored, Salas Tarag spoke. "What about it pilot? What's this mysterious cargo?"

The harbor pilot set down his mug. "Tonight," he said, taking in the whole table with his eyes, "on a ship straight in from Vli Holm, I shipped a lilith."

Vod Penna Osher's boredom vanished. He sat very still.

Tarag leaned forward and said, "A lilith? Are you sure, pilot?"

"If I said I was sure, friend, you'd know I was lyin'. Whoever it was was wrapped in cloak and veil from head to toe. How could I be sure? Even supposin' I knew what a lilith looked like. Some say they're so beautiful no man alive could keep his hands off 'em—and some say they look like a duongnu with swelling sickness. But nobody knows, do they? The Vli know, but they're not tellin'."

"Ah, it's naught but another tall tale," Omur declared. "I put my money on Cap'n Tarag, and I win."

"Hear him out, hear him out!"

"All I know for certain," the pilot went on, "is this: The ship was benched by Vli, fore and aft, no other races. And I heard one of 'em call this hooded one 'my lilith.' I don't know a lot of their tongue, but I heard that right enough. The captain seemed most anxious for me not to speak a word about the passenger. And there was quite a little ceremony when we landed. That Vli merchant Habil Metterner was down to the dock with a sedan chair and two guards wearin' swords, and I've heard how he ties strings on his coppers so when he buys somethin' he can jerk the money back out of your purse. Stands to reason he wouldn't go to all that trouble for a shipload of weltwood."

"What's a lilith?" the downy-cheeked boy at the foot of the table asked plaintively. "Some sort of creature?"

"Your lilith," explained the squint-eyed oar who had told the tale of the weltwood, "is your species of whore. The pilot's got no claim. I shipped five liliths once, and right smart little pieces they were. Very tasty. Why go clear to Vli Holm, says I, when you can buy good lovin' from a lilith or two no further away than the next streetcorner?"

Osher made to rise. "I've got to be getting back to the garrison," he said to Tarag in a low voice. "It's late."

Tarag waved him back to his seat. "Hold. We'll be off quick enough." He turned to the boy. "Don't believe all the slander you hear, lad. A lilith's no whore, no more than I'm a kelg."

"And how would you be knowin' that?" somebody else demanded. "Next you'll be tellin' us you've got your papers for the harbor at Vli Holm, and go callin' on 'em when you're out that way."

"No, I've never been to Vli Holm, no more than anybody

has, that lived to tell the tale. And I've never seen a lilith. But I know a little about them. I had a hint or two from a Vli lad I saved from drowning once, and I got a bit more from the mnoerri, who live in the uplands of Vli Holm just as they do on any other island."

"Well, *I* knew a Vli lad once, and he told me they're whores. They live in brothels, and they put out for anybody that comes to call. That's what he said, Bulon take me if I'm lying." The oar crossed his arms on his chest, daring anybody to contradict him.

"That much is probably true," Tarag admitted. "Or so it would seem to you or me, our customs being unlike theirs. The way I heard the tale, they're priestesses, a sort of living incarnation of their goddess Li. But if we say 'priestess' or 'whore,' we're using our categories, not theirs. The truth, I'd guess, is that they're both. It was the mnoerri who put me on the right track. They kept talking about 'oneness,' and 'two-ness,' and 'threeness.' Have you ever noticed how, with all the Vli men and Vli women you'll find in ports like Falnerescu, there are no Vli babies born? Doesn't that seem odd?"

"Most women choose not to start babies while they're on long voyages," Graio rumbled. "Nothin' odd about that."

"Most women, aye. But *all* of them? Here's the truth of it—as much truth as I've been able to root out. Among the Vli there are not two sexes, but three. There are men, and there are women, and there are liliths. The men and women mean nothing to one another. Only the lilith can satisfy them."

There were several howls of protest. "This is the tallest tale we've heard tonight," somebody objected. "If you've got the equipment, you're a man. If you don't, you're a woman. How could anybody be a woman with men and a man with women?"

"As to that," Tarag said, "I'm as much in the dark as you. The mnoerri did let slip one other item, though. The liliths number no more than one in a hundred among the Vli. Perhaps less. So of course the Vli keep them in what my friend here calls a brothel. And of course each of them must sleep with a hundred men and women, so that the women can bear children. Can you think of a better explanation of why the Vli won't let outlander ships dock in their harbor? They have to keep the liliths to themselves. If they fail to do so, their whole race will die."

"Three sexes?" Zimba turned his head and spat on the floor. "It don't make any sense."

"The world is full of things that don't make sense," Tarag pointed out. "Can you tell me why the Potheqi grow to their enormous size, or why the Berkenders are short a finger and a toe?" He gestured at Osher, who did indeed possess only three fingers on each hand in addition to the thumb.

"It's not we who are lacking," Osher said evenly, "but you who are—oversupplied."

"Deformed, you was about to say," Zimba said in a distinctly unfriendly tone. "We know what you Berks think of us. No need to hide it."

Such a confrontation could easily turn nasty, Tarag knew. He hurried on. "The point is merely that every race is different somehow from every other. How did that happen? Were we all alike once? What was it made us change? I'd give a lot to know. But you've all seen the differences. There are some who say even the duongnué are human, and they're far less like us than the Vli. Whether the liliths are goddesses or whores, they're as human as you and me. The only real difference is, none of them has ever left Vli Holm before, not for any reason. Why do you suppose one's come here now?"

Vod Penna Osher opened his mouth to speak, and closed it again.

"If what you say is true," somebody commented, "it's no surprise Habil Metterner has let loose the purse strings. How long do you suppose it's been since he's been up against it? He'll take good care of her—aye, and keep her busy too." The remark drew laughter. "Too bad, Tarag. You won't have a chance at her."

Tarag's eyes lit up. "You think not? You think this one's beyond my grasp?"

"Your grasp wasn't what I was thinkin' of." More laughter.

"You intrigue me." Salas Tarag rubbed his palms together and grinned. "Here's a wager for you, lads, since you're in a wagering mood. Before Nardis next rises full, I'll see this lilith face to face, with no veil, and speak with her. I'll have once and for all the truth of what she is, she and her kind. Do I have any takers?"

"All you want to do is talk? Don't make me laugh."

Tarag shrugged theatrically. "How will I know till I've seen her? What if she looks, as our friend the pilot says, like a duongnu with swelling sickness?"

"Three silver olmins you can't do it."

"Ten coppers he can!"

"Taken!"

There was another flurry of betting. When the hubbub subsided, Tarag was in for nearly fifty silver olmins, and the side bets amounted to nearly as much. If he won, he would have enough to outfit the *Amera Smiles* smartly for her next voyage. If he lost, the ship would have several new co-owners.

"One thing's still botherin' me," a heavyset oar announced. "How are we to know you've done what you've wagered? You've got to bring back some sort of proof."

Having initiated the betting himself, Tarag was in no position to dodge the awkward question. "Fair enough," he said. "But what sort of proof you'll have to leave to me. I won't know what's practical till I'm there, will I? If I can manage it, I'll have Habil Metterner stand up on his rooftop and announce to all of Falnerescu that his lilith has been keeping company with one Salas Tarag. But you may have to settle for less than that."

Osher was trying to get his attention. Tarag raised his brows, and the Berkender motioned him closer, so that their heads were touching across the table. "You don't mean to go through with this," Osher said through clenched teeth.

"I assure you, I do. It sounds like fun, and it's too late now to back out. Besides, I can use the money."

"There are important matters at stake here. You don't realize—" Osher shifted his eyes left and right at the oar. "We'll talk about it outside."

Tarag sat back and eyed his friend stonily across the table.

"The wager," he said, "is on." To the table at large, he called, "What say, lads? Another round on me?"

"Naw, naw," an oar protested. "You're goin' to be out an olmin or two afore long. This time the table buys for you and your friends."

"I thank you." Tarag put his palms on the table and stood up. "But my friends and I have had a long day. Let us return to this spot at the next full-rise of Nardis—or before, if I send word. Either I'll pay you then, or I'll have my proof, and you may pay me."

Osher was already standing, rather stiffly. Graio got up, and the three made their way between bodies to the aisle. There Osher strode on, but Tarag went more slowly, nearly sauntering, not so much to show the oar how confident he was of the outcome of the wager, but because he wanted time to puzzle out what had so upset Osher. Tarag had no particular aversion to Berkenders as friends, but having one as an enemy was decidedly less than ideal.

Chapter 3

*T*he gray first light of morning blossomed in the east, dimming the Moons Road and silvering the mist that lay along the water of the bay. Ships in the vagueness loomed, dark shapes that creaked gently as waves lapped at their hulls. Slowly the light grew, until the sun burst yellow over the line of low hills that flanked the mouth of the bay, teasing the mist into tendrils and quietly burning it away. The ships at anchor, no longer ghosts, stood out in bold detail.

The *Amera Smiles*, scarcely rocking, rode amid two dozen like her in the Bearth anchorage off Falnerescu. When Salas Tarag's purse was fat, he preferred to dock her rather than row a dinghy back and forth, but currently his purse was far from fat. Not the largest ship in the anchorage but not the smallest, the *Amera Smiles* was low and broad, with one square-rigged mast, whose sail was currently furled at the boom. She had enclosed cabins fore and aft, and in the hold below the main deck she benched sixty oar—fifteen oars at port and fifteen at starboard, each pulled by two of the crew. A small vessel might bench only twenty, and they on benches open to the weather. A Berkender warship, on the other hand, could easily bench two hundred, fifty oars to port and fifty to starboard on two decks of twenty-five each. There was, on the Island Sea, no clear distinction between passenger ships and freighters; Tarag might be hired to carry people one voyage, cargo the next. A galley could never be an efficient way to ship large cargos for long distances, simply because the oar had to be fed before they could row. But bulky goods like food were produced locally on each island anyway; the shipping was in luxuries, and these paid enough that a clever man might do well. Of late a few trading companies had begun building huge tubs powered by sail rather than muscle, to carry huge ladings, but while wind power was more efficient, it was less reliable. Sailing-ships might lie becalmed for weeks, or be driven onto the rocks in a contrary wind, and all self-respecting oar looked down with scorn on "sailors."

The last scraps of mist were steaming from the rails when Salas Tarag shambled out on deck, yawning and scratching his chest. It was a fine morning, clear and nearly windless, the kind of weather a seaman is referring to when he says, "Amera smiles." Blue sky had swallowed the Moons Road, and Gavril, waning, stood at the zenith. Tarag's eye noted absently that there were no storm clouds massing, though that was to be expected when the moons were scattered. Storms most often followed multiple conjunctions and oppositions, when tides were high and winds turbulent.

He padded to the rail on bare feet, loosened the drawstring of his trousers, and urinated into the bay. On the next ship over, a woman was leaning on the rail. She waved to Tarag, who with his free hand waved lazily back. The air was cool without being chilly, and tainted already with the smoke of morning cooking-fires.

After tying the drawstring, he ambled over to the mast and crossed his hands, palms inward on his chest, before the idol, which was carved and painted in the image of a smiling woman. "Morning, Amera," he said. Amera was the goddess of waves and wind, the loving consort of fierce Bulon, god of the depths. Stepping past Her, Tarag went to the foredeck ladder and climbed it far enough to poke his head over the edge. A tattered and stained gray blanket was humped in the lee of the bow rail, one naked human arm sticking out from under it. "Ho, Jutie!"

Tarag called. "Wake up, you lazy bag of bones! Where's my breakfast?"

The blanket flew into the air, and out from under it scuttled a most peculiar little man, in one moment awake and making for the ladder. His arms were too long, and his legs were both short and bowed. His head, a squashed sphere perched crookedly on his shoulders, was favored with a wide, expressive mouth, coarse yellow skin, a broad flat nose, and a thin crop of long greasy hair. Also perched on his shoulder, to the left side balancing the angle of his head to the right, was a glistening green lump a little larger than an open hand. Eyeless and earless, the lump sat pressed tight against the little man's collarbone like a dollop of something disagreeable that had landed there and stuck. Unless one peeled back the lump far enough to see its suction pads, one might never realize it was an animal. The little man's name was Jutie, and he was of a southern race whose proper name was the Wologchim, but who were never called anything but wogglies.

Tarag made way for Jutie, who clambered down the ladder, loped across the deck, and rooted in a covered box for charcoal, which he pitched into the iron brazier in its sandpit and huffed on with a little bellows, all with a show of energy and enthusiasm remarkable in somebody who fifteen seconds before had been asleep. "I'll need four honeycakes this morning," Tarag told him. "No, make that six. This promises to be a busy day, and it may be long before I have the chance to eat again." That prophecy was to prove truer than he expected.

"Here, now. What's all the yellin' and stompin' about?" The door of the forecabin swung wide, and Graio, who had to bend nearly double to get under the lintel, came out on deck, rubbing his eyes with fists the size of hams.

"You've nearly slept the day away," Tarag said. "We've got a wager to win."

"*You've* got a wager to win, you mean."

"Wager? Wager?" Jutie's head cocked up and twitched from side to side.

"Aye, a wager," Graio confirmed. "Fifty olmins. Or was it sixty? Enough to put the ship in hock, anyhow." Not bothering to elaborate, he stepped to the rail and dived over it in a clean arc. The spray from his mighty splash kicked up over the deck and sizzled in the charcoal. After pumping a few more breaths into the coals, Jutie hopped across the deck and down the main hatch. From the hold his muffled voice emanated, crying, "Honeycakes, honeycakes, yes, yes!"

Standing alone by the sandpit, Salas Tarag had a good stretch and finished waking up. There was a wager, right enough. And winning it would be no simple matter. You've steered into it again, lad, he mused. Well, no way now but forward. Losing the wager would cost him a good deal. But the treasure to be gained if he won it wasn't the money. No, the real treasure was the lilith. Whatever a lilith was. What would she be like? A poor bewildered creature who couldn't get through the morning without slaves to dress and feed her? Possibly. But what if she had a mind and soul to match her fabled beauty? That was the possibility not to be lost sight of. Smoke from the brazier tickling his nostrils, Tarag asked himself whether any man in Falnerescu more deserved to see a lilith, or was better equipped to bring it off. He answered no. If it could be done, he meant to do it. And anything—Tarag permitted himself a little smile—anything could be done, if only a man put his mind to it. One could fly to the stars. Well, perhaps not fly to the stars. But most things.

He went back into his cabin, and brushed his hair and beard before the wavering face in the narrow mirror that hung unframed against the wall. From the wardrobe he selected a clean linen shirt and some sober blue trousers with matching vest. He grinned at himself in the glass, and white teeth glinted engagingly against the dark skin. Something more seemed called for, on such an occasion. He dug in a drawer and drew out a necklace of rough-finished white and pink coral beads, and from the bottom of the wardrobe fetched a pair of rope sandals. That, he decided, would do nicely.

Out on deck, Graio was levering himself up over the rail, dripping rivers down his great slab of chest and puffing out his cheeks. He paused to survey Tarag's apparel. "You mean to go through with it," he rumbled.

"Where's your romantic spirit, Graio? When Amera whispers, you're tying line. Of course I mean to go through with it. Wouldn't you, in my place?"

Graio considered the question. "She's an island woman, isn't she?"

"Not a woman, a lilith."

"That's as may be. I'd split her in half. Even not considerin' that, I'm not sure as I'd want to pit myself against the Berks. Osher made it pretty clear last night that this lilith is official business, that you're to steer a wide berth."

"Did he?" Tarag asked with a twinkle. "I can't seem to recall a word he said."

Jutie was stirring batter in a wooden bowl. "How many cakes for Graio?" he asked the bowl. "How many?"

"Fifteen or twenty ought to do it." Graio slogged away toward the forecabin, leaving small lakes behind him on the deck.

Tarag climbed to the afterdeck to have a look around the harbor. The mist had burned off, and the fishing fleet was gone but for a couple of stragglers. Away to the north, where the island's only large river emptied into a vast and fertile marsh, he could almost make out in the wavering haze the clustered dots that were gangs of slaves harvesting the water-crisp. The light shimmered on the bay, and perhaps he only imagined he saw them because he knew they were there, hundreds of them, hip-deep in mud, reaching down between armloads to pry the suckers off their legs. It was a brutal life. Tarag shuddered.

To the east the seeing was better. A Berkender warship was headed out the channel, oars dipping and rising in flawless coordination. You can think what you like about the Berkenders, Tarag mused, but they know how to row a tight stroke. Shading his eyes, he could just make out the ship's pennant. What a pity there was no such thing as a distance-glass, which would bring far things nearer the way a reading-glass made little things bigger. All a reading-glass did to distant things was turn them upside down, which was puzzling. Tarag frowned and scratched his beard. Of course, if one glass turned things upside down, putting a second glass in front of the first might

turn them right way up again, and make them bigger into the
bargain. What a curious idea! He strode across the afterdeck,
took the ladder flying, and dived into his cabin.

There was one reading-glass in the top drawer, a good large
one ground of Olmalinese glass. But did he have another? He
rummaged in the back of the drawer. Not there. What about
that lot he had picked up in Baldoremu? Yes, at the bottom of
the chest, among the wood-carving tools and the chunks of
incense. Unfortunately, he had sold that lot nearly a chetne
ago. One reading-glass was all the ship boasted.

From the door wafted the spicy fragrance of honeycakes
grilling. Tarag wrapped the glass in its cloth and set it back in
the drawer. Perhaps later, when he had no business more pressing . . .

Half an hour later he was sitting in the bow of the dinghy
while Graio propelled them swiftly in the direction of the public
pier. As they swung near the pilings, Tarag had the rope ready
and tossed it. For three pennies to the man in the shed, they
could leave the boat tied there all day.

There were dozens of people on the pier coming and going
on their morning business—lowering bundles into waiting boats,
or merely visiting the public lavatory that overhung the water.
The wealthier districts in Falnerescu had indoor plumbing, but
this wasn't one of the wealthier districts. Tarag and Graio set
off across the planks toward dry ground, but before they reached
it Graio put out an arm to restrain his captain. "Sedan chair
over there," he warned. "Shall we duck out?"

"Graio, where are your manners? We mustn't disappoint
Shuma. Besides, I'm curious what's got her down here at this
hour of the morning. Usually she isn't even up yet."

So they went on boldly, down the center of the dock and
down the ramp to the street. The cobblestones were still wet
from being washed. Tarag bent their course toward the sedan
chair, which was supported by four stolid, well-muscled eunuchs,
and as he hove into its lee the curtain parted and Shuma Borando
peeked out at him. "Psssst!" she hissed theatrically.

Tarag feigned surprise. "How very nice to see your ladyship
this morning." He inclined his head a formal handsbreadth.

"Oh, don't be like that," Shuma said, wrinkling her nose. She was a sultry beauty with luxuriant black hair. Her gold earrings dangled as long as Tarag's fingers, and her perfume coiled into his nostrils. "What are you up to, Tarag? I want to know. You're dressed for a wedding."

"Nothing that final, I hope."

"Come on, Tarag, you can tell me. Hop up here beside me and whisper it."

"I don't think your bearers would appreciate that." The bearers, unblinking, gave no sign that they had heard.

"Well, I suppose I could get down and we could go for a walk. But a girl does like to be asked."

"My lapse was inexcusable, Lady Borando. Would you care to accompany me on a brief inspection of this unexcelled example of Falneresc civic architecture?" He held out his elbow gallantly. Shuma used it to get to the ground, then clung protectively to his arm as they sauntered off.

Watching their receding backs, Graio unlaced a pouch at his belt and drew out his pipe, which he stuffed with dried verlinmoss from another pouch. He stepped up to the lead eunuch. "Any of you got a light?"

Without speaking, the eunuch gravely proffered a little ceramic vial in whose cap was mounted a strange mechanism. Graio accepted the object and frowned at it in perplexity. He had been expecting a wooden match.

"Strike the flint against the iron," the eunuch suggested. "So the spark touches the wick just there." After fumbling for a moment, Graio saw how to draw back the flint on its spring and let it fly forward. On the third strike the wick blazed merrily. He held the flame over his pipe bowl and puffed.

"Now, tell me, Tarag," Shuma said. "What kind of mad scheme are you embarked on? And don't go all huffy and call me 'your ladyship.' Answer me straight."

"A small wager. Osher spoke to you, did he?"

"He couldn't wake my husband. Don't you think it's silly throwing yourself into the middle of something you don't understand? You'll only do harm. Why don't you and I go away today instead and have a nice long picnic in the woods?

Hmm?" Still hanging on his arm, she gazed up at him and batted her eyes appealingly.

Kissing those lips would have been easy. "Much as I'd enjoy it," he said with sincere regret, "my course is already plotted. It's a matter of honor."

"Oh, no, it isn't. It's the money you wagered, isn't it? Well, tell me how much it is, and I'll give you enough to pay it off—that, and enough over you'll think you've won. Say yes."

So she was willing to bribe him if necessary. That was intriguing. He wondered whether she was simply jealous, or whether she was trying to lure him out of the way for some other reason. "Your ladyship seems awfully eager. Can we not have our picnic another time?"

"Damn it, Tarag!" Shuma stamped her foot. "I'm trying to do you a favor. I know what you're up to, and you're going to find yourself in over your head."

"I'll swim."

"You're not listening to me. Do you think you can just waltz into this—this creature's bedchamber, and not cause an uproar? This is a complicated situation diplomatically, and I won't have the cart upset by a sea captain with a roving eye."

So it was political, not personal. Or at least not entirely personal. "You haven't always minded my roving eye," he commented.

"A lot depends on where and when it roves. Come on, Tarag, can't we just go have a nice picnic? You should see the sandwiches I had packed—there's spiced jelly, and sausage, and some mouth-watering, just-picked water-crisp, and a *big* bottle of wine."

"It's a splendid offer, your ladyship—a hundred olmins to spend the day in your delightful company. I can't think when I last had such an offer. It breaks my heart to refuse it." He saw in the set of her mouth that she wasn't finished trying yet. "But I rarely accept money from women as payment for my attentions," he added, to give her a push.

Shuma's eyes went glassy, and her mouth fell open. "I don't believe it," she said. "I don't believe you said that. Apologize, this instant."

Tarag lowered his eyes. "I may have put it badly," he admitted. "But that was the substance of your offer, was it not? Naturally, I understood that your ladyship meant nothing improper. You were moved to unaccustomed generosity solely by your regard for me. I'm deeply grateful."

"Then you'll come with me?"

"Shuma, not only will I *not* go with you, but if you're still standing here when I've counted to ten I'll pick you up by your hot little pink britches and toss you in the harbor. Am I making myself clear?"

After staring coldly at him for a good two-thirds of the allotted time, she spoke through clenched teeth. "You'll regret this. I promise you'll regret it." Turning on her heel, she stalked off.

"Looked like she was about ready to chew you up and spit you out," Graio said as they walked on into the city.

"Nothing serious, I trust. Only a little quarrel."

"You seem to've developed a sudden knack for gettin' Berkenders mad at you."

"I do, don't I? It's plain that they're concerned for the safety of the lilith, though I don't pretend to understand why. You'd think they'd see her as the worst sort of mongrel, and want nothing to do with her. Well, no matter. If they're concerned, her own people will be doubly concerned. The pilot did mention a guard, didn't he? Much as I favor the direct approach, this may not be the time for it. We might accomplish more by stealth. Aye. Tell me, Graio, who's the stealthiest man you know?"

"Pye. You'll be wantin' to talk to Pye."

"Curious," Tarag said. "I'd just had the same thought myself."

Everybody in Falnerescu, it seemed, was out on the street this morning. Tarag and Graio made their way up a crowded thoroughfare, stepping past farmers who had spread out mats on the pavement to sell fresh fruits and vegetables, fat old seawomen in capacious skirts, muscular oar, and innumerable children and small animals. At one corner they paused to let pass three clanking Berkender soldiers, attended by half a dozen kelg. The kelg wore leather breastplates for armor, but carried no weapons; their own fangs and claws were weapons enough. They were evil-looking little creatures with grayish-yellow skin, who stumped along on their hind legs in imitation of their masters, though in a rush they might go down on all fours. Like most Islanders, Tarag detested kelg, and like most Islanders he was prudent enough to make way for them in the street.

Tarag and Graio went on to where at last the pier street debouched into a broad plaza with a tall fountain in the center. On the stone ring around the fountain's pool women were pounding laundry, moss-covered gargoyles watching impassively from behind a curtain of water. The plaza, a welter of open-air booths and stalls where one might buy anything from grain meal to fine weaving and brasswork, was the commercial center of Falnerescu, and perhaps the city's heart. Its head, two thousand tadigs west along the shore but visible from the plaza, was the dark brooding mass of the Fortress Falneresc, a turreted and crenelated jumble of stonework crouched on the highest ground on this side of the bay.

"Fine thieving weather," Tarag observed. "Can't imagine a thief would be abed, a morning like this."

"Best hope not," Graio said. "Could be any of a hundred beds."

They wandered among the stalls, stopping from time to time to finger merchandise. Tarag's eye was caught by a small mechanical water-clock, and he picked it up and examined it. Water dripped from a reservoir into one of the spoons at the rim of a wheel; when the spoon was full, the weight of the water would cause the wheel to turn one notch, allowing a single glass bead to slide down a string. Clocks interested Tarag, because he had a vague idea they might be useful in navigation. Reckoning how far north or south the ship had drifted was simply a matter of sighting on the southern stars and measuring the angle they made with the horizon. But there was no equivalent way to judge east-west position. It was suspected that things rose later in the west than in the east; but without an accurate clock, measuring how much later was impossible. This clock was no improvement on dozens he had seen. It would work well enough on land, if the spoons and the drip-hole were kept clean. In high seas, however, the water would slosh uncontrollably. He put the mechanism down with regret.

Graio, tall enough to see over the heads of the crowd, had been keeping watch. "There," he announced. Tarag followed his lead. They came to an inconspicuous stop in front of a booth displaying rather unsanitary marsh-reed mats. About twenty tadigs on, a fat man whose jeweled rings flashed in the sun was arguing heatedly with a vendor of oils and unguents, waving a slim-necked jar in the hapless merchant's pinched face. With every breath the fat man took to shout, the leather purse at his belt swung and bounced against his hip. Standing quite close to the fat man but apparently oblivious to the argument was a slim, nondescript fellow with the smooth, bland features of a pure-blooded Eloian. Though he seemed entirely absorbed in the activity of sniffing first one jar of scented oil and then another, frowning with the concentration of a connoisseur, the Eloian was using only one hand to lift the various containers to his nose. The other hand, as if it were a small animal with a mind of its own, was tugging delicately at the drawstring of the fat man's purse every time it swung in the right direction. As Tarag and Graio watched, the purse yawned open and the hand dipped into it, to emerge clutching half a dozen gold pieces. When the hand had tucked the money safely out of sight in its new owner's belt, the Eloian sighed softly, shook his head in dismay at the poor quality of the oils, and moved placidly on.

"Quick," Tarag said. "Before he turns to smoke." The Eloian was making his way toward the mouth of an alley at the near edge of the plaza. When they reached the alley he was nowhere to be seen, but there they were free to run. After two turnings and one near-collision with a pushcart they sighted their quarry climbing a narrow flight of stairs toward a roof. "Ho, Pye!" Tarag called. "It's all right—it's us!"

The Eloian paused in his flight, saw who his pursuers were, and came more slowly back down the stairs. "You shouldn't run so loudly," he said. "Anybody else would have doubled back and dropped on you with a knife. How goes it, Tarag my friend?" He and Tarag clasped their four hands in a comradely grip.

"In up to my neck, as usual. You?"

"Times are bad for thieving, I fear. It's all these new taxes, and the slave glut. Folk are hanging tight to every copper."

"You seemed to be doing all right when we caught sight of you just now."

"Ah, that." Pye shook his head sadly. "A shameful business, but typical these days. I give the oil vendor thirty percent to look the other way. He wanted fifty, till I threatened to betray him if I was caught. Still, there's enough here for us to hoist a pint, if we like. What say?"

"Perhaps later. For what I've got in mind it may be to our advantage to move quickly. With luck, we may be able to get in and out again before they think to bar the gate."

"You've got your eye on a hoard."

"Aye." Tarag explained briefly the circumstances of the lilith's arrival and the wager he had made. "I'll not blame you if you don't want to pit yourself against the Berkenders," he concluded. "It's a risky game."

"Risky?" Pye's eyes were glowing. "It's a grand game. Would I pass up a chance like this?"

The three were strolling in a less crowded side street, taking care to lower their voices when passersby came within earshot. "The bet is not for *you* to see her," Tarag said.

"My friend, you do me an injustice. Nothing was further from my mind. I only meant that I've been chafing for something fresh. I'm too good at ordinary thievery. The sport's gone out of it. But this promises to be a rare challenge. Have you got a plan of attack?"

"Not a glimmer. I was hoping you'd come up with something."

Pye pulled ruminatively on an earlobe. "Well, I've seen Habil Metterner's house. Actually been inside it once, but that's another story. We could climb the wall. It's got iron spikes on top, but really they're just right for throwing a rope over, and so dull they wouldn't cut a baby's bottom. Once over the wall, you'd only have to locate an unbarred door. There's sure to be one, with all the clan there going in and out."

"Right now there might be, but by tonight they'll have turned the place into a fortress. If they haven't already."

"And walking in through the kitchen in the middle of the day is liable to get you noticed. Yes. You could climb up to a second-story window, but there's no guarantee it'd be unlocked, and you'd make too much racket, if you climb as well as you run."

"Better."

"That's what I was afraid of. Well, if we can't get you in the back door, we'll just have to get you in the front door. There are several ways to do that, some easier than others. You aren't bothered by being in small, enclosed spaces, are you?"

"Not that I've noticed."

"Good. Then we can get you inside undetected. I'm sure of it. After that, you'll be on your own. Graio, can you lift this reprobate?"

"Sure. Easy." Graio stood behind Salas Tarag, put his hands under Tarag's armpits, and in one smooth motion hoisted him to his shoulder, where he held him without apparent effort, sitting half on a shoulder and half on a hand.

Tarag shaded his eyes with a palm and peered ahead. "Ahoy, ahoy!" he called. Graio set him down again.

"Now, we'll need a piece of apparatus I can get from a friend," Pye went on. "And some trinkets. Jewelry, scarves, lotions, that sort of thing. You don't happen to have a store of such aboard your ship? I thought not. Well, we'll manage somehow. Oh, there's one other thing. Graio, you don't mind being a slave for an hour or two, do you?"

"Not as long as I don't have to put on chains. But you're jabberin', master Pye. What's this apparatus you spoke of? And what are we goin' to do with a mess o' scarves?"

In a few words, Pye sketched out his plan.

The first necessity was to procure for Tarag a long pink cloak, which conveniently tucked itself inside the front of Pye's shirt while the proprietor of a stall in the market plaza was distracted by a clumsy Potheqi. A few minutes later Tarag was standing in the shop of Bim the jeweler, a craftsman and merchant of excellent repute. Bim himself stood behind his carefully arranged display table and sourly regarded his customer. Tarag swirled the pink cloak affectedly and batted his eyes. "*I* don't know why she wants them," he lisped. "She's *so* impetuous about these things. 'Go, Erak,' she says. 'Bring me jewelry.' So naturally I'm supposed to drop whatever *I'm* doing and rush around like a common servant. She insists on having a large selection to choose from, and there's not a minute to be lost." He pulled a kerchief from his sleeve and sniffed at it delicately.

"It's highly irregular," Bim said.

"Well, don't complain to *me*," Tarag said superciliously. "If you don't want the business, I'm sure the Borandos would be happy to take their custom elsewhere."

"Did you want to take the merchandise with you?" Bim asked. "I'll need a rather substantial deposit—"

"Oh, heavens, no. *I'm* not going to carry any nasty old crates of jewelry around, not in this *sultry* weather. Just send one of your slaves up to the garrison, and she'll sign for the trinkets herself."

"Perhaps I ought to go myself," Bim said uncertainly. "Such an important customer—"

"Oh, no, no, no, no, no. She'd only keep you waiting half the day, and then not like anything and send it all back. She hates having a fuss made."

Bim was still suspicious. "You said your name was Erak? What exactly is the nature of your place in the Borando household, if you don't mind my asking?"

"Oh, heavens, nothing official. I'm just a friend of *his*, if you see what I mean. I only run little errands for her now and again to keep on her good side." It was public knowledge that Jakul Borando was more interested in the handsome young officers serving under him than in his beautiful wife, but that was no particular source of disgrace on the Island Sea, where customs varied widely. Borando's dissoluteness was legendary, his homosexuality merely incidental—but useful, at the moment.

"Oh, all right, all right," Bim said. "Just point out what it is you want, and I'll have the boy deliver it immediately."

"Well, I don't think it matters much *what* you send," Tarag said. "I mean, nothing looks really *good* on her, if you see what I mean. Let's see—that tray of rings, to start with, and—"

"The whole tray?" the merchant yelped.

"Well, she has to have some to choose from, doesn't she? Better make it two trays of rings, that one and that one over there." Tarag waggled a finger. "And those necklaces. She likes gold—though between you and me it doesn't do a thing for her complexion. And the shell bracelets, you'd better throw them in too." He gazed around the shop, eyelids drooping. "You don't have any jeweled hair combs, do you? She *expressly* told me to be sure there was a large selection of jeweled hair combs. Perhaps I'll have to go elsewhere after all." With a regretful sigh, he gathered the cape about him.

"No, wait! I've got some. Here, they were just on the bottom shelf. Look, won't these do? All the more stylish young ladies are wearing them."

Tarag inspected the tray of hair combs perfunctorily and shook his head in mock dismay. "I suppose they are. Well, there's no accounting for taste. Let's see, is there anything else? Oh, yes, throw in some silk scarves, if you've got any. And cosmetics. I don't suppose you stock cosmetics."

"I can get some from the apothecary down the block." By now Bim was desperate not to lose the sale.

"Good." Tarag dipped into his purse and drew out two of the gold pieces Pye had filched earlier. He dropped them negligently on the counter. "This is for your trouble. Now mind your slave doesn't dawdle. Lady Borando detests being kept waiting."

"Thank you, kind sir, thank you." Bim bowed and scraped as Tarag swept grandly out the door.

After mincing down the street until he was out of sight of the jeweler's windows, Tarag ducked into an alley, where Pye and Graio were waiting.

"How'd it go?" Graio whispered.

"He fell all over himself. Are you ready for the next bit?"

"Aye."

They watched from the mouth of the alley as Bim emerged from his shop and trotted down to the apothecary at the corner. When he had returned with a small parcel and gone back inside, Tarag emerged from the alley and went swiftly down the street, the pink cape billowing behind him. A wagon was parked near a wall, and he crouched behind it and peered through the spokes of the wheel at the door of the jeweler's shop. After a few more minutes, a gawky adolescent came out of the shop carrying a much larger parcel, embracing it in both arms. Bim was at the door behind him and stood shaking an admonitory finger as he repeated his instructions. The lad nodded, backing up slowly, torn between the need to listen courteously and the need to hurry as he had been instructed. For a moment Tarag was afraid Bim would watch the lad's progress down the street, which would make things difficult, but at last the merchant went back into the shop and shut the door.

Emerging from the alley at a trot, Graio careened squarely into the lad, sending him tumbling to the cobblestones. Tarag winced, imagining that he could feel the shock of the giant's impact even at this distance. Graio got to his feet and began yelling at the unfortunate courier. "Idiot! Dung-brain! Why don't you watch where you're going?"

The lad tried to get to his feet, but Graio was leaning over him menacingly, waving a boulder-sized fist in his face. At that point, however, Pye came striding along. He stopped to survey the scene and, taking the boy's part in the quarrel, interposed himself between the two and began shouting at Graio and shoving him back. After snarling a few more insults, Graio limped away, and Pye helped the lad to his feet. A kerchief appeared in Pye's hand, and as he wiped the dust from the lad's clothing he managed to hold the kerchief under the lad's nose for several long breaths. Already shaken, the lad swayed visibly. Pye had to support him with an arm.

Popping up from behind the wagon, Tarag sashayed down the street toward the pair.

"Are you all right?" Pye was asking.

"A little—a little dizzy," the lad said, pressing fingers against his temple.

"Well, that's only natural," Pye said, stuffing the kerchief back into his purse. "Why not come along to the tavern over there and have one on me while you catch your breath?"

"Oh, I can't," the lad said. "I've got to deliver this package to the garrison. If I waste any time, my master will—"

"Your master wouldn't want you to go on when you've been hurt, would he?" Pye said solicitously. "You're in no condition—"

"No, really, I appreciate it, but I've got to get—"

"Oh, say," Tarag interrupted in his most affected tone. "Are you the nice boy who's taking Bim's little trinkets up to the garrison?"

"That's right," the lad said woozily. "Aren't you the gentleman who ordered them?"

"Mmm-hmm. Say, I'm headed back to the garrison right now. Why don't you and I just walk along together and get better acquainted?" He put his hand on the lad's shoulder and squeezed gently.

"I'm not sure. Maybe I had better go sit down for a minute. I'm not feeling too well. Sorry."

"Well, if you change your mind . . . Say, I'll tell you what. Why don't I just take the package on up to the garrison for you, and you can go sit down and have a nice rest till you feel better?"

"I don't know. I'm not supposed to."

"Well, make up your mind, sweetie. I'd love to have you come along with me, but if you're not feeling up to it . . ."

Pye had the kerchief out again, holding it under the lad's nose. "Come on," he urged. "An ale will do you good. We won't tell your master. Let him take the package."

The lad scrunched his eyes shut and opened them again blearily. "Oh, all right," he said. "I've gotta sit down." He pushed the parcel into Tarag's arms.

"I'll see that it gets where it's going," Tarag promised. "You two enjoy yourselves. Toodles!" Tucking the parcel under his cape, he promenaded off down the street. Around the first corner, he stuffed the cape into a convenient trash bin and doubled his pace. Graio was already at the rendezvous, and Tarag gleefully held up the parcel. A couple of minutes later, Pye joined them. "I ordered two mugs," he reported, "and then went out back to answer a sudden call of nature. I hope he's got the coppers to pay for the ale when it comes."

"Say, what was that stuff in the kerchief?" Tarag asked. "It made me light-headed too."

"There's more to the craft of thieving than I'll confide to any mere apprentice. If you want to know more, you must join the guild."

"I don't know that I've got the soul of a thief."

"Why do you say that?"

"For one thing, I mean to return these baubles"—Tarag hoisted the parcel—"when we're done with them. Or better yet, send them on to Shuma and let her buy or return them as it pleases her."

"After all that trouble?" Pye protested mildly. "It seems a waste." But if he was thinking of diverting part or all of the jewelry to some other end, he kept his own counsel.

Chapter 4

The first thing Zhenuvnili noticed on her first morning in Falnerescu was that her bed was not swaying. She lay for a moment savoring the delicious solidity of the soft sheets and mattress, the not even remotely fishy smell of cooking and trees in bloom, before she yawned and stretched and levered herself up on one elbow. The whitewashed walls of the big room glowed where the sun spilled through the southern windows. The rugs and tapestries were finely woven, and the brass fittings of the square-cut furniture gleamed against the dark luster of well-oiled wood.

She sat up, and her feet found her slippers; she slipped into a translucent dressing gown, flipped her tresses out over the collar, and padded across to look out the window. Outside was a narrow balcony, less than a tadig wide, faced with a low balustrade. Standing on the balcony a window and a half to her left was young Gorin Metterner, staring stonily straight ahead, one hand gripping his sword hilt. Though he gave no sign that he had seen her, she stepped back a bit, not to arouse and embarrass him needlessly. Beyond the railing and below lay the garden, a walled profusion of greenery and blossom five times the area of the mansion itself. Between the house and the garden she could just glimpse through the gaps in the railing a broad patio of flagstone, with a table on it and some

52

chairs. She had a mad impulse, instantly suppressed, to burst out of the window, lever her bare legs over the railing, and drop from her hands to the pavement below. One couldn't, of course. Still, that table at the edge of the garden *did* look a nice place to have breakfast.

"Karanli, wake up! Ehlanli! Wake up, you mosspillows. Come dress me."

In the adjoining room she heard stirrings, and presently water gurgled in the lavatory basin. Karanli, her hair uncombed but her figure already—or still—wrapped in her gray traveling robe, entered and crossed to the wardrobe where the lilith's things had been hung. Stiffly, she ducked her head forward in a little bow. "How shall we dress you, li?" Her eyes had not risen from the rug.

Zhenuvnili's heart sank a little. She had hoped that once they landed . . . "Did you sleep well, pet?" she asked.

"She was tossing and turning all night," Ehlanli said from the doorway. "She kept poking me with her elbows." Ehlanli was wearing only satin shorts and a halter. Her limbs were still rounded by baby fat, but her figure was already budding, and promised to be ripe. She yawned and stretched sensuously.

"Oh, dear." Zhenuvnili went up to Karanli and put her arms around her. "I know it's hard, love. I know there are lots of things here that frighten you. But I need you to be strong. I want you to trust in the blessings of Li. Trust that She will guide you safely and be with you always. Can you do that for me, sweetness?"

Karanli took a deep breath and let it out shakily. "I'll try, Zheni," she said. "I'm sorry I'm such a miserable—I'm sorry you're stuck with me."

"Ssh-tch-tch-tch-tch." The lilith put a finger to the nala's lips. "I'm glad you're here. For one thing, it's the greatest opportunity you'll ever have to become the mistress of your fears, which is something every good lilith has to learn. And for another, I think perhaps you're here for a reason. I think Li sent you to remind me to be careful. Eh?" She beamed affectionately at Karanli, who returned the smile reluctantly. "So if something frightens you, don't give way to your feelings.

Just come and let me know, and I'll look at it and decide whether it's something we need fear or not. I'm counting on you to do that."

"But there are so many things," Karanli protested. "What if the foreigners burst in and kill us all?" She was wringing her hands.

"Love, please. Each moment the Goddess provides all we need for that moment. When you see a foreigner, you have my permission to scream as loud as you like. Until then, don't worry about it, hmm? You'll only make lines in your face." Zhenuvnili touched each side of the nala's mouth and between her eyebrows, as though drawing worry lines with a fingerful of paint. "Now. I want my outdoor cloak."

"What? Are we going somewhere already?"

"No, silly. Only out in the garden. There's a lovely patio just beneath our windows here. It's the perfect place to have breakfast."

"Completely impossible," Ranga Strell declared fifteen minutes later, standing with folded arms in the entryway of the lilith's suite. "Far too much traffic, too much visibility. We'll set up a table in here. Near the window, if you like."

"I *don't* like. Ranga, don't make me be cross. I just want to get some fresh air. I like the air here. It smells different than at home. Now that I think of it—" she paused to twinkle at him "—it's essential that I be able to take the air. After all, you're to meet these Berkender negotiators and take their measure, not I. If I'm to get any useful information at all, I'll have to sniff it in the air. If I'm not allowed to sniff the air, I don't see how I could possibly put my seal of approval to any treaty. Do we understand one another, dear Ranga?"

"Yes, my lilith." Lowering his eyes, Ranga Strell removed his bulk from between the lilith and the door. Drawing her hood forward, she brushed past him. She wondered how often she would be able to cut with that knife before it grew dull.

When she was settled at the table on the patio, the nalas brought a bowl of sliced fruit in tree-milk, and nut bread with honey, and at a sign left her to eat alone. The sun was gloriously warm, and the hint of a breeze rustled among the leaves of the trees. Her guard had descended the balcony's outside stairs and stood at one corner of the patio, his attention fixed on the top of the garden wall. Paradoxically, his motionlessness and silence made him more difficult to dismiss from her thoughts; she spread honey and took a bite of bread, but barely tasted it. What distracted her was the tension in the young man's stance. A lilith's first duty was to soothe away her lovers' tensions, so that she could sense and guide new tensions as they arose. But under the circumstances, soothing the guard's tensions would hardly be appropriate. There was the right of rank to be considered. Last night she had declined to take a lover at all, pleading weariness and the fact that her things were still packed. But Habil Metterner was the master of the house, and as such would be her first lover here, probably no later than this afternoon, followed by whoever was senior among the childbearing women. His nephew would be far down the list.

Thinking back on her arrival the night before, she realized that it was not just Gorin Metterner who was tense, but the whole household. They had all suffered years of abstinence, like dozens of other Vli scattered across the city and thousands on the Island Sea. Or did people choose to live abroad because they were ill-suited somehow to a normal sex life? Every lilith knew such people existed, though one did not talk to the nalas about them. That would account for some of the tension too— the cook laughing almost hysterically when introduced, the footman who looked at her not with joy but with a curious blankness in his eyes. Or perhaps she was only imagining it. If there were a few more here with unusual tastes than one would encounter among a like group at home, it was up to her to love them more freely and completely, that was all.

Spooning the milk over a golden slice of fruit, she permitted herself a small sigh. Had ever a lilith been faced with such difficulties? Vividly she understood Karanli's desire to be home again, safe in a Nest with nothing to worry about beyond smoothing a furrowed brow and making sure the stitching was tight in one's embroidery. Finding time to love all the Vli she could while she was here was her main concern as an individual—but she was not here as an individual. She was here as the representative of Li Ranli, head of all the liliths and chief priestess of Vli Holm, to the emissary from Berkenland. Upon Zhenuvnili's shoulders rested the weight of the fate of her land and her people.

She remembered the long intimate sessions in which Li Ranli had first sounded out her knowledge of foreign affairs. It was little enough—beyond their schooling in the arts of love and a bare ability to read and write, nalas were taught nothing. Living in the Nests, venturing out only on rare ceremonial occasions and otherwise having goods and entertainments fetched in, they needed no more. Most liliths had only the sketchiest ideas about the world beyond their walls. But Zhenuvnili had always been fascinated by books about travel. She knew the name and legend of the first seaman among the Vli to venture to a foreign port and return before she could recite the syllabary. In time, the illustrated storybooks no longer satisfied her, and she sent to the university for texts on geography and foreign languages. Not surprisingly, at her Robing she requested to join a Nest near the harbor, where she could pick up scraps of information from the pillow-talk of the oar. So when Li Ranli asked her opinion of the Potheqi threat, Zhenuvnili replied unhesitatingly. "I'm worried about it, more than I can say. It's not just that their land is growing drier and less hospitable every chetne. From what I've heard, they actually seem to *like* making war. I think it's sad that anybody can be so seduced by the thrill of violence, or by thinking they have no choice. There's always a choice. If they had liliths to love them, maybe they wouldn't be like that. But they don't, and they are, so we've got to take some kind of measures to see that the attacks against our ships don't turn into a full-scale war. We've got to find some way to make them stop. I'm not sure we could survive an invasion, as a people."

"So you think it will come to an invasion."

"Yes, I'm afraid I do."

"What measures would you recommend?" Li Ranli asked. The elder lilith was curled up on a cushiony green couch before a crackling fire.

Zhenuvnili frowned. "I'm not sure. If we gave them what

they wanted, that might stop them for a while, but it might only make them want more. We may have to fight them."

"But they're so many, and we're so few."

"Well, if you can't fight somebody by yourself, you have to get help. We need an ally, don't we? But none of the island kingdoms at this end of the Island Sea are strong enough or rich enough to help us. They're more helpless than we are." She might have said more, but paused.

Li Ranli smiled. "You're very astute, Zheni. I'm sure you know that. I need somebody astute. I'd go myself if I could—but I can't."

"Go? Go where?"

"To a place very, very far away." Li Ranli stared into the fire.

After that they had more conversations about specifics that Li Ranli knew and Zhenuvnili didn't. Only when Zhenuvnili had grasped the situation, and met and been approved by Li Ranli's circle of advisors, were the representatives of the government called in. And only after messengers had come and gone bearing notes sealed with wax on silver salvers did Zhenuvnili find herself for the first time sitting demurely across from Qob Qobba and Ranga Strell as Li Ranli set out her position.

Like any lilith, Li Ranli began with the personal and developed from there into the abstract. "Dear Ranga. Dear Qob. You both know me well." She smiled at each in turn, adjusting herself slightly in the chair with languid grace. "This is Zheni. Zhenuvnili. You will know her as well as you know me."

Zhenuvnili nodded at the funny fat man with the red face and the equally funny and equally solemn skinny man with the tall hair, and murmured agreeably. They looked as if they would be dears, when they loosened up.

"Zheni will be going with you to Falnerescu."

Ranga Strell's jaw dropped. "You're not serious," he said.

"Entirely serious. It's a measure of how serious I am that I'm willing to send her. Nothing less than desperation would prompt me to send one of my own to a foreign shore." Li Ranli leaned forward, elbows on knees. "This treaty is vitally nec-

essary. But it must be concluded on our terms. The safety of
the Nests cannot be compromised. I could not possibly agree
to any treaty that I felt violated certain basic principles." She
did not need to add that without her approval, no treaty was
likely to gain widespread support. "But the Berkenders cannot
land here until a treaty is signed, and I cannot voyage to meet
them.

"The solution is for Zheni to go with you to Falnerescu as
my representative. She need not be present at the negotiating
table—indeed, I assume she will not be. But you must present
to her the text of any agreement that is reached, and have her
signature on it before any others sign. If she does not sign, I
will not permit the agreement to take force. Is that quite clear?"

"But Rani," Qob Qobba protested. "This is so unnecessary.
We have the best interests of the Nests at heart. How could we
otherwise?"

Li Ranli's eyes softened. "I do not doubt your loyalty, Qob
Qobba. But you will be far from here, and subject to many
pressures, many unforeseen circumstances. If a treaty forged
and signed by you had to be disavowed by the Nests for some
reason, it might prove impossible afterward to convince the
Berkenders to ally with us, whatever the advantage. This I do
not intend to risk. So Zheni will go with you. And return with
you. I love my little Zheni very much, and I would be very
upset if she did not come back with you. More than upset, I
would be suspicious. And if I were suspicious, I couldn't possibly acquiesce in any treaty. I'm sure you understand. I want
Zheni to come back and tell me that the Berkenders made no
trouble about our conditions."

Qob Qobba shook his head slowly. "No. No diplomat would
agree to what you're asking. Not to speak of the danger to the
lilith, we would be negotiating with our hands tied behind our
backs. If she wasn't at the conference table—and obviously
she couldn't be—we'd never get anywhere. These Berks are
cagy. They play it two ways, from all I've heard. One is to
get you pinned down on paper before you have a chance to
leave the room. The other is to send in enough ships to burn
your cities to the tideline. Strell and I have got to be free to

exercise our own discretion. Otherwise we can't undertake it. I'm sorry."

"But you are free, dear Qobba. All the matters we've discussed—the location of their garrison, the number of troops deployed, the shipping lanes, even the amount of gold, up to the maximum that I'm sure you know as well as I—are in your care. To me they are nothing. You know this. And you know as well the conditions I do set. The Berkenders, officer and man alike, are to leave the garrison only on official business. Off their garrison, they are to be subject to our laws, and tried in our courts. Those found guilty are to suffer the penalties set by our laws. And any of our people, citizen or slave, if taken into the garrison for any reason, are to be surrendered to our authorities on demand."

Qob Qobba tried again. "I'm not sure you see the reefs in these waters, my lilith. A treaty of the sort you propose hinges on the question of who is the lawful government of Vli Holm. Unless the treaty specifies this, it can be abrogated simply by overthrowing the existing government and putting in a new one. The Berks have done this time and again."

Li Ranli was sitting bolt upright. "There's room for treachery, yes. But if we start spelling out the structure of our government in the treaty, all of it will become subject to negotiation, and the wording might contain a poisonous flower. No, our government must remain our own concern, both as to its organization and as to its laws. You'll have to draw the line there."

Both men conceded the point, reluctantly but without argument.

Five chetnes later, at the edge of the garden in Falnerescu, the weight of responsibility was heavy on Zhenuvnili's fragile shoulders. She felt tired and alone in the bright morning and wished she were back home in the Nest.

At one of the ground-floor windows Habil Metterner's round face peered out, bobbing and hovering uncertainly. If she beckoned, he would come sit beside her, and then perhaps they would go upstairs together. But she pretended not to see, and at last he went away again. She was not trying to avoid having sex with him—she was rather looking forward to it, in fact—

but there was still so much strangeness about this place, these people. She needed time to sort it all out and put her own mind at ease before she addressed herself to the needs of others. So when she had finished her solitary breakfast, she went for a stroll in the garden. The merchant's nephew made to follow her, and she waved him back. He frowned, but when she repeated the gesture he bowed and retreated.

The paths among the garden wove cunningly, so that from curves behind hedges house and wall were out of sight, and she might imagine that the greenery stretched out forever. After picking a blue flower and raising her veil to sniff its faint musk, she sat down on a sun-warmed stone bench and twirled the flower stem absently between her fingers. Amid the buzz of insects she began to feel a little sleepy, and nodded comfortably. The fact that she had snubbed Metterner rose up and nagged at her, and she felt a twinge of guilt. But she wasn't here to love him—she was here because she loved all her people. If carrying out her duty to Li Ranli meant ignoring the needs of every Vli in Falnerescu, she would do it. Or would she? How could two sorts of love oppose one another? Didn't the Teachings say there was only one font of love? Maybe the Teachings that were true in Vli Holm weren't true in other places. No, that was impossible. The Teachings were the Teachings, and love was love. If she loved at all, she loved everybody, and neglected nobody in need.

A shadow fell across the path, and she looked up, startled. Two beings stood before her, regarding her solemnly with dark unblinking eyes. Their heads were squat and hairless, their faces coursed with tiny wrinkles. Their earflaps, translucent, fluttered on their necks below narrow, pointed jaws, and from their delicate arms descended long capes of gauzy many-colored skin, the vestiges of wings. They were mnoerri. Except for stone-tipped spears and pouches slung from straps, both were naked.

The lilith regarded them in silence. She had seen mnoerri in her own land, twice, at a distance. Never had any approached so near her.

The lighter gray of the two took a step forward. "You are

visitor of island," it said in a voice that was half rustle and half squeak. "Visitor from island of threes. You are three." It spoke a strangely accented Olmalin, not her native Vli, but she found she understood it well enough.

"Yes," she said. "I am three."

"To this island welcome you we."

"Thank you." Vaguely she wondered how they had gotten in over the wall. Their wings were too frail to brave wind. "How did you know who I am?"

"To ones are few secrets. Open remains way."

The other mnoerri stepped forward. "Comings bring beginnings," it whispered in an even drier tone. "Beginnings bring new life."

"Beginnings bring new life," its companion echoed.

The lilith repeated the phrase as well. She liked affirmations. That seemed to please the mnoerri, who exchanged a few words in their own tongue. "Why have you come here?" she prompted. It could not be by chance.

"Upon us falls the knife. Come the many twos. Come the slaughter-fiends."

Even knowing the words, she had to struggle with the alien linguistic framework. "You mean the people here are doing violence to your people. Is that right?"

"For you also, open remains way."

"That's very sad. I'm very sorry. Perhaps I could send word to the governor of the island, but I don't suppose that would do much good. He has no reason to listen to me."

"Our wish was not this. Few are ones who remain, fewer at every moonrise. Oneness cries out among us. But stand-the-moons lacks long."

"I don't understand. Stand the moons?"

"When stand-the-moons, Become-All. Ones become all. Glad-flowing, each into each. When stand next the moons, ones before the knife will be scattered. Become-All not."

"This Become-All—" Zhenuvnili groped "—it's important to you. And you can't have it except when the moons are aligned properly."

"Open remains way." In the alien voice she could hear the note of praise, or hope.

"And you're afraid that when the time comes again, you'll be scattered."

"This to my island-brothers say I: Like oneness is threeness. In coming to island of you is new beginning, brings new life. As when stand the moons are you, coming." One oddly jointed arm-wing gestured at an invisible point in the sky.

"You mean you can have your Become-All now, because of my coming."

"Glad we. Of your coming glad."

"Well, that's very sweet. I'm not sure what a Become-All is, but I'm happy for you. I hope you have a good Become-All."

The mnoerri's wings rustled. "Moons not in sky, Become-All not. You stand. You three moons together, stand with us in forest."

"You mean you need me to be there? Oh, I'm sorry. I can't. I can't possibly. You'll have to think about me and pretend I'm there. Do you understand pretend?"

The wings were becoming more agitated. "Among threes," said the mnoerri with the quieter voice, "is not three life-bringer to young?"

"Yes, we are."

"For us also. Stand-the-moons brings young. Without Become-All, without young to fly, joining of ones island to island is lost."

Bit by bit Zhenuvnili puzzled it out. The Become-All was some kind of ritual that was necessary among the mnoerri for making babies. The two before her were hazy on the details; perhaps Olmalin had no words for the alien reality. But it was clear that without the Become-All an entire tribe would perish without issue, and they hinted that this was a tragedy not merely for the locals but for mnoerri everywhere. For equally mysterious reasons, her presence at the Become-All was vital. In the flesh, but only in the flesh, she was an adequate substitute for a lunar conjunction.

She tried to frame a refusal, but before the entreaty in those blank black eyes the words died in her throat. Hadn't she just affirmed that loving meant loving everybody? These gentle beings needed her. How were they any different, any less deserving, than her own people? She chewed on her upper lip. Common sense said it was impossible. Even Qob Qobba would balk at letting her go off into the forest, and Strell would be livid. Clearly, they would never let her leave the house on such an errand. And they would be right. Her duty was here—both her personal duty to the Vli men and women, and her larger responsibilities. Nor was this duty externally imposed. She loved her people. But what was love if one insisted on loving some and denying others? A lilith was trained to deny nobody. If she turned the mnoerri away, would she not be offending the Goddess? And what of the baby mnoerri who would never flock on the wind? Liliths had a special feeling for babies, because they bore none of their own.

"I can't promise that I'll come," she said at last. "Things are difficult here. I may not be able to get away. But I will try to come. If I can join you, I will. Do you understand?"

"You do not know the wind, but you will spread your wings. Yes."

"May I bring others, or must I come alone?"

"Become-All for twos is not."

That made it harder—to venture out without a guard for protection. But the Teachings were quite explicit about the fate of those who loved only when it was easy. "You must tell me how to find this place in the forest. I am a stranger on your island, and do not know the landmarks."

The larger of the mnoerri extended its arm to the south. "Fields, then forest," it said. "Then rock with three heads."

"This rock—is it near a road?"

"Big road. Stone river here—" right wing out. "Three heads rock here—" the left wing.

"Stone river?"

"On legs."

"Oh." It must mean an aqueduct. An aqueduct, and a well-traveled road, and a three-headed rock. She could find the place. "I'll be there when I can. Perhaps not till after nightfall. Wait for me."

Both mnoerri tapped the butts of their spears once, lightly, on the ground. The lilith touched herself thrice. They turned and slipped away between two bushes. After a moment she got up from the bench and went to look where they had gone, but blank wall greeted her, and bright sun and the buzz of tiny flying things. She was alone again. She went slowly back down the winding path toward the house.

On the patio, Ranga Strell was giving Gorin Metterner a thorough tongue-lashing. The lilith paused, half-hidden behind a flowering bush, to listen.

"I don't care *what* she told you. She's not to be alone at *any* time, for *any* reason, except in her own rooms." Strell's face was purple, and drops of spittle flew from his mouth into the hapless guard's face. "If you let her out of sight again while you're on duty, I'll see to it you *never* have the chance to love her. You'll be posted at once as far away from here as the first ship can take you. Do you understand that?"

Zhenuvnili stepped forward. "Ranga Strell," she said loudly. "It is not your affair whom I love, or when. There are punishments you may mete out that do not relate to me. Please confine yourself to such. As to this young man, I ordered him to remain behind. I will accept full responsibility."

"No." Strell shook his head emphatically. "You won't. You have no idea what's safe, or proper. You think you can come and go as you like. But that's not to be permitted."

"I was only in the garden." Ranga, she felt, was becoming very troublesome. But what if he was right?

"What if somebody climbed the wall and saw you? Have you thought about that?"

"Well, I suppose," she said, "that if somebody wanted to see me badly enough, they could climb the wall."

"So you understand why in future you're to remain indoors."

She frowned at him, her expression safely concealed by the veil. What was it that made him so hateful? Well, in his present humor it was no use talking to him about an excursion to the forest. If she was to get away, it would have to be on her own, secretly. "Dear Ranga." she said pleasantly. "I wouldn't dream of arguing with you. Shall we go indoors? Only promise me you won't punish this poor boy. I'm sure from now on he'll do everything in his power to follow your instructions." But I won't, she added silently. I won't.

Chapter 5

*T*he land on which Falnerescu had been built sloped gently up from the waterfront toward a low line of distant hills, often cloaked in haze, which were capped by the dark escarpment of an ancient, eroded lava flow. From the pier where Salas Tarag had tied his dinghy that morning it was nearly a two-hour walk through the warehouse and market districts, past the edge of the longhouse district where some of the old seafaring clans still made their homes, to the heights where dwelt the city's wealthy. There owners of fleets could look out their windows at the owners of vast farmlands, prosperous guild masters, delegations from foreign governments, exiled nobility, and an assortment of moneylenders and dealers in rare and costly commodities. The streets were wide and paved with brick, and the mansions hid behind high walls. Here and there narrow alleys ran back from the street toward garden gates, slaves' quarters, and stables.

At this hour, nearing midday, traffic was light—a one-passenger trap that rattled past drawn by a prancing little roaty, a couple of white-aproned women with tall baskets balanced on their heads, and an Eloian dressed in the flowing robes of an itinerant vendor of wares, accompanied by his slave, a bronze-skinned Potheqi giant who carried on one shoulder a massive iron-bound wooden chest entirely large enough to have contained a man. At the gate of one particular mansion the Eloian halted and peered between the heavy iron bars. Nobody was in sight. Only a few steps back from the gate stood the house—white stucco walls, windows of leaded glass set in arches, blue tile trim. The Eloian pulled the cord that hung down beside the gate, and the brass bell clanged vigorously. "Ho! You within! Entrance, I pray, entrance! Fauxnaster the jeweler is here to display his wares!" Fauxnaster the jeweler, should anybody have noticed, bore a suspicious resemblance to Pye the thief. When no answer was forthcoming, the jeweler repeated his exhortation.

The front door opened and a woman came out. Her dark hair was cropped short, and her bare arms were well-muscled. At her belt was a sword. "What is it?" she demanded, coming up to the gate. "What do you want?"

"Want? Ah, what I want is to make the world a little more beautiful. It's a labor of love. In the name of love I take my wares from house to house, leaving behind perhaps an item or two that might delight a young lady such as yourself, or delight her swain when he sees it, and all of the finest quality—rings from Raneldon, scarves from Scalienu, trinkets from Turenis, baubles from Bayyoum. Is there none within—perhaps even you yourself, fair lady—who desires to see the most precious and scintillating of stones set in necklaces, bracelets, earrings, hair combs of the most exquisite workmanship? And should these perchance not please, I have as well a selection of extremely stimulating scented oils and lotions, to say nothing of a thousand other items sure to delight the heart and gladden the senses. Indeed, I hardly know how to tell in words what a rare opportunity stands here before your gate. Will you not allow me to come inside and set out before you—"

The woman looked at him stonily. "We've got all the trinkets we need."

"Oh, surely not! Is there not anyone in this fine house whose surpassing beauty would be fittingly graced by a uniquely crafted gift tendered by those who cherish her? A hand-embroidered scarf, perhaps, or a gold ring set with rubies and diamonds? I assure you, my prices are extraordinarily modest. But why burden yourself with the decision? Why not simply inform your master that Fauxnaster the jeweler has consented to wait upon his convenience, and see what he says, eh? I'll just wait right here. No, you needn't apologize; I don't mind in the least. Graio, set down the chest, so I can have something to sit on. Careful—all that gold and silver is heavy, isn't it?" Pulling up the skirts of his robe, Pye settled himself on the chest. "Ah, that's better." He gestured impatiently to the woman behind the gate. "Well, go on. What are you waiting for?"

The woman glared at the jeweler, fist gripping her sword hilt. "Wait here," she said. "I'll get somebody."

Only a couple of minutes passed before they were confronted by a tall thin man whose thick curly red hair stood straight up from his bald forehead. He stared at them between the bars of the gate. "You're a jeweler?"

"Your wisdom surpasses all understanding, kind sir. Such indeed is my humble profession. And you, I take it, are the master of this house?"

"Not I. This is the house of Habil Metterner. I am called Qob Qobba. State your business."

"My business, sir, is beauty. To each businessman, it's true, his business is beautiful, for it brings him wealth and the respect of his fellows. But all men's business is not *in* beauty, as mine is. My wares are the most hauntingly and maddeningly beautiful that can be had anywhere on the Island Sea—as, indeed, kind sir, I'm sure you'll be wanting to see for yourself. If you would but unbar the gate, my slave will bring this heavy cask"—he thumped his heel roundly on the chest—"within, where all that it contains may be displayed before your wondering eyes."

"You've come at a bad time."

"All the more need, then, for humble Fauxnaster. For what lifts up the downcast heart like a precious stone, eh? But are cold stones all that I offer? No. In this cask I have perfumes imported from distant lands with whose lascivious fragrance the fair sex cannot fail to delight a hapless clod such as you or I. Also among my wares—"

"Fair sex?" Qobba interrupted. "Don't you know this is a Vli house?"

"Oh. Ah." Fauxnaster lowered his eyes in evident embarrassment. "A thousand pardons. I can only pray that my ignorance will be forgiven. Then I take it there is nobody within who requires finely embroidered scarves, or silver bracelets chased with ivory and jade, or that powder for the bath whose many-colored bubbles tantalize the skin as they soothe and soften . . ."

"Oh, let me think a minute, won't you? Yes, all right. Come on in." Qobba turned to the woman guard, who was regarding him sourly, and spoke in Vli. "It's on my authority."

"I don't like the look of them," she answered.

"Wouldn't you like to have something to give Zheni? I know I would." Qobba put his arms to the bar, lifted it and slid it back, and the gate swung open.

With a grunt Graio hoisted the chest once more onto his shoulder, and they proceeded through the gate, across a narrow courtyard with a brace of miniature fruit trees, and up the blue-tiled steps to the tall wooden door. Behind him Pye heard the scrape of iron against iron as the bar was made fast. It was not a sound that he liked.

Qob Qobba led the way down a long hall whose ceiling arched in dimness far above. Without seeming to, Pye cast an appraising eye over the tapestries and candelabra. Good workmanship, and imported, probably from Vli Holm itself. Worth remembering, if ever he found himself in the neighborhood. Qob Qobba indicated an archway. "In here, please." They entered a room.

"Over there, Graio," Pye suggested. "Where the light's best." In fact, that corner was distinctly gloomier than the other side of the room, where tall arching windows looked out on the patio, but it was near a side door that opened on another, apparently unoccupied, room. Graio complied—but the chest slipped from his grip and landed with a none-too-gentle thump. Pye winced, expecting a muffled stream of profanity, but the chest remained silent. Graio retired to the opposite end of the room, where he stood gazing around restlessly and fidgeting from foot to foot.

"Well, shall we get on with it?" Qobba asked.

"Certainly, sir." Pye unlatched and lifted the lid of the chest, revealing a shallow tray overflowing with sparkling jewelry. He launched into an elaborate sales pitch, waving glittering necklaces one after another under Qobba's nose to dazzle him. Graio, meanwhile, was edging toward the arch that led back into the hall.

But before Graio could commit himself to his part in the scheme, Qobba shook his head and backed away from the supposed jeweler. "I don't know," he protested. "They all look alike to me. Wait here while I fetch somebody who knows about this sort of thing." He stepped past Graio and went out, leaving the woman guard to keep an eye on the two strangers.

Pye cleared his throat. "I don't suppose I could interest you in some earrings," he said. "They're very nice earrings." The woman stared at him and said nothing.

Several uncomfortable minutes later, Qob Qobba reappeared escorting the nalas, who were swathed from head to toe in their hooded gray robes. Pye wondered whether either of these mysterious figures could be the lilith, and decided that was unlikely. Ehlanli was leading Karanli by the hand, Karanli allowing herself, reluctantly, to be dragged forward. When they saw the foreigners, both stopped in their tracks. Karanli tried to wrench her hand free so she could turn and run, but Ehlanli tightened her grip and grabbed the other nala's shoulder. The two tussled. Writhing, Karanli began making a throaty gasping noise, an "aahh-aahh-aahh" that went on and on. The sound was not loud, but it was unsettling, disturbing. Pye felt the hair on his neck prickle. He knew enough Vli to know that the sounds were not words. Ehlanli began dragging Karanli forward, talking to her in a low, firm voice, while Qob Qobba stood by helplessly, clenching and unclenching his hands. He was unsure whether he wanted to discipline Karanli or offer her comfort, but as he was forbidden to touch her he could do neither.

For the sake of adding to the confusion, Pye advanced boldly on the hooded figures, holding out a necklace of amber beads. "See?" he said eagerly. "Pretty. Pretty." The guard stepped toward him, leaving Graio, for the moment, unobserved. Graio sidled again toward the hall. The guard blocked Pye's shoulder with the heel of her hand, and he allowed himself to be pushed back. Over her shoulder he saw Graio vanish through the archway. He waited two more breaths before calling, "Graio! Graio, come back here! Where are you going?"

Qob Qobba and the guard both turned, saw that the giant had vanished, and leaped after him. At the same moment Ehlanli lost her grip on Karanli, who tumbled backward into Qobba, sending them both reeling. Ehlanli sidestepped around Karanli and followed the guard, and after regaining his footing Qobba did likewise, leaving Karanli in a heap on the floor.

The hooded figure's face was turned away from Pye, and he judged that this was the best opportunity he would have. Bending over swiftly, he released a hidden catch. The front of the chest swung open and Salas Tarag rolled out. Pye jerked his thumb in the direction of the side door to the next room, and Tarag scuttled in that direction without straightening up. Pye knelt and fastened the secret panel once more in place. Looking up, he saw that the hooded figure had gotten to its feet and was leaning against the wall, trembling visibly. The hood was still partially averted, the face wholly invisible. Was he being watched? Had the figure seen Tarag? If so, the game would be up at any moment. But except for the shuddering of indrawn and expelled breath, the figure remained silent.

A good deal of shouting echoed from the hall, and after a moment Graio was led back into the room by the woman, at sword point. "What's all the fuss?" he was grumbling. "I just wanted to have a look around. Maybe stop in the kitchen for a snack."

Qob Qobba appeared behind Graio, brandishing a pikestaff awkwardly but nonetheless putting on a bold front. "This misconduct is not to be borne," he declared. "Pack your wares, jeweler, and get out of here!"

Continuing the imposture, Pye glared at Graio. "You've worn out our welcome again, have you?" he snarled. "I'll whip you, I swear it! You'll have no mercy from me!" To Qobba he went on in a sugary tone, "Kind sir, I pray, let not this half-witted barbarian's deplorable manners prevent us from concluding our business. I have anklets with silver bells—"

Another man, stout and red-faced, burst into the room. "What's the meaning of this disturbance, Qobba?" he demanded in Vli. "What are these people doing here? What sort of treachery is this?"

"No treachery, Strell. You've been so hard on poor Zheni, I thought only to cheer her up with a gift. By chance, this jeweler appeared at the gate—"

"Jeweler? How do you know he's a jeweler? How do you know he's not a spy, or an assassin? Can you tell me that?"

Pye decided the conference had gone on long enough. Time to get thrown out. Turning again to Graio, he resumed his harangue. "This time you've gone too far, you useless hunk of meat! I'll sell you to the first swamp-rat slaver I can find, papers or no papers!"

With a howl of protest Graio dived at his supposed master, and the two had to be forcibly separated. "Enough!" Ranga Strell roared in heavily accented Olmalin. "Out! Get out!"

"Oh, very well," Pye said, collapsing suddenly into sullen resignation. "Get the chest, Graio. Mind how you lift it—it's still just as heavy as it was before." Graio made a show of heaving the chest up to his shoulder, and they were escorted at point of sword and pike down the long hall to the tall doors and out into the sunlight. The whole way Strell kept up a stream of Vli, and Qobba listened with his lips pressed together.

But before they could reach the gate, a shout came from the balcony overhead, and the entire party turned to look. A drab-looking older woman was standing on the balcony frantically waving her arms, while behind her thick smoke billowed from a window. "Fire!" she screamed. "Fire! Help!"

The guard who had been herding Pye and Graio turned and raced back into the house, Qob Qobba at her heels. Wasting no time, Pye unlatched the bar on the gate and lifted it aside. But Ranga Strell, who moments before had been determined to see them gone, had changed his mind. "Hold!" he cried. "It's a plot! Stand where you are!" As Graio stepped out the gate, Strell attached himself to his arm and tried to drag him down. Graio unceremoniously and firmly dropped the chest of jewels on the stout man, who fell beneath it. Pye was already away down the street, knees high as he sprinted, and Graio's pillar legs pounded after.

The light hit the Tarag's eyes like a wall, but he was moving. He saw Pye's thumb jerk and lurched in that direction, ignoring the agony in his ankles. Through the doorway, he rose to a half-crouch and looked around warily, flexing the stiffness out of his limbs. He was in an ordinary room, furnished with a square-cut wooden table and chair, a brass wall sconce mounted with three white candles that had burned halfway down, and very little else. He was alone. Good. Now all he had to do was keep from being discovered until he had a chance to find out where they were keeping the lilith.

In the next room he heard Graio being brought back, and the confrontation between Qobba and Strell. He tiptoed toward the opposite door and pressed his ear to the crack. No sound. He carefully opened the door. The next room was empty as well, but there was a curtained archway, low and unadorned, and beyond the curtain lay darkness. A place to hide, if he needed one. Worth investigating.

Dark objects surrounded him, and ahead was another curtain leaking light. Drawing the edge of the curtain back with a cautious finger, he saw Pye and Graio being ushered down the main hall to the door.

Beyond this point he had no plan. Pye had told him the house was two-storied, and he assumed the lilith would be upstairs. But it would be folly to walk boldly up the front stairs if a less trafficked route was available. What he needed was to wait here until he overheard a conversation or two.

At the cry of fire he was instantly alert, and a moment later confused. Had Pye contrived somehow to kindle a fire as a diversion? Unlikely. He peeked out again, and watched as the swordswoman and the tall man with the pikestaff rushed in the front door and up the stairs. From the rear, at the same moment, came two kitchen slaves bearing large wooden buckets that sloshed out wet on the tile floor. A slightly built figure in a hooded gray robe came past Tarag's hiding place, quite close, and nearly collided with a third slave rushing back toward the kitchen. A stout red-faced man staggered in at the front door shouting, "Treachery! Treachery!" He was bleeding from a cut on the head. A man and a woman who might have been scribes rushed by, cradling bundles of rolled parchment in their arms. The stout man seized the arm of another bucket-bearer, and was shaken off. He then accosted the hooded figure. "Where's Zheni? Why aren't you with Zheni?" In the uproar Tarag couldn't hear the low-voiced reply. The first bucket-bearers came back down the stairs. A second robed figure dashed past Tarag and staggered up the stairs, and the stout man followed it, still shouting. A young swordsman appeared, crying, "The wall! We've got to watch the wall!" He waved furiously at a group of slaves who had come from another passageway. "You, and you, get swords and follow me! You, see that the gate is barred!" Smoke was drifting down the stairs. A third robed figure—or was it the first one he had seen, come back?—stopped directly across the hall from Tarag and stared straight at where he stood concealed by the curtain; not breathing, he watched the figure through the coarse weave. After a moment it went on in the direction of the front of the house.

The tempo of the shouting and stamping of feet overhead changed abruptly. There was a ragged scream of fear, followed by the unmistakable clash of blade on blade. In through the front door plunged a raggedly dressed man with drawn sword. A bucket-bearer caught sight of the intruder, and lost no time letting fly first water and then bucket. The intruder, spluttering, pursued him, and the slave scuttled away down the hall, screaming, "Help! Help! Somebody! Murder!"

Tarag gripped his dagger. Obviously, he wasn't the only one who had come to pay a call on the lilith. And the newcomers, whoever they were, seemed little concerned with social amenities. Down the stairway, dueling, came the Vli swordswoman and another of the intruders, she forcing him back one step at a time. Before they reached the foot of the stairs another scream ripped the air, and a human body dropped from an interior balcony to land with a dusty thump on the floor of the hall, where it lay crumpled, unmoving. Somebody else was still screaming somewhere, and the smoke was getting thicker.

Tarag's first impulse was to bolt from the house in the confusion. But after an attack like this, the Vli would be triply cautious. He was unlikely to gain admittance again. Equally, he could not stay where he was. Assuming that the house did not burn to the ground, the victors—probably the Vli, but perhaps the intruders—would soon be searching to root out what enemy might remain. His best course was to stand forward and fight with the Vli. He might even be able to help save the lilith's life from these assassins—certainly a deed worthy of a boon.

He drew the dagger and, holding it point up in his fist, stepped out of the curtained alcove. There were two fights going on in the hallway, Vli swords evenly matched against the attackers. He looked around for a better weapon, but none was to hand. He danced forward on the balls of his feet, looking for an opening to leap on one of the intruders. But as he was still circling, a voice behind him cried, "Aha!" He wheeled just in time to see a bucket spinning squarely at his head. Pain exploded.

He woke to the pain, and waited patiently while it receded to an evil throb. He became aware that a weight was planted firmly on his chest. The sounds of battle had subsided, but not far away he heard somebody sobbing. The air stank of wet ashes. He opened his eyes a slit and saw above him Qob Qobba. The Vli diplomat was standing with one foot on Tarag's chest, holding a pike so that its point wavered a scant fingersbreadth from Tarag's throat. Qobba looked bitterly determined, and also very nervous.

"You can put that down," Tarag said as calmly as he could. "I'm on your side."

"Silence." The point of the pike nicked Tarag's throat.

"Ow. Well, at least use a proper grip. You can't possibly hold it steady with both arms out from you like that. Tuck the butt under one arm and get the fingers beneath the shaft, not on top."

Qobba considered this advice briefly before complying. The point was still less than a handsbreadth from Tarag's chin, but he could breathe now without fear of inadvertently developing

a new orifice for the purpose. Several minutes passed before
Gorin Metterner, still brandishing a sword, came striding in
the front door. "They got clean away," he announced in Vli.
His face was clouded with fury.

"All but this one," Qobba replied.

"With any luck, he'll lead us straight to the others."

"I wonder. He doesn't look the sort to betray his friends."

"He'll talk before we're done with him."

Tarag got the drift of this exchange. For the moment, he
felt, it would be prudent to pretend that he understood none of
their tongue. They might let drop something useful.

Ranga Strell bustled toward them, glowering, followed by
Habil Metterner and the woman guard. "The house and garden
have been searched," Strell said. "The lilith is gone." Gorin
Metterner sobbed once, a raw sound in his throat, and Qob
Qobba blinked back sudden tears.

"Did you question the nalas?"

"One of them is hysterical, and the other is seeing to her.
They know nothing."

Tarag, still on his back on the floor, looked inquiringly from
one of them to another, as if waiting to be let in on the conversation. So, he thought, the intruders weren't assassins; they
were kidnappers. His chance of ever seeing the lilith had just
taken a decided turn for the worse. That, however, was not his
most pressing problem.

"Can I get up now?" he asked in Olmalin. "I won't make
any trouble."

"Are you ready to answer questions?" Qobba demanded.

"Certainly."

A wave of dizziness hit him as he rose, but he managed to
stagger, supported at both elbows, into a room he had not seen
before, a big square room with a stone fireplace, desks, and
several uncushioned wooden chairs, into one of which he was
summarily pushed. He palpated his head gently, and winced.
There was a painful swelling, but skull and skin seemed intact.
The guards took up position at his sides, one holding each
shoulder, and Ranga Strell faced him. Blood was matted in
Strell's hair where Graio had dropped the chest on him.

"What is your name?" Strell demanded in thickly accented Olmalin.

"My name is Salas Tarag. I'm a free ship's captain."

"It will do you no good to lie. Everything you say will be looked into, and if we find you have been lying it will go very badly for you. I ask you again: Who are you?"

"I told you already. If you don't believe me, ask any oar on the waterfront. Half of them know me, at least by sight. My ship is the *Amera Smiles*. May I ask what I'm accused of?"

"You may not. We'll do the asking. Who hired you to come here?"

"Nobody hired me. I came here of my own free will."

"Liar!" Strell's hand came up as if to strike, but he checked himself.

"It could have been the Berkenders," Habil Metterner suggested in Vli. "I've heard of this Tarag. He's friendly with the wife of the commander of the garrison, or so they say."

"Why would the Berkenders want to kidnap Zheni?" Qobba asked. "They must know it would destroy any hope of a treaty."

"True, but how can we be sure they *want* a treaty? We've only their word. What if they've taken the lilith to force her to reveal our weaknesses?"

"You," Strell snapped at Tarag. "Is it true you're a Berkender agent?"

"No. It's true I number among my friends Berkenders, just as I number Olmalinese, Eloians, Vli, Potheqi, Hamil, even a wogglie or two. But as to my being hired by them, absolutely not. This would all be much simpler if you'd let me explain—"

"You'll have plenty of time to explain, after you tell us where your men took the lilith."

"Those were not my men. I've never seen them before in my life. I have no idea who sent them, and even less idea where they've gone." Hearing his own words, he realized how lame they sounded.

The back of Strell's hand struck Tarag's mouth, hard. One of the fingers bore a heavy square-cut signet ring. Tarag licked his lip, and tasted blood. "Where have your men taken the lilith?" Strell barked. "Answer!"

"I can't tell you what I don't know. If I'm to be charged with a crime I demand to be taken before the governor and have the accusation read."

"We'll turn you over to the governor when we're done with you, never fear. But how much of you is left to stand trial depends on how much you tell us now, is that clear? How many of you were in on the plot? Where is your headquarters? Who is the leader? Speak, before you start losing toes!"

Qobba protested in Vli. "I don't know that we ought to be taking so harsh a line, Ranga. Why not listen to what the captain has to say before we reach any conclusions?"

"He hasn't said anything, and he won't unless we force him."

"But Ranga—"

"Bungler! You let Zheni slip through your fingers, and now you want to let this one off the hook. If we do things your way, we'll never get her back."

Salas Tarag took a deep breath. "I'd be happy to tell you everything I know. I don't expect you to believe me, but by the Goddess I swear that every word will be truth."

"How dare you name the Goddess?" Strell came at Tarag again, fingers outstretched to throttle him. Tarag twisted away as best he could with both arms pinioned. In the struggle his coral necklace broke, and the beads bounced across the floor. Qobba was behind Strell trying to restrain him, and one of the guards interceded as well. When order was restored, Strell was standing sullenly on the far side of the room and Tarag was fingering his throat and coughing.

"He won't tell us anything if you kill him," Qobba said, a tremor in his voice.

When Tarag could speak he said, "When I spoke of the Goddess I spoke of Amera, whom I worship. No other Goddess did I mention, nor would I. I'm sorry if I've given offense." He met Strell's eyes for a moment, then let his gaze drop.

"You said you'd tell us your part in the kidnapping," Qobba prompted.

"I said I'd tell you all I know. Unhappily, as regards the kidnapping, what I know is nothing."

Strell snarled.

"Bring in the chest," Qobba said. Gorin Metterner and his uncle went into an adjoining room and fetched the chest, whose false front was now sprung and spilling jewelry. "Is this nothing?" Qobba demanded. "Do you deny that this is the conveyance in which you and your men planned to spirit away the lilith? Speak!"

"That is the conveyance in which I arrived here."

"So you admit it!"

Tarag went on patiently. "My two friends, the Eloian and the Potheqi, carried me in and made a distraction so I could get out of the chest unobserved. We meant no harm. I was in a tavern last night when a harbor pilot told us of the lilith's arrival, and I wagered some friends that I could see her face to face. Kidnapping was never our intent. We three came here alone, and would have left as peaceably as we arrived. Of the others who burst in, and of the fire, I know as little as you. This by Amera do I swear."

"No, no, it was *you* set the fire, isn't that so? Wasn't that your part in the plot—to create a diversion so your comrades could get in over the wall? I ask you again where they have taken her. To your ship? Where?"

"You're welcome to search my ship if it pleases you."

"What of the two who brought you here? Who are they?"

"The giant is Graio, my first mate. You'll find him back aboard the *Amera Smiles* by now, unless he stopped off for a bite. Graio has a big appetite. The Eloian is no more than he told you himself, a jeweler named Fauxnaster." Let them disprove that, if they could. "Graio will confirm everything I've said. He was there when the wager was made."

Qob Qobba pulled tufts of hair between his knuckles, thinking. He was convinced that the dark-skinned stranger was lying, but he saw that the lie had too many strands to be untangled here. They had not the force of arms to hunt down the kidnappers unaided. "Audacious," he said at last. "If all you've said is true, you might still have started the talk of the lilith yourself, and maneuvered yourself into the wager for some reason you've not spoken of." He turned to Strell. "We'll have to take him before Governor Chespid. If their scheme is to get the lilith off the island aboard this one's ship, they've got a fine head start, and we won't stop them unless the governor orders out the harbor patrol."

"Can't you see you're playing into their hands?" Strell fumed. "The harbor patrol is no more than an arm of the Berkender garrison. They'll seize Zheni and turn her over to the Berks, and we'll never see her again."

"We've got to trust somebody," Qobba pointed out. "Our only hope of seeing her again lies with Nule Chespid. Or are you suggesting that we take on the entire garrison by ourselves? As matters stand, we dare not even accuse the Berkenders unless we've got some proof. By using Chespid as an intermediary, we can keep our hands clean. And if the Berkenders are behind this, which I very much doubt, Chespid will have heard a whisper. He knows everything that goes on in Falnerescu."

Hands beneath Tarag's arms lifted him to his feet. He had never imagined the day would come when he would be glad to be dragged before Nule Chespid and branded a criminal, but his heart was far lighter now than it had been a moment before. He would be free of suspicion only when the actual kidnappers were found, and the Vli were not going to find anybody by torturing him.

Chapter 6

The first humans to ply the waters of Falnerescu Bay arrived in outrigger canoes built of tied bundles of reeds. These craft, which seated five comfortably and nine or ten with some danger of swamping, were the product of the most advanced form of shipbuilding known on the Island Sea at the time. That anybody had the temerity to brave open ocean in them was astonishing. Of the science of navigation these early seafarers were almost entirely ignorant. They knew that the sun and moons came up in the east and set in the west, and some few shamans had mastered the secret art of making charts by tying knots in cord. The people wove baskets, and had never heard of firing clay for pots. Their spears they tipped with stone.

At what was to become Falnerescu the first oar—more accurately, in those days, paddle—found a tidal marsh of enormous extent, alive with sting-flies and mudfish, sheltered on all sides from the sea save for a gap in the eastern hills that one might paddle across in a quarter of an hour when the current was fair. Marsh mud was an uninviting place to build huts, however. The most habitable spot was an isolated hill deep in the southern marsh where dry-land vegetation showed the tide never rose. That hill the people called *nechar*—their word for "hill." Somewhat later, their descendants were conquered by a race that built wide, shallow plank boats with hide-covered shields at the prow, still outriggered but equipped as well with a small square sail that could be raised or lowered and benches where twenty men could paddle facing forward. These folk called a hill *vesc*, so the name of the place became Nehar Vesc. Again generations passed, until a more warlike race arrived rowing the first true galleys. Their word for hill was *pfal*. Thus the not very remarkable hummock in the marsh came to be called Pfal-Neirvesc. The *-u* suffix, added still later, was an Olmalinese form that meant "city."

Every succeeding wave of invaders drained and filled in more of the marsh, so that houses could be built—far more houses than the original hill could have held. On the hill was built a fortress where, when raiders came from the sea, the people could retreat behind palisades and rain down spears and arrows on the enemy. As time passed, the hill disappeared entirely beneath the encroaching stonework of the fortress, which, old and smoke-blackened, crouched on it like a hardened lump of dung. Rumor had it that the fortress was shot through with secret passages—not unlikely, in view of the amount of reconstruction that had gone on over the years. The current governor, technically an appointee of an independent council of nobles but in reality serving at the pleasure of the Berkender emperor, was the successor of the old line of island kings, and lived in the fortress as they had. And in its foundations, as in ages past, lay the prison.

Dabbing crumbs from his lips with a smooth white napkin, Governor Nule Chespid permitted himself a tiny grimace of exasperation. How was he supposed to enjoy his luncheon with this Berkender officer standing so stiffly before him? The officer—Vod Penna Osher, and in uniform, helmet clutched under one arm—could not very well be kept waiting. But nothing compelled Chespid to offer him food. The table was set for one, and adding another place would be awkward at best, since the table was precisely the wrong height. Sitting behind the table with his chair on its customary raised platform, Chespid had his eyes at nearly a level with the Berkender's. If they had both been standing, he would have been staring at Osher's brass-buckled chest—for the governor of Falnerescu was a tiny man, not much more than four feet tall. He was small-boned and well-proportioned save for his hands, which were large, red, and coarse, with prominent wrinkled knuckles. Chespid had always looked on the hands as foreign objects, attached to his wrists by an accident but really belonging to somebody else. Fastidious by nature, he kept them out of sight as much as possible. His head was entirely hairless, his features smooth, almost boyish—though the curl of his lip and the glitter in his eye suggested that he was not young in the ways of the world.

Having let the Berkender stew for a bit, Chespid spoke abruptly. "So. What are my orders?"

Vod Penna Osher squirmed inwardly. He did not like Chespid's habit of using tactlessness as a bludgeon. There were several other things he did not like about Chespid, things not material at the moment. "By the Charter, you're not subject to orders. You know that as well as I. This is merely a request for assistance."

"Which I will most graciously grant, if I know what's good for me. Yes." Chespid sawed off a flaky piece of fish, dipped it in sauce, and conveyed it to his mouth. "Well, go on."

"The commander feels that certain measures need to be taken. However, for reasons that I'm not at liberty to explain, we are unable to take care of matters for ourselves."

"Reasons you're not at liberty to explain. Those are always the most interesting kind. What measures?"

"It will require the deployment of a few of your guard."

"I'd already guessed that. I don't know why we pay your tribute. We always end up doing your dirty work for you on top of it. What is it this time? Smugglers? Or has somebody been posting seditious notices?"

"This is no ordinary criminal matter," Osher said. "Last night a ship arrived from Vli Holm, bearing an important diplomatic party. You may already have gotten word of it."

"One hears rumors, certainly." In fact, Chespid had not previously heard about the lilith's arrival, but he was far too canny to let slip the fact. He took a sip of wine.

"The Vli are staying at the home of one Habil Metterner, a merchant of their race. To ensure their safety, a guard must be posted before nightfall outside the walls of the Metterner estate."

"You've got plenty of men. Why not guard them yourselves?"

"The situation is delicate. If we surrounded the Vli with our own soldiers, they would see it as a deadly affront to their independence. Do you see?"

"Independence." Chespid cocked his head as if listening to a distant bell. "The word has a vaguely familiar ring, but I'm not sure what—well, no matter. You expect me to post a guard, probably six men on two shifts, which is twelve men I haven't got. Would you like me to pull them off the streets, and let the thieves have their way? Or would you suggest leaving nobody to take the daily tally and collect the fish tax?"

"Hire more men if you need them. This matter is urgent."

Chespid removed another bite of fish from the fork with his front teeth, set down the fork, and let his hand drop discreetly back to his lap. "I don't suppose you have any idea how I'm supposed to *pay* these men you're so eager for me to hire. Or is Borando going to dig into his own purse for a change? I believe I could provide an adequate force for, shall we say, five gold pieces a day?"

"Impossible. Out of the question. You could feed a squadron for five a day. Your sources of revenue should be ample for such a minor expenditure. You collect the port duties, after all. Without us to hunt down the pirates, you'd have no duties to collect. All the cargo would be putting in up the coast at night. And this is the thanks we get."

"You also get the pirates' cargo, and I see not a penny of it. But let's talk no more of finances." Having made his point, Chespid was prepared to be magnanimous. "When the business is concluded we'll reckon the cost, and I'm sure I can count on the commander to remember the assistance I provided. May I ask exactly what these Vli are doing here that makes them worth so much trouble?"

Osher's eyes were hooded. "You must understand, Excellency. I would not be at liberty to discuss such matters even if

I were privy to them. I may say only that the safety of these foreigners is of grave concern to us. Our confidence in your abilities makes us certain that you will be as concerned for their well-being as we are. May I tell the commander that you will give the matter your personal attention?"

"That's what I'm doing right now, isn't it?" Chespid said testily. Damn, the fish was giving him gas. Fish always gave him gas. Why did he have to live in a seaport, anyway? "What you must understand is that I cannot possibly act without the benefit of more complete information. How many are there in this diplomatic party? And who am I to protect them against? Do you propose to order me to keep them safe and then have my head because somebody gets at them that you knew was a threat and neglected to tell me about? Is the threat such that an agent might already be planted among the household, or need I worry only about an armed assault on the wall? How big an armed assault? Should I station men inside as well, or only on the perimeter? And what am I to do when these Vli take a notion to go into town, eh? Am I to send a contingent with them? You're a military man—why do I have to be the one to think of these things?"

"I think it unlikely," Osher said evenly, "that an agent will be found among the household. All who live there are Vli, and their loyalty will be firm. For the same reason, you cannot station men inside the wall. The Vli would not permit it. I assume they have a guard of their own posted within. There are only three in the visiting party, I believe—our information on this point is uncertain."

"So three gentlemen of Vli Holm come to Falnerescu, and you're worried they're going to have their throats slit. Why? Tell me that. Why should anybody in our fair city be concerned with these? Vli men and women come and go on every tide."

"I suppose there's no use trying to keep it from you. You'll have it one way or another before long. One of them isn't a man, nor a woman either. They've brought one of their—their creatures, their concubines."

Nule Chespid sat quite still for a moment, indigestion forgotten, letting that extraordinary bit of news sink in. "A lilith, you mean." His mind was buzzing. "Why should a lilith come to Falnerescu?"

"Again, Excellency, I am not at liberty to say." For the simple reason, Osher reflected, that he didn't know himself.

"To be sure. Well, since I'm not to have any of the specifics from you, I shall have to do my best to guess at them. I'm sure you won't mind if I try to guess. And since my guesses *will* be merely guesses, I'm sure you won't have any objection if I whisper them to whoever comes in earshot." Osher began an answer, but Chespid hurried on. "Of course, if I knew the facts, I would know what to be discreet about. The risk that I might inadvertently start a rumor that would cause you trouble would be *much* less if you took me into your confidence. You do see that, don't you?"

"I cannot see nor not see, Excellency. I have been given orders."

Curiosity was a burning itch in Chespid's knuckles; he rubbed them hard beneath the edge of the table. "You know, you look quite marvelous in that uniform—the leather, the brass studs, the plume on the helmet. It's a shame Borando keeps his men on such a tight leash. He lets you strut around in your finery, but when it comes time to shoulder the responsibilities and make the decisions that go with rank—well, that's another story, isn't it? I wish *I* could afford to keep a squadron of splendidly outfitted flunkies standing by to wipe my nose and run down to the market for melons."

Osher's face darkened. "I am nobody's flunky. I am Vod Penna Osher."

"Penna Osher. A noble lineage. One of the finest old families in all Berkenland, I'm told. What a shame to have to hew to the whims of a potter's son like Borando, when your own judgment tells you you ought to act differently. You have information that would help me do my job—my job being, after all, to help you. But you can't give me the information." Chespid let out a small sigh. "Very well, I'll tell you what let's do. Your part is simple: You merely stand there. Do nothing at all—especially nothing that would betray your orders. I, for my part, will make guesses. Conjectures. Wild surmises. You will tell me nothing about whether my guesses are correct or incorrect. That is as it must be. All I ask is this—that if you hear me making an assumption so ill-founded that it will actively interfere with my ability to take care of this little matter for you, you will stop me and say as much. Speak when you hear Skavish speaking. If I hear nothing, I will know how I am to proceed. Thus does Nule Chespid receive his orders." The little man bowed his head in an ironic salute. "Well, now, to begin, if it's a diplomatic party, there's got to be a treaty in the offing. And certainly the Vli didn't come here to make a treaty with *me*—I'd know about that, wouldn't I? So it's a treaty with Berkenland. Now, the emperor wouldn't have that fool Borando as his signatory, so you'll have an envoy of your own arriving before long. But why would Berkenland want to make a treaty with Vli Holm? Especially considering your well-known aversion to—what's the term you use?—mongrel races. Degenerates. Obviously you're concerned about the growing Potheqi presence in the Western Sea. You'd like to get a beachhead there yourself, wouldn't you? It's too far away to control the shipping effectively from a fleet based closer to home, so you've got to have allies there, or bases of your own, or both. For allies you have an unappetizing choice—the Potheqi meat-heads, who've got no use for Berkenland, or the Vli perverts, who've got no use for anybody. They're the only ones in that region with warships, and the gold to float them. Everybody else is still putting out to sea in washtubs. Tell me, do you anticipate the arrival of a delegation of Potheqi?"

Osher pressed his lips together and said nothing.

"Come, come, don't balk," Chespid said. "I can't plan effectively until I know how I'm going to have to allocate my resources."

"The Potheqi are warriors," Osher said carefully. "Any that come here will be able to fend for themselves."

"Mmm. Well, I'm going to assume no Potheqi are expected. It's far more likely that you're entering into a treaty with the Vli. That would give you effective control over upwards of a hundred islands, many of them timber-bearing or inhabited. Yes, I don't blame you for being nervous. There are any number of factions that would prefer to see that region kept independent. Pirates, of course. The fewer free ports they've got to run to, the harder it is for them, and the fewer bases you've got for ships, the better they like it. All it would take would be one determined pirate to scuttle your whole scheme. They could slit the throats of these Vli and be gone in the night, and then where would your treaty be? But pirates are rare in these waters. The real danger is sure to come from the Brown Hand. You'd thought of that, hadn't you? Every Berkender galley afloat makes it a little harder for them to run their little boatloads of escaped slaves off to safety."

"Anarchists," Osher muttered. "Damn them."

"Yes, it is hard to understand why anybody would advocate the abolition of slavery, isn't it? Our whole economy would collapse, and their sniveling rabble would starve alongside everybody else. Really, people don't know when they're well off, don't you agree? Still, the Brown Hand is an adversary not to be underestimated. They say the Hand is quicker than the eye. Now where was I? As to the substance of the treaty, that's a matter on which it's more difficult to speculate. But I find it suggestive that a lilith has made such a long and arduous journey to be present at the talks. Extremely suggestive."

"It has no official standing in the delegation, as far as we know," Osher pointed out. "In fact, we didn't know it was going to be here until it arrived last night. It may have been sent merely to provide companionship for the diplomats."

"Oh, I think not. There have been Vli in Falnerescu for thousands of chetnes, some of them quite wealthy, and they've got along well enough without companionship, as you so delicately refer to it. How, I don't pretend to understand, but it's none of my affair. No, the lilith is plainly a person of importance, and we'll have to make sure the best of protection is provided for her—it—whatever the right word is. Her presence trebles the danger, of course. Do you know, I'd rather like to meet this fabulous creature for myself, and find out whether the tales are true." Chespid's grotesquely large hand rose and dabbed a napkin at his lips.

Osher groaned. "You too? I've got a friend who's been struck with the same idea. He doesn't have your influence, but he's got more determination than any three men have a right to. Your men will have to be looking out for him as well. He's a sea captain. His name—"

A knock on the door interrupted him. "Come," Chespid called.

A handsome clerical slave wearing a green velvet vest and knickers entered, looking harried. "A group of individuals requesting to see you, Excellency. I explained that you were occupied, but they insisted that the matter is of the gravest urgency."

"It always is. Tell them I'll see them tomorrow. Better still, attend to it yourself."

"Excellency, I am not empowered to order a blockade of the harbor."

"A what?" Nule Chespid stood up. The backs of his knees struck the chair, knocking it backward off the platform. He was now, temporarily, the tallest person in the room. "Who are these people? Have they been taking drugs?"

"I think not, Excellency. They are most properly dressed, though two of them seem to have suffered minor injuries in some sort of fracas whose nature they were reluctant to divulge. One I believe you met at the grand ball at the last Tide-Sowing— a Vli merchant, Habil Metterner by name. With him are—"

"A Vli merchant? Send them in, you ninny! Send them in! What are you standing there gaping for?" The flunky closed his mouth and rushed out. Chespid looked behind him at the chair, lying on the floor a good distance off, and from the chair to the Berkender officer. An impossible situation. He couldn't stand there behind the table for the next half hour. Wrestling the chair back up onto the platform himself would be extremely undignified, but to ask Osher for help was unthinkable, and Osher seemed disinclined to volunteer. It was barely possible that that twitch at the corner of Osher's mouth was vigorously suppressed laughter. Chespid sighed. He was just going to have to tough it out. He sat down on the edge of the platform, from where his legs barely reached the floor, and stood up. Now the tabletop was as high as his nose. After scowling at the ruins of his luncheon, he paced across the multicolored carpet to the leaded glass window and stood staring out at the harbor. No clouds in sight—if it didn't rain in another aptarne, the public fountains would go brackish, and he would have plague on his hands. Not to mention the risk of fire. Down the slope of the hill directly below him, two enormous grain ships stood at a dock, being loaded from long chutes. Wagons doubled back one after another up a zigzag ramp to where they might dump grain into the hoppers that fed the chutes. The ships were not galleys but sailing-ships—and two-masted, a recent innovation. Under way they would be propelled by one huge square-rigged canvas at the mainmast and another smaller sheet at the foremast. The sails, furled at present, were crosshatched with brailing, thin leather strips that reinforced the canvas and kept it from tearing when the wind gusted. When laden, the grain ships would run down the tide and set sail east from Falnerescu toward Berkenland, where the land was poor and the mouths to feed many.

Salas Tarag was not thinking about ships at that moment. His head still throbbed painfully, and the cut on his lip where Strell had struck him burned. Nobody had offered to tend either wound. Coming to the fortress, he had stumbled a few times on rough cobbles, less because he was groggy than because his escort rushed him along at an unforgiving pace. As they passed beneath the raised iron portcullis, the air of confidence he had been trying to build up began to sag inward like a pricked bladder. The lower passages of the fortress had the lingering dankness of dripping water and fetid moss. As they climbed the narrow flights of stone stairs toward the governor's chambers, Tarag wondered whether this time he hadn't gotten in over his head after all. The grip on his arms was firm, and seemed unlikely to slacken. Then the doors, blackwood with silver handles, swung open, and he was ushered into the presence of the governor.

Nule Chespid continued staring out the window after the newcomers entered, long enough to make clear who was in command. When he turned, he saw that there were five of them—four Vli, by their red hair and long thin noses, and one

Islander of unusual coloring, dark leather skin and white-blond hair and beard. The Islander, who had a purple welt on one temple and a cut in his lip that was still oozing a little blood, was trying to look confident, defiant, and ingratiating all at the same time, and succeeding only in looking dazed and a little frightened.

Tarag saw Osher, and felt immense relief. But when he tried to get Osher's eye, the Berkender ignored him.

"I am told you wish to blockade the harbor," Chespid said. "I trust you have some reason for making such a bizarre request."

Three of them tried to talk at once. When the tangle was sorted out, Qob Qobba had the floor. "One of our people has been kidnapped," he explained. "We fear her kidnappers mean to take her off the island."

"And who is this? One of the kidnappers, I take it."

"We killed another one and captured this one. He claims he's a sea captain. If that's true the rest will certainly be found aboard his ship, making to bend oar."

"Possibly. May I inquire who it was that was kidnapped? When you know who's missing, it makes finding them again *so* much easier."

The Vli looked at one another uncertainly. Ranga Strell appeared to be chewing on something that tasted bad. Finally Qob Qobba replied. "Her name is Zhenuvnili."

"A pretty name. A woman, then?" Hands clasped out of sight behind his back, Chespid smiled like a carnivore that has just sighted something edible.

"No, Excellency," Qobba admitted. "She is of the third sex. A lilith."

Chespid quelled the urge to laugh out loud. "Well, Osher, what do you think? Do we have the sight of oracles, or are we merely efficient? Not quite efficient enough, it seems. You— what's your name?"

"Salas Tarag."

"Salas Tarag. I've heard of you. Can't remember just where. It'll come to me. What have you got to say for yourself?"

"Only that I stumbled into a situation not of my making, and was taken prisoner by mistake. Concerning the kidnapping

I know as little as these worthies. It's true I entered their house
by stealth. But my motive was innocent."

"What *was* your motive? Speak quickly."

Salas Tarag was not above lying when it suited him, but he
judged that in the present circumstances a lie would be more
dangerous than the truth. Besides, he couldn't think of a good
lie. "I was trying to win a wager," he said. "Last night in a
tavern we heard of the lilith's arrival, and I wagered I'd get in
to see her face to face. Wouldn't any man of you have done
the same?" He looked around at the ring of faces, and saw no
fellowship, no acknowledgment. "Osher here will tell you what
I say is true," he went on. "He was there when the wager was
laid. He heard every word."

Vod Penna Osher glared at Tarag for a moment before turning away. "I've never seen this man before in my life," he
stated.

Tarag's heart lurched painfully. Betrayed by his friend? Why?
Was this the Vod Osher who talked endlessly about the value
of truth?

Nule Chespid was cleaning fish scum off his teeth with his
tongue. He was disappointed. He had hoped for fair game—
this sea captain looked intelligent, too intelligent to make such
a crude blunder. Trying to implicate a Berkender officer in the
scheme—ridiculous. Now the prisoner would begin to contradict himself, and he would end by spitting out the names of
his confederates, along with a few of his teeth. The whole thing
was becoming tiresome. "What's the name of your ship?" he
asked.

"The *Amera Smiles*. Anchored at Bearth."

"I don't suppose your confederates are actually stupid enough
to take this lilith aboard her, knowing you've been captured,
but we'll search anyway." Chespid pulled the bell-rope and,
when the green velvet flunky returned, gave orders to have a
messenger sent to the harbor patrol to seize and search the
Amera Smiles. Useless, of course, but he was going to have
to spend the rest of the day doing things that were useless. He
might as well get started.

The Vli took turns reciting their version of the kidnapping, in which Salas Tarag figured prominently. Somewhere along the line he had acquired a sword; he had also been observed setting the fire. Tarag himself kept silent. Plainly, nobody was going to listen to him.

Chespid was listening to the tale with only one ear. He had been struck by a thought. Just before this annoying gaggle of foreigners had been announced, Osher had been on the point of saying something about a friend of his who had more determination than was good for him, who was bent on seeing the lilith. A sea captain. This one? Yes, it fitted. But why, if the Berkender had been about to denounce Tarag, had he turned and denied him? Could Osher himself have something to do with the kidnapping? Unlikely, but possible. If so, Tarag might betray him under questioning, either willingly, having been denied, or inadvertently, or if necessary under duress. Chespid's mouth watered. If a Berkender officer had guilty secrets, he wanted to know what they were—and he wanted to learn about them when nobody else was present to hear. Such information could be of incalculable value.

When Qob Qobba paused for breath, Chespid broke in. "Yes, yes. Tragic, I agree. You ought to have notified the civil authorities of your arrival; all this fuss might have been avoided."

"But what do you mean to do?" Ranga Strell wanted to know.

"I'll take charge of the investigation personally. I'll want to ask more questions of all of you, but for the moment I believe the prisoner would be safer in a cell. I shall ring for the warder and have him taken below."

"You mean you're not going to question him?" Qobba asked incredulously.

"Later, assuredly. But at the moment I'm inclined to the opinion that this one was only an unwitting dupe in the scheme. Probably he knows nothing that will help us. No, in a city this size the only way to find something you've lost is to mobilize men, the more men the better. Speaking of which," he said to Osher, "what do you suppose Jakul Borando will want done about this? If we're to put up roadblocks and blockade the harbor, to say nothing of a house-to-house search, we'll need two or three squadrons at the very least. Shall I put in a formal request, or shall we just get on with it?"

Osher saw that Chespid was trying to goad him into overstepping his authority. "I shall carry your request to the commander," he said.

Chespid's eyes twinkled. "Splendid uniform," he remarked.

Chapter 7

*T*he door clanged shut, leaving Tarag in darkness. The
air reeked of old, befouled straw, and mildew, and fish,
or something gamy but very like fish. The only light
came feebly through the small barred grill in the upper part of
the door, from the torch flickering in the rock-hewn hallway
beyond. Not wanting to sit on anything that might bite, Tarag
waited for his eyes to adjust before moving farther. The footsteps that had brought him receded, leaving only the sound of
dripping water, an occasional murmur or moan from a nearby
cell, and, much nearer, in fact there in the cell with him, the
rasping hiss of someone, or something, breathing. Tarag froze,
stilling his own breath, heart pounding in his ears, trying to
tell where the sound was coming from. Over in that corner.
He could just see the raised shelf cut in the wall, and a dim
shape lying on it. The slow rhythm of the breathing was interrupted by a choking gasp, and a cough, and then resumed. He
tiptoed toward the shape. The fish smell was stronger there, a
miasma. There was too little light to see clearly, but suddenly
Tarag knew what was lying before him. He knelt and put out
his hand to touch the shape, and felt smooth skin, hot and dry
beneath his fingers, a naked arm.

The breathing changed rhythm at his touch, and after a
moment the arm was drawn away. He wondered what language

to try. If the thing even knew language. Finally he whispered in Olmalin, "Don't be afraid. I won't hurt you. Are you ill?"

For answer he saw a yellow flash, which bloomed somewhere deep in his brain while the room stayed dim.

"That means yes. You are ill."

The flash came again, but weakly somehow, flimsy at the edges. After it came a glimpse of caked and cracking dry mud, again seen not without but within.

"I don't know what I can do to help you. Is there anything I can do?"

His mind's eye filled with the cool green lapping of seawater.

"You need water. You're too dry. You're drying out."

Yellow flash.

"I'll see what I can do." Tarag stood up and went to the little window in the door. "Ho, guard!" he bellowed. "Guard! A prisoner sick! Prisoner sick! If you don't want Nule Chespid blaming you for his death, come quick! Guard! Ho!"

Two cells down, a voice called, "Pipe down, fer Bulon's sake, before I cut yer friggin' heart out." The threat was empty, but the tone was venomous.

Tarag continued hailing for several minutes, ignoring the abuse, until a door somewhere down at the end of the passage crashed open and slow steps shuffled toward him. The jailer, when he appeared, cast huge shadows on the stone wall. He was a coarse-featured old man with a big belly and a jingling ring of keys. "What be all the racket about?" he demanded.

"You've got a prisoner here like to die. My cellmate."

The old man scratched his beard. "Yer in there with the dongie, aintcha?"

"The duongnu, that's right. He's very ill."

"Don't matter none about him," the old man said, shaking his head. "They ain't gonna let him out, nohow."

"But he's dying!"

"Like I said."

"All he needs is a bucket of seawater. Is that too much to ask?"

"I can't open up the door to give ye no bucket o' water." The old man shook his head again. "Wish I c'd help, Cap'n, truly I do. I've naught against dongies. But he's a goner. Best you hope they haul you out o' there before he starts to stink."

"Why did you call me captain? Do I know you?"

The jailer squinted at the face in the cell door, and his eyes brightened. "Why, bless my soul if it ain't Cap'n Tarag! Cap'n, what be you doin' here? This ain't no fit place fer the likes o' you."

It was Tarag's turn to scrutinize a face. The shadows were deep, but there was something in the shape of the nose . . . Then he had it. A voyage thirty chetnes ago, or thirty-five. An old man who had begged to bench a galley one last time, and struggled to pull his weight, and in his free time taught a band of youngsters about currents, and knots, and sighting on the stars. "Seve!" he exclaimed. "Seve—Rogas, was it?"

"Aye, aye." The old man's head bobbed happily.

"Seve Rogas. So here we meet. What have they got you doing, eh? Keeping watch over a lot of cutthroats."

"Aye, they're a scurvy lot. No master'll have them, and here they lie buried before their time. But Cap'n, if you'll forgive me, I never expected to be lookin' at you through this door."

"Nor I to find myself on the wrong side of it. At least you've found honest employment. I fear my fate may not be so happy."

"What have you done, then?" The old man leaned closer.

"Not what I'm accused of. I was cutting beans, and I fell into the pot."

"Knowin' you, they was tasty beans."

"I don't know. I was interrupted before I could get a taste." Another gasp came from within the cell. "Seve, can't you do anything to help this poor duongnu? Anything at all?"

Seve frowned. "I'd sure like to, Cap'n. But I'm not allowed to open the door without another guard present. That's to keep folk from escapin'."

"Then call another guard."

"Cap'n, there's not another guard in the whole fortress would take three steps out of his way to *spit* on a dongie."

"Seve, I give you my word. I won't try to escape. I'll move back to the far corner and lie face down on the floor. You need only open the door far enough to put the bucket in, and close it again. Will you do it?"

"Well—seein' as it's you, Cap'n Tarag. I don't s'pose there's another man in the world I'd trust to keep his word, above you. You swear?"

"By Amera I swear. When you open the door to put in the bucket, I won't try to escape, and I won't harm you in any way."

"I reckon that's all right, then. I'll go get some water."

Seve was gone for a long time. The duongnu's unhealthy breathing filled the cell. Tarag had time to worry about his own plight. Certainly Nule Chespid did not mean to leave him buried here indefinitely, and Chespid's methods of interrogation were far less gentle than what he had suffered at the hands of the Vli. Would it not be prudent to jump Seve and escape? He regretted swearing by Amera. But even had he not, such a course would mean the death of the duongnu. Seve was unlikely to be in a humor to see to the other prisoner's needs after being tricked and assaulted. So when at last he heard Seve returning, Tarag went over to the far wall and lay face down in the muck, for good measure lacing his fingers behind his head. Torchlight flared as Seve inspected the arrangements through the window. After a jingling and a scraping, the lock snicked back, the door creaked open, and the bucket thumped on the floor. When the door had slammed shut again, Tarag called, "May I get up? Something's tickling my nose."

"Aye."

Seve stayed at the window providing light with his torch while Tarag took the bucket over to the prostrate duongnu. Its gray-green skin had an unhealthy silver sheen. Over uncounted thousands of years its ancestors had adapted to life in the sea, but unquestionably it was human. Genitals enclosed, but evidently male. Ears very large, intricately folded, lying now slack. Nasal openings not between eyes and mouth but above the eyes, the extension of what had once been sinus cavities. Hands and feet rather large, with webbed fingers and toes. The duongnu's eyes were closed, his mouth open in stertorous breath.

Best not use up all the water at once. Tarag dribbled a little over the merman, beginning at the crotch and moving slowly up to the neck. The merman convulsed, and his breath quickened. The skin seemed to soak up the water; only a few drops ran off. Tarag repeated the procedure a second time and then a third. The last time a webbed hand rose to the green chest to spread the water where it would do the most good.

When the bucket was empty, Tarag set it on the floor. The duongnu lay back, breathing more easily. "Yer only holdin' back the tide wi' yer fingers," Seve said from the door. "I don't know that it's a kindness." The torchlight dimmed, and shuffling footsteps receded.

Tarag upended the bucket and sat on it. "I'm afraid he's right. You can't survive much longer in here. How long have you been here?"

For answer he received only an impression of the blackness of the walls that surrounded them.

"No, I suppose you can't, without looking at the sky. How did you come to land in here?"

There was no reply.

"I don't know about you," Tarag said conversationally, "but I'm here on account of love. Love, pure and simple. If you don't count being soft in the head. Love, we'll call it that, for somebody I've never seen nor spoken to."

An impression of a drifting sandbank, light, insubstantial.

"Naturally, feeling this sort of love for her, I wanted to see and speak to her. But I was netted. I don't know, to be honest, whether it's love at all. Maybe it's only the love of love. After not having been in love for too long. Have you ever felt that way? Do your people know love as we do?"

A kaleidoscope of images surged through his mind, so jumbled he could catch only scraps: a leg darting out of sight behind a frond of seaweed, shell ornaments strung in a necklace on green twine, gentle eyes in a hairless dome of skull with nostrils slanting like second eyebrows above ducking in and out of the briny foam and close, very close.

"Was that some special face? Your beloved?"

Yellow flash, followed by another series of images, a lithe and naked green lady dodging and curling in the current.

"She's beautiful. I've never spoken with one of your people before, though I've seen you swimming from time to time, from the deck of my ship."

A galley seen from the water, a grotesque jumble of oars and people on deck proportioned no better than a child's scrawl.

"Yes. A ship like that."

Figures on the deck of the galley hurling spears. A swirl of blood in the water.

"Not I. There are those who hunt your people for sport, or kill them when they tangle in their nets, but I've never done that, nor would I let my ship be used for it. I'd starve sooner."

A bucket pouring water. Yellow flash.

"Can you tell me, do you understand my words, or do you see my thoughts with the same power you use to send me yours? Do your kind even use spoken language?"

For a time there was no reply. Then the duongnu spoke in a hoarse voice. "Ulloalualiemeh. Song of sea. Under water. Carry far. Speech close, head to head, no sound." The words were nasal, and oddly accented.

"The song of the sea," Tarag repeated. "This is your spoken language? Ulloa—?"

"Ulloalualiemeh." The word was full of resonances, vowels that shifted like undersea currents. A vision of an escarpment where the floor of the sunlit shallows slanted down into murky depths.

"Where did you learn Olmalin, then?"

A stone amulet, carved with some insignia he could not quite make out. "I am son of chief." The merman seemed to feel that this was an adequate answer.

Tarag decided not to pursue the question. "May I know your name? Is it permitted?"

A stone knife slashing through a thicket of knobbly seagrape.

"What is that in far-speech?"

The merman spewed out a rising and falling sound that Tarag could never have repeated, then, mercifully, translated it. "Bravely-Among-Weed, of clan Foam-Thrasher."

"Clan Foam-Thrasher. I am honored. Shall I call you Bravely?"

The duongnu made a gurgling noise that might have been laughter. "Walker speech so short. Not—not—" He ululated an eight-syllable word.

"No, I suppose it's not. My name is Salas Tarag."

"Zalaz Darang." Bravely flipped one webbed hand palm up, evidently a gesture of greeting. "Sad you not see beloved. Hurt much."

"Not as much as what they're going to do to me, now they've got me locked up in here." Tarag shifted on his improvised seat, which was digging into his backside.

"Is same the two, not?"

"No, not at all the same," said Tarag, puzzled. "Even if I was out walking the streets right now, which I'd dearly like to be, I'd not be within a league of the lilith. But I'd gladly trade that sort of pain for this. If you were free, you'd be off swimming with your beloved, am I right?"

A collapsing gray burst that could only mean no. "Dishonor. Shame." Bravely lay back on the filthy pallet and turned his head to the wall, crushing one earflap beneath him.

They sat in silence. Somewhere water was still dripping, a slow, measured *plonk, plonk, plonk*. In a cell down the passage a quarrel had broken out. The stream of shouting and babbling grew more insistent and less coherent until it ended abruptly in a horribly prolonged scream, which was accompanied by mad laughter. The scream sank into sobbing and gradually ceased.

"How were you dishonored?" Tarag asked.

"Not bring love-gift."

"Tell me, what is a proper love-gift, among your people?"

"Thing of beauty. Thing rare, hard to get. Love-gift must bring back from danger place. Go alone, no help, only knife."

"What kind of danger place? And what do you bring back?"

"Most man go to deep. Long-diving. Bring back teeth." The duongnu levered himself up on one elbow to look at Tarag. "I, Bravely-Among-Weed, see many teeth on many girl." He held his hand above his chest and waggled it rapidly so the thumb and fingers blurred, and Tarag saw a necklace slung with innumerable sharp curving teeth. "Think, in other danger place not teeth. More danger, more love-gift."

"I might have done the same. What other danger place?"

"Land. Love-gift steal from walkers."

"Of course. So you came ashore. Now I want to understand. Do you mean you were dishonored, so you needed to bring a love-gift? I thought you said you were dishonored *by* not bringing the gift."

"By walker teeth trapped." Again, this seemed to be all the explanation Bravely thought necessary.

"You were dishonored by being captured?"

Yellow flash.

"What happens to those who are dishonored?"

Bravely's ears waved gently as his head moved from side to side. "Not love. Come back from deep with scars, hands or feet gone. People care for, bring food, help float when old. But not love. Not mate."

"Frankly," Tarag said, eyeing the walls, "I'd settle for a hand or a foot missing. Somebody to help me float would be a pure blessing from Amera, who smiles upon the waves, and no mistake. Do you know what Nule Chespid, our chief walker, is going to do to me when he calls me back upstairs? He isn't going to let off with just a hand or a foot. I could lose my tongue, or my privates. Not that his excellency is especially cruel—he's only efficient. He's going to want me to tell him some things I don't know, and he's not going to believe me when I say I don't know them. And he's the one with the teeth. What I *don't* understand is why Osher wouldn't back me. What's got into the man? We'd quarreled over the lilith, of course, but that didn't mean anything. He was just being stubborn about following orders, and expecting me to follow them as well. As if I were a sergeant-of-kelg. But I'm not. I'm his friend—or thought I was. We'd been talking, not an aptarne back, about how rare a thing true friendship is, how much to be cherished the chance to converse with one's equals. And now this."

"Your love-gift hunt die as mine. But walker want walk, live, not mate?"

"Well, I haven't given up hope, as you seem to have. If I can get out of here whole, I'll mate again, I promise you. Aye, and once over just to celebrate. And you'll not catch me complaining, either, about how the joy's gone out of it."

Bravely frowned, confused, the nostrils above his brow ridges puckering. "Dishonor!" he protested.

"I'm not dishonored, lad, not that I've noticed. Nor are you, from all you've told me. I don't see you've lost any hands or feet yet. Didn't you say it was the maimed who were dishonored? So how are you dishonored? You're bound to die in here before long, you may as well die with honor."

Bravely struggled with the new idea. "Truly? Do I yet float?"

"Your honor floats." Tarag was happy to be able to cheer up his fellow prisoner. A small thing, but in the circumstances flinders were all he had to cling to. They sat again for a while without talking. But Tarag's curiosity was never idle for long. "That trick where you put pictures in my head," he said. "The close-speech. Can all your people do that?"

Yellow flash.

"And they can all see it. It's like talking and listening."

Yellow flash.

"My people saw things in their heads," Tarag said. "Or perhaps it wasn't in their heads. Perhaps it was that I was blind. I've never been sure. They saw the gods. The gods rode chariots through the street, and everybody waved and cheered and threw flower petals, and exclaimed to one another how beautiful and tall and strong and radiant the gods were. When I was little my father would lift me up onto his shoulders so I could see better. But I never saw the gods. The street was empty, only flower petals drifting down. My sister and brother could see the gods, and my father taught me the gods' names, and their sacred symbols. But I could never see them. So as soon as I was old enough to pull oar, I ran off to sea. I was looking for the gods, at first. I couldn't understand what offense I'd committed, all unknowing, that made them turn their faces away from me. But on the Island Sea, I found, nobody claimed to see the gods, only fools and madmen. That made it easier, but somehow more frightening as well. It wasn't I who was singled out to be alone. We were all of us alone. So we pray to Amera, or to Tha, or Bulon, or Dai-Toh. One has to believe in something, even if it's something one has never seen. Perhaps especially then. What one *has* seen is diminished afterward in one's eyes; only a mystery can remain undimmed. All the same, I suppose I ought to thank you for showing me something in my head. I've always wondered what it would be like."

"Head does many things."

"You can plant an image directly in somebody's mind, whether or not they know how to receive it, whether or not they even want to receive it? Is that all you can do, or is there more?"

Yellow, yellow flash. The yellow flash pulsed, receded, flooded back. Tarag found himself drawn into it. There was something irresistible about letting yourself sink deeper into the yellowness of the yellowness of the yes yellow sliding down into yellow traced with red pulsing yellow throbbing oh—

The yellow flash spattered apart and was gone, and he was back in the cold dark cell. He rubbed his head, and let out a shaky breath. "You did that."

"Close-speech thunder. All people know."

"But you let me go. I couldn't have escaped from it otherwise."

"I am son of chief." Bravely squared his shoulders and beamed, perhaps a bit smugly.

"How long can you keep that up?"

"Not when sleep."

"I've never felt anything like it. It's like being swallowed."

"Use to catch fish. Fish sleep, spear fish. Big fish, many spear."

"You mean a whole group of hunters overpowers a big fish with this close-speech so it can't move, and then you spear it? How do you keep from putting one another to sleep at the same time?"

"Every animal have—" Again the merman lapsed into his

own polysyllabic tongue. "Every animal different. Like taste in water. Touch differentness."

Tarag scratched his beard thoughtfully. "What I don't understand is why you didn't put Seve to sleep when he opened the door. You could have gotten away!"

"Dishonor."

"Dishonor, eh? Are you saying what I think you're saying? Are you saying you could have gotten out of here any time the door was opened, but you didn't because you were *dishonored*?"

A small, reluctant yellow flash.

"Okay," Tarag began. "Your honor is important to you. You are the son of a chief. But if you hadn't been so weak for lack of water, you would have been able to think clearly, and you would have seen that you haven't been dishonored at all. You've only been delayed. You still have your hands and feet. There's not a wound on you. You could return to your people right now and be hailed a hero, am I right?"

"I would know dishonor."

"That's what I'm trying to explain," Tarag said patiently. "You're not dishonored. Isn't it a proof of strength among your people to be able to dive deeper and stay down longer than anybody else? How is staying on land any different? You've only been proving your strength by staying here. This is a rare opportunity for you! Think of it. Among the dwellers in the deep are fearsome fish with sharp teeth. But no fish is as fierce as the Islander with his iron, eh? You said as much yourself. And what is the sharpest tooth the Islander has? Not the sword, not the harpoon, but the *key*. Those metal implements Seve carries about with him. The key is all Seve needs to be safe from the most vicious criminal in this place. Wouldn't your lady-love be impressed if you returned to her and presented her with Seve's ring of keys? Has ever any swain given such a love-gift? And how else could you get the keys but by diving into the very deeps of the land? You've come this far unscathed. You have only to catch the jailer in that net of yours and snatch his teeth, and you'll be free to return to the sea a hero!"

The duongnu set a hand on the edge of the pallet to lever himself up, but fell back. "Weakness," he said.

"I'll carry you if need be. Your part is to knock out anybody who tries to stop us. Once you get to the water you'll be all right, won't you?"

Yellow flash.

"All right. When we hear them coming we'll be ready. As soon as the door swings open, but not before, you put everybody in the corridor to sleep. We'll get Seve's keys on the way by. Then all we've got to do is find a way out of this place. Are you with me?"

"Not dishonor?" Bravely said.

"Not dishonor," Tarag assured him. "Great honor. A marvelous love-gift."

More time passed, perhaps half an hour, though in the darkness there was no way of telling. Now that his own future showed some faint promise, Tarag began, belatedly, to worry about the lilith. Who had captured her? Were they treating her well, or badly? Impossible to guess, unless he knew why she had been taken. Tarag knew nothing about the intended treaty or the political intrigue surrounding it. As far as he could see, it was the person of the lilith the kidnappers had been after. Quite possibly she had fallen victim to slavers. He shuddered. There were people in Falnerescu whose taste in bed-partners ran to the exotic. Some of them had the money to buy what they required, even to have it hunted out and procured for them. What if the lilith were destined to become the plaything of one of those? Or would such an arrangement suit her? Was being a bought bed-partner any different from what a lilith did all her life? It was the most degrading form of servitude, Tarag had always felt, but he had met slaves who were content with it, even boasted of it. Impossible to tell how the lilith would feel unless he were able to find her and ask her; and his prospects for that were rather dismal.

Not far off a door scraped and creaked open, and several sets of feet came down the hall toward them. "Are you ready?" Tarag whispered.

Yellow flash.

He got his arms beneath the merman's and lifted him to his feet. Bravely was as hot and dry as when Tarag had first touched him, and his breathing was labored, but once standing he managed to carry his weight on his own legs, swaying only slightly. Outside, Seve's voice said, "This one here," and the footsteps ceased. "Best we use manacles," another voice said. "He's a wily one, and he'll be wild by now." There was more clanking of keys and chains. The door swung open, and a guard stepped into the cell, his stout wooden cudgel swinging at the ready. Seve was behind him. Both stopped suddenly, staring at the air in front of them. Seve fell first, crumpling in a heap and partially blocking the doorway. A moment later the guard's legs went slack. From the hall the angle of the light shifted as a torch fell clattering.

Tarag let Bravely lean against the wall while he peered out. Two more guards were sleeping peacefully on the stone floor. He dragged Seve out of the doorway. "Do you want to pick his teeth yourself?"

Bravely knelt and tugged at the big iron ring with its twenty or so variously shaped keys; it was fastened to the old man's belt, and wouldn't come loose. "We'll cut it," Tarag said. "One of them must have a knife." But before he could make a search, Bravely had untied the belt and drawn it out of its loops, bringing the key ring along with it. The merman put his hand through the ring and wrapped the belt around his wrist, securing it crudely but effectively. In close-speech he sent Tarag an image of two figures swimming swiftly.

"I couldn't agree more." Tarag picked up the fallen torch and carried it in one hand while supporting Bravely with the other arm. They passed down the hall between facing rows of cells. On either side, prisoners had realized an escape was in progress. Shouts urged them to stop and open doors, and threatened dire injury if they didn't. They kept moving. Tarag glanced back at the recumbent forms. "How long will they stay like that?"

"When I stop, they wake."

"Can you keep doing it from far away?"

"Not far."

"Then they'll raise the alarm before long." They went through an open door into another, longer passageway. "I don't imagine there's a clear way out from this level. We're under the hill itself. The stairs I was brought down are just ahead."

At the end of the tunnel Tarag turned right, toward the stairs, but Bravely balked. "This way," he said, pointing to the left. "Smell sea."

The tenor of the shouting behind them had changed. Boots were running, and somebody was shrilling a whistle. Tarag had no time to make a conscious decision. He let Bravely lead the way to the left. They went down a flight of stairs, and the dampness increased. The floor was slick with puddles and slime. Halfway along the passage they came to the dark mouth of an opening. "Here," Bravely announced. Holding the torch aside, Tarag peered into the new tunnel, which was no higher than he was tall. Even he could smell the sea now.

But the way was barred by a padlocked iron gate.

"Give me the keys," Tarag said. When Bravely hesitated he went on, "I know how these iron teeth work. You don't. Quick." He inspected the padlock, which was bigger than his two fists together. Bravely unwrapped the belt and handed him the keys. Three whistles were sounding, one of them not far off. Tarag pulled Bravely into the shelter of the tunnel mouth, where they were pressed together against the bars of the gate but out of sight of anyone at the end of the passage. Deliberately he dropped the torch in a puddle, where it sputtered and died. Darkness closed in. Clutching the key ring tightly, not to drop it in the dark, he selected a key and tried it in the lock. The key would not turn. He tried another, and another. Torchlight was dancing toward them, and a voice said, "They might of come down this way."

"That don't lead nowhere, only to the sea-gate."

"Aye, and where would a stinkin' dongie make for, if not the sea-gate?" Boots clomped and splashed closer.

The fifth key turned somewhat, but the lock was stiff with rust. Tarag gripped the key harder and twisted. When he had his shoulder into it, the lock sprang open, and he fumbled at it, freeing it from the hasp. Behind him the guards called out,

"There, ho!" "Halt!" But the duongnu close-speech silenced them. The gate creaked open, and the two fugitives groped their way hurriedly down another long flight of stairs that ran straight into the water. There the darkness was absolute, the sea-smell stagnant, unclean. Tarag was in water to his knees, and Bravely sat down on the stairs and wriggled, bathing himself.

"Where do we go from here?" Tarag asked. "This tunnel has got to lead to the sea, but Amera knows how it twists and turns; I don't. It may be entirely under the tide for part of its length. And swimming indoors in the dark is a sure way to bump your head and drown."

His voice echoed wetly. Bravely's splashing subsided to a gurgle that ended in the lapping of ripples against stone. "Well?" Tarag prodded. There was no answer. He squatted on the stairs and felt around him in the greasy water. He was alone. The merman had swum away.

Chapter 8

The night before, escorting her on a tour of the mansion, Habil Metterner had boasted how well drilled the household were to fight fire. Otherwise she never would have thought of the trick, nor risked it. She didn't want to burn the house down, after all, only create a diversion. After borrowing from the nalas' wardrobe a gray robe, which she judged would be less conspicuous than her own white one, she tore down some curtains, stuffed them into an empty bathtub, sprinkled a little lamp oil over them, and set them alight. The sudden whoosh of flame frightened her, but it was too late to change course. Creeping toward a narrow side stairway, she nearly collided with one of the household slaves. "There's a fire in the front bedroom!" she cried, pointing. The woman rushed to see, leaving Zhenuvnili free to descend to the ground floor. When the shouting erupted and the bucket brigade swung into action, she was waiting at the rear of the long hall to make her way to the front door.

Halfway down the hall she paused, eerily certain for no reason that somebody was hiding behind the curtain in the alcove directly opposite, staring at her. Almost she stepped to the curtain and pulled it aside—but seconds were precious. She hurried on.

The gate had been left ajar—a piece of luck, since she had

not considered how difficult it would be to unbar it by herself. In the street was a large chest, its lid sprung to spill a cascade of jewelry across the paving-bricks. Gold and precious gems glinted in the sun. Such an odd thing to find lying there! Were the people of Falnerescu so rich that they strewed the streets with jewels? She knelt and tucked a teardrop pendant of opal and silver into a pocket of her robe. "What Li bestows," she murmured. She had no money—a lilith needed none—and Metterner had neglected during the tour to point out the location of his coffers. So perhaps the Goddess had chosen this unusual method of seeing to Zhenuvnili's welfare. She went swiftly down the sunlit street, nearly running. Behind her there seemed to be a great deal of commotion for such a little fire, but she had no reason to go back and find out the cause. Probably they had noticed her absence, and not yet received the message. She had drawn Karanli aside and left word that she was off to see the city for the day. They would still worry, but there was no help for that; she had seen to it that there would be no needless alarm. As it happened, Karanli's terror at being dragged before a pair of foreigners, one a dreaded Potheqi, and then seeing people fight and die in the hall, had reduced her to hysterical incoherence, and the message had foundered and sunk undelivered. But Zhenuvnili knew none of that, and went on unconcerned.

Crossing the city after nightfall in a sedan chair, she had not seen how the streets of Falnerescu twisted and turned like twining branches, nor how many of them there were. Streets at home, the few she had seen, were laid out in a plain square grid, obviously a more sensible arrangement. What had seemed a simple matter when she was talking with the mnoerri—strike out to the south until she saw the three-headed rock—now posed bewildering difficulties. For one thing, Falnerescu had no street signs. She could only keep on until she found a major thoroughfare, and then follow it to see where it led.

After taking several turnings at random in the mansion district, she found a sloping walkway that led down between two blank-faced adobe buildings and deposited her in one of the smaller market plazas that dotted the city. There crude carts drawn by plodding paum lurched and jostled between rows of produce vendors hawking their wares. The odors were many, and exotic. The lilith slowed to a stroll, drinking it all in. The market was so marvelously alive! People young and old, in all manner of outlandish native dress, going about their daily business as they always did. What a luxury to be able to walk among them and be not the center of attention but merely another ordinary human being! To be a lilith, to give love, was a privilege, but it was an obligation as well. The liliths were given every gift in gratitude for their love, save only the gift of freedom. And now, for a few precious hours, she had freedom as well. Praise Li!

A group of boys, she saw with a start, were pointing at her, laughing and nudging one another. Why? A nala, which her robe proclaimed her, would never appear on the street alone, but these people did not know that. They had never seen nalas, so could have no hint of what she was. She should have been entirely unremarkable. A man at a stall stared wide-eyed at her and dropped the pot he was holding; it crashed in the dust, splattering cooking oil. She walked faster. Had she alarmed the man somehow? An old woman with whiskers snarled at her, chewing on an oath with toothless gums. Cold slime congealed in Zhenuvnili's gut. She felt nauseous. She was alone in a throng of foreigners, and people were staring at her. The utter alienness of the city pressed in on her.

She stopped and leaned against the wall of a building, suddenly dizzy, her heart hammering. Behind her she heard a little boy say, "Daddy, look! Is that Lord Death?" With a sharp rush of embarrassment she realized the boy had been speaking of her. So that was what the fuss was about—her hood and veil! In all this crowd she was the only one whose face was hidden. She laughed aloud. Such a simple thing, and she had thought nothing of it!

If she wanted to avoid attracting this sort of attention, she must throw back the hood. But she found she was unable to do it. From childhood she had been taught that only her lovers were to see her. According to the Teachings, a lilith must remain veiled because her naked face would drive men and women

mad with desire. And certainly, for her to appear unveiled in
public in any city in Vli Holm would cause a riot. Might not
these foreigners react the same way? Her beauty, inescapable,
shining like a beacon, would betray her. Even if she were not
assaulted, she would surely be stared at as much as if she
stayed hooded, perhaps more. She began to tremble. To stand
forth unveiled before a city of foreigners—suddenly she felt
very cold and naked and alone, infinitely small and standing
in a place infinitely vast and chaotic, a leaf on the wind, a
grain of sand tumbled by the tide. For a moment she could not
remember her own name, or how she had come there. The
buzz of voices in the market was menacing and incomprehensible, as if heard in a fever. The wall beside her swayed. She
needed desperately to be back in a Nest, safely surrounded by
the warmth of her own people. She turned and ran. Her soft
slippers beat on the hard ground, and breath rasped in her throat.
She elbowed people aside without seeing them or hearing the
curses they called after her, and ran on.

When the ache in her lungs would let her run no more she
slowed, staggered a few more steps, and sagged against the
edge of a paum-trough to rest. Looking around, she saw that
she was lost. While a few of the foreigners peered curiously
at her, they passed on without molesting her. She drew up her
shoulders and tried to collect her wits. Had Li Ranli sent her
all this way to make a fool of herself in the public street? Her
mouth was dry, and the moss-edged paum-trough was nearly
full of water. She leaned over it, saw the hooded figure reflected,
and laughed again. She did look mysterious; no wonder they
were staring. But the water did not look clean enough to drink.
Only a few steps on, however, was a tavern, its sign sporting
three red mugs side by side. She could get wine, or tea, or
whatever they served there. And perhaps some food as well.
The mnoerri might offer her food at the Become-All—she had
no idea what the ceremony entailed—but there was little chance
that she would find it palatable.

Inside, the tavern was black as pitch. Shapes shifted dimly
in the gloom, but she saw that she would surely fall over a
table or bench and cause more trouble. All right, then. If it

was too dim to see, nobody would see her, would they? Taking a deep breath, she lifted the veil and defiantly threw back the hood. If she expected thunder to resound from the firmament, she was disappointed. The tables were but sparsely occupied, and the glance or two that strayed her way drifted away again. The lilith was offended. Was she so unremarkable, then? Why was nobody taking any notice? Not that she wanted to be noticed, of course, but all the same . . .

She made her way to the bar. After a long moment, the leather-aproned barman raised his head to stare incuriously at her. "I would like something to eat and drink," she said in careful Olmalin. When he continued to gaze blankly at her, she added, "If it pleases you." Her heart was bumping like a drum.

"Somethin', aye. Somethin' we got. What'll it be, then?"

"Do you have any spiced wine?"

"Spiced wine?" The man rubbed the side of his nose with a greasy forefinger. "Aye, a keg out back, I seem to recall. If it's not gone bad by now. You be wantin' eats too, then?"

Zhenuvnili looked around at the tables. A man and woman were sharing a plate of crustaceans in sauce, picking out morsels with their fingers. "Whatever they're having," she decided. "But just a little plate."

The barman looked at her with bored suspicion. "You be meanin' to pay?"

"Oh." She had forgotten. From her pocket she dredged up the opal pendant. "Will this do? It's all I've got." She laid it on the counter.

The barman picked up the pendant and squinted at it in the bad light. "Aye," he said, nodding solemnly. "Food and drink both this'll be buyin' you." He did not bother to tell her that the pendant was worth the price of a meal fifty times over. He tucked it into a pocket in his vest, patted the pocket proprietarily, and shuffled off in the direction of the kitchen.

The lilith found an empty table in the darkest corner of the room and sank down on the bench behind it. She drew her knees up and hugged them. If the other customers were even aware of her, they gave no sign. And this was as deflating as it was liberating. Since childhood Zhenuvnili had been alternately fussed over, venerated, and lusted after—especially lusted after—but she had never been ignored. Were they all teasing her? Were they being polite? Or did they have some malevolent design? No, that was fancy. That she wasn't one of them simply had not occurred to them. Perhaps after all she wasn't as beautiful as she had always been told. Or had some change come over her? She wished for a mirror for reassurance, but none was at hand.

The barman brought her a plate with a steaming heap of small many-legged creatures, and a dented goblet of some dark liquid. He set them down carelessly and went away again. The wine, if it was wine, tasted horrible, strong and bitter, but the crustaceans were surprisingly savory. No utensils were provided, so she ate with her fingers. After a few bites the wine cut through the sauce nicely, and she didn't mind the bitterness so much, though she still wished she had ordered tea instead.

The man and woman who had been eating what she was eating were no longer eating, but they were still drinking. The man had come around the table to sit on the same bench with the woman, and had his arm around her. He was wearing a vest of coarse brown cloth, and his unruly hair had not been washed recently. The woman's dress was lighter in color but of as coarse a weave, and her hair was pinned with several clasps from which it was escaping in loops and dangles. The man whispered something in the woman's ear, and she whooped with laughter. He picked up his mug and presented it to her lips, and she drank. After taking another swig himself, he leaned forward and began kissing the woman on the mouth. His tongue and lips lasciviously explored hers, and his arms crushed her close. Zhenuvnili watched, repelled and yet fascinated. The technique was atrocious, of course. A six-year-old nala could kiss better than that—and did, every chance she got. But these two didn't know any better. Neither of them was a lilith. She was watching perverts kiss. What a disgusting spectacle!

Still, what choice did they have? In this land there were no liliths to love them. Even if they yearned for normal sex, they had only one another to turn to. Her heart went out to them. How wonderful it would be to come between them, and so fulfill them both! Their pleasure would be far deeper than the feeble spasms they could manage by themselves. But her caution outweighed the impulse. There were too many people on the Island Sea. She could not love them all; all the liliths together could not love more than a handful. Somehow the Islanders managed to make babies without help, which was puzzling. But how could a lilith see all these poor deprived people and remain unmoved? Was it not her duty to love everybody? Perhaps this was why Li Ranli had sent her—not to safeguard the treaty, but to know the pain of standing by and watching, unable to love. If the ports of Vli Holm were opened, as eventually they must be, all the liliths would know this pain. Their generous spirit might turn into something twisted and shrunken, which would infect all the Vli and destroy them. Or the frustration might drive the liliths mad.

The man and woman pushed back their bench and rose, still entwined, and staggered together toward the door. She watched them go, blinking back tears. She bit into another crustacean, and found she had lost her appetite. Perhaps her promise to the mnoerri had been a mistake. If men and women were to go unloved, could she rightly concern herself with aliens? But a promise was a promise. Besides, she wasn't ready yet to give up the bit of freedom she had snatched.

Three hours later, under a westering sun, she had left the outskirts of the city far behind. She strode confidently along the main south road, hood thrown back on her shoulders, pausing now and again to wince and hop when a sharp rock dug into the soft soles of her slippers. Her long dark hair flowed out behind her in a curling wake. Her complexion was a pale olive, the bones of cheeks and chin prominent. Her long thin nose ended in flat flaring nostrils above plump, slightly everted lips. Though her eyebrows were plucked to a thin line, her features were stronger than they were delicate. The green of her eyes nearly matched the green of the soapstone studs in her earlobes.

Before her in the distance, the lava escarpments that delineated the edge of the highlands stood, brown and crumbling and covered here and there with patches of scrub trees. She had been studying the lava outcroppings as she walked; none of them looked especially three-headed. Traffic on the road was about what might be expected—ahead half a dozen farm wagons were visible, and a woman herding five small children and a couple of grubblers, and two men in dark robes and broad-brimmed hats who paced along with the aid of stout staves. On either side stretched out a carefully tended orchard, shoulder-high bushes bearing alternately a fleshy red fruit called oba and a tangier yellow fruit called jehnad, which grew well together, replenishing one another's soil. On the right, somewhat more than a thousand tadigs off, ran the line of stone arches that carried the aqueduct that fed the city's reservoirs. Ahead on the left, however, the orchard gave way to forest, a dark mixed stand of swatleaf and conetop. And beyond, partly eclipsed, loomed one of the lava formations. After another half hour she could see that it was possessed of three flattened domes. She would not have called them heads.

By the time she reached the uncultivated land that sloped up to the irregular and often broached old lava line, the sun had set in a burst of crimson, and as the world faded to gray the Moons Road brightened silver into view. Cheth stood higher that night in the west, and Nardis had not yet reached the zenith. Aptar would rise late. She looked for a path on her left, but none appeared. Perhaps the mnoerri avoided paths. There was, however, a meadow that she might cross. The flowers were folding up for the night. Some flowers had teeth, she knew. Their bite might cause madness. But would the mnoerri hold a ceremony in a bad flower place? Skirting only the thick stands of blooms, she walked on boldly, the hem of her robe catching from time to time on thistles or twigs.

Under the trees the going was rougher, the ground uneven and the darkness nearly impenetrable. Only an occasional slash of moonlight dappled the forest floor, and here and there a patch of lightmoss pulsed palely. She had heard of lightmoss, but never seen any. On a tree trunk, a patch taller and broader than she undulated in irregular ripples that cast a ghostly luminescence. It was said by those whose business took them to the forest at night that lightmoss crawled from tree to tree during the day, for it never marked the same trees twice; it crept along the ground among the underbrush and fallen logs, feeding on decaying matter, and at nightfall found a high spot on which to display itself and signal to its kind.

When she judged that she was underneath where the three heads were, she slowed, stopped and listened, and went forward cautiously. The chittering of the tree-babies told her she was not alone, and once she surprised something large that snorted and lumbered away. But of the mnoerri there was no sign. Had she come to the wrong place? Had they been detained for some reason, or given up hope of her coming and left? She angled to the right, in the direction of the cliffs—from high ground, she might be able to spot them.

But before she reached a vantage point, she heard the singing. Soft and lilting, with a falling inflection, it tendriled its way so slowly up out of the night noises that it had wrapped entirely around her before she realized she was hearing it. But suddenly it was as palpable as a fragrance. Around her shapes slipped among the trees, chanting in some unknown tongue. The mnoerri paralleled her, escorted her, coming no nearer. She merely walked on. When it was time to stop or turn aside they would give the sign.

They emerged in a moonlit meadow, she and the mnoerri who flanked her and more who came behind them straggling out from beneath the trees singly and in twos and threes, wing-flaps spread somewhat in a ritual or instinctive posture. High above in the double moonlight rose the three-domed rock; from below, it did indeed resemble a trio of gigantic mnoerri. The meadow sloped gently upward to the foot of the lava cliff, which was tumbled in jagged boulders. The singing had grown no louder, but it was more unified. A rough melody had emerged whose contours all the mnoerri were tracing, each adding its own embellishments and inflections, so that the air was gravid with intertwining strands of song. The lilith stood silent, listening, floating on the river of sound.

As they sang, the mnoerri moved across the meadow, form-

ing gradually a rough circle where they sank down to sit or lie
on the ground, casting their spears and pouches behind them
in the tall grass. As each joined the circle the tenor of its song
changed, so that the ebb and flow of the melody melted slowly
into a low irregular hum to which the last few arrivals sang
counterpoint. Zhenuvnili stood a few paces back from the circle, facing it and the cliff beyond. The night air was cool, and
she shivered a little. None of the aliens had acknowledged her
presence directly, yet she could feel that they were aware of
her, as surely as they were aware of Nardis, whose green light
bathed them. If she had not been there, the circle would not
have been formed. The last remnant of the song subsided as
the circle grew tighter, mnoerri touching mnoerri, wing-flaps
outstretched and rustling as they slid over one another. The
lilith did not understand precisely what she was seeing, but she
could see it was an outpouring of love. What was it her visitors
had said? "Glad-flowing, each into each." Somehow the sixty
or seventy mnoerri in the meadow were joining in a single
indissoluble circular bond, a ring of flesh. It was a solemn
spectacle, and silent, and terrifying in its intensity. The bodies
of the aliens seemed to flow into one another, immingling,
glistening wetly—or was the wetness only the scintillation of
iridescent wings rippling in the moonlight? She could smell
their musk now, an odor of old leather and freshly snapped
green shoots. Truly, Li visited each people differently, but she
had not neglected the mnoerri.

For an unmeasured time, the lilith stood bearing witness to
the slow writhing of flesh. The beauty of the moment moved
her, but it also excluded her. A catalyst she might be, a par-
ticipant never. These were the beings, primitive and reluctant,
who retreating before encroaching human civilization might
never inherit their own world. And however she might feel for
them, there was no place in their circle for her. After a while,
slowly and carefully so as not to disturb them, she stepped
back under the shelter of the trees.

Behind her a twig snapped. Her breath caught in her throat,
and her ears probed and sorted among the small noises of the
night. The tree-babies had fallen silent. Off to one side there

was rustling among some bushes, and from another quarter a mutter of low voices and the crunch of footsteps. Her heart was thudding against her ribs. She darted glances back among the trees, but the darkness pressed close, ominous and impenetrable. The footsteps halted, and the voices came again, guttural, in no language she knew.

Out from the shelter of the trees toward the circle bounded ten or twelve kelg, trampling through the grass, moonlight gleaming on their fangs and unsheathed claws. Though they scampered on four legs like animals, they wore the leather breastplate of trained Berkender battle-kelg. The lilith tried to cry out, but her voice had stuck fast. She watched, powerless, as the leader of the rush gave a gargling cry of triumph and leaped upon the nearest of the mnoerri, razor claws shearing through soft flesh. The spasm of pain coursed around the circle like a wave in a bathtub, but that was the only visible effect of the assault. Not a mnoerri moved to rise or defend itself. The other kelg fell upon the helpless mnoerri, biting and slashing. Pale blood ran from their jaws down over their uniforms, and still the mnoerri made no resistance, though a few, groping and swaying as if wrapped in a thick fog of sleep, had begun to struggle to rise or crawl away. The kelg were not stopping to feed; the attack was no meal, it was a massacre. Having ripped one mnoerri open they moved on to the next, leaping atop the sundered circle and digging in with fore- and hind-claws, bouncing on springy limbs among the carnage and stopping to tear and chew wherever living flesh still moved.

Without kneeling or turning away, the lilith vomited a thick half-digested fountain over the forest floor. Her stomach contracted again and again, and bitter bile bubbled down her chin.

Chapter 9

*S*alas Tarag stood knee-deep in foul water, waiting for
Bravely to return. He was fairly sure the duongnu meant
to do so; he had swum off without his precious love-gift,
the ring of keys. There were no sounds of pursuit, only the lap
and gurgle of the tide. Probably the two guards knocked unconscious by Bravely's power were so frightened by the mysterious
spell that they felt it safer to wait for reinforcements. Tarag
wished for a lantern or a torch, if only to inspect the ancient
stonework of this dismal vault. He had heard that the fortress
possessed secret underground channels leading down to the
harbor, built in the days when a siege was a real threat. Such
a channel would run now beneath city streets, perhaps joining
the main sewer somewhere this side of the seawall. If it had
not caved in at some point, the channel should offer a safe
means of escape. What he was going to do after he reached
the harbor was a question altogether murkier than the stagnant
water sloshing around him. By now his ship would be
impounded; he would have to contrive somehow to get it back.
He wondered what had become of the lilith. Wherever she was,
she must be in danger. If he could find a way to help her, he
would do it. What he would do if compelled to choose between
the ship and the lilith, he had no idea.

Eventually, splashing told him Bravely had returned. The

merman hissed breath through his elevated nostrils. "Way clear," he announced. "No air only one tunnel. Walker swim good?"

"Probably not as fast as you. Especially not in the dark. Is there light in the no air tunnel?"

"No light. Walker not—allieohvehme—not call, listen, hear in dark?"

"No, I don't know how. You'll have to lead me. I can't see anything. Do we swim the whole way?"

"Swim, crawl, swim, dive, swim. Zalaz Darang have teeth of walker prison?"

"Aye. Here." He held out the key ring. The keys jingled.

"Hold ring of iron. Hold tight."

Tarag did as he was bidden. Bravely gripped the key ring as well, so that their fists were knuckle to knuckle, and led him into the swirling unpleasant water. When the stairs were too deep to touch with his toes, Tarag kicked free, paddling with his free hand, and spluttered when his head dipped beneath the surface. He tried not to think about the decaying matter bobbing around him. His sandals proved to be an encumbrance, and he kicked them off.

They came, after what seemed a long time, to the place where the water was shallow enough to crawl. The ceiling was too low to stand upright, as Tarag found when he bumped his head, so Bravely led him forward on hands and knees, Tarag's left arm advancing with Bravely's right over the rough slimy stone. Then there was another stretch of swimming before they arrived at the tunnel where they would have to dive. "How long?" Tarag wanted to know. Bravely put an image in his mind of a strand of seaweed with seven fronds. Tarag narrowed his eyes in exasperation. He didn't even know whether the fronds were a measure of distance or of time. He began rapidly filling and emptying his lungs. Like most oar, he thought nothing of being on the sea, but was uneasy at the thought of being beneath it. *I mean no trespass, Bulon. I will leave Your domain as I entered it.*

They plunged into the stinking brine, Tarag tugged along by powerful webbed feet and a ring of keys, stroking awkwardly himself with one arm and scissor-kicking. How long could a duongnu stay under water? Long enough to go down to the deep for teeth, and fight and be injured, and still float back up to the light. Tarag's lungs were beginning to ache. He kicked harder. Bravely changed direction, and Tarag nearly lost his grip on the keys. He grabbed the ring with his other hand and let himself be towed. Red spots were pulsing in front of his eyes. He let out a few bubbles to ease the pressure, then a few more.

Nearly unconscious, he barely noticed when Bravely angled upward, but suddenly they broke the surface. Tarag coughed and spat out water, and gasped and coughed again. The red spots dissolved into golden sparks, and he saw gray daylight glancing from dripping walls. "You—dragged me—the last—quarter of—of the way," he managed. "I couldn't have—done it. By myself. That makes us even. I saved your life. You saved mine. Even."

An image of two forearms wrapped around one another, elbow to elbow, wrists and fingers entwined.

"Aye. Like that."

"Pledge of friend."

"Then we're friends, aren't we?" They were treading water, clutching the ring of keys between them. Tarag brought his arm up and wrapped it around Bravely's in the gesture the merman had shown him. "Give the teeth to your lady-love." He let go of the ring.

"If Zalaz Darang fall in sea ever, call as this: 'Ulloeyyah. Ulloeyyah.'"

Tarag repeated the sound. Bravely corrected his pronunciation.

"What does it mean?"

"Duongnué find. Help float."

Together they swam down the tunnel toward the open harbor. When they reached open air Bravely held the keys aloft in a salute and, in a single smooth motion, dived. Ripples spread out from where he had been and were lost in the general swell. Tarag snorted to clear salt water from his nose, and looked around. The mouth of the sewer behind him was an arch set in the stone bulwark of the seawall. The sun stood low in the west, and the pitch-smeared pillars of the nearest pier cast long shadows. Turning on his back, he surveyed the activity topside. No guard yet—but there might be at any moment. Nule Chespid would have a shrewd guess or two about how his guests had escaped. Not caring to climb up onto a public street dripping wet, and not caring either to swim conspicuously across open harbor like a swamp-rat, Tarag edged his way along the waterfront, diving like a duongnu and coming up in the shelter of the piers to breathe. In that manner, he swam a thousand long tadigs to the point nearest where the *Amera Smiles* rode at anchor. The sun was a yellow blaze afire in the western hills, the reefed spars of a hundred ships silhouetted black against it. The air was cooling, and the muscles of his shoulders rippled in a shiver as he clung to the inside of a dock ladder to catch his breath. There were dark figures moving about on the deck of his ship, three or four of them, and that was too many, because nobody ought to be there but Graio and Jutie. Not knowing Tarag had been captured, Graio had no reason not to return to the ship, where he would certainly be arrested in turn. What had happened to Jutie could only be guessed at. He was not guilty of any crime, but Chespid's guards could be relied on to detest wogglies, as did most folk in Falnerescu. And Jutie was sure to fly into a rage if he heard anybody accuse Tarag of misdeeds. One way or another, the wogglie was in for a bad time. But at the moment there was little that Tarag could do. Even if Jutie were still aboard the ship Tarag would accomplish nothing by swimming out to it and attempting a rescue. Item: He would be observed swimming. Item: The guard aboard the *Amera Smiles* would be armed, and Tarag had not even a table knife. Item: He couldn't snatch Jutie and swim off with him, because Jutie couldn't swim. Like all Wologchim, the little bowlegged man was symbiotically attached to his pet. Separate them, and both would die. The pet was descended from what had once been an aquatic species, closely related to the common swamp-sucker. But its ancestors had long ago climbed up into the trees, where they hung motionless until the moment came to drop upon their prey. They could no longer breathe in water. And they had no lungs to store air.

There remained the remote possibility of getting Jutie aboard the skiff that was tied alongside the *Smiles*—but maneuvering a skiff short-handed in a crowded harbor was not a task that Tarag relished. Better by far to climb ashore, get some dry clothes, and then worry about rescuing his crew. His crew and his ship. His crew, his ship, and if possible the lilith. Wherever she was. Whoever had taken her.

A few short steps from the top of the ladder was a convenient public lavatory. He slipped into a booth, jammed the stick on its string into the latch, and stripped out of his shirt and trousers. The chill draft puckered his skin. He wrung the clothes so they dripped mostly through the hole in the board seat, and ran his hands through his hair and beard. He would have liked to wash, but there were no basins in public lavatories, and certainly no running water. He put the clammy clothes on again. When he stepped back out on the pier nobody seemed to be paying any special attention to him. Not wanting to catch a chill, he stepped lively.

Pye, Tarag knew, had no fixed abode. He might sleep one night on a rooftop, the next in the well-appointed chambers of this or that lady. But at sunset he was more predictable. There were half a dozen taverns where Tarag might hook his fish, the nearest only a street or two off. He remembered an Olmalin proverb: Only a fool thinks two eyes see more than four. And of all the eyes in the city, Tarag most hoped to enlist Pye's. Eyes, arms, whatever was needful; even a bit of Eloian philosophy might prove useful in a situation like this.

In the first tavern he hooked nothing, nor in the second. The third was boarded up, the iron rings on the doorpost hanging dispiritedly where the sign had been torn down. By now the light was failing, and Tarag no longer was stepping lively; he was trudging. Before long he would have to find a good hot fire to stretch out by.

In the fourth tavern, a small, grimy, sour-smelling place lit only by a few lumpy candles, he spotted his quarry. Pye was deep in conversation with an old man with long stringy hair and beard and very few teeth. Tarag slid in on the bench beside his friend without speaking and folded his arms on the table.

The two men looked at Tarag. "Plogi, we'll talk of this another time," Pye said. The old man nodded and slid off the bench, eyeing Tarag with discreet but unmistakable curiosity. Tarag nodded politely, and the old man lowered his eyes and slipped away.

"You hardly look a bridegroom," Pye observed. "Nor smell one."

"I've been swimming."

"I never would have guessed it."

"Did you know there's an underground waterway from the fortress to the harbor?"

Without seeming to, Pye glanced around to see who might be listening. Of the folk who might be in earshot, two were arguing in low voices and the third was slumped forward on the table, dead to the world. "I knew things had gone wrong. How wrong?"

"As wrong as can be. Chespid's men are aboard the *Amera Smiles*. As he sees it, I'm a kidnapper. The lilith is gone, nobody knows where."

"There was a fire. That was when we ran."

"I don't know who set it. But no sooner had the cry gone up than half a dozen swords at least were in full attack on the house. They were all killed or escaped, but I got hit on the head."

"So you had to swim for it. These waters are shallow, Tarag. Don't underestimate Nule Chespid. He looks a bit of a fool, but he's not one. He'll have your heart on a stake, or at least your ship on a reef. He's already nicked you, I see." Pye touched with a fingertip the cut Tarag had had from Ranga Strell's square-cut ring. The wound still burned, but the water seemed not to have set it festering. The salve he kept for such emergencies was on the ship. In another day he would know whether it would heal clean or cause him trouble.

"Not Chespid," he said. "One of the Vli. They've got an evil one there."

"What of the others, those who broke in?"

"Ill-dressed, and sour-faced. If they'd been enjoying the

scrap, I'd say they were pirates. As it is, I'd put them down for the Brown Hand."

"So the Hand has got the lilith."

"And Chespid's got my ship."

"Stealing a ship should prove a stimulating challenge," Pye said.

"It may not come to that, if we can convince Chespid of my innocence. The thing I don't see is why Osher should deny me like that, when a word from him could have saved me. I'd thought we were friends."

"Osher?"

"He was in Chespid's audience-chamber when we got there. I tried to explain about the wager, and nobody was of a mind to believe me, so I turned to him. He was there when it was laid. But he told Chespid he'd never spoken to me in his life."

"Odd," Pye mused. "You don't suppose he's in league with the Hand, do you?"

"Osher? Impossible. As a matter of principle, he's opposed to everything they stand for."

"No, wait. I see. They all supposed you meant to kidnap the lilith. So if Osher acknowledged you, he'd be as much as admitting complicity in the kidnapping."

"True. He's not subject to arrest, of course, but he might have other reasons for not wanting it supposed that he was involved."

"Such as wanting to keep on the good side of the Vli," Pye suggested. "You don't suppose there's a treaty in the offing, do you, between Berkenland and Vli Holm? That would explain what the lilith is doing here, it would explain Osher's behavior—and it would also explain the Hand's interest."

"Aye, you've hit on it, I'm sure. What good the knowledge will do us, if any, remains to be seen. We've got to plot a course."

"That will wait," Pye said, "until you've gotten a hot bath and some clean clothes."

"Lovely sound those words have. You know a place? I'm penniless."

"I know a place. Good folk that I've helped out from time to time."

Pye led the way across the moonlit city. Traffic was lighter than during the day, but they passed a number of pedestrians— garishly dressed young dandies lounging under a streetlamp, homeless beggars rooting in a trash bin, a religious procession in red robes pacing silently, icons held out before them. At one intersection Tarag and Pye saw ahead a good-sized mob carrying torches and shouting angrily. They stepped back into the lee of a building and waited for the mob to pass. The only words they could make out in the tumult were "Death to the poisoner!"

At length they reached the longhouse district, whose sober citizens were at that hour indoors. A typical longhouse, two-storied, might house thirty or more members of one clan, most of them related by blood and all sharing in a loose communal marriage. In days gone by the longhouses had been the back-bone of Falnerescu, putting out a fishing fleet that fed the hungry during the period of collapse that preceded the birth of the Olmalin dynasty. Since then, many of the clans had fallen upon evil times, though a few still thrived. Pye tapped on the door of a longhouse, and shortly the top half of the door swung back and a skinny, bright-eyed old man peered out at them. He was holding a candle. "Oh, it's you," he said when he saw Pye. "Come on in." He unlatched the bottom half of the door.

"My friend needs a place to stay the night," Pye explained. "Also a bath, and some clean clothes. Can you help us, Freeman Chaluman, or have we come at a bad time?"

"No time's a bad time for a friend. In truth, I'm glad of your coming. The old woman and I have nobody left but each other, and the evenings are long. Chala, come see! We've got visitors!" An old woman wearing a dark floor-length skirt and holding some needlework appeared at an inner door. "Eh?" she said. "What did you say?"

"Visitors," Freeman Chaluman shouted. "Boil some water for a bath!"

"What?"

"Boil some water! For a bath!"

"You had a bath, only the day before yesterday," the old woman complained. "What you be wantin' another for?" Then she got a good look at Pye. "Oh, it's young Pye, is it? Why didn't you say so, Chalis? We've not got much," she said, shaking her head sorrowfully, "but I'll set out the bread and cheese."

Pye kissed her on the forehead. "That's good of you, mother." Clearly the term was one of endearment, not of familial relationship. "My friend will need some clothes, after his bath. Do you have any that would fit him?"

"Clothes? Yes, Nupta left some here when he went off to Baldoremu. They should be just about the right size. If only I can find where I put them." Limping painfully on an arthritic hip, but still obviously pleased to have something to do, she went to see to the newcomers' needs.

When he had steamed and soaked the grime away and toweled himself dry, Tarag put on the clothes the old woman had laid out. The white linen shirt was too tight across the shoulders, but otherwise the garments fit well enough. Pye had gone out again briefly, and returned with a small earthenware pot. It contained a soothing salve that Tarag rubbed onto his cut lip.

"In order to pry her loose," Pye observed, "we'll need a lever. Or is it the ship that concerns you? We can as easily let the ship be, and trawl for the lilith."

"We may be able to accomplish both at once," Tarag said. "With luck, we might manage to free the lilith from the Brown Hand and then use her as a lever against Chespid, to convince him to declare me innocent."

"It might work. But I thought you were opposed to using people without letting them know about it ahead of time and striking a bargain."

"True," Tarag conceded. "So we'll find her first and then ask her to help. Where do you suppose the Hand have got her hidden?"

Pye frowned and shook his head. "Too many places it could be. Not just in the city. There's thousands of tadigs of open country out there, and slave barracks that are never inspected. The Hand have been hiding folk for a long time; they're good at it. Nor would it be wise, I think, to jump in without knowing where the shoals are. We'll have to begin by learning what the Hand are up to."

"Is that all? It'd be quicker and easier just to hole up until Chespid decides to sell the ship."

"The Hand are secretive, it's true. We won't get a whisper from any of the small fry. We'll have to go straight to the top."

"From all I've heard," Tarag said, "we could *build* a ship sooner than find out who guides the Hand in Falnerescu. Or do you know of a channel that I don't?"

"I know somebody who knows somebody."

Tarag stood up and flexed his shoulders in the too-tight shirt. "We've got to have a line ready to play out," he said. "Some bait they'll strike at. Now, we're assuming that there's a treaty afoot between the Berks and the Vli. So it's a fair bet the Brown Hand is out to scuttle the treaty. Nothing they could do would be likely to budge the Berkenders. Therefore—"

"Therefore," Pye said, "they plan to use the lilith as a lever to force the Vli to denounce the Berkenders, or insult them publicly, or some such. It's possible they've already sent word to the Vli, naming their terms. But if I were in their shoes I'd be holding back, to give Metterner and his friends time to sweat a little. In which case *we* might be able to make a dip before the purse is emptied. We need only say we're acting for the Vli, and I'll wager somebody will take us to see somebody."

"Why should they believe us?"

"It's not public knowledge that the lilith is gone. Who could we be, if not who we claim?"

They bade good night to the old couple and went out again. The streets were nearly deserted. Once they saw a pair of Chespid's guards strolling, helmets and pikes gleaming in the moonlight, but they went boldly on without changing gait, and were not challenged nor pursued.

The somebody Pye knew was out for the evening, but his wife suggested they try another somebody. Following her directions, they arrived at the rear door of a large, weatherbeaten old house squeezed on a narrow strip of land between a slaughterhouse and a brewery. A big, balding, square-jawed man let them into his kitchen and listened, arms folded impassively, as Tarag explained that he had been sent by Habil Metterner to negotiate with the Brown Hand for the return of the lilith.

"Your oars are in the air," the square-jawed man said. "Do I look like a slave? I'm a law-abidin' man, and I mind my own business. Got no time for swamp-rats."

"I believe you," Tarag assured him. "We have no business with you. However, we heard it whispered that you might possibly know somebody who could help us, somebody who might be happy to learn that the Vli were willing to do whatever proved to be necessary . . ." He let the sentence dangle. When there was no answer, he added, "Why burden yourself with the decision? If, as you say, you know nothing of the Brown Hand, you can hardly be the best judge of what will interest them. Why not send word, at least, and see what reply comes back?"

The man made up his mind. "You wait here," he ordered, putting on his vest. "Be here when I get back. And best you hope there's nobody watchin' from any rooftops to see where I'm bound, or you'll be fish food before the sun comes up." He went out, leaving them alone in the kitchen. Tarag sat down on the hearth and held out his hands to warm them at the banked coals. The room was sparsely furnished, with nothing in the way of personal decoration, only a large broad-bladed knife hanging from a nail on a thong, and a few dented pots. Anybody might pass through such a room and be equally at home, equally a stranger. Perhaps this was one of the safe houses where the Hand sheltered escaped slaves.

Overhead a board creaked. Tarag and Pye exchanged glances, both struck by the same thought. Almost certainly, somebody was upstairs watching them through a peephole. Tarag felt a little show might not be out of order. "Do you think he means to help us?" he asked. "Or has he only run out on us?"

"We have to trust him," Pye said. "He's our only hope, if we're to get the lilith back."

"I don't like what he said about fish food. You don't think we're in danger, do you?"

"The Hand are not cutthroats," Pye said, picking up the

cue. "They've an honor of their own. As long as we deal squarely with them, we can expect the same in return."

Tarag leaned back against the brick of the fireplace and closed his eyes. He had nearly dropped off to sleep before the big man returned. They heard him come in by way of the front room and climb the stairs. After a brief murmur of conversation, he descended again. Entering the kitchen he took no notice of them, but crossed straight to the back door and opened it to admit two others, who regarded Tarag and Pye warily. The newcomers were both small and wiry, one dark and one fair. They wore daggers.

"You will be taken to a place," the big man announced. "You must not know where it is. You will allow yourselves to be blindfolded." The two others brought out dark cloths and stepped behind Tarag and Pye to bind the blindfolds. Then their hands were roughly seized and pulled behind them, where their wrists were bound, none too gently, with cord. Tarag was not happy about the arrangement; it reminded him uncomfortably of the manacles he would have been wearing by now had he not escaped the dungeon.

They were led out the kitchen door and down the steps to the yard. Tarag had no trouble telling by the smell when they left the neighborhood of the slaughterhouse and the brewery, but their route twisted and turned so that he quickly lost all sense of direction. By the reek of trash bins, he knew they were traversing alleys rather than thoroughfares. Now and then they surprised a swamp-rat that skittered away squeaking. Once they were jerked to a halt and stood waiting in silence for some other footsteps to pass. At length they were led up more steps and, after a coded knock, through a door into a room. Their blindfolds were removed, though their wrists remained bound. The bleak, cheerless little room was lit only by two flickering candles. Scraps of this and that were collecting dust in the corners, and there was no furniture save a rough-hewn plank table and behind it a chair. A woman was sitting in the chair, her eyes leveled at them.

The woman was Jaima, the drummer from the Brass Paum. Jaima and Tarag locked eyes for long seconds. Her nostrils dilated as she breathed, the only sign that she was furious. "Of all the men in Falnerescu," she said, "I might have known it would be you." Like the men, she was wearing a vest and trousers. The brass armbands she wore when playing in the tavern had vanished.

"Well, since we're all old friends," Tarag said, "why don't we sit down and make ourselves comfortable? You could start by having your men untie us. They are your men, I assume. You're—?"

"Who I am is no concern of yours—or wouldn't have been if you'd been anybody else. You've just become rather a dangerous person to be let run around loose, Tarag. Can you think of any reason why I ought to let you and your friend go on breathing? And don't start talking about what we once meant to one another."

"I wasn't going to, believe me." Not when her eyes had that iron glint, he wasn't.

"I suppose that story about your speaking on behalf of the Vli was a fabrication. Not that it's any concern of mine, since I have nothing to say that would interest the Vli, nor they anything that would interest me."

"If not," Tarag countered, "why did you agree to see me?"

"I didn't. You're not seeing anybody. But if you value your life, you'll explain what you're doing here, and quickly."

"All right. I won't pretend to be speaking directly for the Vli, but it's true that I've their interests at heart, and yours as well. I know you've got the lilith, and I know pretty well why. You'd like to get her back to Habil Metterner safe and sound, but only on certain conditions. I'm here to carry your terms to him. I don't see any difficulty in that."

"I don't know what you're talking about," Jaima announced promptly. "There has never been a lilith away from Vli Holm. You should know that as well as I. But if a lilith *did* come to Falnerescu, it would still be no concern of mine. What makes you think I'm involved?"

"You wouldn't have had me brought here if you weren't involved. Do you deny that those were your men who attacked Habil Metterner's house this morning?"

"I have no men. And I know nothing about any attack. You still haven't explained your own interest in the matter. And I'm running out of patience."

"All right. I'm in a tight spot. Nule Chespid is convinced that *I've* kidnapped the lilith. In order to show him that I'm innocent, I've got to make sure she's returned to her own people. And in spite of your denials, I know you've got her. But I also know you don't mean her any harm. Both because I know what the Brown Hand stands for, and because I know you. All I'm asking is that you let me help you get whatever you're trying to get out of this, so that the lilith can go home and I can get my ship back."

"Has it occurred to you that she might not want to go back to her own people? I know no more of the Hand than you do, but I know they free slaves. How can you be certain the liliths aren't slaves? That if the Hand offered one freedom, she wouldn't seize the chance?"

"In that case, I'd not interfere," Tarag said. "If you know me at all, you know I count all men as free, and would return none to his master against his will. You have only to bring me before her so she can tell me she's found freedom, and I'll find some other way to get my ship back from Chespid." And if nothing else, I'll have won the wager, he added silently.

"You persist in assuming that I'm lying," Jaima said. "Yet you've said nothing to convince me that you're telling the truth. Why should Chespid think you've got the lilith? Tell me that."

"Because I was in the house when your people attacked. I was hit on the head and captured. When I woke, the lilith was gone."

For the first time, Jaima seemed unsure of herself. "Gone? Are you sure?"

"You ought to know."

"No, no. Who told you she was gone? How did you learn of it?"

"The Vli were talking of nothing else. They seemed quite distraught. Is there something remarkable in that?"

"I don't know." Jaima thought for a moment. "You were in the house, you say. So it was you set the fire."

Aha! She had admitted knowing something of the events of the morning. But still Tarag was perplexed. "I didn't set the fire," he protested. "I thought your people set the fire."

"Why should we set a fire? There's more here than I can fathom. But I see now we've been talking at cross-purposes."

"Then you see more than I do," Tarag said. "Perhaps you'd care to enlighten me."

"I may as well. You've already guessed most of it. Since dawn we'd been waiting in a hiding place near the Metterner estate—exactly where doesn't matter—hoping to learn where the lilith was being kept. When the fire broke out, we saw it was the best chance we'd have, to come in over the wall while the household were distracted. But when we got in, we couldn't find the lilith. We lost two brave men, and nothing to show for it. We assumed she was in some part of the house we weren't able to reach."

"That was a lot of trouble to go to just to free one person that you aren't even certain is a slave."

"There are other factors as well. I've had reports of a shift in alliances—well, I needn't burden you with rumors. That's why I agreed to speak with you tonight. I was curious who else would be concerned about the lilith, and what they might know that would be of use. But you know less than I. Disappointing."

"Can you tell me why I should believe you?" Tarag said. "You could easily have her, and be lying."

"The Hand *has*, as you put it, nobody. All are free to come and go as they choose."

"Blindfolded and tied up, some of them, I notice. It's possible we can help one another; I don't see that our ends are opposed. But my hands are getting numb, and I can't think when my hands are numb. Now that we've dropped the pretense, and you're assured we mean no harm, why not tell your men to cut us loose?"

Jaima made a motion with her finger, and the men who had been standing behind Tarag and Pye loosed their bonds, thriftily not cutting the cords but untying them. Tarag chafed the raw creases in his wrists.

"You haven't introduced your friend," Jaima pointed out.

"My friend has several names that I know of, and probably several more that I don't. He lives by his wits. If I told you his name, I'd be honor-bound to tell him yours."

"Then we'll skip the introductions. Perhaps his wits can find a way out of this swamp. I'll admit I'm foundering. And on the bodies of the two who died, I'd dearly like to know. You don't know where the lilith is, and I don't know where she is, but she's gone. Could there have been some other hand that succeeded where we failed? Surely one of us would have seen them, coming or going."

Pye was busy rubbing his arms and wrists, and inconspicuously flexing his ankles as well. "I don't think she went anywhere," he announced. "I don't think she ever left that house."

Jaima and Tarag stared at him.

"Look at it from all sides," Pye said. "Here's what you see. You folk have the house under your eye. You see the Potheqi and me arrive with the chest containing friend Tarag, am I right?"

Jaima nodded.

"Did you see anybody else come or go before us?"

She shook her head.

"So nobody came or went. And is there any reason to suppose that any third party might have been involved?"

"There's always Osher," Tarag pointed out. "But he plays by the book. I can't quite see him for this."

"Right," Pye went on. "Anybody else? Tarag learned of the lilith's arrival from a harbor pilot. Does anybody want to suggest that the pilot's involved in this, or any of the oar at the table? No? Good. Now, we don't know what your source of information was, but unless you see some reason for suspicion we can discount it. Agreed? It wasn't somebody in the Vli house, was it?"

"No."

"So we arrive, and then a fire breaks out, and then Gr—and then the Potheqi and I leave, just as you arrive, and then you leave, and Tarag stays. The gate is barred, and nobody else comes or goes. Am I on course so far?"

The other two nodded.

"Then it's clear as sky." Pye shrugged. "There was no time when she could have been taken away, and nobody to take her away, so she's still there."

"It does make a kind of sense," Tarag admitted. "But where's the advantage to them in pretending she's been kidnapped when she hasn't?"

"There the fog is thicker. Maybe they're so fearful that a second kidnap would succeed that they elected to protect her by claiming she's gone. Maybe it's a charade to give them some leverage against the Berkenders. Or maybe one of them is a traitor, and is deceiving the others. We've all heard what a beauty the lilith is, or at least what a beauty the Vli think her. Might not there be somebody in that house who wants a lilith all his own, who doesn't want to share her with anybody, and who seized on the opportunity to imprison her in a secret place in the house? Those who live there have lived without a lilith all their lives. Who knows what deprivation might do to them? If we can get into that house again, and search, I'll wager we'll find the lilith."

Jaima looked at Tarag. "I see what you meant by wits. This one has a glib tongue, if nothing else; but I believe his bread has nuts in it. All we lack is a means of gaining entrance to the house. What worked once won't work a second time."

"Why should you be with us?" Tarag asked. "Why should you care where the lilith has got to?"

"I don't like to see anybody imprisoned," Jaima said. "Also, there are some questions I'd like to ask her. Whether she answers is her affair. I'd not threaten her, but I'd make it plain to her she was free to answer if she chose, without fear of retribution from those who had held her in chains."

"You'll have your chance to ask your questions, if I can manage it," Tarag promised. "But you're right about the difficulty. By now Chespid's guard will be all around that house, and the gate will be barred to strangers. Even should we gain entrance, the Vli would stand in the way of a search. Could we talk them into standing aside? I doubt it."

"If we can't manage the search," Pye suggested, "we need somebody to manage it for us. Chespid?"

"We can't go to Chespid," Tarag pointed out. "The first thing he'll do will be to throw me back in the dungeon."

"Osher, then."

Tarag considered the idea. "Aye," he said slowly. "Osher we might persuade. And I'd trust Osher above Chespid, to do as he's agreed. Chespid is tricky, but Osher is very unimaginative. Offer him the right line, and you can tow him wherever you want."

"I didn't know you were so friendly with the Berkenders," Jaima said.

"I'm friendly with who suits me. You ought to know that." Tarag crossed his arms on his chest and grinned at her. "You know, I'd always felt there was a part of you that I was missing. I'm glad I finally found out what it was."

Jaima glowered at him and lowered her eyes. "You haven't said what bait you mean to dangle before the Berkender."

"Oh, that." Tarag yawned and stretched ostentatiously. "I'll think on it as I'm dropping off to sleep. Are you going to blindfold us again on the way out, or are we all friends?"

Chapter 10

*I*n the waning of the afternoon, at an hour when Zhenuvnili was still striding along the south road, sobbing and murmured prayer echoed from the house of Habil Metterner. Although Karanli had been instructed to tell the Vli that there was no cause for concern, the nala's hysterical fear had convinced her that the message was of no importance, that the kidnapping had occurred as those around her described. So Zhenuvnili was mourned as dead, for she had fallen into the hands of strangers.

When Nule Chespid had succeeded in shooing them out so that he could interrogate his prisoner in peace, Qob Qobba, Habil Metterner, and Ranga Strell had gone back to the mansion and waited, in vain, for a messenger to arrive with news, growing more fretful by the hour. In the large front room where Salas Tarag had been questioned, they were still waiting when the last of the sun sank beneath the spiked wall outside the arched window, and the sky burst red and faded to gray. Qob Qobba was lounging sideways across a dark wood chair with square arms and no cushions, absently tapping a short-handled reading-glass on one bony knee. In a matching chair against the far wall Habil Metterner sat slumped forward, wringing his hands. Strell, too impatient to sit, was pacing back and forth, pausing at one end of each traverse to stare malevolently out the window at the little fruit tree struggling up out of the bare circle of soil in the pavement of the narrow forecourt. "Why is there no word?" Metterner fretted. "Surely they've searched that madman's ship by now!"

"Plainly, she wasn't on the ship." Qobba spoke to the reading-glass, not raising his voice. He felt very tired.

"Or else she *was* on the ship," Strell said nastily, "and they've found her and brought her back to Chespid and he isn't telling us for some reason. I don't trust that runt. He's slick."

"They say he's the most honest, efficient governor this island has had in a thousand chetnes," Metterner said reassuringly. "He's especially known for his impartiality toward people of all races."

"You've been living among this foreign filth too long," Strell said. "You don't smell the stink. Chespid didn't fool me. He's just a pervert, like all the rest. The only difference is, he's got armed men to back him up. Think he'll pass up a chance to get poor Zheni locked up where he can slobber all over her? Who's to prevent him?" Strell flung his arms wide in rhetorical appeal. "And these are the people we propose to let into Vli Holm! Less than a day, and they've stolen the lilith, to soil her with sacrilege! It's no more than I've been saying all along."

"So you have," Qob Qobba said drily. "I was hoping you'd forbear to remind us of the fact." He held up the reading-glass, and through it saw a smaller Strell standing upside down. "But whether or not we subscribe to your view, it will prevail. I can smooth things over a bit with the Berkenders, take their proposals under advisement and so forth, but without Zheni I can't commit us."

"And a good thing!"

"Is it? Tell me, friend Strell, when somebody swings a sword at you do you shut your eyes to ward off the blow, or do you raise up a sword of your own?"

"I don't see what you're talking about," Strell said sullenly.

"How can we live in this world, as a people, with our eyes closed, cringing away from every blow? Had we not better get ourselves a sword?"

"If it were only a sword. But you're forgetting, or maybe

it's that you hope to honey-talk me into forgetting, that there's a hand attached to that sword, a foreign hand that's shy a finger. Can you will another's hand to strike, Qobba, or to refrain from striking? Can you will even *my* hand to do your bidding, in place of my own? I think not."

"We are all in the hands of the Goddess," Qobba pointed out mildly. "It is Her will."

"Aye, it's Her will and Her hand have snatched Zheni from us. She it was That let the lilith be taken, so that the treaty would be broached below the waterline. Speak me no more treason. The signs are plain: The Goddess Herself opposes our mission."

"I cannot believe," Habil Metterner protested, distraught, "that the Goddess would allow Her child to fall victim to such evil! Surely a storm at sea or a sudden illness would have been more merciful."

"We don't know what the Goddess wills," Qobba said, "except by studying what She does. If I'm speaking treason, you're speaking heresy, friend Strell, to claim to know the will of Li. Li will reveal, in Her own time, what is to be. The lilith may yet be returned to us, safe and whole. We can only wait, and pray."

"I'd pay any amount of money to get her back," Metterner moaned. "I'd sell myself into slavery in a minute."

"Money may be called for," Qobba observed. "I've been wondering whether we might expect a demand for ransom. If it becomes necessary to buy Zheni back, friend Metterner, I will certainly take advantage of your offer. I'm hoping it won't come to that. Chespid's men are searching the city. They may find a trail."

"How do you know they're searching?" Strell demanded. "How can you be sure those cutthroats this morning weren't under Chespid's orders? He may have planned all this from the start. You notice how he let that sea captain off without questioning him closely. Why? Because the man would have betrayed him! As soon as we were gone, I'll wager, he let him walk out of prison as free as a ship. Mark my words: We'll see that fellow Tarag walking the streets long before we see Zheni again."

"I don't mind who took her," Metterner said miserably. "I only hope she's all right."

"If she's dead by now, she's well off," Strell rasped. "The touch of foreigners is contamination. Not that our dear Zheni is concerned by little things like that! Do you know this morning I caught her walking in the garden without an escort? I shouldn't wonder she invited the whole band of filthy grubblers into her bedchamber and then went off to carouse with them in the streets!"

"I won't listen to such slander!" Metterner cried.

"How are we to know what she's capable of? She's criminally impulsive and irresponsible, we know that well enough. But what does it matter? You heard that sea captain declare what he'd do to Zheni if he had the chance. They're all like that, I tell you!"

"Not all foreigners are depraved, friend Strell," Qobba pointed out mildly. "No more than all Vli are to be trusted."

"What's that supposed to mean?" Strell snapped.

"Nothing. Merely an observation."

"You haven't liked me from the start, have you? You're jealous that Li Ranli has been my lilith for a hundred chetnes, and yours for only forty! You've opposed me at every turn, sneaking around behind my back trying to get me removed from this mission, spreading lies about me! You were the one letting the lilith run about the ship half naked, and undermining my authority when I tried to put things right. Don't deny it! You'd rather I was out of the way, wouldn't you? That would leave you free to do with the treaty as you liked. If I weren't here to stop you, you'd be free to sell our whole beloved island to your bed-friends the Berkenders!"

Qob Qobba regarded his fellow diplomat, whose face was flushed a dark blotchy red, with patient distaste. Strell's behavior was disturbing, but the whole day had been disturbing, and Qobba was too tired to attach any special significance to the outburst. He sighed. "Friend Strell, we're all overwrought, and with good reason. So I will take no offense. I'm sure you'll feel better after a night's rest. Perhaps cook can prepare a soothing warm drink for you."

"Oh, you'd like that, wouldn't you? You'd like to slip me some poison so you'll have me out of the way too! How much are the Berkenders paying you? How much, Qobba? Tell us!"

Qob Qobba uncurled unhurriedly and got to his feet. His back ached where the chair had dug into it. "I'm not going to listen to any more of this," he announced. "I'm sorry that events have upset you so, friend Strell. I'm sure that when you come to think on your words, you will repent of them." At the door he paused. "I will be in my room," he told Metterner. "If the lilith is found, or if a demand for ransom is received, please notify me at once." He turned away. He was faintly surprised to see that his fingers, on the door handle, were trembling. With a slow and measured tread he went out, and shut the door behind him.

The horrifying thing about the massacre was the stillness; the only sounds were the gnawing and snuffling and the scrabble of claws in the dirt. Zhenuvnili stood watching, unable to cry out or even look away, while the kelg finished dispatching the last unresisting mnoerri and began to feed. Their appetite, like their enthusiasm, was prodigious, but among the dozen of them they could not have downed a fraction of the meat. She felt the vomit congealing on her chin, and reached up a hand to wipe it away.

One of the kelg saw the motion and raised its head to survey the shadows beneath the moonlit stand of trees. It barked, and two of its fellows also looked up from their meal. After sniffing the air and exchanging glances, the three trotted toward the lilith on their stubby hind legs. She knew that she must turn and run, but the silver moonlight wavered a thick undersea green, and her limbs were too sluggish. Long before she could stir herself, the three kelg had ringed her and were picking at her garment with the sharp pincers that were their fingers. She flinched from the touch, and the kelg before her opened its mouth wide and hissed breath in its throat, displaying a narrow blood-flecked tongue that writhed among the fangs. She whimpered, and backed away, but missed her footing, twisted her ankle, and fell. The sharp end of a fallen branch jabbed painfully into her hip. She tried to rise to her elbows to crawl, but fell back, trembling. She knew they were about to slash her flesh from her bones and suck the juices from her organs, but suddenly that seemed not to matter very much—it was all happening to somebody else, somebody very small and far away.

But the moment stretched out, and the attack did not come. More of the taloned feet had joined the ring around her. She could smell the rank, bitter smell of kelg, and the rich forest loam where it pressed against her cheek. The kelg were snarling and bickering among themselves. Here and there she could make out a word that might be Berken, but she did not speak Berken. Evidently they were deciding her fate. The one standing at her head, whose belt bore insignia of brass, gained sway over the others and made a short speech, punctuated with grunts, which the others took up one by one until they were all chanting "Uh! Uh! Uh!" and jumping up and down in the moonlit forest.

They left off chanting at a barked command, and many small gore-bespattered hands clasped and clenched around her, claws digging into her skin. She felt herself lifted into the air. At another command, the kelg set off through the forest at a trot, bearing her unharmed aloft. Gradually the numbness that had cushioned her evaporated. She began to wonder where she was being taken. And suddenly she was convulsed by terror, so she jerked out of their grip and fell, jarringly. After some grumbling and recrimination she was picked up again and carried on. She found that it was a soothing way to travel, horizontal among the trees, with only a little disruption when the kelg broke stride to make their way up or down the sloping side of a gully. After a while she slipped into a reverie in which the recurring images of carnage were no more than abstract dancing designs, the mnoerri in their love-ceremony passively lying down to submit to the merciless caresses of the kelg. Bodies broken, blood seeping into the soil, the mnoerri were mnoerri no longer. They had become all.

She wondered vaguely what the kelg meant to do with her.

Her fate could not be pleasant. Perhaps they would take her back to their cave, and lay their eggs in her paralyzed living body, if eggs they laid. She would become, as all liliths dreamed, a mother. But then she remembered the brass belt buckle. These were Berkender kelg, kenneled at the garrison. They could only be taking her back to their masters. Why? So she could be put in a glass pickle barrel, naked and dead, for the edification of students of anatomy? Because they had been ordered to search for and kidnap her? Or merely to make a present of her to their human sergeant?

When they reached the road the pace quickened, and the ride acquired an unsettling bounce. After a few minutes she threw up again, weakly, and got a little on the kelg at her shoulder, which earned her the back of a hand across the mouth. Her lip split on a tooth. The stomach acid burned agonizingly in the cut, bringing tears to her eyes. She tongued the wound, and swallowed repeatedly until her stomach lay back in peace. And though it was little enough, that caring for herself began to restore her. She flexed her arms and legs very slowly, not to arouse suspicion, and found that no bones were broken. She could run, if need be. But how was she to escape? The kelg were battle-trained. Still, by the angle of the moons she knew they were carrying her toward Falnerescu, not away from it. She need only lie quiet and wait. Once they entered the city, an opportunity might present itself.

What end they had in view for her she never learned. The outlying villas, wrapped in sleep, slipped by, and the kelg phalanx trotted into the same market street from which she had set off that afternoon. The stalls were vacant, the awnings folded, but the market was far from deserted. On the contrary, a riot was in progress. The most imposing building on the plaza, a pillared edifice of great antiquity, was being besieged by upwards of a hundred people bearing torches and chanting, "Death to Harcot! Death to the poisoner!" One especially determined group was trying to maneuver a battering ram into position in front of the tall, ornately graven doors, while those on the fringes of the crowd were content to throw rocks and vegetables. Ranged against the mob were four of Chespid's guards,

who were trying without much success to force them back with
pikestaffs. Roused by the noise, the lilith twisted her neck to
look, but saw only confusion. The building was a temple of
Tha, the sun-god. As it happened, a man named Harcot had
bought moldy grain and, knowing it was bad, fed it to his
slaves. Worse, when they fell ill he refused to call for a physician. Several had died. He had taken refuge in the temple.
Not all of the mob were slaves, but they all believed slaves
had rights that masters must respect, and they wanted Harcot's
head on a pole. Not more than six or eight of the most vocal
among them were fingers of the Brown Hand.

Kelg, although capable of speech and the use of simple
tools, were not noted for their ability to concentrate on a single
task for long periods of time, especially in the presence of such
an attractive distraction. Seeing a fray, they were delighted to
drop everything and pitch in. The lilith landed on her shoulder
with an impact that sent knives from her wrist to her neck.
Then her feet had been let go, and she was free. The kelg were
scampering off in the direction of the temple, and already the
near edge of the crowd was shrieking and shying away from
them. The kelg had no doubt whose side they were on—the
side of the men wearing helmets. At the same moment reinforcements were arriving from another direction. Four more
guards came down a side street at a run and passed no more
than three tadigs from the lilith, chain mail jingling, without
seeing her.

She got to her knees, rose shakily, and stood, swaying,
clutching her injured shoulder with the other hand. People were
running past her, fleeing the kelg. She had no time to lose; one
kelg could have recaptured her, in her present condition, without trouble. She got her legs moving and staggered away.

A few streets off, Ranga Strell heard the shouting at the
temple. Unable to sleep, he had not even lain down, only paced
his bedroom endlessly. Outside the window twilight turned to
night, and inside Strell lit more and more candles and set them
on every available surface, so that his window was a beacon
shining over the wall. The burning knot in his stomach was
worse than usual, so bad he could hardly think. He had risked

some wine with honey, standing in the kitchen to watch while cook prepared it and snatching the cup away before she had a chance to add any poison, but the drink had done nothing to soothe the pain. Li speaks to us, he repeated to himself. In the bending of the bough, She speaks. As we walk the paths of our lives She walks beside us, and Her hand is in our hand. She it is has caused this false lilith to be cast out. She sets the days of my life in order, and commands what I shall do. She makes my lust a burning flame, so I must follow Her. Always Her sweetness is a wine that fills my heart with bliss. But whom Li casts out, truly shall be cast out. This false lilith. He could see plainly that Zhenuvnili had no Li in her heart. Zhenuvnili was not li at all, but a traitor and an abomination. To dare to come so far from Vli Holm! And more, to display herself so shamelessly! That Li should condemn the false lilith to dishonor among strangers was the final proof.

The house, noise by noise, sank into sleep, and Strell lit candles and paced, his viscera throbbing slow strokes of pain like a soft tormented bell. When he heard the disturbance at the temple he leaned out in the cool night air and saw the flare of torches. The whistles of the guard were answered shrilly from just below him, and four sets of feet dashed off in the direction of the market. Apparently, civil disorders were common in Falnerescu. Not surprising things were run so badly— foreign rabble. At home the cities were peaceful at night. In Falnerescu the Vli had to stay penned like animals, so the other animals couldn't get at them. Not that that runt Chespid cared a seed for their safety. Posting men outside the walls was just a ruse; before long he would find an excuse to demand that they throw open the gate and make the soldiers welcome in the house. But for the moment, the guard had withdrawn. Why not a breath of fresh air, while he could still get one unmolested? Strell picked up a candle in its pewter candlestick and padded downstairs. Setting the candle on a table in the hall, he unbolted the front door and stepped out into the forecourt. The cool night air revived him; he breathed deeply. Perhaps he could manage a little supper after all, if he watched it being prepared. He went back inside, picked up the candle, and, not noticing that he had left the front door ajar, went down the main hall toward the kitchen. Shadows shifted among the arching rafters far overhead. In the kitchen, a dim red glow still emanated from the banked oven. He poked among the cupboards and in the shelves in the pantry, but found only pots and skillets and tableware, and a large sack of hard unappetizing knob-roots. In order to get any supper, he would have to wake cook. The cellar stairs opened downward at the rear of the pantry, and he descended, candle held out before him. In the uncertain light the cellar looked very different than it had when Metterner was showing his guests the house, and Strell could not remember which direction the slave quarters lay. So he turned right, into a passage that led not back under the house but out under the patio and garden. The ceiling was low, the floor was dirt, and the walls were of rough stone blocks set together with crumbling mortar. Spinner-webs clotted with dust hung from the heavy overhead beams. The first door creaked back on an empty room, and the second. Where were the slaves? The third room was a jumble of barrels and crates and stacked lumber, but all of it looked old, disused. Habil Metterner's fortunes must ebb and flow like the tide. At moon-crest this wing would be filled with slaves and stored merchandise. But lately nobody had been there.

Strell made his way back to the foot of the stairs. His stomach was still gnawing at him, but dully. The idea of waking six or eight slaves in order to find cook no longer appealed to him. He trudged heavily up the steps.

Entering the main hall, he saw that he had left the front door standing wide open. Who knew what filthy foreigners might be prowling outside, waiting for such an opportunity? Cursing his own stupidity, he went to shut and bolt it—

—and, looking out, saw the lilith standing disheveled at the gate.

"Ranga?" she said. "Ranga, is that you? Dear Ranga, come let me in." Her head was obscenely bare, her robe torn in several places, her lip bruised and swollen. She was leaning against the bars of the gate, too weary to stand.

So, the she-devil had returned. It had had its fill of obscene rutting with foreigners and had come back to contaminate and destroy the virtuous people of Li. It was trying to entice him to pity, but he knew its wiles, and was unmoved. His first impulse was to let it stand out in the street and rot, as it deserved. But then he had a better idea. Liliths were privy to many secrets. This one might know whether it was truly Qob Qobba who was his enemy, or that fool Metterner, or somebody else. He might learn much if he could force the gutter trash to answer questions. He got the gate unbarred without much noise, and Zhenuvnili pushed it open and staggered in. He replaced the bar with care. No point waking anybody else. In fact, stealth might serve him best. The others would only raise a fuss and ignore his wishes. Better to talk to this one privately. He'd get the truth. But not to alarm it. Be friendly. Be friendly, and get it down into the cellar.

"Zheni!" he exclaimed in a whisper. "What has happened to you?"

"It was horrible. They—they—"

"Don't try to talk. Just come with me. I'll take care of everything." Strell wrapped his free arm firmly around the lilith's shoulders, and she winced and shrank from his touch. So—she found him repulsive. Probably she always had, in her heart, and had concealed it. Oh, what treachery! After bolting the door as softly as he could, he supported her down the hall and into the kitchen.

She stirred feebly. "This isn't the way to my room," she protested. "Where are my nalas? Nalas, where are you?"

"Ssh. Quiet. They've prepared a room for you in the cellar, where you'll be safe. Safe, do you understand? Nothing to worry about. I'll take good care of you. Trust me. It's down this way. Everything will be all right." She shut her eyes, and he led her down the stairs.

The passageway into the deserted wing was long, and took several irregular turns before ending in a blank stone wall. Strell opened the last door on the left and thrust the lilith through. She took two steps and slumped in a heap on the floor. His candle revealed that this room was more decrepit than those he had seen earlier; in one place the wall had actually collapsed, and bare stone and loose dirt lay tumbled. In the black depths of this cavity something scuttled away from the light, and its claws loosed a tiny landslide that sifted down the mound of rubble. There was no furniture but a single hardwood chair.

Zhenuvnili lifted herself on one elbow. "Nalas? Nalas? Where are the nalas? You told me—"

"That's right, that's right. No need to worry. I only want the answers to some questions. Is it true Qobba means to kill me?"

"Qobba? I don't understand. Ranga, are you sure you're feeling well?"

"You needn't lie to protect him. It won't do any good. I know the truth, you see. You thought you were fooling me, but you weren't. You ran off with that sea captain, didn't you, that Salas Tarag, and defiled yourself with him." Strell had conveniently forgotten that he had seen Tarag locked up in Chespid's dungeon.

"Defiled? Who—who is Salas Tarag?" It was the first time she had heard the name.

"Don't pretend you don't know! Was he the only one, or did you entertain all the beggars in the street?"

"Ranga, I'm dreadfully tired. I'd like to rest. Could you please send for my nalas now?" Nothing Strell said made any sense. Obviously he was distraught, but if he expected her to soothe him he would have to wait until morning.

"Not until you've answered. You're just like all the others. You think you can keep secrets from me. You think I don't know what you're whispering behind my back. But I'll not be deceived! I'll have the truth out of you, I swear it!" Bending over, he gripped her shoulder and shook it.

She cried out in pain. "Stop it, you're hurting me!"

"It's no more than you deserve. You like to pretend you're fragile, so we'll all run around taking care of you. But that trick won't work with me. I'll take care of you, all right, and we'll see how you like it!"

"Ranga, if you love the Goddess—"

"Speak not to me of the Goddess! Such filth as you should be ashamed to utter Her name. Why did you betray the Goddess? Why? Why did you strip off your robes and commit abominations with foreigners? You're foul with the stink of sin!"

"What abominations? What foreigners?" Strell's fingers gripped her shoulder, and her eyes filled with tears of pain.

"So you won't tell me. You refuse to talk. Very well." He had been planning only to question her until she blurted out the truth of the conspiracy. But he saw she meant to be stubborn. Perhaps she was in the pay of the Berkenders, and meant to sell them all of Vli Holm by getting him and Qobba out of the way so she could forge her own treaty. But she hadn't deceived him. He would teach her what fate was proper for traitors. Yes. Nobody would hear, and afterward they would thank him. But what if she struggled? She might escape from him and spread her lies among the others. He unbuckled his belt and drew it out of its loops. Before Zhenuvnili could react, he had caught her hands forcibly behind her and wrapped her wrists tight. Dragging her over to the chair and lifting her into it was harder; the pain in his stomach lit up like the sun. But at last he got the free end of the belt looped around one arm of the chair and secured it. Breathing hard, he looked down at the pitiful figure, which was slumped forward, seemingly unconscious. He prodded with a toe, and got no response—but that might be a trick. To be safe, he would have to tie her ankles. There would be some rope in the storeroom he had found earlier. When she was bound and helpless, he would deal with her as she deserved. He went out, taking the candle with him, leaving the lilith alone in the dark.

Chapter 11

Between the ancient fortress on its unlikely hill and the mouth of the bay lay several thousand tadigs of gently curving marshy shore. Near the fortress the marsh had been filled in and city built on it, and the shoreline was clearly delineated by the stone bulwark of the seawall. But at its eastern end, the seawall angled inland and degenerated into a mere earthen dike, reinforced here and there with irregular stonework and elsewhere washed outward in an alluvial spill of soil. Beyond the dike there were no structures of any consequence, for the highest tides ran far up into the marsh. Only one road cut east through the tall tufts of marsh-grass, on a dead line aimed at the gate of the Berkender garrison. In laying out the road the Berkenders had disdained to take topography into consideration, with the result that the low spots were most often mudholes. Walking out to the garrison on a bright and shining morning, one might come upon a gang of slaves, overseen by six or eight idle Berkender pikemen, putting down paving-brick in one of those hollows.

The wall of the garrison, while less a feat of engineering than the seawall, was more imposing as one approached it, looming higher and wider to the eye every time the road topped a hummock. The wall was earthenwork faced along the bottom with stone and higher up with close-set brick that would give no purchase to a climber. Near the top, slots in the brick let archers command the bare ground before them. The wall enclosed a large compound, nearly a town for its number of buildings and inhabitants, though few of the latter were women or children. At a private harbor, protected from the rest of the bay by a fortified breakwater, a dozen sleek war galleys rocked gently on the tide. No wall stood at the rear of the garrison, and none was needed, for the long-dead lava flow that formed the crest of the south hills meandered northward there, capping the ridge behind the compound with a frowning brown-red cliff that no force of any size could traverse. The mouth of the bay was a wide gap eroded through the lava line in ages past by the river that now fed the north end of the bay. Beyond the gap the towering rock formation emerged again, running north along the shore of the island until it merged with the distant hills.

At this hour of the morning the garrison gate, massive wooden beams bound with thick bands of hammered iron, stood open to let the daily traffic through. But guards were posted to make sure nobody entered who did not have proper business. On occasion civilians were detained in the gatehouse while a messenger ran to get authorization from whomever they had come to see. And having been through this procedure more than once, Salas Tarag had already determined what to tell the guard. Obviously, Osher would be in no mood to make him welcome. Osher had last seen him hustled off toward Chespid's dungeon, and might well send back word not to admit him but to arrest him. Shuma Borando was a much better bet. True, she had been furious at him the morning before, but Shuma's moods were short-lived. She might not even know that Tarag was an escaped prisoner, and if she did she might be more curious than hostile. So he strode confidently up to the guard, whose three-fingered hands clasped his pikestaff at the prescribed angle. "Salas Tarag, to see the Lady Borando, if she will. Accompanied by his friend Fauxnaster, a dealer in fine jewels."

The guard replied in Berken, as he had been addressed. "Well, I know you, sir. No need to send for word, I guess. It'll be all right. Her ladyship hasn't left the garrison yet this morning, not since I've been on duty. If she's of a mind to toss you out, don't tell her 'twas me let you in." With a wink, the guard stood aside.

In an open quadrangle a squadron of soldiers, a hundred or more, were drilling in full battle armor, and on all sides dour-faced armed men trudged on various business. "I'd be happier swimming among sharks," Pye said in a low voice as he and Tarag tramped down the dirt street between the barracks.

"Ah, friend Fauxnaster, your jewels are safe here. What thief would dare to cast his nets in such waters?"

"There's a game young men play in Eloia," Pye said conversationally. "A game that makes use of a very sharp knife and the outspread toes of one's feet. It's a game for two players. One player spreads his toes as wide as he possibly can, and the other tries to stick the knife into the dirt between his opponent's toes by flipping it end over end."

"Naturally, it would be impolite to flinch."

"Naturally. The winner is the one who finishes with the most toes. I'll show you how to play it sometime."

"Delighted. Is there really such a game?" Flirting with danger sounded distinctly un-Eloian.

"No, but if everybody lived the way you do, there would be."

Falnerescu was at the end of the Island Sea nearest Berkenland, and the garrison there was of considerable age. On the slope above the barracks, over the course of a thousand chetnes and more, an ornately fenestrated warren of steep-roofed dwellings had been built up, most of them constructed entirely of wood—for Berkenland was bare of trees, making wood a luxury that officers and their wives were proud to boast, despite the hazard of fire. The houses pressed in on one another, for the land they occupied was narrowly circumscribed by the lava wall above and the barracks below. Having nowhere to grow but up, the houses peaked in a forest of slender towers and minarets, the taller of which were buttressed ostentatiously by open webs of wooden beams. A breath of breeze, it was said, was enough to set the top tower of a Berkender house groaning and swaying like a ship in a storm. The tallest tower of all, naturally, stood atop the house of Jakul Borando, commander of the garrison. But before they reached the foot of this structure Tarag and Pye turned aside toward the bachelor officers' quarters, a long, imposing building whose left side was supported on stilts where the slope fell away. This was more than a barracks, for each officer had his own suite, compact but functional, a sitting room and bedchamber that he might furnish as he chose, and for the senior officers a private lavatory as well.

Vod Penna Osher had one of the suites with private lavatory. On the bare wood walls he had hung only a few items—a crossed pair of dueling swords, inscribed on hilt and blade; a dim and faded icon of the first sage among the Berkenders, a stern-looking fellow with a long gray beard; and a scroll with several lines of flowing calligraphy and a seal impressed in a blot of red wax. The furniture was austere and unremarkable. Osher had grilled some fish for breakfast on the little charcoal brazier, and was standing at the window cleaning his teeth with his tongue and staring out at the city in the distance when the knock came at the door. He assumed the orderly was there to take the dirty plate. "Enter," he said without turning.

"Lovely morning, isn't it?" Salas Tarag said.

Osher whirled. "You! What—" Words failed him. He stood gaping.

Tarag sniffed the air appreciatively. "Ah, grilled darters. I had half a seed-melon."

"How did you get in here? And who is this?"

"A friend of mine, Fauxnaster by name. We arrived by the main gate. Did you think I'd scale the wall in broad daylight?"

"I wouldn't put it past you. Why wasn't I notified you were seeking admittance?"

"Would you have told them you'd see me?"

"Of course not. Not in the present circumstances. I had word last night you'd escaped from Chespid somehow. I expected you'd be halfway to the Drachth Puel by now." The Drachth Puel was a narrow, rocky channel at the farthest end of the Island Sea, legendary for its ship-swallowing whirlpools. "Didn't I warn you you were letting yourself in for trouble?"

"You didn't warn me you meant to compound it yourself. You might have saved me the inconvenience of being locked up. But let's not quarrel about that. I'm willing to be broad-minded."

"Good of you. I hope you'll be so forgiving after I've summoned the guard and had you taken back where you belong. You must be mad to come here, Tarag. Do you know what they'll do to me if they find I've been entertaining an escaped prisoner in my room instead of reporting him?"

"You've weathered storms before. But do your duty, if you must. I only risked coming here out of friendship. But I wouldn't expect you to be swayed by that. I happened upon some information that I thought you might find helpful. But if you don't want to hear it . . ."

"Information? What sort of information? And why wouldn't I want to hear it?"

"No, no. Your duty is more important. My tale would take some little time to tell, and if anybody chanced to walk in on us, you'd be in a very awkward position. It's too bad, in a way. I know you'd like to learn where the lilith is. But I wouldn't dream of letting you jeopardize your good name by sanctioning my presence here."

"Oh, leave off, will you? What's this about the lilith? Have you got some news?"

"Perhaps. Do I have your word you'll hear me out, or do you still mean to call the guard?"

"I don't know why I listen to you. You've caused nothing but trouble so far."

"I've caused no trouble," Tarag objected. "I'm trying to help you find the lilith, and you accuse me of causing trouble. I don't know that I ought to say anything more, if you're going to take that attitude."

"If you've got information that will help resolve this incident, it's your duty to speak."

"Oh, so now it's my duty we're discussing. You haven't given me your word yet."

Osher made a face as if he were tasting something disagree-

able. "I suppose I owe you a chance to redeem yourself. Very
well, you have my word. I'll hear you out."

"And you won't call the guard and have me turned over to
Chespid."

"That depends very largely on what you have to say."

Under the circumstances, Tarag saw, that was the best assurance he would get. "Then I take it you are interested in finding
the lilith?"

"Interested? I was up half the night arguing with that fool
Borando about what we're to do. We've got to do something—
our own envoy will be arriving any day now, and if we have
to tell him that the Vli won't sit down at the conference table
because we let their plaything slip through our fingers like
some worthless bauble, we could all be sent home in disgrace.
But Borando dithered and whined and ended by staggering off
to bed without issuing any orders at all. I wanted to mobilize
the entire garrison for a house-by-house search, but he seems
to feel that will get him in worse trouble—with his wife, or
with the paymaster, I suppose. He's still hoping the lilith has
only wandered off somewhere like a roaty pup, and will find
her own way back if only we whistle loud enough. Ridiculous
idea, but typical of the man. But you don't care about my
troubles. You said you know where she is. Spit it out."

"It might be more accurate to say I know where she isn't."

Osher groaned. "I've no time for riddles."

"Then listen closely." In a few words Tarag sketched their
encounter with the Brown Hand. Osher, predictably, demanded
names and places and details, and refused to be put off; the
Hand was a thorn festering under his skin. But at length Tarag
got him soothed, and went on to explain Pye's conclusion that
the Vli had only pretended that the lilith was kidnapped. "It's
to their advantage in the negotiations," he finished. "They
won't refuse to sit down with your envoy, as you fear. Rather,
they'll claim injury and use the claim as a lever to pry conces-
sions out of you. That may be the main reason they brought
the lilith here."

"You're saying they'd deliberately do one of their creatures
harm just to gain an advantage at the bargaining table?"

"They'd never harm her. You misunderstand. But they'd willingly put on the *appearance* that harm had befallen her. It would do no good to accuse them. They'd only deny it, and take steps to cover their trail. Your only hope is to march up to Metterner's gate with a detachment of men, taking them by surprise, and demand to make a search."

"You're mad, Tarag. You don't know what you're asking. Forcing entrance to that house, whatever the justification, would be a worse affront by far than failing to protect a concubine that we hadn't officially been notified was there."

"Not in the least. They're demanding that the lilith be found, aren't they? How can they fault you for finding her? Anyway, once you uncover their duplicity, you'll have the advantage over them, and can name your terms."

"Impossible. I won't even consider it." But by the uncertainty in his eyes, Osher was considering it.

"You might also want to consider how much good it will do your reputation at home when you solve the mystery of the lilith's disappearance and so ensure a favorable climate for negotiations. The emperor himself might well decorate you. You could be in for a promotion, to say nothing of a transfer to some outpost more civilized than this one. You might even be posted to the Emperor's court itself."

"And you're kind enough to offer me this juicy tidbit out of friendship, asking nothing in return. Or is there something you expect to gain?"

"There *is* my ship. Chespid has it. I'd like it back."

"Why not take this ridiculous tale to Chespid, then?"

"I don't trust him. If the lilith is known to be missing, and he can get his hands on her, he might decide to keep her. Or sell her. And do the same to my ship. You, on the other hand, are a man of honor."

"The weak link in your chain, Tarag, is that you accept the word of a bunch of damned subversives when they say their kidnapping was a failure. Why should I put any trust in their assurances? Especially when they have every reason to do me false? How do I know you're not a member of the Hand yourself? You've spoken out against slavery often enough. No, take me to them and let me ask my own questions. Then we'll talk about searching Metterner's house."

"You're a Berkender. If you think any member of the Hand would answer questions put by you, you're the one that's mad."

Without warning the door burst open and Shuma Borando breezed into the room, dark eyes snapping. She was wearing a close-fitting vest and knee-length breeches of suede leather, and her perfume blossomed in the room. "Don't listen to the man, Osher," she cautioned. "He's a born liar. Also, he's got the manners of a swamp-rat. I wouldn't trust him to clean my shoes, not even if he begged to. Especially not if he begged to. I'd know he had something up his sleeve. Do you know what he said to me yesterday? Of course you don't, but I'm not going to repeat it. And he's not, either, if he knows what's good for him. He could get his tongue cut out if he's not careful. How are you, Salas darling? Your face looks dreadful. Trip over your knees getting out of bed and fall into the night-bucket? I had word from the gate you'd been asking for me, and when you didn't show up I knew there was only one place you could be. I'm a bit perturbed at you, Tarag. You shouldn't go using my name, not unless you're coming straight to me to apologise. Do you know what I think I'll do? Somebody committed a jewel robbery yesterday, using my name. Unless you're very, *very* nice to me, I think I'll tell them you did it. It could have been you, couldn't it? The description matches—and here you are again, waving my name about like a flag. There were three of them in the gang. Who's this, Osher? Your new Eloian orderly? I didn't know we were buying civilians for the barracks."

Osher clicked his heels and inclined his head. "Salas Tarag and I were just discussing some private business, Lady Borando."

"Were you, now? Nothing's private in this garrison, Oshie, not for long. Just go ahead. Don't mind me. You wouldn't have been talking about this lilith, would you? I keep hearing so much about her. Or it. Whatever. Lilith this, lilith that. It's quite tiresome. Nobody's paying any attention to *me*. I think it's time Salas Tarag paid some attention to me. If he doesn't

want to be denounced as a jewel thief. Doesn't that sound like
a grand idea?"

Tarag was wondering what he had ever seen in Shuma. She
was extremely beautiful, of course—that helped. And when
in a good mood she could be attentive, perceptive, provocative,
quite shameless. This was his first undiluted exposure to one
of her bad moods. Without any assistance, she was a strong
argument in favor of castration—her father's, at the very least.
In most circumstances, Tarag would have been content either
to humor her or to insult her further so she would go away,
but just now he could afford to do neither. "You look quite
fetching this morning, Lady Borando," he said. "No man could
fail to pay attention to you. But time is short. Penna Osher and
I had just agreed on a course of action to recover the lilith.
I'm sure you'll agree how important an objective that is; it far
outweighs mere personal quarrels. Once we've concluded our
business, I'll be happy to steal as many jewels for you as you
like."

"Hmp. I knew it'd be something about the lilith. You say
you've found her?"

"We know where she's been hidden, yes. We were just on
our way there when you—"

"Oh, good! I'll come with you."

Tarag looked to Osher for support.

"We'll be spending the day in the marsh at the north end of
the bay, Lady Borando," Osher said. "We'll be using small
boats—you know, the kind that capsize so easily? I've already
notified the medical officer to have his store of sucker-sting
balm ready against our return."

"Oh." Shuma considered this deflating bit of news. "Well,
perhaps I'll wait to make the acquaintance of the creature until
you've brought it back. And Tarag and I can have a nice long
talk then too. I'm sure he'd like to explain to me why I shouldn't
have him arrested."

"With great pleasure," Tarag assured her. "Shall we go,
gentlemen?" He opened the door and let Osher and Pye precede
him.

Behind them Shuma said wanly, "Happy wading."

They strode in silence to the end of the hall and down the wide wooden steps to the ground. The air was warm, the sky a cloudless blue. "You might have warned me," Tarag said.

"Would you have believed me?" Osher asked.

"I suppose not. Infatuation leads us to do strange things. So you have to contend with that as well as her husband's incontinence."

"On the whole, I prefer him. He drags his heels, but he doesn't interfere."

"Well," Tarag said, heartily rubbing his hands together and gazing around at the sun-flooded garrison. "Where are we to get our detachment?"

"You're treating the matter as if it's been settled."

"I thought it had been. Or would you prefer explaining to Shuma why you did nothing to get the lilith back, after telling her that was what you meant to do? She's far from powerless. She could make your life rather unpleasant."

"Damn Shuma. I'd like to be rid of her, her and her husband both."

"The way lies clear. You have only to raise your finger, and you'll be a hero. You'll have enough influence to get posted wherever you like."

"All right, then. I don't know why I trust you, Tarag, but I do. Do you think sixteen men will be sufficient? There was a riot down that way last night. Some fool wasn't taking proper care of his slaves, and the mob nearly got him. I'll tell the sergeant we mean to search for the perpetrators. No point in starting rumors flying."

Osher led the way to a weathered gray barracks building and left Tarag and Pye standing before it in the dusty street. To their right in a little quadrangle a flag was flying from a tall pole, the six gold stars on a blue field of Berkenland. Not far away, a hundred twenty-eight voices were counting to four over and over in unison. Osher came out of the barracks, a line of soldiers behind him. The soldiers halted, pike butts thumping the dirt, at the order of their sergeant. Approaching Osher, the sergeant held up his clenched right fist in salute. "Do we be wantin' any kelg today, sir?" he inquired crisply.

"I think not."

"Beggin' your pardon, sir, but against the kind of trouble that broke out last night, kelg can be mighty handy. An outfit of them, off duty you understand, happened to be passin' through that area at the time, and they was a great help, from what I heard."

"I appreciate your suggestion, Sergeant, but for today I think we'll skip the kelg. You and your men follow us at eight paces. Close to four paces when we reach the city. I'll give you further orders when we reach our destination."

"Very good, sir." The sergeant snapped a salute and took up position at the head of the column.

"I've never liked kelg," Tarag said as they walked in the direction of the gate.

"Nor I," Osher agreed. "They're nasty brutes. I know a lot of influential people who would rather be rid of them, only nobody wants to be the first to bar them from his castle, for fear his enemies will set theirs on him while he sleeps, or on his children at play. And of course they *are* useful in controlling the Islanders."

"How long have your people consorted with them?"

"They were brought back from South Berkenland when that was first discovered—five thousand chetnes ago, long before the unification of the six kingdoms. The kelg had their own towns built of dried mud—little more than warrens, really. They still do. South Berkenland has never been settled by human folk. It's too dangerous. But I'm told the wild kelg are not all as fierce as those we breed. These are the pick of a hundred litters. We have to let them run wild in the countryside occasionally, and turn a deaf ear to the complaints about the mayhem they commit. If we keep them penned up, they start killing one another." He shrugged. "Better a few butchered paum."

They passed through the gate and walked out along the marsh road. "Your friend's silence is remarkable for its tenacity," Osher said. "I don't believe he's spoken a word since he entered my room. Or am I being tactless?"

"He still has his tongue."

"Friend Tarag was being so eloquent," Pye said, "I saw no reason to interfere." He did not add that fading unobtrusively into the background was a skill that had saved his life more than once.

"He said your name is Fauxnaster, but he didn't say what your business is."

"Ah. He was being discreet. As it happens, I have the honor to be a dealer in fine jewels, rare commodities, and valuables of every sort."

Osher looked closely at the Eloian. "And what, if I might ask, led you to close up your shop on such a fine morning to come with your friend to see me?"

"I thought I might be of service. Like you, I was instrumental in getting Salas Tarag into his present difficulties, and like you, I felt an obligation to help extricate him."

"Oh, you were instrumental, were you? This is becoming interesting. How?"

"He's going to find out when we get to Metterner's," Tarag pointed out.

"I'd already thought of that." Pye turned to Osher. "It was I who smuggled Tarag into the Vli house in the chest."

"That's an odd thing for a respectable businessman to get mixed up in. Where did you say your shop was?"

"I didn't. As you'll discover if you consult the tax rolls, I have no fixed place of business. My operations are too small to warrant the expense of keeping a shop. I find it more convenient to carry my shop about with me."

Osher regarded Pye dubiously. "Isn't that dangerous, with valuable wares? Don't you worry about thieves?"

"There are those who would like to take from me what little I have. But I've never worried much about thieves, no."

Tarag had to bite his lip to keep from laughing. But he saw that it would be wise to distract Osher before the inquiry went much further. "I asked Fauxnaster to come," he explained, "because he has some small experience with false-bottomed cabinets and secret panels. You or I might miss a hiding place."

"That's an odd thing for a jeweler to be knowledgeable about."

"Not at all. He not only deals in jewelry; he teaches people how to keep it safe. When we reach Metterner's, though, we'll need some story to account for why the two of us are with you. When last the Vli saw me, I was bound for the dungeon."

They were approaching the first houses now, low ramshackle dwellings with flat roofs and crooked walls. Children playing in the road scurried out of the way. Behind them the sergeant snapped an order, as he had been instructed, and the phalanx double-timed briefly to take up position four paces back.

"You're my prisoners," Osher said.

The statement hung naked in the air. It was a workable explanation, Tarag saw, to give to the Vli. But it was also a threat. If for some reason they failed to find the lilith, Osher could simply take them both back to Chespid. They would have little hope of escaping the armed escort. The lilith would have to be in the house, that was all. "It would be easier," he suggested, "if you told them they'd accused me wrongly, but that I had graciously consented to help you in your investigation."

"I'd do that," Osher said darkly, "if I were sure you'd been wrongly accused. I'm still wondering how you roped me into this, Tarag. You've got the keenest mind of any man I know, and I suppose that ought to reassure me that you know what you're doing, but somehow it doesn't. You haven't got a shred of evidence."

"The only way to get evidence," Tarag pointed out, "is to go in there and find the lilith. It doesn't take a keen mind to see that."

Metterner's gate was shut and barred, flanked by a brace of Chespid's guards, who stood a little straighter when the Berkender detachment rounded the corner and marched toward them. Osher halted before the nearer of the two. "I am Vod Penna Osher, here on the lawful business of Berkenland. Are there more of your men watching the alley?"

"Two more, sir."

"Sergeant, send two of our own men to join them. Nobody is to leave this estate for any reason, without my authorization. If you see anybody trying to escape, stop them if you can, give chase if necessary, and see that I'm notified at once. But you're to cause no injury to anybody. Is that clear?"

"Yes, sir." The sergeant chose two men, who jogged off in the direction of the alley.

Osher addressed the guard again. "Are they all inside?"

"Nobody's left yet this morning, sir, save the cook and two of her helpers, bound for market."

"Were their faces covered, or bare?"

"Bare, sir. Why should they be hidin' their faces?"

That was less than reassuring, Tarag realized. Would any of them even recognize the lilith if they saw her? The easiest way to hide her would be to dress her as one of the Vli women. They could search all day with her standing boldly before them and find nothing. Still, the tradition-bound Vli could hardly avoid showing signs of deference; if he was sharp-eyed he might see through such an imposture.

Osher pulled the bell-cord, and a moment later Qob Qobba opened the door and came slowly down the steps. He looked as if he had slept badly: There were dark pouches under his eyes, and his high mop of red hair was in worse disarray than usual. If he was surprised to see Salas Tarag, he gave no sign. He gazed at the soldiers quite expressionlessly through the bars of the gate. "Yes? How may I help you?" he said in careful Berken.

"We can speak Olmalin, if you'd rather," Osher said in that tongue. "I'm quite fluent."

"Very well. Penna Osher, is it not? I am honored. What brings you here? Has Zhenuvnili been found?"

Tarag smiled. Zhenuvnili. A pretty name.

"We believe we know where she is. But rescuing her from those who have imprisoned her presents certain difficulties. We'd like to ask for your cooperation."

"Certainly. Anything. Is it money you need? Perhaps I ought to fetch Metterner."

"It's not money," Osher said. "But perhaps I should speak to Habil Metterner, yes."

Qobba turned to go back into the house, then halted. "What are those two doing with you?"

"They are my prisoners."

"They don't look like prisoners."

"They have provided me with certain information about the whereabouts of the lilith. If it proves accurate, they will be released. If not—" Osher shrugged.

"So he *did* know more about it than he admitted."

"Salas Tarag is a resourceful man."

Qobba's eyes made clear what he thought of resourceful men. He went back into the mansion.

Habil Metterner bustled out of the door. "Anything," he said unceremoniously. "Whatever it takes. You understand, esteemed sir. It is our lilith who has been taken."

"Yes, of course. So I can count on your full cooperation?"

"Absolutely. Unhesitatingly."

"Good. I thank you, Freeman Metterner. You are making this somewhat disagreeable task much easier. You will understand that my men and I have no official standing." Behind him one of Chespid's guards snickered. Osher ignored it. "The city of Falnerescu lies entirely within the jurisdiction of Nule Chespid."

"Yes, yes. What is it you wish us to do?"

"If you would be so kind, Freeman Metterner, I would like you to unbar the gate and allow us to search the premises. We have reason to believe that the lilith is concealed within this house."

Metterner and Qobba goggled at Osher, exchanged glances, looked back at him. "You're mad," Metterner declared. "Feverish, or you've been taking some sort of drug. Concealed in this house? We'll do no such thing!"

"It grieves me to press the point, Freeman Metterner, but a moment ago you were promising your full cooperation."

"What reason have you got? You owe us that, at least."

"Certain of my information has been received in confidence. I may say no more than that the people who broke into your house yesterday have been found and questioned, and it has been ascertained that, while their objective was to kidnap the lilith, they failed. They know nothing of her whereabouts."

"They're lying! They've got to be! Who are these people? I demand that you let us question them ourselves."

"Perhaps later that can be arranged. First we must satisfy ourselves that she is not still in this house."

"Of course she's not in the house. That's ridiculous. You don't think we'd lie to you, do you?"

Qob Qobba put a restraining hand on Metterner's arm. "That is precisely what he does think," he said. "He has no evidence, other than our word, that the lilith is actually gone. Perhaps we may take this as an indication of how difficult it can be to work with the Berkenders on a basis of mutual trust. As to the present question, I see no harm in convincing them of our veracity. When Penna Osher has seen that he is wrong, I'm sure he will be more than willing to carry a message back to his superior officers protesting this unwarranted incursion in the strongest possible terms. Until then, we may take it that he will do as he likes."

"I am sorry to hear you put that interpretation on it," Osher said. "Our only wish is to offer you our assistance in these tragic circumstances. Surely it has occurred to you that one of your number might be a traitor."

"That is our concern, not yours," Qobba countered.

"When you accuse the citizens of Falnerescu of a crime, it becomes my concern."

"I thought you said you had no official standing."

"We can take our disagreement to Nule Chespid, if you like," Osher offered. "I assure you, he will see matters as I do, and much time will have been lost. Far simpler for you to open the gate now."

Seeing that it would be futile to prolong the argument, Qob Qobba unlatched the bar and lifted it aside. Metterner stood clenching and unclenching his hands indecisively. When Osher and his party had stepped through into the courtyard, Qobba spoke. "Only one request do I make, beyond our obvious wish that your men be respectful of the furniture. One of our number is very ill—delirious with fever. He is in a room upstairs, attended by a physician. Whether it would be harmful for you

to enter that room is a decision I must leave in the hands of
the physician. I'm sure you understand."

Tarag and Osher looked at one another. Surely the Vli didn't
expect to fool them so easily! "I will speak to the physician,"
Osher said, carefully not agreeing to bow to the physician's
judgment.

The house was large, and the search was long and mostly
uneventful. There were four stairways from the ground floor
to the floor above, and Osher posted a man at the foot of each,
so that the lilith could not be moved from one hiding place to
another while his back was turned. Another stairway and a
ladder led down into the cellar, and those got the same treatment. Osher, Tarag, and Pye went from room to room, poking
and prying into anything large enough to contain a human body.
Tarag made a point of being forward to the women he encountered, to see how they and those around them would react, but
he got only the expected rebuffs, and Qobba and Metterner,
who were never far from his heels, did not feel it necessary to
intervene, though their opinion of Tarag, never high, was
declining by the minute.

When they reached the suite that had been the lilith's, they
encountered the two adolescents, robed and hooded, who had
come to look at Fauxnaster's jewels the morning before. One
was cowering back on the far corner of the big bed, trembling.
The other, bolder, stood up when the men entered. "What is
the meaning of this intrusion?" she said in Vli in a flat, colorless
voice.

As Metterner was explaining the situation to her, Tarag
considered whether one of these two might not be the lilith
herself rather than an attendant. The nervous one, probably.
"Who are these two?" he demanded.

"These are nalas," Qobba explained. "They are here to see
to the lilith's comfort."

"There are only two of them? Not three?"

"No," Qobba said, puzzled. "Only these two were sent with
Zheni. Why should you think there might be three?"

Why indeed? Tarag remembered standing behind a curtain
watching pandemonium erupt. His memories were confused—

a great deal had been happening at once—but he did recall dimly that in the course of a few minutes three different nalas had passed by. The third had actually stopped and stared at where he was hiding. "Does the lilith dress as these do?" he asked.

"I don't see what—" Metterner began, but Qobba interrupted him.

"The lilith's robe is white," he explained.

"How are we to know one of these is not the lilith?" Osher wanted to know. "One robe looks much like another."

So it does, Tarag mused. Now, what if that third nala had been not a nala but the lilith herself, disguised? Where did that line of thought steer him?

"You will have to accept our word, I'm afraid," Qobba said with a shrug. "It is a thing forbidden among us for any man or woman to look upon a nala; even I do not know these two by their faces. Nor would it do you any good to look upon them, if we permitted it, for you don't know what the lilith looks like. I'm surprised you hadn't considered that."

Osher saw that going on with the search would be futile. If he accepted Qobba's word that neither of these was the lilith, he might as well accept that the lilith was not in the house. He would accomplish nothing except further offending the Vli if he demanded to see the nalas' faces. Still, he was committed to a course of action that, for good or ill, he would have to explain eventually to Jakul Borando. The commander was just obtuse enough to upbraid his subordinate for not finishing the search; it smelled of slack procedure. "Very well," Osher announced. "For now, I will take it that these two are what you say they are. That being the case, we shall have to search elsewhere. Let us continue." After peering under the bed and pawing through the tall wardrobe, which Pye measured with a critical eye and thumped the sides and back of to hear how it resounded, they left the nalas and went on to inspect the next room.

The physician was a small, white-haired man who held a monocle to his good eye and squinted through it at the party while Osher explained that they must search the invalid's room.

Predictably, he thought badly of the idea. "My patient's condition is delicate," he asserted. "You can't all come trooping in. One or two of you, perhaps, but you'll have to be quiet. Best if you don't even speak." Osher loosened his sword in its scabbard and motioned Pye to precede him into the room. The doctor toddled after them, leaving Tarag and the Vli standing in the upper hall, alone with a pair of silent Berkender pikemen.

Qobba faced Tarag. "All this is your doing, isn't it? I don't so much care how you sold him the story. What does concern me is why you're determined to destroy us. First you break in and take Zhenuvnili, for what reason we still don't know. No sooner are you captured and put in jail than you're out again, not even manacled, walking around with a Berkender officer for an escort. What's your game?"

"I told you yesterday. You chose not to believe me."

"Surely you've had time by now to come up with a more convincing story."

"Have you ever read Calthurnas? He says that truth is like clear water, which is why so often people look straight through it and don't see it."

"Did your Eloian friend teach you that?"

Tarag was mildly impressed that Qobba knew Calthurnas was Eloian. "My Eloian friend," he said, "rejects most of Calthurnas for philosophical reasons so subtle I've never been able to grasp them."

"You still haven't answered my question. What do you hope to gain by all this?"

"I'd be satisfied to get my ship back, and my crew out of prison. Beyond that, I'd like to see the lilith returned safe to you. We're not enemies."

"Why should I believe you?"

"There are reasons, but it would take some time to explain. If we find what we're looking for, explanations won't be necessary." But Tarag was less confident of the outcome of the search than he had been earlier. What did it mean that there had been three nalas? One had gone upstairs weeping. But he couldn't remember where the other two had gone.

Osher and Pye were finishing their examination of the sick-room. The physician had refused to let the curtains be thrown back, claiming that bright light would be injurious to his patient. The patient, Ranga Strell, was lying on his back on the bed, face bathed in sweat. His eyes were closed, but from time to time he mumbled something through cracked lips, or cried out incomprehensibly. Standing over him, Pye spoke suddenly in rapid-fire Vli. "What have you done with the lilith?"

Strell's eyes popped open; he gazed in unfocused terror at the ceiling. "She—" he said, and gasped and gagged. "She—" His face went slack, the eyes closed, and he began to shiver.

The physician felt Strell's brow and turned his head to glare at Pye. "I told you not to speak," he snapped.

"Aye, so you did," Pye said. Plainly the sick man knew something—but just as plainly, they had no way of finding out what he knew.

So they proceeded at last to the cellar, a thick-walled warren of tiny rooms. Pye was obliged to examine every foot of every wall, tapping with his knuckles and running his fingertips along the mortared cracks for the gust of air that could bespeak a hidden doorway, scanning the dirt floor for signs of traffic that led into blank masonry. Fortunately, the slaves' quarters were sparsely furnished and offered few places of concealment. One wing, which angled back from the house under the patio and garden, was not even occupied, and the searchers stirred up a good deal of dust, which sizzled and snapped when it drifted into the candles. One room was a disused storeroom, and they spent some time dragging barrels and crates into the middle of the floor so they could inspect the wall. The deeper into the wing they went, the plainer the evidence of abandonment—a door sagging crookedly from one hinge, and in the corners dried animal pellets.

Holding his candle high, Pye knelt and examined the floor of the passageway. "Somebody has been this way recently," he announced. "Look at the footmarks."

"Those could be ancient," Osher objected.

"I think not. Here's a drop of fresh candle wax. And another." Still crouching, Pye led the way slowly to a door at the far end of the passage. "In here," he said.

Osher pushed the heel of his hand against the latch lever, but it failed to yield. "It's been pegged," he announced. "Where does this go?"

"Only another room," Metterner said.

"Is there any other way out?"

"Of course not."

"Then there's still somebody in there." Osher motioned his men forward, and they applied the butts of their pikes to the planks, unleashing thunder that rolled through the cellar.

"You promised you wouldn't damage my property," Metterner fretted.

"We'll buy you a new door."

At the fifth stroke one of the hinges pulled free of its mounting with a tearing noise, and after three more strokes the latch gave as well. The pikemen reversed their points and looked uncertainly at Osher. Stepping past them, Tarag entered the room, candle aloft.

The far wall, he saw, had collapsed inward at some time in the past, spilling stone and dirt across the floor. Except for a single chair that lay fallen on its side, and a strap of leather curled beside it, a man's belt, the room was empty.

Metterner knelt and picked up the belt. "Whose is this?" he asked, displaying it to them draped across his open palms like a dead thing. "Whose is it?"

Tarag was inspecting the latch. "It wasn't pegged," he decided. "If the peg had been in the hole when we broke in, it'd be scarred. The latch stuck fast, that was all."

Pye stared at Osher's candle, and from it to the hole in the wall. Going up the mound of rubble, he crawled forward until they could see only his knees and feet. After a moment, he slithered back down into the room. "She's not back there," he said. "Nobody is."

Chapter 12

They spent a little more time searching the rest of the cellar, though by now they were only going through the motions; nobody expected to find the lilith. Tarag's sense of confidence had evaporated, leaving him downcast and gloomy. He had been so sure she must be in the house—he was still certain, for that matter, that she had been, in that little cellar room, though he had no evidence other than a few drops of candle wax. But he was at a loss to explain the connection between the candle wax and the puzzle of the third nala. The expedition had had only one positive result that he could see: He had learned the lilith's name. Nobody with such a beautiful name deserved to be in the trouble she must be in. But Tarag was the only one, it seemed, who was truly bent on rescuing her. Her own people had locked themselves up in their house rather than risk the contamination of mingling with foreigners. It had taken Tarag himself to goad the Berkenders to act. And Amera knew what steps Chespid was taking; probably none of any great consequence. Having an excuse to seize a ship was enough to keep him purring and preening for days. To him, the lilith was no more than a foreign visitor who had gotten lost, hardly a remarkable occurrence in a large seaport. Taking steps to find her would be expensive, and Chespid was a thrifty man.

Having reassembled his detachment in the street, Osher thanked Metterner and Qobba for their hospitality in stiff, formal tones. He apologized for the inconvenience. He regretted the bad information that had made it seem necessary. He assured the Vli that steps were being taken on many fronts throughout the city, of which this was only one. He promised to have them notified by messenger as soon as there was progress to report. Qobba mouthed the correct responses; Metterner was too upset to do anything but wring his hands and glare.

"Disappointing," Tarag said when they had marched a little way.

"That's not the word I'd have used," Osher said. "I can think of two or three stronger words that might be more appropriate. You're in serious trouble, my friend—and somehow you've managed to drag me in with you."

"You'll get used to it after a while."

"I don't know how you do it."

"It's a knack I have. But all that's behind us. The question is, what are we to do now? She's got to be in the city somewhere."

"The question," Osher stated, "is not what *we're* to do. It's what *I'm* to do. And I've already figured it out, without any help from you. I'm taking both of you straight to Chespid, and then I'm going back to report to Borando. It may not be too late for me to patch my career together. I haven't been rammed below the waterline yet, and I don't mean to be, so it's no use trying to snare me in any more of your schemes. You're far too clever for your own good, Tarag."

"I'm not clever. If I were clever, the lilith would have been in that house, as I expected her to be."

"No argument."

"There's more to this affair than meets the eye," Tarag went on, ignoring his friend's dour expression. "Did you notice how the tall one insisted there were only two nalas? Only two, you see? But yesterday, at about the time the fire started, I was standing behind a curtain in the lower hall, and I distinctly saw *three* nalas pass by, one after the other."

Osher rolled his eyes. "So now we're missing a nala as well

as a lilith. Is that what you're saying? More likely, you saw
one nala three times. You're not going to convince me you can
tell them apart."

Seeing that it would be folly to debate this point, Tarag
hurried on. "There's another thing. Who set the fire? The Brown
Hand didn't set it. We were told they had to jump into action
before they meant to, because they saw they'd not get another
such convenient distraction. They'd have no reason to lie about
such a minor point. So a mysterious fire breaks out, and immediately afterward there's an extra nala in the lower hall. You
see what I'm driving at?"

"For my money," Osher said, "Strell set the fire. He's gone
mad. If you'd seen him, you'd say the same yourself. He was
mad yesterday, only nobody knew it yet."

"He couldn't have set the fire," Pye pointed out. "He was
with Graio and me the whole time."

"There is one way to tie the strands together," Tarag said.
"What if the lilith set the fire herself, and disguised herself as
a nala for some reason?"

"Why should she do a thing like that?" Osher asked.

"To do exactly what we know she did—to get out of the
house unobserved. If we knew *why* she wanted to get out, we'd
know where she is now."

"Could it be," Pye offered, "that Strell was molesting her
somehow, and she had to flee from him? I was able to ask him
one question before the doctor intervened, and I'm certain he
has guilty knowledge."

"It's possible, I suppose. But why run away? She need only
complain to somebody. And if she had, we'd have got a whiff
of it." Tarag spread his hands. "Why make things complicated?
She lands in a foreign city, she'd like to have a look around.
Perfectly natural. But they won't let her out. You saw how
closed and protective that place is. So she concocts a scheme
to sneak out unobserved. It's what I'd have done."

"I've no doubt," Osher said drily. "But even if all you've
said is true—and I haven't said I buy it, mind—it still gives
us not a hint about where she is now. Why didn't she simply
go home last night?"

"Oh, I don't think that's mysterious at all," Tarag told him. "Falnerescu, you see, is shaped like a funnel. You and I don't notice, because we've got our wits about us. But for a visitor who doesn't know the ways of the place, perhaps doesn't even speak the language, the sides are slippery, and a slide once begun is hard to halt. I can think of any number of mishaps that might have befallen Zhenuvnili, but if she's still alive, she'll slide straight down to the bottom of the funnel, and that's where we'll find her. I don't know why I didn't think of it before."

"I seem to recall hearing this refrain once already today," Osher said. "You'll pardon me if I'm not wildly enthusiastic."

"We have led you a bit of a chase, haven't we?"

"I don't know why I listen to you."

"Because you're an intelligent man. Few men have the wit to follow a line of reasoning, and fewer still the boldness to act on it. You're not going to back off and turn tail now, are you, when the lilith is so nearly in your grasp? Aren't you even curious to know where she is?"

"You can tell me when I've turned you over to Chespid. He can look into it, or I'll look into it myself."

"It won't work. You'll need our help on this one."

"Would you mind telling me why?" Osher asked, exasperated. "What can you two overgrown street urchins hope to accomplish that the official weight of Berkenland can't?"

"I can't explain that without telling you where she is," Tarag said. "And you don't want to hear about it. Well, all right, lock us up if you choose. Without us, you'll be free to bobble the whole thing, and probably get posted to the worst stink-pit of a garrison they can find, for having stirred up so much trouble and having nothing to show for it. But don't let that stop you. Go ahead—play it by the book. But don't expect us to cooperate. We have nothing further to say." Tarag folded his arms impassively. Pye worried a little that Tarag might be overplaying it, and estimated his chances of breaking away from the Berkender phalanx before they reached the fortress. A few more streets remained, and traffic was heavy enough to cause some confusion. A man not encumbered by a pike could

easily clamber up the nearest rain barrel to the roofs, especially
if he knew the roofs well, as Pye did. He had no compunction
about deserting Tarag; it would serve no purpose for both of
them to be thrown in prison when one might go free.

Osher stopped abruptly in the middle of the street, and the
detachment, which was no longer following at a discreet four
paces, piled into them before the sergeant could order a halt.

"All right, let's have it," Osher said when they had untangled
themselves.

"Not unless we're in on the play. You agree not to turn us
over to Chespid?"

"If this new idea of your turns out as badly as the last one,
I won't have to turn you over to Chespid. I'll strangle you
myself. And I'm not committing myself until I hear what it is.
The lame stunts you've pulled in the last two days do not inspire
confidence."

Tarag shook his head. "No deal. I tell you, I know where
she is. She's *got* to be there. If she wasn't, she'd have been
home by now. But it's simply not a place you can walk into
and demand that they hand her to you. A certain subterfuge
will be called for. And if there's a man in Falnerescu better at
subterfuge than I, it's Pye here." Tarag put his hand on Pye's
shoulder.

"I thought his name was Fauxnaster."

"You see? You've spent the whole morning with him, and
you don't even know his name. He's perfect. You've a lot
riding on this, Osher. If you have any hope of finishing the
race with your oars in the water, it lies in trusting me. This
morning you were willing to act first and add up the cost
later."

"A lot has happened since this morning."

"To be sure. But has anything really changed? Nothing has
changed. Only that we're a step closer to the lilith than we
were before. But now suddenly you'd rather give up and go
back to letting Shuma Borando lead you around with a ring in
your nose. I seem to recall you'd had enough of that this
morning, and I can't say I blame you. So what's it to be? Are
you going to betray the friends who've tried to help you and

condemn yourself to a career as a junior officer in some dreary outpost in the mountains of Hamilia, or are you going to order the sergeant to take his men back to the garrison and come sit down in a tavern where we can discuss strategy like gentlemen?"

"This isn't just a trick, is it?" Osher said doubtfully. "You really do know where she is?"

"I really do know where she is." The grotesque exaggeration slid smoothly across Tarag's tongue. He smiled his most engaging smile.

"What if we need the men?"

"We won't, I promise. They'd only frighten the quarry."

"Oh, very well. I don't know why I listen to you." Osher drew the sergeant aside and spoke to him in a low voice. The sergeant snapped a crisp order, and the column about-faced and trudged off down the street, pikes on their shoulders in perfect array. When they had vanished around a corner Pye took a deep breath and straightened his shoulders. Suddenly he felt much better. "I'm warning you," Osher said, waving a finger under Tarag's nose. "This had better work. It's your last chance. And you're still under arrest, both of you, so don't try to give me the slip. I'm not a man to be trifled with."

"Indeed you're not," Tarag assured him. "Now, what say to a mug of ale and a bowl of stew? I seem to recall we passed a tavern just back that way."

When they had been supplied with foaming mugs of dark ale and steaming bowls of paum stew by the proprietor of a small but tidy establishment, Osher said, "Now, what's this about a funnel, eh? All I can see is that it would empty into Chespid's dungeon. And if you wanted to force your way in there you wouldn't have had me dismiss my men. Or would you?"

"I've seen all I care to see of the inside of the dungeon. And she won't be there. Chespid would find a way to turn the situation to his advantage, no doubt, but he'd know how dangerous it would be not to let you know he had her. There's another place nearby, though, a place a lot like the dungeons, through which passes many an unfortunate on the way to something worse. Think, Osher!"

"The pens. You think she's been taken to the pens."

"If your arm is as keen as your eye, we'll have her out in no time. The course of events seems simple enough. The lilith leaves the house to wander about the city. Perhaps she becomes lost, perhaps she's robbed, perhaps even drugged by an unscrupulous tavernkeeper when he hears her foreign accent. From there it's a short chute to the pens. Which explains why she hasn't returned home. It also explains why nobody has come forward asking the Vli to pay for her return. She can't be sold legally, because she's got no papers. So if the slaver who has her learns her identity, he still can't approach the Vli without putting his own head on the block. The only way to sell her is to a private bidder on the black market. I fancy a lilith would bring quite a price. But we've got to act fast, because whoever has her will be in a hurry to get rid of her. Selling nobles as slaves is risky, but keeping them penned up while word gets around is riskier. Most of them can read and write, so it's no use cutting out their tongues."

"I had an uncle who lost his tongue," Pye remarked. "When he couldn't lie anymore, he had to take up an honest trade. It was a terrible blow to the family."

"There are dozens of licensed slavers in this city," Osher pointed out around a mouthful of stew. "Any of them could have her. If this is your stroke of genius, I could have done better consulting a soothsayer."

"Ah, Osher, your great shortcoming is that you have no faith in me. There are dozens of slavers in Falnerescu, true. But most of them are dull-witted whip-wielders whose only custom is with the land barons and the shipping companies. They're too frightened of Chespid to touch merchandise this rich. There's only one man with the daring to offer a lilith for sale. If he doesn't have her in his own pens, he'll have heard a whisper where she is. He'll know where to lay hands on her and turn a profit doing it."

"I knew it," Pye said. "The moment you said 'funnel,' I knew you were talking about Ashubeleth."

"I've heard the name," Osher said. "I may even have met him. A huge fat man with a pockmarked face?"

"The very same. Fatter every year. I've heard it said he eats the slaves he can't sell, but I doubt it's true. More likely he just lets them starve, and saves their portions for his own table. Nobody likes Ashubeleth, but I imagine the other slavers trade with him when they've got something special. They'd know what might happen to them if they didn't."

"The easiest course," Pye said, "would be to offer to buy her from him."

"And once we confirm he's got her," Osher said, "my men can march in and seize her. I knew it was a mistake to dismiss the men."

"Knowing he's got her is one thing," Tarag pointed out. "Knowing *where* he's got her is another thing entirely. Have you ever been in Ashubeleth's pens? They're a worse maze by far than Metterner's basement. Even if he's got her himself, and not somebody else for whom he's brokering, his men would have her out the back way before you'd finished marching in the front."

"We'll surround the place."

"That would take ten times the number of men we used this morning. Do you seriously think Borando will be in a mood to let you stroll out the gate at the head of a whole platoon, when he hears how you've offended the Vli?"

"How *I've* offended the Vli? You miserable—"

"Temper, temper. I only meant that's how Borando, in his usual muddled way, will look at it. No, we can't rely on force. We'll have to play Ashubeleth in such a way as to get him to produce the lilith and hand her over to us voluntarily."

"And knowing Ashubeleth," Pye added, "no amount of slick talk will avail. He's got to have coin to bite down on. What do you suppose the going rate is for liliths?"

"Well, a trained courtesan was about five hundred gold, the last I heard. Whether the lilith is worth more than that or less will depend on her condition—and also on whether she's as beautiful as we've been led to believe. But considering the exotic appeal and the one-of-a-kind nature of the merchandise, I'd expect to pay as much as a thousand."

"Agreed," Pye said. "The question is, where are we to get it? The number of coffers in the city that could belch up a thousand gold on demand is very strictly limited, and access tends to be difficult to arrange. Habil Metterner might be able to scrape that amount together, if pressed. But asking him for it would be a touchy business. He would naturally assume that we were the ones had had her all along, that we were claiming to act as go-betweens merely to keep our hands clean."

"I think we can rely on his putting that interpretation on it," Tarag said. "He wouldn't give us the money; he'd only demand that Osher lock us up and torture the truth out of us. We'll have to find the money someplace else. Still, it's best to worry about only one thing at a time. Why not talk to Ashubeleth, confirm that he's got her, and find out how much he wants? Then we'll know how to proceed. If she's badly injured, or ugly, he might be happy to see a hundred. I'm sure a man of your accomplishments would have no trouble getting a hundred to stick to his fingers."

"The rumors are mostly exaggerated," Pye said modestly.

"What are you two talking about?" Osher said. His stolid military demeanor was beginning to show cracks. "You're not seriously contemplating *stealing* the gold to buy the lilith back? Tell me you're not."

"Kindly lower your voice," Tarag cautioned. "Yes, we're talking about stealing it, because we've got no other way of coming by it. Unless the Emperor of Berkenland would care to advance the necessary sum." He raised his eyebrows expectantly.

"Don't be ridiculous. A thousand gold! I could advance you as much as fifty out of my own pocket, though it would leave me nothing to buy my ale ration. Even fifty I'd have to go to the garrison strong room to get, and that would mean signing papers and explaining what I was about. But a thousand! Not even Borando himself could authorize that. He might as well try to sell a ship. And speaking of ships, Tarag, that tub of yours ought to be worth at least a thousand."

"You forget—I don't have the *Amera Smiles*; Chespid does. There isn't a moneylender in the city would give me fifty coppers on her. No, raising the money will be a problem, if money is what it takes. But I say again, let's talk to Ashubeleth first, and find out. Perhaps he can be tricked. Perhaps he can be frightened into wanting to get her off his hands."

Pye snorted. "Frightened? That one?"

"We'll see. Friend Osher, I suggest that you find some pleasant way to amuse yourself in Falnerescu for a couple of hours. Rent a fishing pole and catch some dinner."

"Oh, no you don't. I'm sticking with you. You'll not give me the slip."

"Nobody is trying to give you the slip. Far from it. We may need your help later. But Ashubeleth is going to be bargaining to sell an illegal slave. Do you think he'll do that while you stand there listening? You'll have to wait elsewhere while we make our approach."

"I don't trust you, Tarag. How am I to know you won't simply take to the hills when I'm out of sight?"

"Osher, do you remember the night a chetne or so ago when we fell to talking about Gidelon's observations of the movement of the moons and planets?"

"Aye."

"On the *Amera Smiles*, unless Chespid's lunkheads have used it to kindle the charcoal, is a manuscript copy of all of Gidelon's calculations. In monetary terms, it's nearly worthless. But as a clue to the workings of the universe, it's beyond price. Would I run off to live in a cave and leave behind such a treasure? Do you think so little of me? I tell you, this thing throws the theory of epicycles completely overboard! I can see you're worried for your own skin, if I run off. But the truth in that manuscript is worth more than my skin or yours. If you can't trust me, at least respect me. Respect my devotion to truth."

Osher was getting tired of arguing with Tarag; he always seemed to lose. "Very well. I'll wait here. Try not to be too long." Tarag and Pye pushed back their bench and rose, leaving the Berkender officer in his leather armor and gleaming brass buckles sitting in solitary splendor in the little tavern, staring into his mug of ale.

"That last was a pretty speech. What's an epicycle?" Pye said when they were well clear of the tavern. The afternoon was advancing, and the crescent Gavril stood mere fingers above the western horizon.

"An epicycle is an awkward and unconvincing attempt to explain something complex and mysterious."

"If you say so. There was one thing he said that gave me an idea."

"Probably the same idea I had."

"You'd have made a good thief."

"I'm flattered."

"It would be difficult," Pye said, frowning thoughtfully.

"You said yesterday you were ripe for a challenge."

"We couldn't do it alone. We'd need inside help."

"There's no shortage of that."

Coming straight toward them were a pair of Chespid's guards, pikes on their shoulders, pointed helmets gleaming in the sun.

"It wouldn't hurt to be conversing in a foreign tongue," Pye said out of the side of his mouth.

"Good," Tarag said in somewhat creaky Eloian. "Oftener conversation we in your highly confusion tongue did. Will."

"Converse and confusing, not conversation and confusion. But it's not confusing, once you've got the inflections straight."

"I remain confusing. Confused. Up-tone progressive, high-tone infinitive, down-tone past is. Yes."

"That's in the first conjugation. In the second, up-tone is infinitive, high-tone is past, and down-tone is conditional."

"Please, will my ship are in those port yesterday? Is slaves noisy? Your grandmother eats things found floating in the harbor."

"Better not let my grandmother hear you say that." Deep in conversation, they strolled past the guard. "Your grammar took a sudden up-turn there at the end."

"What say I will? Say I did? An Eloian oar teaching me to say this, your grandmother about. What are 'eats things found floating in the harbor'?"

Pye translated in an undertone, and Tarag laughed. "To this noble I was an apology. Surely in Eloia no grandmother eating things are floating in harbor found. Your people should civilization."

"Civilized. Too civilized. That's why I left."

They turned a corner, and reverted to Olmalin. "I dislike having to dodge the guard," Tarag complained. "How do you put up with the strain?"

"I never think about it when I'm not doing it. Isn't it a strain for you to command a ship, knowing you're charged to bring your crew and cargo safe through treacherous weather and hidden shoals?"

"Not really. I just do what has to be done. I see what you mean. Isn't it remarkable that human beings can learn so easily to swim in such different waters? Without even knowing how we do it. We're a marvel, friend Pye, and I don't mean just you and me. I mean the lot of us, Berkenders and Eloians and Vli together. It never ceases to pleasure me to have the privilege of walking the streets of such a world."

"So much for the taking." Pye held up a leather purse that had not been on his person a moment before. The purse was fat, but when he emptied it into his palm he held only coppers. Still, coppers were coppers. He poured them back into the purse and tied it at his own belt.

The slave-pens stretched across a good many acres on the west side of the city, the side farthest from the garrison. As Osher had pointed out, two dozen slavers and more kept premises there, some larger than others. Agricultural slaves—the bulk of the trade—were kept in open stockades, where they sweltered in the sun and shivered in the rain. On a given day a given stockade might be empty, or it might be so full there was no room to lie down. Demand and supply both fluctuated.

Household slaves, and those with special skills like metalworking, shipbuilding, and writing, could expect somewhat better treatment. While waiting to be put on the block they were kept indoors, space permitting, and the meals were at least regular, if less than tasty. Open barnlike buildings divided into sections or cages by bars were the norm, and such structures sometimes rambled on crookedly for considerable distances, abutting their neighbors side-to-end and enclosing bare, cheerless exercise yards. All the buildings were old, and most were poorly kept up. Nowhere in this quarter of the city could the stink of human misery be entirely flushed out of the nostrils.

As Tarag and Pye approached, an auction was in progress on the main block. Thirty or forty bidders stood in small knots, whispering to one another or raising their voices and arms to call out bids, while the auctioneer paced back and forth on the platform, praising his current lot in extravagant terms. Standing in front was an adolescent girl wearing manacles so large they seemed in danger of sliding off. She was frightened but smiling nervously, hoping to attract a buyer who would not whip her too harshly. She was naked from the waist up.

"You don't suppose that's the lilith," Pye whispered.

"Not on the open block. But your question raises another. How are we to be sure we've got her? What's to keep Ashubeleth from selling us just anybody? If the whole transaction's illegal, we can't very well take him to court. We'd have no papers to prove we'd been cheated."

"My friend, I trust you. You'll know this lilith when you see her."

"I wish I shared your confidence."

Ashubeleth's place of business was a huge barn just off the auction plaza. A wide, high doorway yawned on an interior cavern lined with a double tier of cages, one row running around the outer wall at ground level and another, just above it, accessible from a catwalk a little more than a tadig high. Bidders were free to stroll in and out, examining the merchandise that had been brought out to the cages for display and dickering with the three well-muscled, brutal-looking salesmen. As he entered, Pye looked around unobtrusively for ways to get out again. The entrance could be closed, he saw, by dropping the solid slab of door that hung suspended among the rafters. Probably it could be dropped swiftly, closing off the barn in the event of a riot or an escape attempt. The only other exit was the much smaller barred door that must lead to Ashubeleth's offices. The barn smelled of straw and urine; a large store of

fresh straw for lining the cages was heaped in a mound in the
far corner. Not far away somebody was sobbing quietly.

Tarag accosted a salesman. "We'd like to see Ashubeleth,
if we may."

"Oh, you would. What about?"

"Private business."

"And what sort of business might that be?" The man was
surly by temperament, and making no special effort to hide the
fact.

"We'll tell him when we see him."

"And will you tell him your name as well?"

"My name is Ranga Strell," Tarag claimed. "I'm a merchant
from Vli Holm."

The man's eyebrows rose. "Wait here." He turned on his
heel and left by the small barred door.

"Was that wise?" Pye asked.

"If he's got her, he'll know the Vli will bid high."

"You don't look the least Vli. They're a very distinct racial
type."

"Then when he sees me he'll know I'm lying—and a man
who lies is a far better market for illegal slaves than a man
who tells the truth."

The invisible sobbing continued unabated, as did the oppressive stench. In a couple of minutes the salesman returned and
growled, "Follow me." He led the way down a long narrow
hallway and opened a door.

They found themselves in a small, untidy room. Stacks of
paper spilled from a writing-desk along one wall, among them
a couple of dinner plates that had not been cleared away. The
window was narrow, and heavily barred, and looked out only
on a gray exercise yard and the wall beyond. Sitting behind a
cluttered table regarding them, and making the room seem even
smaller and more crowded by his bulk, was the fat slaver
Ashubeleth. His little eyes glittered, embedded deep in folds
of flesh. His complexion was coarse, his nose somewhat lop-
sided, and longish hair hung down in a fringe around the knobby
dome of his skull. He was wearing a purple shirt and a vast
black vest. He made no move to rise, but only sneered at his

visitors. "So," he said. "A gentleman of Vli Holm. We so seldom trade with your people. You seem to prefer bringing slaves out from your homeland, and taking them back when you go. A needless expense, I've always thought. What occasions this visit, if I may be so bold?" His labored breath wheezed in his hairy nostrils after every utterance.

"We'd like to buy a slave."

"Remarkable. What a curious idea. Do you know, if there were more like you—Strell, was it?—I might actually be able to go into business selling slaves. I know it sounds far-fetched, but I'm in your debt for bringing the possibility to my attention." Ashubeleth tapped two pudgy fingers on the tabletop with ill patience.

"You might prefer to discuss the details privately," Tarag said.

But Ashubeleth showed no inclination to dismiss the muscular salesman. "Details?" he exclaimed. "Then I take it there *are* details. You've thought this thing through. Admirable. It's not just any slave will do. You must be a clever man, to know that all slaves aren't alike. I myself discovered the fact only recently."

Plainly, Ashubeleth was waiting for his visitors to make the first move. Tarag pushed on boldly. "Yesterday, a person who is greatly beloved of myself and others of my race disappeared from the house of my countryman Habil Metterner. Perhaps you have already heard of the incident."

"One hears many things."

"I am desirous of bringing about her return. I am willing to pay."

"Again, I am astonished by your sagacity. To understand that merchandise when purchased must be paid for—ah, if the gods could hear you, they would sing your praises." Ashubeleth paused after this poetic flight to catch his breath. He fixed Tarag with his gaze. "How much?" he snapped.

"Then you have her here?"

"I have not said anything of the sort. How much can you pay?"

"That will depend on her condition. Dead, though I pray to

the Goddess she is not dead, perhaps ten gold pieces, so those who love her can see her properly put to rest. If harm has come to her, perhaps as much as fifty. Well and whole, somewhat more. You understand, I can make no firm offer until I have seen her condition for myself."

"There are lots of female slaves about," Ashubeleth said absently, toying with a small dagger that had been lying on the table. "I can offer you excellent bargains—or Brugo here can, which is the same thing. I understand you Vli don't go in for such amusements, but doubtless your—secretary?—would enjoy having a plaything to warm his bed. Or are you yourself inclined that way?"

It was too broad a trap for Tarag to walk into. "I want nothing to do with female slaves," he said stiffly. "There is only one purchase I wish to make. Zhenuvnili is not a female, she is a lilith. As you must already know, if you are an honest businessman and can sell what you undertake to."

"Inasmuch as I *am* an honest businessman," Ashubeleth wheezed, "I haven't got the faintest idea what you're talking about. Are you suggesting that I have somebody in my pens who has not been properly sold to me, with documents to prove it? You insult me. I am a slaver, sir, not a kidnapper. Just speculatively, however, if I *did* happen to learn where this creature of yours might be found, and if she were well and whole, how high might you be prepared to go?"

"Two hundred. No, three hundred. Three hundred gold. I can raise that much, if you'll give me a day or two. Is she all right? Can you tell me if she's all right?" A show of concern seemed to be in character.

Ashubeleth laughed. The sound was chilling, and the amusement seemed to afford him as much pain as pleasure, for he pressed his palms against his sides and stopped laughing to breathe. "Brugo, show these gentlemen out. They no longer amuse me."

"No, wait," Tarag said hurriedly. "How much? Tell me how much!"

"I can't set a price on something I don't have, can I? I'm sure you take me for a fool, but even for a fool there are limits."

"Five hundred," Tarag offered.

"Indeed. You seem most anxious."

"Six hundred. It's as high as I can go. I'll have to sell all my furniture, even Fauxnaster here. How can I do business without a scribe? But if it will bring Zhenuvnili back . . ."

"Yes," Ashubeleth said. "A touching gesture. You know, people are so careless when they come to Falnerescu. A big city, crowds of strange people speaking foreign languages. It's so easy to get lost. Sometimes visitors wander about in the streets for days, suffering horribly from hunger, to say nothing of violence and depravity of every kind. None of this has anything to do with me, you understand. My business is strictly in slaves. But once in a while, I have the opportunity to do a favor for such an unfortunate. It falls to my lot to reunite them with those dear to them. In return for this service, those involved sometimes see fit to make me a gift. It's not a transaction, you understand. Purely a matter of mutual generosity."

Tarag tried again. "How much?"

"Ah, the young are so impetuous. *If* I happened to learn of the whereabouts of this lilith, and *if* she chose to be given into your care, I would be most gratified by a donation of, shall we say, two thousand gold?"

"Two thousand?" Tarag stared at the floor and bit his lip. It was important not to agree too quickly—but also, the amount was more than he had any hope of raising. "I don't know," he said. "I'll try. I'll let you know. When might you have any more definite information?"

"I won't have any information. Bring the money here, to my showroom, by midnight tonight. Perhaps by then I'll have the lilith; perhaps I won't."

"If anybody bids higher, will you let me know? I'd like the chance to—"

Ashubeleth held up a fat palm. "Please, friend Strell. Nobody is bidding. Nothing is being sold. In a situation like this, there are far too many uncertainties. To mention only one possibility, if you should happen to speak to Nule Chespid about the gift you were making me—or if I even suspected that you meant to speak to him—I think we can take it as conclusive that you would be disappointed. If anybody—your scribe here, for instance—should even breathe a suggestion that I might be involved in anything unlawful, my dignity would be injured. And when my dignity is injured, it can go very badly for anybody who happens to be languishing in my pens. Very badly indeed. Do we understand one another?"

"Yes. We won't tell anybody."

"Good. I'm so pleased that you understand the value of discretion. You have until midnight. I'll be waiting. So unless there's anything else—" Ashubeleth put his palms flat on the table as if about to rise, and waited while his visitors bowed and backed out. He motioned for Brugo to stay behind and shut the door. "Follow them," he ordered. "I want to know who they are, where they go, who they see. Don't lose them. Understand?" Brugo nodded knowingly and slipped out the door. "If that one's Vli," Ashubeleth wheezed to himself, "I won't eat for a month. They're running a line. And if it's got two thousand gold dangling at the end, I want to know who's holding the pole. Chespid? He'd love to catch me selling illegally. But he won't. I'll squash his two messenger boys like bugs." He bared his yellow teeth in a snarl.

Chapter 13

As soon as the door slammed, Zhenuvnili opened her eyes. Darkness pressed in on her. Her arms were twisted behind her and tied to the arm of the chair; Ranga Strell's belt cut unmercifully into her wrists. Something was dreadfully wrong with the man—but to her shame, she felt no sympathy, only revulsion, only a frantic desire to get away from his damp touch. She worked her wrists back and forth to find out how much play was in the belt. Not much, but a little. By hunching her shoulder backward, she got a little more. She felt at the pattern of the knot. Through there, then up that way—a lilith's fingers were clever. Ah, a little slack in that loop would let the end feed through. Pinching the edge of the leather strip between one thumb and the other middle finger, she began forcing the slack through one loop into another. That left no slack at all around her wrists. She chewed her lip in frustration. But at last she got a bit of the free end to feed through, and used that slack to get more slack, and suddenly the knot fell open and she was free.

Rubbing her wrists, she stared around at the unrelieved blackness. The door was that way. Over the other way was some kind of opening, only dimly glimpsed. Outside the door, soft footfalls were approaching. She dropped to her hands and knees and crawled, groping, across the spilled dirt and stone toward the caved-in wall. The ground sloped, and she crawled up the slope, one hand out before her to feel for projecting edges.

Behind her the door creaked open, and candlelight flared. She rolled over onto her back. Strell was standing in the doorway, candlestick raised, staring at the empty chair. For a moment he seemed not to see her. On her elbows she scrabbled backward, deeper into the cave-in, and at the sound Strell's eyes swung around to her and he moved forward, a hideous grimace on his face.

"Ranga! Stand back! The Goddess commands you!"

For answer he only groaned like a dumb beast and reached out for her with his free hand. She kicked at the hand, and he evaded the kick and came on. She kicked again. He was trying to seize her ankle to drag her back, but one of the kicks struck his wrist, knocking the candle away so it fell and bounced on the floor, made a little spitting noise, and went out.

"Hear me, Ranga Strell," she said in a low, trembling voice. "The Goddess commands that you die." The words chilled her blood, but the death-command was her only weapon. "Die, Ranga Strell. The Goddess wills it."

Two hands clamped on her left leg, nails digging into her flesh, and her back scraped painfully on loose stones as he dragged her toward him. He might not even have heard the death-command, for all the effect it had. Reaching up over her head for something to cling to, anything, to keep from being dragged down to her death, her fingers and then her fists wrapped themselves around iron bars. Iron bars sitting firmly horizontal. The kind of iron bars sometimes used as gratings in the pavement. Face pressed against the grate from below, she looked up and saw Nardis, green disc nearly full, a little westering at this late hour. The first flush of the Moons Road would be rising now in the east.

Using the grate as an anchor, she jammed her free leg downward sharply and felt the heel glance off something. She kicked again and connected with solid flesh. There was a muffled exclamation, and the hands let go of her leg. She kicked twice more; the second time met only air. After lying limp for less than a moment thanking the Goddess, she stiffened her shoulders and pushed upward on the grate. It didn't budge. She pushed harder, strained against it. Still nothing. She began to whimper. She tried twisting while she pushed, tried rattling it back and forth, tried sliding it sideways.

Sideways it slid. Then one edge was free of the projecting rim above, and lifted easily. She wriggled upward, got her elbows on the rim, hoisted, and was sitting on the pavement of the alley in the dim green moonlight, legs dangling down into the hole, shivering. This must be how the slaves got out of the house when they didn't want the master to know, she thought. Perhaps rain leakage had led to the cave-in, or perhaps it had been engineered intentionally, to disguise the lower end of the tunnel. In any event, she was free—for the moment, anyway. She drew her legs up, clutched her knees, and leaned her forehead on them, too exhausted to stand. She had used the death-command on Strell. Had it really been necessary, or had she spoken too soon? The death-command was the liliths' only weapon, one rarely invoked. It was known to be effective—in some cases, at least. It had not seemed to slow Strell the way a good kick had. The death-command was only to be used when no other recourse was available, and its use had to be reviewed afterward by a panel of liliths meeting in secret court. When Zhenuvnili returned home, she would have to stand before the court and explain what had happened. But she didn't know what had happened, only that Strell had attacked her at a time when she was too drained to control him properly. So perhaps it was her fault. The death-command had always seemed a sensible precaution to have available in an emergency, but now, bitten by conscience, she saw that it could hurt those who used it as deeply as those it was used upon.

The hole in the pavement was dark and silent, but Strell might erupt from it at any moment. She wrestled the grate back into place, and got shakily to her feet. Where to now? She could circle back to the front gate again, but if she hadn't knocked Strell unconscious he might be lying in wait for her. She would be safer staying outside until dawn, when the household would be stirring and others near to protect her from the madman. But was it safe to stand here in the alley, exposed to view? What if more kelg were roaming the streets? The memory of the massacre flooded back, and she leaned against the garden wall for support. Those same kelg might be hunting for her now. Where could she go?

At the end of the alley, a helmeted figure appeared bearing a pike. Zhenuvnili gasped, and the guard turned toward her. "Ho, who's there?" he called. She had no idea that the house might be guarded, or why it should be. All she knew was that an armed man—possibly one of the dreaded Berkenders—was coming toward her at a lumbering trot. With the swiftness of panic, she dashed away from him, turning left at the rear of the estate to run past the stables of some other prosperous citizen. The footsteps were still pounding behind her, so she took another turning and another at random in the maze of alleys. The sounds of pursuit grew gradually fainter, and at last ceased. Crouching behind a rain barrel and gasping for breath, she looked back the way she had come, but the guard did not appear. Unfortunately, she was lost. And retracing her steps would do no good—she might only run into her pursuer again. So when she was rested, she stood up and walked on.

Falnerescu in the dead hours before dawn had a cold and silent beauty. Her slippers crunched on gravel, and she pulled her robe tighter against the chill. Nardis and Aptar cast double shadows. A couple of times she surprised small animals that raised their heads to peer at her with huge eyes before scuttling away. At one house candles were glowing already in the kitchen, and voices murmured, but she could make out no words. She had an impulse to tap on the door and ask if she might come in and warm herself at the hearth. But she was learning to be wary. What seemed a friendly greeting might conceal some unfathomable evil. Back among the ramble of houses and small shops, the star-thick sky pressed close enough to touch. She wished she had wings to fly up and live among the stars, wished she could be as perfect and unchanging as they. In the last day, the ordered world she had lived in all her life had collapsed in ruins, stone crumbling to dust beneath her fingers. Or had the ruins always been there, just beneath the surface, unsuspected?

She had never known that such cruelty as the kelg's could exist, such suffering as that of the mnoerri. In the Nest there might be disagreement or, rarely, outright anger. And of course one heard of people dying. But actually to see and hear a tragedy of such magnitude . . . What was worse, it was she who had brought the mnoerri together in that meadow—and in the name of Love. She had lured them to their deaths, and later done her best to kill Ranga Strell. What was happening to her? Was it something in the air of this foreign land that caused the violence, or was it a poisonous flower that had sprung up in her heart? Had she failed Li Ranli through not loving the Goddess enough? But she had been trying to love! From childhood she had been taught that the light of love was the great power in the world. Love healed, love strengthened, love brought joy and contentment and peace. The Goddess, said the Teachings, warmed every heart with Her inexhaustible love. But not, it seemed, the hearts of the kelg. Could the Goddess be so cruel, to turn her face away from the suffering of the mnoerri? Or was Li as powerless as Zhenuvnili herself? What sort of Goddess could be so powerless?

The questions spun in the lilith's head, and she had no answers, no answers at all. Walking on through the moonlit city, she saw how ignorant she was of the world. Li Ranli had called her "one of our brightest, as well as fairest, jewels." But Li Ranli knew as little of the world as she. Could a race prosper in an increasingly complex world when at its heart lay such ignorance? Not mere innocence; the liliths acknowledged their innocence; they gloried in it. To look at the world and see only love, love flowing everywhere, love unending! It was a grand dream. But they had bought innocence by sealing themselves away from knowledge. And they had bought ignorance along with it, and compounded the two until the one could not exist without the other. How many liliths could witness what she had witnessed that day and still feel love? Zhenuvnili felt revulsion, and confusion, and sorrow, but no love, not even the faintest whisper. And for a lilith, not to feel love was the most frightening feeling of all. Her heart was stripped raw, for the wind to blow through it; and the wind was cold, and bitter.

The Moons Road was arching higher now, the sky graying at its base. In Vli Holm, the Moons Road was also called Li's Promise, because it reached out from the sun, which was the Heart of Li. But to Zhenuvnili, standing alone in an alley in a foreign city, the promise was empty, deceitful, a streak of paint on cardboard that somebody had set up in the east to tease and mock her.

In this mood of sullen uncaring, the residue of grief, she wandered aimlessly. The sound of voices in the darkness at first failed to register, so that she had drawn quite close to the speakers before she heard them and stopped, heart thumping, to listen. Two men were engaged in a desultory and rather drunken argument.

"Don't blame me. I can't make her cough up if she won't."

"It was your idea to go to her in the first place."

"I didn't hear you objectin' too loud."

"That was when I thought we was in for a bit of money."

"Well, I don't like it any better than you, but it's no use complainin', so shut yer yap. The Hand only pays for value received. It's not my fault the game went sour."

"We should of gone to Ashubeleth in the first place."

"Oh, you're loyal, you are. The Hand no sooner gets you free of that fat grubbler than you're wantin' to run straight back to him."

"He's got money," the other man whined. "And we don't."

"Well, there's that."

To Zhenuvnili the discussion had no significance. Jamming her hands deeper into the pockets of the robe, she sauntered on.

"Here, now. Just a minute. You."

She turned to look. A ragged, skinny man sitting on the ground against a wall was beckoning to her with a bony finger. He had a hooked nose and long stringy hair, and from one eye descended a crooked silver scar. Beside him in the dirt was a shorter man clutching a jug.

"What might you be doin' out at this time of night?" the skinny man demanded. "You a whore? Yeah, you look like a whore. C'mere."

Fascinated, she took a few steps closer. The man seemed not evil, merely incomprehensible.

"Listen, you an' me oughtta team up. You could pick up the coin, an' I could protect you. Take care of you. Thass a good idea, hunh? How much you got on you right now? Have a good night?"

"She ain't no whore," his companion objected. "You ever see a whore got up in a long robe like that?"

The two beggars, struck by one thought, turned to look at one another, then turned back to the lilith.

Zhenuvnili had never heard of whoring. Though the liliths' needs were met by a tithe on all Vli citizens, the idea of sex for pay would have been difficult for her to grasp, the taboo against it impossible. So she took no offense, but merely stood looking at the curious scruffy derelicts.

"Listen," said the man with the scar. "You talk at all? You got a name?"

"Zhenuvnili. My name is Zhenuvnili."

"Some kinda foreign name?"

"Yes. My people are the Vli." In her mouth the words had a lilt.

"Tha sends down the gold out of the sky," the short man said reverently.

"Amen, brother."

In unison they rose and came toward her. Zhenuvnili was considering, in an abstract way, how one could love such as these. She knew it would have been very easy for her only a day ago, but now she felt nothing. One ought to love, if one's life was devoted to loving. But how? She was locked in a dark room, and somehow she had mislaid the key.

"This time," the short man said, "we'll try Ashubeleth."

"And we'll see the color of his gold before we deliver."

"Aye."

The man with the silver scar lifted something small in his right hand and swung it at the lilith's head. The object landed with an impact that sent her spinning into darkness.

Chapter 14

*I*t was a long walk back from the slave-pens to the tavern where they had left Vod Penna Osher, and the afternoon was fast advancing. "Two thousand," Pye said. "For an illegal slave. The man's audacious; I'll give him that."

"Where in Bulon's teeth are we going to get that kind of money?"

"I thought we'd already discussed that."

"There's a difference," Tarag said, "between discussing it and laying hands on it."

They were walking down a wide curving avenue with the fortress looming up on their left. In the street a juggler was performing, and now and again a passerby flipped a coin into his hat. Tarag was about to suggest that they take up juggling when Pye said, "We're being followed. Don't look back."

"I wasn't going to."

"We could split up."

"You're better at this than I. I don't even know who I'm trying to shake."

"All right. I feel a sudden need to purchase some candles." Ahead on the right was a candlemaker's shop, and Pye angled toward it without changing pace. "Quick," he said to the plump girl behind the counter. "Is there a back way out?"

The girl giggled. Her eyes were wide. She giggled again.

Pye unhitched the purse of coppers from his belt and dropped it on the counter. "If anybody asks, we haven't been in here. You haven't seen us."

Still giggling, the girl pointed toward the rear of the shop. They went in that direction, past candles plain and scented, candles white and tinted, slim spires and fat long-burners, and out a rear door to an alley, where they doubled back and emerged on another street. "What's remarkable," Salas Tarag commented, "is that that purse you stole on the way to Ashubeleth's should be just what was needed to oil that girl's hinges. How do you do it?"

"It's a knack I have."

"I think I said that first."

"There is a great deal you don't know about thieving, my friend."

"Such as?"

"There is no such thing," Pye said, "as thieving."

"How so? When my purse is gone, it's gone."

"Ah, but who says it's your purse?"

"I say it's my purse."

"And I say it's mine. Though in fact I don't say that. It's not mine, nor is it yours, nor anybody's. It's only a purse. It passes from hand to hand, as you just saw. The first necessity, if you would be a master thief, is to banish the concept of property from your mind. There is no such thing as property. These are merely objects, you see? Nowhere in them—in *them*, mind you—is there any substance called belongingness. The belongingness is in us." He tapped his head. "And what is in our minds, we have the power to unravel."

"I'm not sure I quite see how one would do that."

"If you bought a ship," Pye suggested, "would you change its name?"

"I might."

"Then you'd unravel the old name from your mind. Or better, consider those documents on your ship, that you said threw an earlier scientific doctrine overboard. The earlier doctrine was in your mind before you encountered the new ideas, wasn't it? What did you do with it afterward?"

"I unraveled it. I begin to see."

"The idea of property is no different than one of your scientific doctrines. And it's the cause of endless suffering. It's the idea that causes the suffering, not the thief. A man who suffers because I have taken his purse is creating his own suffering."

"But what if he's poor," Tarag objected, "and needs the money to buy bread?"

"If he has unraveled the idea of property, he cannot suffer. He simply steals the bread."

"And what if he gets caught, and has his hand chopped off?"

"Ah, my friend, you ask too much. Is it up to me to see to it that all thieves are skilled at their craft?"

"Unraveling the concept of property," Tarag mused. "The Eloians must be a remarkable people."

"We are a contemplative people. We strive not to be remarkable. Just the opposite. To attract attention is painful for us. Have you ever been to Eloia?"

"No."

"It's a vast and flat and foggy land. Always cool, though seldom to the point of frost. There are no mountains, not even high hills, only an endless low roll of green fading into the mist."

"You make it sound beautiful. Why did you leave?"

"I was a disturbing influence. My teachers found me disrespectful of tradition. Eventually I committed a crime."

"You? A crime?" The tale was new to Salas Tarag.

"There was a manor house, lying well out in the country, that hadn't been lived in for generations. Still, the people who lived nearby tended it, and kept it up as carefully as if it were tenanted. One day, wandering about, I came upon this magnificent dwelling, and after admiring it went up to tap the gong beside the door. Nobody came to see who had come to call— but in Eloia, you'll understand, it's quite normal for folk to be home and not answer the door. Never having seen or heard of the place, I had no idea it was unoccupied. I was hungry, so I thought I'd step around to the kitchen for a bite. All the food in the larder was fresh. After I'd had a snack, I thought I'd curl up for a nap. When I woke, there was still nobody there, and since I had no reason to move on, I stayed. It was some days before it finally dawned on me that nobody lived in the house at all, though the peasants came in every morning to dust and bring fresh bread and cheese and fruit. They were unfailingly polite, and I was polite in return. Nobody ever suggested, or even hinted, that I was unwelcome—until one day a chetne or so later, when the local constable arrived to tell me that I was desecrating a shrine. I was taken before a judge and sentenced to be deported."

"But from what you've said," Tarag protested, "you had no way of knowing it was a shrine."

"Precisely. That is why I was deported."

"I don't follow you."

"I ought to have known," Pye explained, "without being given any sign. In Eloia, one is expected as a matter of course to perceive the imperceptible. Failure to do so is a punishable offense. Nonetheless, living in that house taught me something about the concept of property."

"My friend, you ought to be a philosopher, not a thief."

"All Eloians are philosophers. So are all thieves."

"You'll have to tie that one down for me. Thieves philosophers?"

"Assuredly." Pye raised a finger. "For one thing, we're masters of the dialectic of pragmatism and exigency. We have to be, if we're to keep our heads on our necks and off the ends of stakes. If you want to know what's practical, ask a thief. But that's not all. We also teach men and women the nature of true happiness."

"And how, pray?"

"The man who believes that happiness lies in material things can never be happy, for he is always at the mercy of the thief. Only the man who has transcended such concerns can be truly happy. For him, possessions are of no importance. He gives, he takes, he takes no notice."

"Then if all men were happy, they'd all be thieves."

"No, none of them would be. Without property, there'd be no such thing as theft."

"We have shaken whoever was following us, haven't we?"

Pye was silent, listening. "I think so."

"You're not sure."

"The wind is wrong."

"Then let's move downwind."

They were within a street of the tavern where they had left Osher. They sidestepped into an alley and clambered swiftly to the roof. From that vantage they watched as Ashubeleth's henchman turned into the mouth of the alley and, not seeing his quarry, trotted in the direction he assumed they had gone. When he was out of sight, Tarag made to lift himself over the edge of the roof again, but Pye put out a restraining hand. "I was careless once. Let's give him time to get clear." So they waited, crouched on the roof, for several minutes, until Pye judged it safe to descend.

Osher was still sitting at the table where they had left him, but the customary military rigor of his posture had slackened. He seemed to have sunk in on himself. The mug before him was plainly his sixth or seventh. When he saw them he looked up inquiringly, but his eyes held little alertness.

Tarag slid in beside him, and Pye opposite. "He's got her," Tarag announced. "He's selling."

"Congratulations," Osher said, pronouncing the word with great care. "I've just been thinking what a wonderful hon— *hic*—honor it is to be an officer in the Imperial Navy of Berkenland. I'm a leader of men. And kelg. Mustn't forget the kelg. The responsibility. The respect. It's so wonderful I don't know how I stand it." He leaned his jaw on the heels of both hands and stared into the mug.

Tarag cursed silently at the unexpected setback. "Responsibility is a sword with two edges," he said, patting Osher on the back. "Only a man with a real dedication to duty could put up with the bureaucratic frustrations, the misplaced antagonism of ignorant peasants, the constant pressure—"

"Misplaced antag—They hate me, don't they? They hate me. What did I ever do to them?" He peered into Tarag's face.

"Nothing, friend Osher. Nobody hates you. But you've got a rare opportunity just now to do something really noble and heroic."

Osher ignored him. "I'm just trying to do my job, make my—my family proud of me. Does your mother ever send you a letter, Tarag?"

"My mother doesn't know where I am. Hasn't for a very long time."

"My mother never sends me a letter. Just my allowance. You know what's wrong with being a leader of men?"

"What?" Tarag said patiently.

"It's no fun. I never get to have any fun. Do you ever have fun, Tarag? Sure you do. That's why I like you. You're fun. But you're under arrest. I've got to take you to jail, because you have too much fun." Having delivered himself of this pronouncement, Osher blinked unsteadily, as if trying to figure out what the words meant.

"Joabbi," Tarag said to Pye.

Pye nodded. "Joabbi." Joabbi was a powerful stimulant, yellowish and bitter, brewed from a pulverized root. Tarag fished some coppers from Osher's purse and threw them on the table, and Pye scooped them up and went to order a mug of joabbi.

"My mother never let me have any fun," Osher complained.

"That's a shame," Tarag told him. "How would you like to do something that's fun, and help save the lilith at the same time?"

"You've got a scheme to get me in trouble again. You can't fool me, Tarag. I'm too—hic—too smart for you."

"That's right. That's why we want to get you sobered up." Pye set the mug of joabbi on the table, and Tarag slid it into Osher's fingers. "You'll need to have your wits about you."

"Sober? I'm sober! Are you saying I can't hold my—I only had, I don't know, how many did I . . ."

"Drink up." Tarag nudged the mug in the direction of Osher's mouth, and got him to take a sip.

Osher made a face. "What is this stuff? You trying to poison me?"

"It's good for you. Make you feel like a new man."

Osher got about half the mug down, and then, with a stricken look, got up hurriedly and made a staggering dash for the back door. After a few minutes he returned, pale and shaken and moving with great care. His medical advisors had a second mug of joabbi waiting for him, which he drained without further incident. They then prescribed a brisk walk. But in sitting down, it developed, Osher had gotten his sword in its scabbard trapped between the slats of the bench. In trying to stand, he hit his helmet with his elbow and knocked it off the table, bent down to retrieve it, was jerked off balance by the still-entangled sword, and fell headlong on the floor, where the bench, the overturned table, mugs, and candle swiftly joined him. Public laughter greeted his performance. Tarag and Pye bent to help him up, but he waved them away, got to his feet slowly, brushed himself off with great dignity, tucked his helmet under his arm, and walked straight into a wall. They took his elbows and gently steered him out the door. In the street there was less to collide with, but he still tended to veer erratically, so they stayed close by his side. If they had not been so encumbered, they would surely have noticed Brugo standing behind them in the street, watching them go. Brugo was not bright, but he was tenacious, and he had stayed in the vicinity hoping to find out what his master had sent him to. So, they had tied up with a Berkender. And not just any Berkender, but a high-ranking officer. Brugo had no idea what this might mean, but he was confident Ashubeleth would.

Half an hour later the trio were striding down the garrison road. Osher had given up complaining about his splitting head to listen to Tarag's plan. After it had been explained to him three times he said, "What you're asking is absolutely impossible. I couldn't possibly authorize it."

"Nobody's asking you to authorize it," Tarag pointed out. "All you have to do is do it. What will it matter? You'll have the money back before it's missed."

"You're a pirate, Tarag. You realize that." In Falnerescu, the word "pirate" was not used lightly.

"I prefer to think of myself as a master of pragmatism and

exigency. Or at least an apprentice. I wish we had other options, but there's no time. Another day and he'll have sold her to somebody outbound for someplace very far away. Even if he has to take a loss. She's too dangerous for him to keep around, especially now that somebody knows he's got her, and he's wily enough to see the danger and old and fat enough not to want to dance with it. You're the only man who can save her, Osher. I won't ask you whether you want to let down your friends and leave them to escape Nule Chespid's goons as best they can. Nor will I bring up the plight of the lilith, who is surely a gentle-born person not deserving such rough treatment as will be her lot for the rest of her days unless you come to her aid. I'll say no more than this: This treaty that's in the offing is plainly important to Berkenland. You and Shuma wouldn't have been so bent on keeping me from putting my oar in if it weren't. But as things stand now, there'll be no treaty. The Vli are grievously offended, as well as bereaved, and will probably turn around and row straight home again. Whereupon the Western Sea will fall to the Potheqi, and you'll have yourself personally to blame for it—whether or not your superiors choose to call you before a board of inquiry to explain your part in the events of the last two days. If, on the other hand, you succeed in rescuing the lilith, the treaty can go forward as scheduled, and you'll be in line for a commendation from the emperor. Am I right?"

"Tarag, you're twisting things. You've got a habit of doing that."

"Of course, if you *want* to let the treaty slip through your fingers out of fear of a few petty regulations, and be sent home in disgrace, don't let us dissuade you. But if you'd rather rescue a legendary beauty and return home a hero, all you have to do is close your fingers." Tarag illustrated by making a fist. "Granted, what we're asking is technically beyond your authority. But are you content to let the scope of your power be dictated by regulations? What's the money there for, if not for emergencies? In an emergency, do you play by the book? Is that any way to show greatness as an officer?"

Osher paced onward, scowling. "That's a pretty speech,"

he said after a minute. "But even if I wanted to get into the strong room—and I assure you I don't—I couldn't. There's a double guard posted at the door of the vault, who take note who goes in and out and what they deposit or remove. The door itself is locked with two keys. The guard on duty has one key, and only two people have the other one. I'm *not* one of those people."

"Is there any other way in? Through the ceiling or the walls?"

"The strong room is set in rock. If you'd like to tunnel through, I'll gladly provide you with a pick and a wheelbarrow. But somebody's sure to hear you at work sometime during the next chetne, which is how long it would take, and you've convinced me you're in a bigger hurry than that. You see? It's hopeless."

"Who has the keys?" Pye asked.

"Jakul Borando has one. The paymaster has the other. And neither of them is likely to be kindly disposed toward this little enterprise."

"Where does Borando keep his?" Tarag asked. "Could Shuma get it for us?"

"Tarag, you're mad. The last time that woman saw you she was ready to carve you into little pieces to feed to the kelg."

"Only a quarrel. Easily mended—I hope. A lot depends on it."

"Even getting the key won't help," Osher pointed out. "There's still the guard. Do you think they'll stand idly by while we load two thousand in gold into a cart and make off with it?"

"We'll lie to them."

"They won't listen to lies. They'll make us wait while they consult the captain of the guard. And he'll make us wait while he consults Borando. The first thing Borando will do will be to lock you up, and the second thing will be to stew for three or four days about what to do next."

"Well, if we can't lie to them, we'll have to draw them off."

At this point, Pye made a couple of suggestions. Osher listened and criticized, and Tarag added a suggestion or two. At last Osher nodded reluctantly. "It might work. It might just possibly work. Not that I like playing that kind of trick on them. But tomorrow we'll be able to put things right, and no harm done. Unless you manage to double-cross me again, Tarag. I wonder if you don't secretly hate me."

"Osher, my loyalty to you is as Amera's to me. Or nearly that, anyway," he added with a furtive glance skyward. "This do I swear: If ever you're in need, you have but to speak. I'll do as much for you as you've done this day for me. I'll walk the Moons Road."

"You've been walking the Moons Road all your life."

"It keeps me light on my feet. You mean to do it, then."

"Let's just say I'm tired of arguing with you."

In the company of an officer, the two foreigners were admitted to the garrison without question. Behind them the setting sun blazed, framed by the massive beams of the gate; as they watched, the gate itself was swung shut for the night. Ahead, the reddish light bathed the gingerbread terraces of the homes of the Berkender elite.

Three floors up in the most ornate and imposing of the structures, behind the small square panes of a large window, Shuma Borando was reclining on a couch gazing lazily out at the sunset. She was wearing lavender lounging pajamas, loosely draped here and tightly tucked there. The color went well, she knew, with her black hair and pale skin. She had just noticed a long curving mark in the high gloss of the burnished wood floor and was debating whether to have somebody whipped or merely have them in to polish everything again when a slave entered and bowed. "Penna Osher, my lady. With two others."

Shuma's eyebrows arched. "How intriguing. Show them in."

Her visitors entered. Salas Tarag inclined his head a little more deeply than was strictly necessary. "Thank you for receiving us, my lady."

"I thought it might be amusing. How were the swamps?"

"The swamps, my lady?"

"The swamps you were so inconveniently bound for this morning. Not too many sucker-stings, I hope."

"As it happened, our plans changed after we left you. We spent the day in the city."

"Oh, really. I may as well warn you, Tarag, I haven't made up my mind yet whether to forgive you for behaving so disgracefully to me yesterday. If you've come to apologize, I *might* be willing to listen. But you're going to have to make it awfully convincing." She smiled at him, without warmth.

"In truth," Tarag lied smoothly, "it's been on my mind all day how to frame a heartfelt apology. But events have moved forward so quickly that I've had no time, poor and stumbling with words as I am, to compose a speech that would do justice to my abject feelings. I fear that if I tried to extemporize, I might inadvertently stumble, as I did once before, and speak words that would injure where they were meant to soothe. When the matter at hand has been resolved, I promise to do whatever is in my power—hire a poet to write you sonnets, if necessary."

"I didn't know they even had poets in the provinces. And I'm not sure words will be sufficient. There are also some missing jewels to be accounted for."

"I know nothing of the whereabouts of any jewels," Tarag said. That at least was true.

"Time is passing," Pye pointed out.

"There speaks the philosopher," Tarag said. "The plain fact, my lady, is that we've come to ask for your help in a matter of the gravest political urgency."

"Why not go to my husband, then? I'm only a civilian, after all."

"More than that, my lady, as you well know. Still, your status works to our advantage, because our errand is unofficial. It seemed safer to trust to your discretion, as well as to your wit. Your husband would only consult his regulations, and meet with his advisors, and by the time he acted it would be too late. You are under no such constraint."

"It's about the lilith, isn't it? What is it now?"

"We know where she is, and how to rescue her," Tarag explained. "But to do it we need your help."

"I knew it must be something like that, else you'd never have dared show your face here again. Very well. I'm not saying

I'll lift a finger. But I'll listen to a few more of your outrageous lies before I make up my mind. You're a scoundrel, Tarag, but you're amusing."

In a few words Tarag sketched the situation as he understood it. Shuma's first reaction was that the lilith ought to be left to rot, but after a little argument her political astuteness got the better of her jealousy, and she admitted that it would be wise to attempt a rescue. Persuading her that two thousand gold pieces were needed as bait took somewhat longer. Even then she maintained that it would be impossible to get the money from the strong room, so Tarag had no choice but to explain the entire plan to her. He was reluctant to do so, because if she balked they would have no other recourse. But when he had finished Shuma laughed merrily. "I think it might just work," she declared. "It's ingenious. But I don't know you," she said to Pye. "Can you do what he says you can?"

Pye shrugged. "It depends on several factors—on what's lying around loose in the strong room, and even more on what sort of uniform the guards are wearing. I've thought of an additional imposture that should make the job easier. But as to the dexterity required, a child could do it."

"You've had experience in this sort of thing before?"

"A modest amount," Pye admitted.

"He's the best there is," Tarag said.

"That's encouraging. There's just one other thing: You *do* mean to bring the money back, don't you? It would be rather embarrassing if I had to explain my part in this scheme to my husband, unless I had the money back to make him happy. And I'm sure you understand just how inconvenient it would be for you if I were embarrassed."

Tarag feigned nonchalance. "Penna Osher will be escorting us with a detachment. The money need never be out of his sight. It's never going to leave the safekeeping of the Berkenders—so really, there's no impropriety involved."

Shuma rose from the couch. "All right," she said. "I'll go get changed."

The first necessity was to relieve Jakul Borando of his key. As it happened, the commander was in his own rooms, sleeping off the effects of a perhaps excessive quantity of wine imbibed during a somewhat protracted lunch. His wife, attired in dark trousers and vest and a matching broad-brimmed hat, had only to slip in, unhook the key from the ring on the table, and slip out again. She had done this sort of thing before, and knew how to manage it without jingling. Back out the door, she held the prize up and wagged it at Pye.

"Are you sure that's the right one?" he whispered.

"You're a distrustful sort." Shuma pouted.

"In my profession one learns skepticism."

"What exactly is your profession, by the way? I don't believe Tarag mentioned that."

"I'm a philosopher. A teacher of philosophy, to be more precise. And like most of my colleagues, I'm blind as a stone." Pye's eyes went slack and opaque. "You'll have to lend me an arm, my lady. Fauxnaster's wisdom is unrivaled on a thousand islands, but he does have difficulty negotiating a flight of stairs."

"I still say it's ridiculous," Shuma protested, guiding Pye down the hall. "Why would I, of all people, hire a teacher of philosophy?"

"You wish to improve your mind. You have sunk too far into the swamps of life. You wish to cultivate and reap from a more elevated plateau. You wish to develop your mind. Who better to converse with, then, than an itinerant teacher whose inner eye has been opened in proportion as the outer have been shut forever?" Nobody, meeting him, would have doubted that Fauxnaster was blind. He moved his head from side to side, listening, and his unfocused eyes angled upward into the air, attaching themselves to nothing. His fingers traced the wall as they descended the stairs, and at the bottom he waited for Shuma to lead him in the right direction. "As it happens, in the last hour you and your teacher have begun to quarrel over the nature of wealth. Your teacher, whose sight is set on higher things, insists that wealth is a spiritual quality having nothing whatever to do with crude physical possessions. But you, in your customary practical manner, maintain that physical beauty has real meaning, and desire to show your teacher the truth of this by letting him examine for himself the kind of wealth you can command."

They were passing along a narrow lane that sloped steeply downward. The twilight was thick upon them, and the Moons Road at its most glorious arched up out of the west. Cheth was high in the west, Nardis in the east, both moving serenely in their time toward full. "Everything you've been saying," Shuma said, "is kelg dung. Honored teacher. How can something be wealth if I can't hold it in my hand? When I'm hungry, am I supposed to go sniveling about spiritual truth and expect to be fed?"

"It has been tried, with some success. I myself have made a profession of it."

"But you don't practice your profession on the baker or the fishmonger, do you?" Shuma said nastily. "Only on those who have coin to spare."

"I practice upon whoever is in need of philosophy," Fauxnaster said. "I make no such distinctions. Do we have much farther to go?"

"It's just up ahead."

"I believe you're one of the most difficult pupils I've yet encountered. Or perhaps one of the most astute. I confess I am curious to learn what sort of treasure you set such store by. Never having seen gold, of course, I know it only by its touch. It is cold and hard. But still, my pupils esteem it above all else. For my part, things that are cold and hard please me less than things that are warm and soft. Perhaps I see something by not seeing. Do you think?"

The building that housed the strong room was the main administrative center of the garrison. Functional rather than ostentatious, it squatted low to the ground at the foot of the slope, abutting a rock face that was not lava but exposed bedrock. Slit windows and stone walls said that the building antedated the garrison wall. Its main entrance was to the harbor side, and it was there that Shuma led the blind man. By that hour the functionaries and underlings had departed, and no lamps burned. Shuma looked left and right for Salas Tarag. Where was the man? His absence could mean trouble. But it would mean worse trouble to leave the blind man to go search for him. Wherever Tarag was—wrangling with the wagon master, probably—he would have to extricate himself.

At intervals along the hallway oil lamps flickered, perched on shelves and backed with brass reflectors to increase their luminescence. Midway down the long building Shuma turned down a side hall, the blind man at her elbow. The passage was short, wide, and straight, and ended in a massive iron door flanked by two uniformed guards standing at ease, leaning on their pikes. When they saw Shuma they snapped to attention. "The thing you haven't grasped," Shuma was telling her teacher, "is that this spiritual quality you claim to find only in pure thought is present in material things as well, if only you have the wit to perceive it. Just wait till you see my jewels! Oh, I'm sorry. Excuse me. I didn't mean—"

"That's quite all right. What a blind man does when he encounters things is a form of seeing. Pray don't be embarrassed to use the word. From the sound I believe we are nearing the end of the passage. And there are two others here. Am I right?" Fauxnaster's eyes regarded a spot high up on the door.

"These are the guards."

"Ah. You see the sort of violence physical wealth brings in its wake. The sort of riches I have been speaking of need not be guarded, for they cannot be stolen. I may give them away, and yet retain as much as I started with."

"This is Fauxnaster," Shuma told the corporal of the guard. "My new teacher of philosophy. I have come to show him my jewels, which he insists are mere worthless trinkets."

"Is it by the commander's authorization, my lady?"

"Of course. Who do you think gave me the key?" She brandished it.

"One of us must go into the vault with you, my lady. Those are the orders."

Shuma shrugged. "Whatever you like. Only don't get underfoot." She stood aside while the guard inserted his key in the lock and turned it, then did likewise in the other keyhole. The latch snapped open, and the guard lifted the bar and slid it scraping back. At no time, under the scrutiny of the other guard, did Fauxnaster's eyes stray in the direction of the lock.

The guard lit candles for himself and Shuma Borando, and the trio entered the strong room, leaving one guard in reserve at the door. The air was cool and dank, the tang of metal sharp in the nose. Behind it was a drier flavor. "Ah," Fauxnaster said. "The walls here are of stone. I can smell it." The natural contours of a cave had been hewn away to make a room whose ceiling was partly supported by thick beams standing upright. The room was long and narrow and somewhat crooked, as if following the line of an ancient fissure. High on one wall, whitewashed over but still traceable, was the outline of some unidentifiable wild animal, spears protruding from its back. And on all sides were piled hoards of bounty. Intricately worked silver candelabra jostled against little jewel-encrusted statues. In one corner stood an urn taller than a man, painted with pastoral scenes in delicate white and gold brushwork. And on all sides sat heavy wooden boxes bound and nailed with iron. The lid of one of those was propped up to reveal half a dozen linen sacks bulging with gold pieces. Poor Fauxnaster was hard put not to see any of it.

In this room were gathered the taxes levied on a dozen nearby islands, to be paid out again in soldiers' keep, sent home to Berkenland, or, more rarely, spent on public works. Also in evidence was the plunder recovered from pirates, little of which ever found its way back to its previous owners. And, in one niche, the personal valuables of the ranking officers, here for safekeeping. Not even glancing at the chests of gold, Shuma led her teacher toward this niche. "There's one piece I especially want to show you," she said. "It's a necklace that my husband gave me not long after we were married. I never wear it—it's too heavy. But the workmanship should please you."

Fauxnaster banged his shin painfully on one of the chests of gold, and nearly fell. Shuma caught and supported him. "You'll have to be careful," she cautioned. "There's a lot of clutter down near the floor."

"A remarkable place," the blind man said. "One senses a

certain vibratory energy. It's quite distinct. I've never felt anything quite like it before."

"That's the gold, you shriveled-up word-monger. Anybody can feel it. I can feel it. So you still say true wealth is in the mind?"

"I am willing to consider new evidence. It is possible that I might be persuaded to alter my view. This expedition is proving most illuminating. Pray continue—show me your trinkets."

Selecting a small key from a pouch at her waist, Shuma unlocked the doors of a tall wooden cabinet and slid out one of its interior drawers. On black velvet were displayed a dazzling array of costly pieces, central among which was a rather gaudy silver necklace whose variously shaped beads were concatenated in interwoven strands. "Well," Shuma demanded, gesturing with an open palm. "What do you think?"

Pye kept his thoughts to himself. He was thinking that in presenting the jewels to his vision, Shuma had made a bad slip. But the guard seemed to have noticed nothing. Raising his hand toward where he had heard the drawer slide out, Pye groped. "Ah, a number of pieces," he said, running his fingers lightly across them. "Which is the one you were referring to? This one, I fancy." He lifted the silver necklace and let the beads trickle back and forth between his fingers. "Yes, quite nice. Quite nice, I must admit." Two smaller pieces, a ruby ring and a jade pin, were now nestled securely in his sleeve. In setting the necklace back in the tray, he contrived to scoop two more pieces into the other sleeve.

Shuma pulled out three more drawers, one higher than her chin, and pawed through them looking for some special item she just had to show off to her teacher. Pye stepped forward to try, clumsily, to help, and succeeded in treading on her foot. Lurching sideways, the hapless blind man clutched at the tall jewel chest, which swayed forward on two legs, threatening to topple. The corporal stepped forward to right the chest and prevent Lady Borando from being crushed. He succeeded in catching the blind man under one arm while blocking the teetering chest with his other hand, but somehow in the confusion a drawer slid free anyway, spilling precious jewelry all over the cave floor. Then all three were scrambling on hands and knees to pick up the jewels. The private, hearing the commotion, poked his head in the door. "Everything all right?"

"If you could just lend a hand for a moment," Shuma suggested. The lad snapped to obey.

A few minutes earlier, in a building a few tadigs to the west, Vod Penna Osher was explaining to the captain of the guard, a man named Volk, that he could not, much as he regretted it, reveal the source of his information. "You understand, captain. I'm sure you have your own ears here and there around the garrison, whose names you would divulge only with the greatest reluctance. Do you believe you're the only officer so equipped? You'll simply have to take it on my word: The strong-room guards on this shift have been stealing valuables. We must investigate at once, before any further theft can occur."

Captain Volk was a compactly built little man with meticulously trimmed black bangs framing a long rectangular face. He was still wearing the slatted leather breastplate of his uniform, but had taken the shoulder guards off for the evening. Now he picked them up from the bench, lowered them over his head, and tied the thongs with military precision. "Very well," he conceded. "I don't believe a word of it. I know those men. Came out from home on the same ship. But it's got to be checked."

They marched across the compound to the command building and down the long corridor that ran its length. When they turned into the short corridor that led up to the rock wall, the iron doors of the strong room were ajar, and neither guard was in sight. Volk stopped and glared. "I see," he said.

"Perhaps they have merely gone inside to help the paymaster lift something," Osher suggested.

"We'll find out." Volk strode up to the door and through. Osher stopped to take a breath before following.

Inside, he found Volk bowing apologetically to Shuma Borando. The two guards stood by at attention, and Fauxnaster, holding Shuma's elbow lightly, was gazing at a corner of the ceiling and bobbing his head this way and that as he listened

to the newcomers. "My apologies for the interruption, Lady
Borando," Volk said. "Certain accusations have been made that
require immediate attention. Would it be possible for you to
postpone your business here until another time? I must speak
to these two privately."

"What is the matter, Captain?"

"Nothing that you need concern yourself with, Lady Borando. A breach of security."

"Captain." Shuma's voice was sweet, but there was a whip
in it. "I should like some explanation. You spoke of accusations?"

"On Penna Osher's information, these two are accused of
theft."

The two guards exchanged bewildered glances.

"Theft?" Shuma said. "Of things in here? But they seem
like such nice boys. They've just been helping me pick up
some jewels that spilled on the floor."

Volk looked at Osher. "We must search them," he said.

"Agreed. Out in the corridor?"

Volk nodded. "Left, *face*. Forward, *march*." The two officers followed the guards out the door, leaving Shuma and Pye
alone in the strong room.

Pye jerked his head in the direction of the open gold chest
with its bags of coins. "How much in one of those sacks?" he
whispered.

"I'm not sure. Sixty-four, I think."

"You've got to be sure. We can't come up short."

"It's sixty-four."

"How many bags per box?"

"It may vary. Best we open them and count before we carry
them out."

Outside in the corridor, Volk had directed the two guards
to drop their pikes and unbuckle their belts. A soldier's belt
hung eight or ten leather pouches, which might contain anything
from a whetstone to a snack. Osher took one belt, Volk the
other, and they began emptying the pouches into a pile on the
floor. Delving deep into one pouch, Volk grunted and drew out
the ruby ring.

Terror blossomed on the corporal's face. "It's not possible," he protested. "I don't know how it got there. I didn't steal it. I never stole nothin' in my life!"

"Then how do you explain this?" Volk waved the ring under the corporal's nose. "Speak quickly!"

"Look at this." From the private's belt Osher produced a finely wrought gold bracelet. "It's both of them. They're in league."

"You're crazy!" the private said. "Sir. It's that Eloian. He done it. He planted the stuff on us!"

"Best you march these two off to the guardhouse at once, Captain," Osher suggested. "They may be guilty and they may not, but plainly there's meat here for investigation."

"I'll bet he's not blind at all," the private said. "You shine a light in his eye and see if he don't flinch."

"Captain," Osher said coldly. "This man is insulting Lady Borando's teacher, a highly respected philosopher. The idea that such a person might be implicated in a common theft is absurd. Next they'll be accusing Lady Borando herself, and you know how angry she can be when she's insulted. Take them to the guardhouse at once. I'll wait here and guard the strong room myself until another pair can be summoned."

"Yes, sir. But I can't leave those two in there. It's against regulations."

"Come, Captain—a blind philosopher and Commander Borando's wife? What harm can they do?"

"It's regulations, sir. I've got no choice."

Osher wrinkled his mouth in annoyance, noticed that he was doing it, and stopped. "Very well. You're right, of course. Let's get them out and lock the door." He stepped into the strong room. Shuma was sitting on one of the ironbound gold chests. The blind man, standing at her side, was resting one hand lightly on her shoulder. "If you please, my lady. Captain Volk insists that we lock the vault."

"Oh, he does, does he? Do you think I ought to speak to him?"

"I doubt it would do any good, my lady. He seems quite determined."

"It's of no great importance," Fauxnaster said. "We can easily return another time, my lady. Perhaps quite soon."

"You're sure?"

"There are few things in the world of which one may be entirely sure, my lady. I am sure only that we should not keep the other officer waiting needlessly."

They left the strong room, and Volk and Osher locked the door again, each with one key. Osher handed Shuma's key back to her, and Volk tucked his into his belt. "I appreciate your volunteering to stand watch, Penna Osher," Volk said. "We'll have a replacement for these two out here in no time."

"No hurry. I have no plans for the evening. Best you get these two locked up first, and then worry about replacements. But aren't you forgetting something, Captain?"

"I don't think so, sir. What?"

"The key. The other key. I should keep it here, in case somebody needs to get into the strong room before the next shift arrives. I happened to overhear the paymaster saying he might need a sum tonight to cover some sort of emergency."

"Sorry, sir. This is the guard key. Begging your pardon, sir, but you're not a member of the guard. If the paymaster comes, you'll just have to ask him to wait." Volk saluted apologetically, picked up the two fallen pikes, and escorted his charges away.

The footsteps receded. "What are we going to do now?" Osher whispered urgently.

"Patience, patience." Pye had knelt to examine the keyholes. "Give me yours," he said to Shuma, holding out his hand without looking up. She frowned dubiously, but complied. He turned the key over to look at both sides, and tried it in both keyholes to feel the lock's response. Then, from somewhere about his person, he produced a long narrow piece of metal, which he inserted in the proper keyhole and stirred delicately. They watched as the seconds stretched out. "I'm not good at this," Pye whispered apologetically. Almost immediately the lock snicked. Swiftly he inserted Shuma's key and turned it. "We're in," he announced.

Osher stepped forward to help Pye slide the bar. Over his

shoulder he said to Shuma, "Go find Tarag and tell him to bring the cart up." She nodded and slipped away.

"There are sixteen bags in each chest," Pye explained. "We had a look. And Shuma said there were sixty-four in each bag."

"The paymaster oversees the bagging himself."

"Then two thousand is just a little less than two chests." They hoisted one between them and staggered with it toward the door. Once they got their paces matched, they were able to move faster. Osher's shoulder and back muscles cried out under the strain, but there was no time to stop and rest. They turned and went down the long hall. Oil lamps gleamed in the dimness. At the door, finally, they set their burden down. After breathing hard and flexing his shoulders for a moment, Osher opened the door and poked his head out.

Salas Tarag, leaning casually against the side of a sturdy two-wheeled cart with his arms folded on his chest, looked up. "Oh, there you are," he said cheerfully. "What kept you?"

Chapter 15

*I*t was Ashubeleth's habit every morning to inspect the inhabitants of his pens. In his youth it had amused him to gloat over the fact that he was the master of all these unfortunates, and could do with them as he chose. But they were such a dreary lot that the gloating turned gradually to loathing and finally to indifference. He had reached an age at which the slaves were no more than walking sides of meat to him, meat that had to be fed, and got sick far too often, and once in a while fought, and once in a great while actually said something worth listening to. Still, he never gave up the daily tour of inspection. For one thing, it eliminated the embarrassment of putting a lot on the block that was diseased. A diseased slave could be isolated from the others and tended until it was well enough to be sold or, if incurably ill, given its freedom to wander off and die in the street. The inspections also kept his keepers reasonably honest. They were brutal men, and would think nothing of withholding food from a lot that had caused them trouble so as to sell it elsewhere and pocket the money. An underfed slave was as useless as a sick one, Ashubeleth had found. They looked bad on the block, and brought little. Some few of the keepers had crueler tricks they liked to practice; Ashubeleth knew who those were, and what the tricks were, and saw to it that no irreparable injury was done. Getting

220

rid of the cruel ones was no use. The ones hired to replace them might easily be worse, and might not be found out before they had damaged valuable merchandise.

At an hour when Salas Tarag was still poking fruitlessly through Habil Metterner's basement, Ashubeleth's morning tour of inspection was interrupted. He had just finished in the long shed and emerged in the brilliant sunlight. Brugo and Velch flanked him—the pens were not a safe place for a fat old man by himself, especially if he was well hated, which he was, and Ashubeleth was no longer indifferent to danger. Breathing meant a lot to him—especially as it required constant effort. Just ahead were the punishment pens, iron boxes too small for a man inside to stretch out to his full height, ventilated only by a few narrow slots. In the open exercise yard the boxes got the full benefit of the naked sun. A defiant northerner had had to be put in one a few days before. Eventually he had gone crazy, and screamed all day long, and bitten his own limbs bloody. Ashubeleth had taken a loss on him. Currently, the punishment boxes were empty. Before he could proceed past them to the stockade, his attention was arrested by an approaching stranger, an ill-clad, skinny man with a large hooked nose, long unkempt black hair, and a crooked silver scar descending from one eye. The man sidled forward deferentially, stopped at a suitable distance, and dipped his head in a stiff bow. "Beggin' your pardon, sar," he began, "but might you be in the market for rare goods?" He attempted a conspiratorial leer, but it fell rather flat.

Ashubeleth wheezed. His first thought was to have Brugo and Velch drag the creature away. But slaving held little enough anymore that was of any interest. It was remotely possible that what was being called rare goods might be exactly that. "What sort of rare goods?" he asked.

"You know what a lilith is?"

"Of course."

"What would you say if I told you I got a lilith for sale?" The man rubbed his bony hands together.

"I'd say you were drunk."

"Not I. By Tha I swear." The man clasped his left shoulder with his right hand in a ritual gesture.

"Save your oaths. You'd lie to Tha as soon as to me. And spare me your guessing games. If you don't want your elbows broken, explain how you came by whoever you've got, and how you arrived at the idiot notion it's a lilith." Ashubeleth planted his stout legs in the dust and regarded the skinny man sourly.

"All right, I'll tell. Just don't hurt me. Night before last, me and me chum was on the dock, see? And we seen a ship land. It was a Vli ship. And on it was somebody *robed like a priestess*, who come ashore. Then last night we finds this one wanderin' the streets, wearin' a long robe, and she says she's Vli. So me and me chum thought what to do, and we clobbered her." The skinny man leaned closer. "Once we got a look, we knew. It's a lilith, all right. Bulon take me if I ever seen anythin' like it. Goes out and goes in, all at the same time." He giggled.

"She told you she was Vli? And she's of noble birth?"

"Aye. Aye."

"Probably just a deformity." But if the captive was of noble birth, Ashubeleth saw, she might be worth money in any case. "Where have you got her?"

"Now, not so fast, old man. Me and me chum would like to be paid for our trouble."

"I'll give you five gold pieces. *If* it's a lilith. If it's not, perhaps two, perhaps nothing."

The scar-faced man worked his tongue around in his mouth. "I was thinkin' more like twenty-five."

"Ten."

"Twenty."

"Ten."

The man chewed on his lip. "Fifteen. That's eight for me and seven for me chum."

"Twelve. That's six for each of you. But only if it's what you say it is. Bring it to my showroom. Just off the main block."

"How do I know you don't mean to take her and cheat me out of my money?"

Ashubeleth looked at the beggar with utter contempt. "I wouldn't stoop that low," he said. "You're the one trying to make a sale. Bring her or don't, as you choose." He turned and waddled off, swinging wide around the scar-faced man so as not to have to smell him.

Inspection tour abandoned, Ashubeleth went straight back to his office and sat brooding. A lilith in Falnerescu? Why? The world was changing, and too rapidly to suit him. Slave revolts, taxes and regulations, and respectable people doing things they never would have done when he was a boy. Doubtless the Vli were changing too. Before long the wogglies would swarm up out of the south and begin breeding their parasitic pets to sell to prosperous householders, and everybody would sit around in a happy stupor with the disgusting little creatures glued to their shoulders, and nobody would be buying slaves at all. Ashubeleth shuddered. He was getting old. His bones ached.

He was still sunk in that mood when Brugo opened the door to admit the tall skinny man and his shorter, scruffier companion. Between them they were carrying the shoulders and ankles of an unconscious figure clad in a ripped and stained gray robe. Above one eye was a swollen purple welt. The two men slung their burden onto the floor, and the scar-faced man jerked the robe up above the lilith's waist. "Take a look," he offered.

Ashubeleth levered himself with difficulty to his feet, and stalked around the table. Not being built to stoop, he stood staring for quite some time at Zhenuvnili's genitals. These were unlike anything he had ever seen, though they showed no sign of disease or surgical mutilation. He had heard that the Vli were three-sexed, and scoffed at the idea, but there before him was proof. He had also heard that the liliths were beautiful. Zhenuvnili's skin was smooth, her bone structure fine, but at the moment she was not beautiful. Her head sagged sideways, and saliva from her open mouth had puddled on the floor. Ashubeleth beckoned Velch forward and pointed to the swelling and discoloration at her temple. "How bad is it?"

Velch knelt and pressed his fingers gently against the contusion. Then he lifted both of the lilith's eyelids, one with each thumb, to look at her pupils. Last he felt the pulse at her neck. He shrugged. "I'd guess she'll live."

Ashubeleth picked up a purse from the table. "You didn't say you'd injured her so badly," he said to the beggars. "For this I can pay only ten, not twelve."

"You said twelve," the scar-faced man said with some bitterness.

Ashubeleth regarded him sourly. "Very well. I said I wouldn't cheat you, and I won't. But if she dies, you'll pay me the twelve back, and another twelve besides, or find yourselves picking suckers off of your legs, papers or no papers. Are those terms agreeable?"

"Yeah, yeah, we'll take it. She ain't hurt. Yer own man said so."

Ashubeleth held the small pouch out at arm's length by its drawstring, and the man greedily snatched it away. He poured the coins out in his palm and counted them, his lips moving. "All right," he said. "It's here, right enough."

"Get out of here." Ashubeleth scowled at the two beggars as they backed, bowing compulsively, from the room. When they were gone, he turned to Velch. "Put her in a private pen. The less word gets around, the better chance we have of keeping her hidden until we learn which way the tide is running. If she regains consciousness, see to it I'm told at once." Velch got his arms under Zhenuvnili's and dragged her out of the room, and Ashubeleth went back to sit behind the table and think. His earlier gloom had evaporated. Now that he was certain of the nature of his acquisition, he had to work out what to do with her. The question was stimulating; rather to his own surprise, he found he was enjoying considering it. Perhaps she had been worth twelve gold, even if she provided no more than that diversion, even if she died without waking or could not be disposed of and had to be killed. The legal situation was the main source of difficulty. According to Falneresc law, a slave was not a slave unless the owner could produce proper documents, or unless, in the absence of documents, the slave had been registered as such with the governor's office and could produce no proof of manumission. Ashubeleth could easily forge a bill of sale to show how he had acquired Zhenuvnili, but he couldn't sell her again without a bill of entitlement. A bill of entitlement required the governor's seal, and if he took her before Chespid, Chespid would certainly ask her where she had come from and how she had come to land in the pens. In some parts of the Island Sea such legal questions would not have arisen, but Falnerescu was a civilized community. Selling a black-market slave was something one could get a hand lopped off for. A slaver could lose his license as well, and with it his livelihood and property, which the governor would be only too happy to confiscate. Still, that was preferable to the penalty for forging a bill of entitlement, which was death by flogging. Everything considered, the prospect of being caught trying to sell the lilith did not appeal to Ashubeleth at all. But he couldn't very well keep her; word spread like fire through the pens— and besides, he was offended at the thought of paying good money and getting none in return. Obviously he would have to sell her and avoid getting caught. The simplest course would be to find out where she had come from. If somebody had gone to the trouble of bringing her out from Vli Holm, surely they would be willing to pay to get her back. When she woke up, he could question her, learn which of the Vli in the city she had been visiting. But could he approach the Vli openly? No— they might easily denounce him to Chespid and get her back free of cost, while costing Ashubeleth all he had. Sell her to a private bidder, then? He knew a few whose tastes might run in that direction.

The arrival of the man claiming—a transparent lie—to be a Vli named Ranga Strell changed matters somewhat. Naturally, Ashubeleth denied knowing anything about any lilith. Just as naturally, he assumed that "Strell" and his companion meant to betray him for selling illegally. But still he was glad they had come—at least he had a bidder. And two thousand was far more than he had hoped for, nearly enough to make him greedy. All he had to do was take their money without letting himself be trapped.

He guessed at first that his visitors had been sent by Nule

Chespid. If anybody knew what a lilith was doing in Falnerescu, it would be Chespid. And the governor, chronically short of funds, would jump at an excuse to revoke a prosperous slaver's license and seize his pens. It was even possible that Chespid had sent the beggars to bring the lilith here solely as a plot to trip him up. But when Brugo returned to report that the dark-skinned man and the Eloian had been seen in the company of a Berkender officer, Ashubeleth had to reconsider. What was the Berkenders' interest in the affair? If they were financing the purchase, could they be relied on to wink at the local laws and abide by an agreement, or were they planning treachery? Was his best course perhaps to send word to the merchant Habil Metterner, whom "Strell" had mentioned, even if it meant parting with his captive for far less gold, so as to have her off his premises when the Berkenders arrived? Or would that be making a bad bargain? Ashubeleth saw that he was adrift in shallow waters. He needed more information, and he needed it quickly. Better, he needed an ally, somebody who could pilot him around the shoals in exchange for a portion of the gold.

In other words, he needed to talk to Nule Chespid.

He hated going to see Chespid, because it meant climbing stairs. He was never entirely sure he was going to make it to the top. As always, he had to rest after every step in the last flight, with Velch supporting him. They were announced and admitted by the flunky in the green velvet knickers, then the latter and Velch ceremoniously withdrew, leaving Ashubeleth standing gasping like a huge beached bladder-fish. The governor, too agitated to maintain his usual theatrical arrangement, had abandoned his elevated chair to pace up and down in the audience-chamber, stopping at one end of the path to glare morosely out the leaded glass window at the harbor. For a time he neglected to acknowledge Ashubeleth's presence, partly to assert his dominance and partly to allow his guest time to recover. But at last he stopped pacing, and clasped his hideous hands behind him. "Well. What brings you all this way?"

"I wanted to—breathe some clean—air, Excellency." Ashubeleth's thick lips were still slightly blue.

"To be sure. Pardon me if I'm not amused by witticisms."

"You seem—disturbed, Excellency. Is something wrong?"

"Wrong? Of course not. Only the usual. Two escaped prisoners, an attempted lynching, a kidnapping, a bunch of dead mnoerri that nobody seems able to explain, and, according to a report I just had, a ranking Berkender officer who's gone mad and is rampaging about the city barging into people's homes with a detachment of soldiers. Just a typical day. I suppose you've come to tell me there's been an outbreak of black spot fever in the pens."

"The slaves are in monotonously—good health, Excellency." Already Ashubeleth had guessed a good deal. The kidnapping victim must be the lilith. And the Berkender could only be the one Brugo had seen. But what did that jumble of facts add up to?

"Good. Then it can't be important. Come back tomorrow."

"At my age, Excellency, one such climb in an aptarne is taxing. Two would kill me."

"Well, then, go on." Chespid resumed his pacing. He was wondering why he had ever sought this post.

"You will forgive me, Excellency. I must sit down." Ashubeleth created an interval in which to think, but it did him no good. The situation was too complex to grasp. To gain a little more time, he diverted the conversation in the direction of the irrelevant. "You spoke of escaped prisoners. If they're anything like escaped slaves, they're Skavish himself to find, once they're loose in the city."

"Oh, this one won't get far. I've impounded his ship. You haven't said why you came."

"I thought I saw the possibility of a profit that we might share. But I'm beginning to suspect that there might be complications."

"A profit? How much?" The little man's expression was avid.

"First, your assurance that the seal won't be revoked."

"That depends on what you've done, and what you're planning. I can't offer you blanket amnesty. But knowing you, you've not been drilling holes in the bottoms of ships. I imagine we can reach some accord. Now what is it you've got your teeth into? And how much is it worth?"

"What if it meant crossing the Berkenders?"

Chespid eyed his guest. "Naturally, I would do nothing to oppose the Berkenders."

"Naturally."

"Still," he went on, "their concerns are far-flung, while mine are purely local. There are many matters on which it's not necessary to consult them."

"It may not be that simple," Ashubeleth said.

Chespid brought out one of his hands to rub the finger along the side of his nose. "How much?"

"A thousand. Five hundred for each of us." No point in being too generous.

"Gold?"

"Gold."

"You intrigue me. For five hundred there are risks I'd be willing to take, though I'd want to be absolutely certain no word would leak back to Borando."

"That goes without saying," Ashubeleth said.

"It may go without saying, but it bears repeating. I'm sure you realize how unpleasant I could make life for you, if there were a slip-up. Now what have you got? What do you need me to do that's worth five hundred to you?"

It was Ashubeleth's turn to weigh a question. "I'm not sure yet," he said. "The situation is complex."

"Then I suggest you tell me the details and let me see the complexities for myself."

"Ah, but I don't know the details," the fat man said. "And you do. You're the one who ought to begin. After all, I'm the one who's offering money."

"My dear Ashel, what makes you think I know anything that would bear on this scheme of yours?"

"You spoke of a kidnapping."

"So I did. Have you got any information about that?"

Ashubeleth shrugged. "How will I know, until I know who was kidnapped? Of course, if you feel you must remain silent,

I have no way to compel you. Having rested, I feel sure I can get this bag of guts back down the stairs without further trouble."

"*If* I decide to let you go."

The two glared at one another.

"I *could* have you whipped," Chespid pointed out.

"Useless. It would only kill me, and you'd be none the wiser. I would suggest, Excellency, that at this moment there is very little that I can do to hurt you, whereas you might easily find a way to turn my tale against me. If we're to work together to our mutual profit, we had better do so as equals. And we will only be equals when I know all that you know. You wouldn't have humored me this far if you didn't suspect that I have something you want. So tell me: What is it you want? What is it I've got? And I don't mean the gold. Tell me."

Chespid rarely let himself be put in this position, but he could see that the old man could not be budged, and the promise of gold was awfully tempting. "Oh, very well. I'll empty the bag. But afterward you do likewise, or I'll see you live to regret it." He began by telling of Osher's concern for the lilith's safety, and how they had been interrupted by the Vli with their captured kidnapper. He explained how Tarag had mysteriously escaped from the dungeon, only to reappear with Osher at the Vli mansion that very morning. "I'm wondering whether the Berks haven't got agents among my jailers," he finished, "to get this Tarag out so quickly. I'm also wondering what their game is. I'm tempted to think they arranged the kidnapping themselves, to scuttle the treaty. If so, they may mean to put the blame on me somehow. And I don't mean to let them. But it seems things haven't gone entirely according to their plan, if you're about to say what I think you are. You've got her in your pens, haven't you? Don't balk. As you pointed out a moment ago, if we're to work together, we'll have to be frank."

So Ashubeleth told how the scar-faced beggar had offered him the lilith, and how little he had paid—they both had a laugh over that—and how a dark-skinned, bearded man who could only be Salas Tarag had arrived soon after and agreed to pay a thousand gold for her. He finished with Brugo's report of whom Tarag had gone straight to meet.

Chespid nodded thoughtfully. "You don't suppose those beggars of yours were in the pay of the Berks as well? They might mean to drag you down along with me."

Ashubeleth shrugged. "I can't see it matters. The question is what we're to do now. I've never liked foreigners," he added, half to himself. Ashubeleth and Chespid had in common that their ancestry, though highborn in the one case and marsh-poor in the other, was Falneresc for many generations.

"I can't think Borando's behind this," Chespid said. "He hasn't the wit. It's Osher's game. He drags this fellow Tarag into it and puts him in charge of the kidnapping, to keep his own hands clean. Don't think I missed it yesterday when Tarag slipped and implicated him. Tarag's accomplice, this scar-face, sells her to you. Then Osher deliberately alienates the Vli by forcing his way into their house. I'd say he's probably a member of a faction that opposes the treaty. That would explain it. When you try to sell the creature to Tarag, he means to burst in with his men, seize her, and have you arrested."

"Aye. Aye."

"Once he gets her, he'll find an excuse not to give her back to the Vli. Claim she's seeking asylum, or something. And he'll certainly kill Tarag, to keep him from giving the game away. What bothers me is that if I were Osher, I wouldn't bring any gold down to your showroom at all. I'd march in and arrest you at once, once I knew you'd received the lilith."

"But he didn't," Ashubeleth pointed out. "He sent an agent. Why, do you suppose? He must want her alive. He must know that I would know she's illegal and would kill her before I'd let her be found. Yes, he wants me to bring her forward alive. But I've already told him, through his messenger, that there'll be no lilith until there's gold. So he'll have to bring gold."

"That has such a nice sound," Chespid said appreciatively. "But I am wondering where he's going to get it. He's only fifth in command, and from what I understand, he doesn't have a key to the strong room. Of course, there are ways into strong rooms. Let's say he steals it, gives it to Tarag to hand over to you, and as soon as the lilith is in his hands he marches in and seizes it back again. He's got the lilith, and the gold, and in the bargain he's got you for selling an illegal."

"You can see why I felt it wise to come to you." Ashubeleth opened his eyes wide and blinked amiably at Chespid. The conversation was turning out very nicely.

"Yes. Well, an honest merchant has nothing to fear in this city. He pays taxes, and he buys protection. If the Berks are up to something underhanded, and plainly they are, I'll not stand idle. There may be steps we can take to stop them."

"Please. Don't mention steps."

"Sorry."

"It's difficult, you see," Ashubeleth said. "There is the testimony of witnesses who might be brought against us. This Tarag will testify to the transaction, and the lilith that she was in my pens."

"That only affects you," Chespid said. "Not me."

"But if I were brought to trial, I would have to tell what had become of the gold. Knowing you, you'd see to it I was never brought to trial. But that won't do. I won't go along unless we can find a scheme whereby I'm as safe as you. And I fear that means we have to kill both Tarag and the lilith."

"We have to repay treachery, you mean. There may be a way to catch Osher in our net, as well. But let's you and I understand one another. If there's murder to be done, I'll not do it alone."

"Nor will I."

"Then we'll do it together, and neither of us can be called to account. Your part is to kill Tarag," Chespid said. "I'll see to Osher and his men."

"How do you propose to do that? You can't order your men to attack his. That'd be war."

Chespid smiled humorlessly. "You don't think I'd risk war, do you? I know an Olmalinese wizard who knows a trick or two."

Ashubeleth snorted. "Surely you don't mean to trust to a hex. That's as good as putting your head on the block."

"This wizard has something better than a hex. It will work. I've seen it work."

"Tell me what it is, then, if you want me to go along. I don't trust wizards."

Chespid told him. "It will cost us fifty each," he finished.

"You'll have to tell me who this wizard is," Ashubeleth said. "I might find a use for such a spell."

"Come now, Ashel. You don't expect me to share all my secrets, do you? If you've occasion to use the man's skills, you can reach him through me."

"There's one other matter. What are we to do with the lilith? Kill her as well?"

Chespid said, "Not unless she promises to make trouble. I might find a use for her."

"Then you mean to buy her from me?"

"Perhaps. If the price is within my means. If not, doubtless you can unload her elsewhere."

"Doubtless. Then we're agreed."

"Aye. You can bring me my five hundred fifty in the morning. See you're not delayed. And don't let that Tarag fellow give you the slip. I want him dead."

"Never fear." Ashubeleth set the heels of his hands on his knees and ponderously rose. He saw how easy it would be for Chespid to do nothing and let him fall into the hands of the Berkenders. But he also knew how badly Chespid would like five hundred gold, and it seemed highly unlikely that the Berkenders would pay more than that merely to ruin the career of one fat, elderly slave-dealer. His was the high bid. The whole affair was proving most satisfactory. The lilith, as he had guessed, was worth the price he had paid. He had not felt this much excitement in a long time. His fingertips tingled. Such an adventure would never come his way again. If it meant a death or two, what matter? Death was no stranger in the pens. He made his farewell and lumbered heavily from the room.

Chapter 16

Gold being gold, moving it from one place to another is troublesome. They got the first chest into the cart, and went back into the strong room for the second while Shuma stood guard. Pye stayed behind to bar the door again while Osher and Tarag strained their muscles. They got the chest loaded, and Pye slipped out the door to join them.

"Thank you, Lady Borando," Tarag said, "for your most gracious assistance."

"You don't think you're going off without me, do you?" she said sweetly.

"This is a difficult and dangerous situation," Tarag pointed out. "Surely you'd rather stay here, where you'll be safe."

"I seem to recall that it was my safety that concerned you so this morning, when you went off to the swamps. And you've got a great deal of gold here. Would you like me to let out a yell right now? Tarag, darling, do you have any *idea* how many young bucks would come charging to my defense? Don't make a fuss. Just let's go on to the gate together, like civilized people. I've decided it's about time I found out what this lilith creature of yours is really like."

Arguing with her would take too long. Tarag shrugged, and Osher shrugged, and Pye shrugged. Tarag and Pye picked up the traces of the cart, and Shuma, smiling regally, descended

233

the wooden stairs and seated herself on the chests of gold in the cart, where she reclined in comfort. "Drive on," she commanded airily.

Osher had a detachment waiting. He strode off with only a veiled glance backward at Shuma. Tarag and Pye leaned into the traces, and the wheels and the axle creaked. They were nearing the gate when a column of soldiers emerged from between two barracks buildings and took up position behind the cart, slowing to half-pace so as not to overtake it.

"You don't suppose they'd like to lend a hand," Tarag muttered.

"Oh, hush," Shuma said. "This is for your own good, Tarag. You're getting far too lazy. Always expecting other people to do your work for you."

The accuracy of the barb stung Tarag. "All right," he said over his shoulder. "That's one for me, and one for you."

"Then we'll have to break the tie, won't we?"

It was full night by now, the stars profuse overhead, and Nardis was in the east and Cheth in the west. The gate was closed, and six guards were there to meet them. Tarag and Pye halted, and Shuma sat up in the cart and waved her arm. "Open," she said pleasantly.

The sergeant-of-guard came forward. "If you'll forgive me, my lady. I would not impose, if my orders did not require it. May I inquire what errand takes you out at this time of night, and in such company as this?"

"These are my paum. We mean to take in a tavern or two this evening. I'm concerned about rioting slaves, after last night, so I'm taking along an armed guard. And if that is any business of yours, you'll find yourself posted among the Worogikh Islands. I'm told the swamp-suckers there are exceptionally venomous. And prone to crawl into the barracks at night. But if you'd rather stand here discussing it, by all means, let's."

The sergeant blanched. Turning on his heel, he commanded that the gate be opened, and the thick ironbound beams lurched and ground their way to one side. Standing beside Tarag, the sergeant said out of the side of his mouth, "Just between you and me, pal, what's goin' on here?"

"Well, just between you and me," Tarag explained, "my friend and I have worked out this marvelous way to steal two-wheeled carts. First we enlist the aid of the commander's wife, and then, just to be safe, we borrow sixteen or seventeen armed men, with a ranking officer to command them, and we make sure to leave the fortress not by day but by night, when questions are sure to be asked—"

"Never mind," the sergeant said. "I don't want to know about it."

The gate slid back, and Tarag and Pye dragged the cart out into the night. The detachment fell in behind them. When they had passed safely under the portal, Tarag spoke. "We couldn't have done it without you, Shuma. I kneel at your feet."

"Just keep pulling. You'll have plenty of time to kneel later. And I'll see to it that you do. Somebody's got to teach you humility; you've become convinced you can get away with anything."

A meteor streaked brilliantly across the western sky.

"I'll be satisfied if I can get my ship back. I'd not ask for more than that."

"Oh, come now. Don't tell me you wouldn't run off with this gold if the opportunity presented itself."

"The gold will be back in your strong room before morning my lady, never fear."

"So it's your gold," Shuma said haughtily, "that you're promising where it will be, and when? That's what I mean about humility. You're not modest. Also, you're a liar. You'd say anything, absolutely anything, if you thought it would help you gain your ends. I wouldn't be in the least surprised to learn that you'd cooked this whole lilith business up yourself, just to have an excuse to steal our gold. There may not even *be* a lilith. Who's seen her? Nobody's seen her."

"That's because she vanished."

"So *you* say."

The road rose and fell over the hummocks in the marsh. One slope proved too steep for Tarag and Pye to manage unaided, and Osher had to order three soldiers forward to push the cart from behind. But at the top it began to roll under its own weight, and Tarag and Pye could do nothing but trot before it as it picked up speed. Shuma squealed. "Do something! Slow it down!" The next low spot was one of the sections paved with brickwork, and the wheels hit the raised edge with a jar that nearly threw her from her perch. "You did that deliberately, Tarag," she fumed as they wrestled the cart to a halt. "You were trying to throw me off so you could run off with the money."

"Where would I go with it?" Tarag asked reasonably. All around them was a maze of moonlit marsh, tall clumps of grass and squelchy bog that could swallow a cart and leave only bubbles. For a moment they all fell silent, feeling as one the desolate strangeness of the marsh and the immensity of the star-clotted sky overhead. Looking up into the vastness, Tarag heard again the voice of the oar who had told the tale of the weltwood: "We're still out there." Could the myths be true? Had humanity come to this world from another, and been marooned here? Were whole worlds no more than islands in a greater Sea? If so, and if he could find a way to make a distance-glass, perhaps he could see those other worlds! He must find a chance to try it.

The mood broke as the detachment trotted down the hill to join them. Shuma wriggled her bottom uncomfortably on the ironbound chest. "Hmp. If you weren't trying to throw me off, you were trying to humiliate me, and that's just as bad. Well, what are you waiting for? Drive on."

They resumed their laborious progress. After a while Shuma spoke again. "Tell me, what's the plan? How are we to ransom this creature?"

"She's in the hands of a fat old slaver named Ashubeleth. We're to meet him at his showroom and make the exchange."

"I've met him. A thoroughly repulsive person. I take it you're sure he's got her."

"He's got her."

"Did he let you see her? Or are you going by his word?"

"Actually, he swore he'd never heard of any such person."

Shuma sat bolt upright. "He *what*? Tarag, you're playing me for an idiot. This is another one of your tricks."

"No trick. By Amera. Look at it from his position. He can't admit to having an illegal slave. But without admitting it, he manages to fix a price. Can there be any doubt?"

"And when we get there she'll have conveniently fallen into his hands through the intercession of the gods. Very neat. But he's still taking a risk in selling her illegally."

"We can be sure he's aware of that. But the price makes it worth the risk. And remember, he thinks I'm a Vli named Ranga Strell, whose only concern is to return the lilith to her people. He won't be expecting treachery—least of all a detachment of armed men come to take his gold from him. Crossing him will be so simple, I'm almost embarrassed to be a party to it. It's too crude. It lacks finesse."

They were entering the outskirts of the city, and Tarag and Pye were breathing hard from their exertions. But Shuma showed no inclination to get down and walk. "How can you be certain he doesn't mean to cross you, and take the gold without delivering the lilith?" she asked.

"If he tries it, we'll be no worse off than we are now. You and Osher simply march in and take back the gold, we search his pens, and if she's not there we think of someplace else to look."

"I suppose you're right—all except the part about my marching in with Osher. I'm going in with you. I'm not letting the gold out of my sight."

"That won't work," Tarag said. "You said you've met Ashubeleth. But even if he doesn't recognize you as Jakul Borando's wife, he'll see you're a Berkender by your fingers. Do you suppose he'll break the law in your presence? You'll have to trust me to make the exchange."

"I wouldn't trust you to give coppers to a beggar without pocketing a few for yourself."

"Then why have you come this far? In truth, you do trust me. You know we'll have to play it just as I've said. You only want to insult me because you're still angry at me. And anger is a poor reason to steer us onto a rock, after all the trouble we've been to."

"You are infuriating, Tarag. But you may be right. I want to talk to Osher. Stop the cart."

Glad of the chance to rest, they did as they were bidden. Shuma hopped down and strode back to the column of soldiers, where she drew Osher aside for a whispered conference. To Tarag, Pye said, "Ashubeleth may not be as easily duped as you let her believe."

"I know. He's a sly one. We'll have to be ready to jump."

"I wish I had a dagger," Pye said. "Normally I detest the things, but if there was ever a man who'd kill for gold and think nothing of it, Ashubeleth is the man."

"We could ask Osher to lend us weapons. But I'm afraid that would add fuel to Shuma's fire. Anyway, we'll be safe enough with a force that size at our backs."

"Don't use your persuasion on me. I know the danger as well as you."

"Then send a prayer Amera's way. That's what I'm doing. You're right about the danger. But we've no choice. If we try to back out now, Osher's men will collar us, and that'll be the end of the game. Our only hope is to get the lilith and let Osher deal with Ashubeleth."

"I dislike looking to a Berkender for protection."

"True. We'll have to look to ourselves."

Shuma came back and ordered them to march on—but mercifully, she was content to walk now, so they made better time. Still, it was a long way from the edge of the warehouse district around the fortress to the pens. The night traffic was light. A few passersby stared at the procession momentarily before slipping away into the shadows; too much curiosity about soldiers marching by night might be unhealthy. Tarag was weighing his options. Charting a course through such a morass would take all his skill. Could he even count on Pye? Also, the gold was getting damned heavy, and the lurching of the cart on the cobbles was giving him blisters. Too many years since he had bent oar.

When they had approached within a street of the main slave

block, Tarag guided the wagon over to the wall of the nearest building. Setting the traces down, he stepped out and beckoned to Osher and Shuma. "I'm going to take a look," he said. "Stay here." He crept stealthily forward to the corner of the building and, crouching, peered out. The barn door of Ashubeleth's showroom was a yellow square yawning on the night. The open space before the auction block was entirely empty. He scanned the roofs. Silence, thick, everywhere. That a single wizard lurking nearby might have a weapon that could overpower sixteen armed men never occurred to him. He crept back to the others and nodded. "They're waiting. Pye and I will take the cart forward to the middle of the square. He'll wait there with it while I go inside. When they've shown me the lilith, I'll come to the door and call him in. If there's any treachery, the gold will be out in the open where you can get to it quickly. The risk will be mine. Satisfactory?"

Osher nodded. "We'll need a signal when we're to move."

"At the first sign of trouble, come up fast. I don't want to get butchered any more than you do. If all goes well, we'll signal." He turned to Pye. "Can you whistle? Good. Pye will whistle like this when it's time for you to attack." Pye whistled softly: long, short-long—long, short-long. "If there's trouble," Tarag went on, "he'll whistle like this." Pye warbled a long rising note. "If you hear nothing after the money goes in, you," Tarag said to Osher, "go forward and have a look. Leave your men back till you've seen what's to be seen. They're far too noisy. Show him the signals again." Pye did so. "Also, see you don't let them show themselves in the square till they move. The moonlight off that armor shines clear as day."

"We know how to conduct a campaign," Osher said stiffly. "And I'm warning you, this had better work. You've had all the leniency and cooperation you're going to get."

"We're all in the Goddess's hands, my friend." There did not seem to be much else that needed saying, so Tarag turned and walked back to the cart. He and Pye raised the traces and pulled it creaking out into the open. The wheels rattled across the uneven pavement.

Midway across the square Tarag stepped aside while Pye

slipped between the traces and took one in each hand. Tarag gripped his friend's shoulder. "Amera willing, tomorrow night we'll be sitting in a tavern boasting of this and getting stinking drunk."

"A boastful thief is a short-lived thief."

"Well, I'll not take the credit when you deserve it. This has been your game from the beginning. You're a true friend, and I thank you."

"There are not many folk I'd have come this far with. It's curious. But when you no longer know anything about property, you find that friendship has a greater worth than ever you suspected."

"Aye. And just now it's time to befriend a lilith." Squaring his shoulders, Tarag turned and marched across the moonlit square toward the open showroom door. The night air was cool and still. His knees were watery. He kept walking. Framed by the big doorway he paused and looked left and right in the barn. The double tier of cages lining the walls had been emptied for the night, the unsold slaves taken back to the shed or the stockade. Only their odor lingered. Three torches were set in sockets along the catwalk. Nobody was visible, but the room did not feel empty. "Ho!" he called. "Ho, Ashubeleth!"

From a dark alcove floated a dry chuckle. Ashubeleth stepped forward, seemingly fatter and slower-moving than he had been that afternoon, supported at one elbow by the silent muscular presence of Brugo. Though Brugo was aiding Ashubeleth, his attention was fixed on Tarag. He did not look friendly.

"So," Ashubeleth said. "Friend Strell has returned. Admirable. I have told our Zhenuvnili to expect you. But you haven't brought the money. Were you unable to raise it?"

"It will be brought in when I've seen she's all right."

"Oh. Oh, that. A mere detail. Velch?"

An iron door scraped as it slid sideways, and the lilith, writhing as she fought the hands that held her, was wrestled into the torchlight by the slaver's man. Her long dark hair hung loose in a tangle around her face, and bits of straw clung to her robe. But before Tarag she fell still, and the terror in her eyes gave way to confusion. "You're not Ranga Strell," she said.

Tarag put a finger to his lips. "I'm here to get you out. We'll talk later." Inwardly he was exulting. Her reaction left no doubt about her identity. But it was too soon to congratulate himself. The danger was far from past. He addressed the fat old man. "My scribe is waiting outside with the money. Let us step out into the square to make the exchange."

Ashubeleth ponderously shook his head. "Too many eyes in the shadows. Call him in. We'll do our trading here."

The request was not unexpected, but something about the big silent barn made Tarag uneasy. He gauged whether he could simply snatch the lilith from Velch and run. But he was out-muscled, and Zhenuvnili did not look as if she was up to running. Her eyes were imploring, but still uncertain; she did not know him, and might not even be willing to run with him. Better to let the old man have a look at the gold, and grab the lilith while the others were distracted. "All right. I can see she's been shamefully treated. You ought to knock off a few hundred for that."

"She arrived here in this condition. You insult me. If you don't want the price to go up, call your man and let's get on with it."

Tarag went back to the doorway and beckoned to Pye. The cart came rattling forward, and Tarag stepped aside to let it pass.

Ashubeleth raised his hand and gave a signal, and the massive wooden door fell from the rafters on its ropes and landed with a booming crash, completely blocking the exit. Tarag spun and stared, and saw that the trap had been sprung. He would have to play for a delay, to give Osher and his men time to force entrance.

"I suppose you mean to keep the money and the lilith too."

"Something like that," Ashubeleth replied.

"I knew you drove a hard bargain. I didn't know you were a thief."

"Before you begin flinging accusations, you might explain

how you happened to come here in the company of a Berkender detachment, friend Strell. Or should I call you Salas Tarag?"

So he knew! "You'll not get away with this," Tarag threatened. "If you value your life, you'll let us go in peace."

Ashubeleth's laughter was drowned by a loud *whump* from outside, closely followed by a second and a third. Somewhere nearby a man began shrieking, a hideous raw sound that went on and on. "You needn't bother looking to your friends for help," the slaver said. "I fancy they've been dealt with."

Zhenuvnili gasped. Looking where she was looking, Tarag saw that two more of Ashubeleth's men had been lying concealed on the catwalk that led around the upper tier of cages. Now they were standing, looking down at the group gathered around the cart. Each bore a naked sword.

"You can have the gold," Tarag said hurriedly. "I'll answer to the Berkenders for it. Only let these two go. They've done you no wrong."

"You think I'm a fool. You're beginning to annoy me."

The two swordsmen were coming down the narrow stairway to the floor. Tarag looked around wildly. There must be a mechanism for raising the door, but operating it would take far too long, even if he knew where it was. They needed weapons. But the barn was bare—a sensible precaution when slaves were being led in and out. There was only one hope. "Torches!" he snapped. Not waiting to see if Pye had understood, he leaped for the nearest torch and tore it from its mounting. He was only a little ahead of the first swordsman, who rushed at him with raised blade. But that little was enough. He swung the torch between himself and the attacker, blocked the falling stroke, and slid the flaming oil-soaked wad inward toward the man's face. The face was handsome in a coarse way, and the teeth were bared in a snarl. The man pushed Tarag off, and the two circled warily, half crouching, each looking for an opening to strike. Tarag risked a sideways glance and saw that Pye, also armed with a torch, was keeping the cart between himself and his much larger attacker. Shadows in the dim barn danced as the torches shifted.

A torch, Tarag knew, was a poor weapon. The wood would

quickly splinter under a sword, and the flaming wad might easily come loose and fall. Without fire, it would do nothing to deter an attacker. Unless some other resource were to hand, he and Pye would be dead within seconds. Tarag's opponent was pressing him backward, leaving him no time to look back to check his footing. He tried to remember what he had glimpsed down this way. And remembered. And had an idea. But before he could put it into operation, there was an interruption. Pye had been easily eluding his adversary by scrambling up across the laden cart, leaping, ducking, and in general manifesting an inexhaustible agility—all without striking a single blow. Ashubeleth, growing exasperated, said to Velch, "Go help him, idiot. I'll hold the freak." Zhenuvnili found herself transferred to the far less taxing grip of the old slaver. She did not know who the two foreigners were, nor what their intentions might be. So far, nobody in this city had been very friendly. By aiding them she might only be buying worse trouble. But they had come here unarmed, and they were in grave danger. She cast her lot. Swinging around suddenly, she drove the heel of her hand hard into Ashubeleth's chin. The old man gawked, and swayed a handsbreadth backward—that was all the force her blow had against the mountain of flesh—but as he leaned forward to grab her again a peculiar, bewildered expression came into his face. Clutching at his chest, he toppled forward onto the ground.

Zhenuvnili and Brugo eyed one another. He lunged at her, and she sprang away. One of the two men harrying Pye was in her path—Velch, armed with a dagger. She used her momentum to hit his back with her shoulder, and he fell to his knees. She danced lightly to one side, and Brugo collided with his comrade and went sprawling. Tarag watched all this as he retreated. Seeing the lilith standing uncertainly as Brugo and Velch untangled themselves, he called out, "If you love the Goddess, get the door open!" She stepped toward the door. "Not that way!" he added. "There's a mechanism! A crank! Find it!" His opponent took the opportunity to lunge, forcing Tarag to sidestep. As he did so he flung the torch deliberately into the mound of straw that was heaped exactly where he remembered it. Before his attacker could regain his balance, Tarag was dashing back toward the center of the barn. He leaped and landed with both feet in Pye's opponent's back. They both fell, and the sword skidded free. Tarag saw the dark form of Brugo above him, and rolled under the cart. He got to his hands and knees and looked out at the assorted ankles and at Velch, who was still lying on his face and, evidently, on his dagger, for around him was a dark pool of blood.

Zhenuvnili had traced the ropes with her eye and seen that the crank must be at one end of the catwalk. She scrambled for the stairs. One of the slaver's men was at her heels. She was moaning, and her arms and legs were stupid and heavy, but she kept moving. Pye, meanwhile, had retrieved the fallen sword. When he saw Brugo lean forward to poke at Tarag under the cart with his dagger, he leaped and brought the hilt down at the base of the man's skull. Tarag rolled in the other direction and stood up. Only two of the slaver's men remained to be dealt with. The one who had first attacked Tarag was climbing to the catwalk after the lilith, and the one who had attacked Pye was standing swaying, swordless and groggy. Pye called, "Here. Catch." The sword executed a half-circle in the air, and the hilt slapped into Tarag's outstretched palm. "After him," Pye said, pointing at the catwalk. "I'll take care of this one."

Tarag dashed to the foot of the narrow stairway, but he was too late. Above him the swordsman had wrapped his free arm roughly across Zhenuvnili's neck. "Out of my way, or I'll gut this one," he snarled at Tarag.

Raising his own blade, Tarag sighted across the point. "Gut her and you've gutted yourself. Let her go and you can walk out of here. We've no quarrel with you."

"I'm walking out right enough, but with this one as a shield. Don't try to stop me."

Pye stepped up beside Tarag, brandishing the dagger that had been Velch's. Blood smeared the blade and his hand. "You can't shield yourself on both sides at once," Tarag said. "We can outflank you. I say again, let her go, and you won't be harmed."

"You expect me to believe you, after what you done to the rest of them? You throw down your sword, and make way."

"Not until you've let the lilith go."

It was a standoff. With his sword Tarag could easily reach the man's ankles, but he was unwilling to risk what might happen to Zhenuvnili if he tried.

That was when they smelled the smoke.

The swordsman raised his nose first. "What's that?" They looked, and saw that the torch Tarag had flung had done its work. One corner of the barn was blazing merrily. "You did that."

"Aye."

"Then put it out! This whole place will go up."

"I've no water. Where do you keep the buckets?"

"They're out in the stockade," the swordsman said.

"Then open the door!"

The man set his jaw. "I'll not. That's my master's gold, and you mean to run off with it."

"Your master's dead," Zhenuvnili said. "I killed him."

Tarag set himself for a lunge. But the man tightened his arm across Zhenuvnili's throat and backed away from the head of the stairs, out of range. The smoke was getting thicker. The cages lining the walls were of iron, but the walls themselves were wooden. The flames licked higher, and dark smoke roiled, more of it every second. Unless they could raise the door and get out, they would all suffocate, and afterward cook.

"I'm going up after him," Pye said.

"Don't be silly. *I'm* going up after him."

"Since you insist."

Tarag started up the stairs. At every step the smoke was more oppressive. By the time he reached the top his eyes were watering, and he had to stop to cough. He advanced along the catwalk, and the swordsman, clutching the lilith before him, retreated. But Zhenuvnili had had enough of being carried about by others. Stretching her jaw wide, she sank her teeth savagely into the man's arm. He yelled and struggled to free himself, and she sank to one side dragging his arm with her, exposing enough of his flank that Salas Tarag could leap forward and drive a sword deep into his side below the ribs. With a choking gasp, the man crumpled. Zhenuvnili let go with her teeth, and he slipped, slid beneath the crude railing, and fell heavily into the gathering smoke. She wiped her mouth hard and spat.

"The crank," Tarag gasped. "The door." He stepped over her, and she rose and followed him. The crank was only another tadig along the catwalk. Belatedly Tarag wondered whether the swordsman had been meaning to go to the crank and save them all. After one had killed, one thought to ask such questions. Together man and lilith grasped the crank and pulled, and the wheel, stiffly and with great effort, turned. The door was dreadfully heavy. After every two or three cogs they had to let the catch take the weight while they got a new grip. There ought, Tarag reflected vaguely, to be a better way to do this—some system of gears, like those on mechanical clocks, whereby many turns of the crank would be easy where now one was nearly impossible. But after eight or ten complete revolutions, Pye called out from below. "Enough! Get down here! The roof is going!"

In the direction of the stairs, flame glinted through the smoke. They rolled beneath the railing and dropped to the ground. Pye had already brought the cart around to face the door. Overhead, flame was spreading, and embers showered down. The door was only half lifted, and the sides of the cart were so tall that it jammed and would not go through. Coughing, they had to back up and roll forward again at a place where traffic had worn a trough into the ground. Even then, Tarag had to stand beneath the door and lift it a last fingersbreadth with his shoulders while Pye and Zhenuvnili maneuvered the cart. When it was through he ducked and sprang clear, just as the roof behind them collapsed with a roaring tearing sound. Scorching air and sparks billowed out under the door. A moment later the door itself sagged sideways and fell. Thinking what would have become of him if he had still been beneath it, Tarag shuddered.

The night air was cool and sweet and still. They drew the cart a few steps into the square and stopped to catch their breath. Nobody spoke; they were stunned by the narrowness of their escape.

Zhenuvnili was the first to recover. "What was the name he called you?"

"Salas Tarag. I'm a ship's captain. This is my friend Pye. And you're the lilith."

"I am called Zhenuvnili. You came here to buy me?"

"We came to rescue you. We mean you no harm. Once you were safe, we meant to give the signal for our friends to march in and seize the gold. But it seems Ashubeleth anticipated us."

Pye was looking around uneasily. "Whatever became of them may yet become of us. Also, the fire brigade will be here before long." The insistent clang of an alarm bell echoed across the sleeping city. The slaver's barn was now a blazing pyre, and sparks were arching among the stars to settle on nearby rooftops. "Let's take ourselves somewhere else."

He got no argument. But at her first step Zhenuvnili cried out in pain. "My ankle," she said. "I twisted it getting down from the catwalk." So Tarag lent her a shoulder, and she hobbled, while Pye pulled the cart.

Looking at the person beside him, Tarag found himself smiling. "I've been to quite a lot of trouble finding you," he said.

"Oh. I'm sorry."

"Don't be. It was worth it."

At the far side of the square they found what had become of the Berkenders. Nine or ten of the soldiers lay scattered across the ground, as if struck down at one blow by a giant fist. Several were horribly mutilated, and both uniforms and flesh were singed and blackened with ash. A strong acrid odor still lingered.

Moving among the bodies, Tarag found neither Osher nor Shuma, but one of the soldiers was still breathing. Tarag knelt and lifted the man's head. One eye was red pulp, the cheekbone laid bare by a massive wound. "Fire," the man gasped. "They threw fire at us, out of the sky." His remaining eye closed and his head dropped. Tarag gently let him back onto the ground.

On all sides a clamor was rising from the pens as the caged slaves awoke and called out to be freed before the fire spread. For a moment Tarag debated going to free as many of them as he could. After all, he had created the danger. But fire fighters were arriving now, dashing across the square with axes and buckets, shouting instructions to one another. They could do far more good than he alone. And in the confusion of a throng of escaped slaves, he might easily lose lilith, gold, or both. He went back to the cart. "We can go faster if you ride," he said. The lilith nodded, and let him help her up. Towing the cart, they plunged into the night-shrouded city.

Chapter 17

"*H*e said somebody threw fire at them," Tarag mused. "Out of the sky."

"There's no shortage of roofs nearby," Pye pointed out. "But how could anybody throw fire? You could pour a vat of lamp oil and throw a torch into it, but you couldn't kill anybody with it unless they were very slow and clumsy, or very unlucky. And the place didn't smell of lamp oil." They had left the area of the pens and were passing south of the fortress. Behind them fire alarms were still ringing, and the skyline glowed an evil yellow.

"No, I've never smelled anything quite like it. But some things burn quicker than others, am I right? Lamp oil is among the quickest. But there may be others quicker, much quicker, that we don't know of. If there was a substance that burned almost instantaneously, it would create a great wash of heat when it ignited, which would char men's flesh and the ground around them in just the way we saw."

"But if it burned instantaneously," Pye objected, "it would burn you when you ignited it. You'd have no time to throw it off the roof."

"No, no. You could attach a candlewick to it, and light the other end. Just before the flame reached this other substance, you'd throw it. It'd be a terrifyingly effective weapon. You'd

never come in sword range, and you could kill far more than
with a bow and arrows, because there'd be no need to take
aim. The fire would engulf whoever was near it."

"I pray the Berkenders never discover such a weapon."

"Aye. Warfare's a gruesome enough business, without fire-
throwing."

"Have you thought where we're headed?"

"This gold weighs heavy," Tarag said. "I'd feel easier if it
were back in the garrison strong room. But it might be prudent
to wait, rather than marching straight there. I didn't see Osher
or Shuma among those fallen, but they might easily have been
injured and wandered off elsewhere to die. Without their word,
Borando won't believe we were working on his behalf. He'll
lock us up." He did not need to add that possession of the gold
would be a potent lever in negotiating the release of his ship.
"What say we make for the longhouse where we stayed last
night? Will we be welcome?"

"I'd think so. Do you mean to take her with us?"

"That's not mine to decide." Over his shoulder Tarag said,
"You're free to go where you will, but I'd suggest you come
with us. We've a place where you can sleep and be safe till
morning."

When there was no reply he turned and saw that Zhenuvnili
had curled up atop the chests and was fast asleep. That seemed
to settle the question. They turned aside toward the longhouse
district, and came within a few minutes to the door of the
Chaluman house. Pye pounded, and waited, and pounded again.

"Who's there?" a querulous voice within cried at last.

"It's Pye. My friend and I are back."

The top half of the door opened, and Freeman Chaluman,
in nightcap and pajamas, appeared with his candle. "If you
come here much oftener," he said, "you'll be wantin' to take
initiation."

"We may do that. I'm honored, friend Chaluman."

"You're welcome to stay the night," the skinny old man
said, "but unless you've got money there'll be no breakfast."

Pye laughed. "We've got money," he said. "But just now

we're wanting to get in off the street. May we stable the cart out back?"

"Aye. I'll lock up here and open the kitchen door for ye."

When the cart was safely tucked in a shed, Tarag lifted the lilith and carried her into the longhouse, leaving Pye to watch the gold. She stirred, and looked up at him, then closed her eyes again and let her head fall on his shoulder. The room to which Chaluman led him was larger than the one they had slept in the night before, a children's room perhaps, long deserted. He lowered the lilith gently onto one of the five beds. She opened her eyes again. "I did not thank you for saving me from those men. Thank you."

"We'll talk of it in the morning."

They brought the gold in, and Chaluman went away taking the candle with him. Tarag lay on the too-short bed with his fingers laced behind his head, aching and weary but too restless to drift into sleep. He remembered the lilith's face, her eyes, her voice. She was not, somehow, quite what he had expected. Beautiful? Perhaps, under more favorable circumstances. Exotic? Certainly. Courageous? Evidently. Without her daring they would never have escaped the fire. But there was something elusive about her as well. He found himself drawn to the mystery. Amera willing, he would have the chance to plumb its depths. Perhaps it was only that she was a foreigner. He had had plenty of foreign women, and knew how quickly the thrill could dissolve into irritating obtuseness and misunderstanding. But this wasn't a woman, he reminded himself. Nor a man, either— he'd leave the latter to Jakul Borando. A lilith was—who knew what? Wondering, he fell asleep.

When he woke, daylight was pouring through the cracks in the shutters. He sat up, and groaned at the stiffness in his shoulders. Zhenuvnili lay curled beneath a blanket on her bed, and in the middle of the room the chests of gold were undisturbed. Pye, however, was already up and gone. How very like a thief! Tarag got to his feet, and stretched, and groaned again. His back and arms were complaining loudly. When he had worked out a few of the worse knots, he slipped into his sandals and shuffled out back to relieve himself.

The morning was milky with a glaring bright haze that lay thick over the city, and every breath brought a noseful of smoke. Evidently the fire in the pens had not been easily contained. To the west a dark column was still rising. Tarag looked at it and sighed. Putting Falnerescu to the torch had not been part of his plans. When he was finished in the outhouse he found a rickety ladder and set it where he could climb to the roof. Up there he could see much of the city spread out before him. In the western quarter there appeared to be three or four major blazes, plus numerous traces of smaller ones smoldering, and the few streets he could see were clogged with traffic. The citizenry, knowing how easily fire might engulf the city, were fleeing, burdened with satchels and carts of household goods. The fire was still a good way off; for the moment, he judged, he and the lilith were safe enough. Trying to go anywhere else, in that mob panic, would be difficult. And if his stomach had anything to say about it, they weren't going anywhere until after breakfast. He climbed back down.

After looking in on Zhenuvnili and finding her still asleep, he went back to the kitchen and began poking in the cupboards. The room was large, clean, and well lighted, but disappointingly bare of provender. At last he found some meal and began, unhandily, whipping up batter for honeycakes. His own poor cakes would never compete with Jutie's. And that thought set him wondering how Jutie and Graio were faring, languishing in Chespid's dungeon. Getting them out was not the least of his problems. Perhaps his best course was to take the Berkender gold straight to Chespid and offer to buy both ship and men. It would bear thinking about.

The old woman hobbled into the kitchen. "Here! What be you doin'? Let me." She took the bowl from him and began stirring vigorously. "This was meant to last us through the aptarne," she said.

Tarag took the hint. "Just a minute." He went back to the bedroom, untied one of the sacks in the nearest chest, and dug out a dozen gold pieces. All but two he put in the pouch at his belt. Back in the kitchen, he tossed the two coins on the table. "Is this enough?"

She picked one up, brought it to her eye, and bit it. "Aye." The money disappeared into a pocket in her apron. "You be wantin' tea wi' yer cakes?"

"Some tea would be nice. Do you know what's become of my Eloian friend?"

"Him? He was out and about at dawn."

"Did he say where he was bound?"

"That one?"

Tarag turned to leave, but turned back. "You know about the fire?"

"Aye, you've built it up too hot. For cakes you only need a little fire."

"Not that one. The big fire."

"Oh, that. Chalis has gone to look. He'll be back to tell us, if he's not trampled to death." Apparently unmoved by her own dire observation, the old woman added another judicious handful of meal to the bowl and resumed stirring. Tarag left her there.

Zhenuvnili was sitting up on the edge of the bed, gingerly putting a little weight at a time on her bad ankle. Tarag knelt to feel the joint, and she flinched away from him. "I'm only going to see if it's broken," he said. "It's swollen, but not too badly. I'm going to move it from side to side, and up and down. Tell me if it hurts."

"It already hurts." She pouted.

"I mean if it hurts more than that." She let him manipulate her foot slowly, and pressed her lips together but did not cry out. "Nothing broken," he announced. "It'll heal. Best you try walking on it a little. I'll lend an arm, if you like."

"I'm not sure I want to walk. Perhaps I ought to stay in bed until word can be sent to my people."

"In ordinary circumstances," he said patiently, "I'd be proud to carry the word myself. But the fire we set last night's not been put out yet. We may have no choice but to move, and quickly, if the wind drives it this way."

"Can't I ride in the cart?"

"I said last night you were free to go where you would. I don't know if you heard me. You were asleep. But the obverse is also true. I'll not carry you, or draw you like a draught animal. You can run, or burn."

"I'm not sure I like you."

"If I decide I want you to like me, I'll let you know." Tarag was getting a little annoyed. Perhaps she was spoiled after all. Or perhaps her intransigence was only an understandable reaction to all she had been through in the last two days. For the moment, he would reserve judgment. But he stood back and let her get to her feet unaided.

She took a few faltering steps, then a few more. "I don't remember all of what happened last night. It's too confused. But I remember that horrible fat man holding me, and I remember hitting him. I killed him, didn't I?"

"Probably."

"He's not the first. Ranga went mad. I had to use the death-command on him." She used the Vli term untranslated, and Tarag did not know what she meant. "And the poor mnoerri . . ." She bit her lip, and tears welled in her eyes, and suddenly she was shivering and sobbing. Tarag stepped forward and wrapped his arms around her and held her close. Her hair smelled very nice. She wept for a while, and then snuffled and wiped her eyes, and he let her go. "Thank you. I—it's all been such a— I don't know. It's not how I imagined it being."

"How you imagined what being?"

"The Island Sea. I always wanted to come here, ever since I can remember. But nothing's the way I thought it would be. Those horrible beasts, and then being hit and locked up—it's done something to me." She wiped her nose on her sleeve. "You must forgive me. It is I who should be strong, and lend comfort to others. I may not show weakness, except before my Nest-mates." She began to pace agitatedly about the room, and at her first step winced and said something in Vli and kept on pacing.

"I know little about you or your ways," he said. "But I know we all have weaknesses, and if you show yours before me I will not be offended."

She stopped with her back to the window so the smoky light rayed out around her in a halo. "I think perhaps you are a good man. I was not sure at first." Then she let her eyes drop to the floor. "Of course, you are a foreigner."

"You're not supposed to see foreigners at all, are you? Only your own people."

"It is true I have disgraced myself before you by allowing my face to be seen. But I did so yesterday before a whole marketplace." The thought sobered her.

"So you've disgraced yourself," he said with a trace of bitterness. "And I've lost my ship and crew, and Nule Chespid is looking for my head on a pike. I think you've got the better of the bargain."

"I do not understand. How have you lost your ship?"

"It's a very long story."

"I should like to hear it. But first, can you tell me, where is the—oh, I don't know the word. The place where one empties." He pointed her in the direction of the outhouse.

When the old woman heard them coming she began flipping the honeycakes up off the griddle onto a platter. They sat at the table, and she set the steaming platter between them and poured fragrant tea from a pitcher into two mugs. Tarag unceremoniously grabbed a honeycake and stuffed half of it into his mouth. The lilith ate more daintily, but with an appetite. The old woman saw that they had all they needed, and discreetly withdrew. Tarag wondered whether she would be hovering just outside listening, then remembered that she was hard of hearing.

"How big is your ship?" Zhenuvnili asked between bites.

"Sixty oar. She's called the *Amera Smiles*."

"Amera is your goddess of the waves."

"Aye."

"It's a pretty name for a ship."

"She's a pretty ship. She can take a wind on the beam without yawing, and she rides tight through the worst weather."

"When I was a nala I used to dream of having a ship. But the others laughed at me, so I learned not to talk about it. But I was forgetting. You said you'd lost her."

"Aye. And on account of you. Oh, it's not your fault," he

added when she looked up, stricken. "Only a foolish wager I
made."

"What is 'wager'?"

So he told her the tale. She laughed when he told how they
had got the money from the strong room. "You are very brave,"
she said, "to dare so much to see me. I fear I must be a
disappointment."

"Well, you're not quite as I imagined you. But a disappointment, no. Certainly not. You *have* led me quite a chase,
I'll say that. It would have been simpler if you'd stayed put."

"But in that case you wouldn't have been allowed to see
me at all. You would have lost your wager, and now you've
won." She frowned at the table. "But at what price? You were
right to say it was my fault you lost your ship. It's all been my
fault, even the mnoerri. Especially the mnoerri."

"You keep talking about these mnoerri," Tarag prompted.
So she told him of the visitors who had come to her in the
garden, and the invitation they had brought. When she described
the circle in the woods, he nodded. "I've heard that they do
that. I'd give a lot to have seen it. It's how they reproduce.
Afterward, some of them are quickened, or perhaps all of them,
and they build nests in the trees to bring forth their young."

"These will never build nests." After another bite of cake
and a sip of tea, she described the attack of the kelg. Tarag
swore a foul oath, but the lilith barely noticed. Her gaze had
turned inward, and her voice was dispassionate. "I had not
known such cruelty could exist in the world," she said. "And
these were not wild beasts. They wore uniforms."

"They were Berkender battle-kelg, then," Tarag told her.

"I guessed they might be. Tell me, do the Berkenders turn
their eyes away from such slaughter, and do nothing to stop
it?"

"I'm afraid they do."

"So. It is good that I have learned of this, though I wish it
had not been at such cost."

"You said they captured you," Tarag said. "How did you
escape?"

She described the riot in the square, and her return to the

Metterner mansion, and how she had fled from Strell's madness.

"My friends saw him the next morning," Tarag said. "Delirious with fever. If this death-command is as potent as you say, I imagine he's dead by now. And I'm sorry I said you'd got the better of the bargain. You've seen as much suffering as I. Amera willing, we've seen the last of it. But we've still got to decide where we're to go from here. I assume you want to go back to your people."

"Yes, I must. Nalas! Oh, how can the nalas be faring?"

"Your attendants?"

"My attendants, and my charges as well."

Tarag remembered groping for a way to explain to an oar how one human being might be both priestess and whore; this was a similar conundrum. "I guess I don't understand your ways. The nalas—?"

"Are young liliths," she told him. "Until they reach the age of two sevens of tens of chetnes, and have their Robing, none may look upon them but those in the Nest. The older ones serve us, as no male or female slave can be allowed to dwell in the Nest. And we teach them to be proper liliths, as we were taught by the elder liliths before us."

"Forgive me if I ask what is forbidden to answer," Tarag said boldly, "but it is said by some that among the Vli there are not two sexes but three, that the liliths are neither men nor women but a third sort of being who completes and fulfills the other two."

Zhenuvnili nodded, and met his eyes gravely. "You have earned the right to know of this, Salas Tarag. What you say is true."

"But I'm still in the dark. Among us, men and women need one another, and very little else. How can it be that Vli men and women turn to the lilith instead?"

Zhenuvnili blushed at the obscenity. "I have heard legends, strange tales passed down by the liliths in their pillow-talk from before the time of seafaring, from the time when there were no Nests. I should not speak of them before a foreigner." She sighed. "But many things are not as they were, and perhaps

Li will forgive me. It is said that among us too, men and women once loved one another, and were content, and there were no liliths. Then Li sent us to our people. We were few, and we did not know our nature. It was the time of Testing. We were not loved in the beginning but feared and despised, because we were thought deformed. We were called the spawn of demons. Later, when we had learned the secret arts of herbs and healing, we were tolerated. We lived in huts on the edges of the villages, and took no lovers.

"But a time came when the women ceased to bear children, though they coupled with men as before. And they and their— what is your word?—husbands came to us, and asked us to intercede with the gods of healing, so that the women's wombs might bear again. This was when the first of the liliths, Zharoli, discovered that our private parts, which had been thought a sign of the gods' displeasure, had the magical power to make the women fruitful again. Our seed of itself does not quicken babies in the womb, but if we couple with a woman before the man does, as was the old way, or receive the seed from the man and pass it to the woman, as has been the way for many generations now, since the revelation of Li, then the women may bear children, and the continuance of the Vli is assured."

"It's a great responsibility," Tarag said.

"To live is a great responsibility, I think, whether one is man, or woman, or lilith. Our road is no harder. It is only different."

The outer door opened and Pye burst into the kitchen. Spying the honeycakes, he pounced on the platter and gathered up three of them. Dropping onto a bench, he munched greedily.

"I don't know when I've seen you so stirred up," Tarag observed.

"I don't know when I've seen the city so stirred up. People running this way and that, furniture lying abandoned in the street. It's not proper thieving weather. Too much competition from amateurs."

"What news?"

"All bad. The fire's still spreading. Most of the garrison has been called out to make a firebreak across that end of the city—and, unless I miss my guess, to keep a weather eye out for you-know-what. Civilians are being urged to stand out on the rooftops with wet sacks to snuff out sparks. Most of the slaves have been let loose. They're not being burned to death, which is good, but they're running in packs through the city, which is not so good."

"All this from one little torch. I'll never light a candle again."

"Don't blame yourself. It's the lack of rain. They're bringing up water in caulked wagons from the harbor; the cisterns are too low. I saw a paum go wild when a cinder landed on its back, and overturn the water wagon on its driver." Pye shuddered, and took a swig of Tarag's tea. "Also, I saw Osher. He's down in the thick of it, directing the fire fighters. Looks as though he hasn't slept."

"Thank the Goddess he's alive."

"Say that again when you've heard the rest. The word is, he's denounced you for setting the fire. Before the smoke clears, every man in Falnerescu will be hunting you. There's a reward."

"Bulon!" Tarag smote the table with the flat of his hand. "I thought he was my friend."

"That's as may be. My thought is, he's laying groundwork. Sooner or later he's going to have to explain to Borando about the gold. The blacker he paints you, the easier time he'll have of it. Also, he wants you found, but he can't have the heralds announce the real reason, or you'll have your throat slit by some treasure-hunter and he'll never see the gold again. Once you're brought in and it's safely in his hands, he can withdraw the accusation."

"Can he? It's a civil accusation. It's Chespid's to prosecute."

"Chespid listens to the Berkenders."

"When it suits him. But once the lilith is back among her people, he'll have no kidnapping charge. The fire will be just the excuse he needs to keep my ship. No, he'll have my head, if he can arrange it—and yours too if you're not nimble. We've got only one weapon to use against him. We've got the gold. I'm thinking we'd be best advised to sit on it until the fire is put out. Then we can use it to buy our freedom."

"But it's Chespid who threatens your freedom," Pye pointed out, "and it's not Chespid's gold. Giving the same gold to two different people can be tricky. Sooner or later they get around to counting it."

"And are very disappointed. Yes. It seems we're bound to disappoint somebody, no matter what course we steer. And there may be more danger than we suppose in simply giving it back to the Berkenders. What if Osher thinks we arranged to have fire thrown at his men? Or what if he believes we're innocent, but Borando doesn't believe him? What if Borando gets the notion we and Osher meant to keep the gold for ourselves, but couldn't get safely away with it because of the fire?"

"Shuma would gladly whisper a story like that in his ear," Pye said. "It would be malicious enough to suit her, and she could twist the tale to minimize her part in the theft. But there's a worse danger. If Osher tells the truth about our errand last night, he'll have to take responsibility for letting us walk into Ashubeleth's trap—in which case, blame for the fire will be laid at *his* feet. He might find it prudent to kill us first and afterward arrange a better tale to tell Borando."

"I doubt he'd stoop that low. But he's betrayed me twice in the past three days. I don't think I care to try for a third time. What it comes to is this: If we take the gold back to the Berkenders, we can't trust them to let us go free. And even if they do, I'll not have an easy time with Chespid. The best course may be to duck the Berkenders entirely and offer the money to Chespid in exchange for the ship. With luck, I can get her manned and out of the harbor before Borando hears of it."

"I fear that won't work either," Pye said, shaking his head sadly. "Do you think he'll trust you to hold your tongue? He can't risk having it whispered he's got the Berkenders' gold. You wouldn't draw three breaths after you'd delivered it to him."

Tarag leaned back against the wall and clasped his hands over his stomach. "So we can't give it to the Berks, or to Chespid either."

"So it seems."

"I never thought gold could be so useless."

"You'd say the same if you were starving. But it hasn't come to that, has it?" Pye dabbed at the crumbs on the platter and licked his fingers appreciatively. "Those were very good cakes."

"Well," Tarag said, "if you've got two thousand gold, and you can't give it away, you may as well keep it. Seems simple enough."

"Spoken like a true thief."

Tarag acknowledged the compliment with a formal bow. Then he turned to the lilith. "Are we boring you?"

Her eyes were twinkling. "What is 'boring'?"

"Making dull, uninteresting conversation."

She considered the question. "I do not think a lilith can ever be bored. We are trained to enjoy listening. You really mean to keep the gold, then?"

"I don't see that we've got any choice."

"You are a remarkable man. Are there women like you on the Island Sea?"

"Not enough of them to suit me."

Zhenuvnili blushed. She had nearly forgotten for a moment that Salas Tarag practiced what was to her unnatural sex.

"The question remains," Tarag said, "what we're to do with it. We can't carry it about on our backs."

"We could bury it," Pye suggested.

"Won't work. If the fire sweeps through this area, the landmarks will be gone. We could dig for the rest of our lives and not find it. If we could get it aboard the ship . . . I seem to remember your saying, a day or two ago, that stealing a ship would be a stimulating challenge."

"It could be done," Pye said. "Provided some escaped slaves haven't already commandeered her and set out to sea. Where you'll get a crew is another question."

"Leave that to me. I can send word to some lads I know. But we can't have them down to the dock to wait. They'd attract attention."

"And they can't come here," Pye said.

"What say to the Brass Paum? It's close to the docks, and oar gathering there will cause no talk."

"Aye. But I'm still not keen on taking it through the streets, as they are now. Best I go up roofside and see which way the wind is blowing." Pye pushed back the bench and rose.

"What about you?" Tarag asked Zhenuvnili. "Where are you bound?"

"I must go back to my people. My absence will have caused them great pain. I only wish—"

"Wish what?"

Their eyes met, and it seemed to him that she was about to say, I wish you were my people. But instead she said, "I wish I had been a better lilith to them. If I had behaved as I ought, and not gone off wandering the Moons Road, none of this would have happened. Perhaps I am not fit to be a lilith. That will be for Li Ranli to decide." She seemed close to tears again.

Watching her, Tarag felt that he was seeing two Zhenuvnilis. The first loved adventure, was amused that her new friends were planning to run off with a cartload of gold. But the second was dutiful and highly orthodox. There was something ironic in the fact that the orthodox Zhenuvnili was the one who might easily make love to a hundred different people in fifty nights. But more important at the moment, it seemed inevitable that when she returned to her people, the orthodox Zhenuvnili would assume control, and would find the adventurous one a source of shame. Salas Tarag decided he did not much care for this. "I'm the one responsible for my actions, not you," he declared. "If you had never set foot outside Metterner's house, I would still have done whatever I could to see and speak with you, even if it meant setting a dozen fires and sinking my ship with my own hands. You've suffered as much as any of us, and through no fault but curiosity and a desire to help others. But now you want to blame yourself not only for your own suffering but for everybody else's. If that's what it means to be a lilith, you'd be better off a slave."

"We are called the slaves of love. We may not be bought and sold, as men and women are, but all may command us."

"Haven't you ever wanted to be free?"

"Oh, yes! But it's impossible. Without our love, our people would die. Have you never been needed?"

"The oar need a captain. But a captain needs oar. The tide flows both ways. Have you ever asked yourself whether you needed your people?"

"Well, of course I do," she said indignantly. "They're good and kind, and they take care of me. I have everything I could desire."

"Except freedom."

"Except freedom," she conceded.

"Do they love you as you do them, or do they only buy you trinkets?"

"The good-hearted ones do," she said slowly. "Qob Qobba loves me. Dear Qob. I must be getting back." She stood up.

"The streets are not safe. I'd best escort you. I only hope you'll remember one thing. In leaving that house the other morning, you were doing something noble and courageous. You were declaring your own freedom. Whatever you do, don't let them convince you it was wrong. Promise me."

She swallowed. "Yes. I promise."

"Good. Now let's get going."

Pye was squatting on the roof. When he saw them, he slithered to the edge and climbed down the ladder. "Smoke's letting up," he announced.

"Good."

"No, bad. I've changed my mind about getting the gold through the streets. It's far safer to do it now, while everybody is running around towing carts and wagons. Once they see the danger's past and make their way home, the guard will have nothing to do but look for a white-bearded northerner and an Eloian pulling a cart. Shall we be off?"

"I've another errand first," Tarag said.

Pye raised an eyebrow. "It's a load for one man. A tempting target as well."

"Throw a blanket over it. And buy a roaty somewhere. It's a roaty cart, isn't it? What could be less conspicuous?"

"*Buy* a roaty? What do you take me for? Mind you stay clear of Metterner's folk," he called after them. "They'd as

soon turn you over to Chespid as pick up a copper lying in the
street."

"Aye. I'll stay out of sight."

In the side street before the longhouse were only scattered
pedestrians, a few running, none sauntering, and an enormous
rail-sided wagon drawn by a pair of spotted paum that was
drawn up crossways so that it nearly blocked traffic. The driver,
enraged, was standing at the head of the paum swearing a steady
stream, and the bewildered beasts, trying to back away from
his wrath, were succeeding only in wedging the wagon more
firmly between two stout fenceposts. Fortunately, the wagon
cleared the street nearly waist-high, and Tarag and Zhenuvnili
ducked beneath it and out the other side.

The main street when they reached it was all the chaos Pye
had described, and more. Mothers crying for their children,
children crying for their mothers, all manner of vehicles large
and small, ancient and new, drawn by man and beast, men
carrying sacks on their shoulders, baggage dropped and split
open spilling out clothing and cookware and foodstuffs and
candles and toys all trampled in the dust, and everywhere throngs
of people shouldering one another aside in their eagerness to
be anywhere other than where they were. A merchant in bro-
cade and a tall blue hat strode past, leading a line of bearers
laden with huge bundles, and collided with an old woman, who
swung her knobbed cane viciously at his back. Tarag took the
lilith's hand, and when that was torn from him forced his way
back to her and wrapped his arm securely around her shoulders.
With his other arm out before them like a prow cutting through
seaweed, he opened up a path.

The avenues of the elite were a thousand tadigs and more
uphill. There the panic was less in evidence; perhaps the aris-
tocracy had faith in the water from the aqueduct, which they
could divert if necessary to fight the fire. Or perhaps they
simply had too many possessions to think of evacuating. Some
of the gates were open, wagons visible inside and slaves bus-
tling back and forth. But atop other walls observers perched,
watching the spectacle in festive comfort, brandishing flagons
of ale and roast joints.

Tarag realized he was still walking with his arm around the lilith, though there was no longer any need. She had been matching him stride for stride, limping only slightly. He looked down at her, and she smiled. "I would have been trampled," she said.

"You're not used to cities."

"I've never been abroad in one, except in a sedan chair."

"You have now." He let his arm fall to his side.

She felt for the hood of the robe, and pulled it forward over her hair. "They mustn't see me unhooded. It would be indecent."

"You expect them to believe you've gone about for two days and nights without ever taking that thing off?"

"A few will wonder, perhaps, but I'll tell them what I choose, and they'll believe it. In the absence of proof, accusing a lilith of dishonor goes harder on the accuser than on the lilith."

"I'm sure it does." He was beginning to see how Zhenuvnili must be revered by her people. Perhaps he had spoken rashly in condemning the arrangement. Too late now, though, to worry about that. He cleared his throat. "There is one thing, if I might ask. A small favor."

"Anything."

"The wager I spoke of. I must be out of the city quickly, but some of those I wagered will be among those I call on for crew, so the wager will have to be settled. I told them I would try to get some proof that I had seen you—a trinket, any small worthless bauble you were about to discard. Would it be asking too much?"

"For saving my life, I would give you all the finest satin sheets from my bed, and sleep on straw. But I have nothing with me. Even my earrings were gone when I awoke in the pens." She spread her hands.

"Could you go into the house and get something, then, and bring it out? It would take only a moment."

She smiled. She guessed, rightly, that he was asking less for a trophy to show his drinking companions than for a keepsake to remember her by. "Once they know I am returned, I will have no peace for hours, or days. And they must not know you are near; it would be dangerous for you. I don't see how, unless I throw something over the wall—no, wait. There is a better way. Let us come up to the house from the rear. I know a way in that no one knows. I'll enter secretly, and make my way upstairs, and return with a token. Then you may take your leave, and I will walk up to the front gate as if just then returning, and all will be well."

Tarag's admiration grew. She was not only courageous, she was nearly as devious as he or Pye.

She was uncertain of the turnings, and twice they had to retrace their steps, but at length they found the right alley, which was deserted. Zhenuvnili pointed at the grating. "This leads to the slave quarters," she whispered. "It is how I escaped from Ranga, when he went mad. I pray the Goddess has by now taken him into Her. It would be best for him, and for the rest of us as well." Tarag was wrestling with the grate, to no avail. She knelt and showed him how to free it.

He looked around at the walls of the adjoining estates. "I'd best not be standing here exposed. Will it be safe for me to come below and wait?"

"The room, if I remember, seemed long unused."

The opening was narrow, and he had an awkward time dragging the grate back into place from below. Then he had to work his way feet first down the dirt tunnel into the dark.

Her hand on his arm halted him. There was enough space to stand, but the darkness was complete. "Can you find your way?" he asked.

"I think so. There's sure to be light at the end of the passage. Wait here, and don't make a sound. I don't know who may be about."

"What if somebody sees you?"

"Did I not tell you? This is the robe of a nala. If I'm seen, they'll think I'm Kari or Ehli."

"Be careful."

"If you can steal the Berkenders' gold, I can steal my own brooch. I'll be back before you know I'm gone."

He tried to think what to say, some word of his that she might carry with her if they were separated now by mischance and never met again. But before he could frame the words, he realized she had slipped away and left him alone in the dark.

Chapter 18

*F*rom the garden wall to the kitchen was not so very far, but it seemed far in the narrow, twisting, unlighted passageway. Zhenuvnili went forward haltingly, toes testing for obstructions or holes, hands groping. She began to fear she had taken another wrong turning, but at last yellow light shone dimly ahead, and in a few more steps she was at the foot of the stairs. A voice above, cook probably, was saying, "We all go to the Goddess at last. But still it seems a shame. He was yet young." Her heart leaped with relief. Ranga Strell was dead! She would still have to face an inquiry when she reached home, but for now she was safe.

After a minute the small noises above had not abated, and she had to consider whether to wait or go boldly up. Certainly cook had not seen a nala go down to the cellar, and might be puzzled. But equally, she could not wait there. She was square in the path to the slave quarters, and sooner or later somebody would pass by. After pulling the hood well forward and taking several deep breaths to steady herself, she set foot on the stairs and climbed. Her slippers, she saw, were dusty on the wood slats, and the hem of the robe was torn.

At the top she took another deep breath, reminded herself not to hurry, and marched through the pantry into the kitchen. Her heart was thudding in her throat. Cook, a large-waisted woman whose long faded hair was tied with a simple thong at the back of her head, was slicing jar-roots, and her sharp-faced assistant was pounding grain to flour in a stone pestle. Cook stopped slicing. "Well, if you aren't a mess. I declare. How did you get lookin' like that? And what were you doin' down there?"

She remembered to use the nala voice. "I went to search for buried treasure." The words came out flat, uninflected, as nalas must speak to men and women, but there was a tremor in the tone.

"Oh, there's nothin' down there but a lot of old crates."

"I was told there was gold."

"Gold, eh? Well, if you find any, share a bit of it with us. And get yourself cleaned up. What would Zhenuvnili say? Just because she's gone is no excuse to run wild." Cook punctuated the admonitions by waving the knife. "Now get along with you."

The long high hall that ran from the front of the house to the back was empty. Light from the window above the front door blossomed on the polished square tiles of the floor. Zhenuvnili tiptoed toward the back stairs. But before she reached them she heard voices, and stopped. Beyond an archway two men were speaking. She strained to hear, but caught no words, only a low murmur. She tiptoed nearer, and still could make out no words.

Reaching the wall beside the arch, she knelt, and risked a peek around the curtain.

Standing in the center of the room, seemingly in ruddy good health, a goblet in his hand and smug satisfaction on his face, was Ranga Strell. She gasped. He heard the sound, and cocked his head. She ducked back out of sight. From that angle she could still see the two others in the room, standing together at a window that looked out on the patio and the garden. Habil Metterner had his hand on his nephew Gorin's shoulder. "Don't blame yourself," the elder man was saying. "It's no different than when that mad sea captain stole away the lilith. You did all you could have done. There was no way any of us could have prevented it."

Gorin Metterner was choking on tears. "We were so h-happy they were coming. And it's turned into a nightmare."

"Aye. First Zhenuvnili, and now Qob Qobba."

A chill washed across the back of the lilith's neck. Suddenly she understood Strell's smug expression. The one cook had been speaking of as dead was Qobba! Trembling, she slipped back into the shadows. How could it be? Poor Qob! Patient, tender Qob! Her eyes flooded with tears. She remembered the red hair on the pale backs of his arms, and the tone of his voice as he had lectured her, solemn and stuffy but always kindly. Never again. He was with the Goddess now. Zhenuvnili snuffled and wiped her eyes. What was she to do? Qob had gone leaving her without a friend among her own people, only the nalas. She would have only them for companionship on the voyage home—them and Strell. Mad Strell. For three chetnes and more, on a tiny ship with a minimum of privacy. Suddenly she was terrified. What atrocities might he commit? Strangle them as they slept? Chop a hole in the bottom so they drowned? To ship home with him would be insanity. Far better to refuse to go. But would he let her refuse? With Qobba gone, she was in his care. If only there were another ship that could take her home.

Not being especially slow or obtuse by nature, she had no trouble thinking of one: The *Amera Smiles*.

But Tarag might not be able to regain his ship—and if he did, he would be off on the morning tide. She would have no time to love even one or two among her people, when they had waited for so long. Could she take such a step? Wouldn't she do better to trust to the Goddess to protect her from Strell?

From beyond the archway footsteps were approaching. She scurried to the stairs and went up them two at a time. She did not know what to do. She only knew she had to see that the nalas were all right.

She stepped into the room that had been hers and shut the door. The nalas were sitting cross-legged on the big bed, Ehlanli in a short white shift with blue embroidery and Karanli in her traveling robe with the hood back. When they saw her, their eyes and mouths opened wide. Zhenuvnili whipped back her

hood and pressed her fingers against her mouth in the sign of
silence. Karanli got out half a syllable before Ehlanli's palm
clapped over her mouth. As they stood up, the lilith rushed
forward and embraced them, one on each side. The three clung
to one another, rocking slightly. "Oh, my nalas," she whispered. "How I have missed you!"

"Where have you been?" Ehlanli demanded. "We thought
you were dead!"

"I'll tell you the story later. Now tell me—is Qob truly
dead, or only missing, as I was?"

"He was stabbed in the night," Karanli said in a tone so
doleful it was almost melodramatic.

"By more of the foreigners," Ehlanli added. "They broke
in again, but Ranga Strell discovered them and drove them off
before they could assault us all."

"Did anybody else see the foreigners, or only Ranga?"

"He said there were two of them. He showed everybody the
marks where they had climbed in the window."

"Oh, nalas, what are we to do? Ranga has gone mad. He
can only have killed Qob himself. We are not safe."

"He wouldn't harm us," Ehlanli said confidently.

"He has already attacked me once, dear one. If we voyage
home with him, he is sure to try it again, and this time he may
succeed."

Karanli began to tremble.

"If you had to, you could use the death-command on him,"
Ehlanli said.

"You must not speak of it thus," the lilith instructed. "It is
not a source of strength, but an admission of weakness. I was
weak. I could not control Ranga. To my shame, I used the
death-command. But it did no good."

"That's not possible," Ehlanli said indignantly.

"Nonetheless, it happened. I can only think that in his madness Ranga has convinced himself that I am not Li. Perhaps I
gave him cause. But if in his eyes I no longer speak with the
Goddess's voice, he need not pay me heed. You see? He may
do with us as he likes; we are helpless." She touched the nalas'
faces tenderly. "If it were only myself, I would risk it. But

what might he do to you, my little ones? No, the Goddess put
you both in my care. I *will* not see you savaged by that monster.
We must pack. Quickly."

"Pack? Where are we going?"

"There is another ship that can take us home, a ship where
we will be safe. Its captain is a good man. But he is not," she
said, speaking straight to Karanli, "he is not Vli. He is a
foreigner. He saved my life, and I am sure we may trust him.
You must believe me, dear heart. He will deliver us straight
home, and protect us from harm."

Karanli began shaking her head jerkily. "I would rather die,"
she announced.

"Then think of me, love. I need you to be with me. If you
go with Ranga, I will worry about you until I cannot eat or
sleep. Is that what you want?"

"No, Zheni. But—but—"

"Please trust me, Kari. I know what's best for all of us.
Didn't Li Ranli tell you you were to obey me? Do you want
to disobey Li Ranli?"

Ehlanli was bouncing impatiently from foot to foot. "Shall
I pack?"

"Yes, li. Bring only what you can carry. It's a long walk.
And choose swiftly. We must be gone before anybody comes."
She turned to Karanli. "Must we leave you here alone?"

Karanli lowered her eyes. "No, Zheni. I'll go, if you say
we must. Only promise you won't let the foreigners hurt me."

"I promise." She gave the nala a swift hug. "Now pack
what you'll need. And hurry!"

She rummaged on the dressing-table, whose contents the
nalas had obviously pawed through, trying things on, while
she was gone, and at last found the brooch. It was a heavy
oval of yellowish-brown horn into which, in inverse relief, had
been carved an image of Li, Her arms outstretched in eternal
welcome, Her legs tucked beneath Her in repose. Clutching
the brooch, Zhenuvnili went to the wardrobe. She picked out
first a fresh traveling robe and cloak, and passed over the red
satin slippers with the high heels in favor of a pair of thick-
soled canvas walking shoes, which she had packed among the

finer clothes for no reason she could have explained at the time. When she was dressed again, the brooch safely in the deepest pocket of the robe, she looked around the room. What else? A couple of changes of underwear for herself and for the nalas, who would undoubtedly pick less practical articles. She scooped lingerie out of a drawer and into a pillowcase. As an afterthought she added a vial of perfumed oil and a little pot of rouge.

Ehlanli had also filled a pillowcase. Karanli was clutching before her in both arms only a largish painted wooden statue of the Goddess. Zhenuvnili glared at her, and she glared back. "Don't you want the Goddess with us?" Karanli demanded.

"Dear heart, the Goddess is always with us. But if it makes you happy, bring it. Only don't complain to me when you haven't got a hair comb."

Karanli clung stubbornly to the statue.

"Now we must get down to the cellar without being seen."

"The cellar?" Ehlanli protested. "Aren't we going out the gate?"

"No. If we try to get out the gate we'll be stopped. There's a secret way out, through the cellar. And the ship's captain I spoke of, Salas Tarag, is down there waiting for us. But cook is in the kitchen. If she sees three nalas, she's going to let out a yell. We can't let her see us all at once. So you'll have to wait in the lower hall, out of sight, while I go back down to the cellar and get Salas Tarag. He and I will get cook out of the way. When I come back into the hall and beckon to you, you'll follow us through the kitchen and down the stairs. Do you understand?"

They nodded. Karanli was chewing on her upper lip. Ehlanli gripped her pillowcase determinedly.

"And whatever you do while you're waiting, *don't speak*. Don't make a sound. It could mean all our deaths."

They went silently down the stairs together, and the nalas slipped into the same curtained alcove from which Tarag had watched the attack of the Brown Hand. Zhenuvnili marched into the kitchen.

"You again?" cook said. Cook's assistant was gone. "Or is it the other one? What is it now?"

"The buried treasure," the lilith said in a monotone. "I found it, so I'm going to bury it." She patted the pillowcase.

Cook shook her head sadly. "It's gotten to them," she said. "I don't wonder. It's affected us all. Well, go on with you. Don't mind me. I'll just be gettin' supper ready." She went back to her chopping.

"It's dark down there," Zhenuvnili said. "May I have a candle?"

"They're on the sideboard. Help yourself."

She held the wick in the stove to light it and cupped the flame with her hand until it burned steadily, then picked up the pillowcase and went on. With the candle, negotiating the passage was quick work. The roofbeams, she saw, were hung with dust-thick clots of spinner-cotton. She met nobody. At the end, the door beaten down by the Berkender pikes yawned blackly, and there, sitting comfortably on a pile of dirt that sagged out of a collapsed section of the wall, was Salas Tarag.

When he saw the pillowcase slung over her shoulder he smiled and rose. "You meant it about the sheets. A brooch would have done nicely."

She shook her head swiftly. "Ranga Strell did not die. He lives. Qob Qobba is dead. I dare not return to Vli Holm on a ship with Strell; he is mad. He will kill us all. Will you take us with you? I cannot pay—"

"Us? How many of you?"

"Myself and the two nalas."

"Gladly, if I can. If I still have a ship. And no payment do I ask. But where are the others?"

"Waiting upstairs. Cook is between us, at the top of the stairs. You must think of a way to distract her. She has a knife."

"Is she alone in the kitchen?"

"She was when I passed by. Somebody else might come along at any time."

"I'd rather not hurt her, but we can't have her raising the alarm. I wish I had some rope. Wait—I saw some, when I was down here before. Yes. Come on." He led the way to another deserted room, where a coil of stout rope hung looped over a peg. He lifted it down and tested it by seizing a section between two fists and pulling. A few fibers popped as they snapped. "It'll be rotten before long, but it should hold her. You must get her to the foot of the stairs. I'll do the rest."

Zhenuvnili left her bag of belongings by the tunnel entrance. Tarag crouched beneath the stairs in musty shadow and watched the lilith's shoes ascend past his face, taking the light. He wished he had a small cudgel; he would have to manage somehow with bare hands. If cook cried out before he could silence her, they would have little hope of escape.

In the kitchen, cook had finished slicing the jar-roots and was stirring a steaming cauldron with a large wooden spoon. Zhenuvnili entered more quickly than she had before. "You must come see what I've found," she said. "You must."

Cook wiped her hands on her wide apron. "What is it now?"

"You must come see. It's a secret."

"Later, perhaps. I've work to do." Cook began scraping the sliced root off the cutting-table into her extended apron. When the apron was laden she waddled across the kitchen holding the bottom hem out before her and transferred the root by handfuls to the cauldron.

Doing her best to sound and act like a nala, Zhenuvnili came closer and reached out as if to clutch cook's arm. "It will only take a moment," she insisted. "It's important. You must come now. I don't know what to do. You must help me."

"Well, can't you at least tell me what it is?"

Zhenuvnili shook her head savagely. "I'm not sure what it is. You must come see for yourself."

"Oh, very well." With ill grace cook wiped her hands again and followed the supposed nala through the pantry and down the stairs.

"Just over this way." Zhenuvnili moved toward the corridor of the deserted wing.

"Oh, there's nothing in there but a lot of nasty crawling things. You don't want to go down that—"

The sentence went unfinished as Tarag brought the edge of his hand down on the nape of cook's neck. The stout woman collapsed like a sack, and he grabbed her ankles and dragged her into the dark passage. Zhenuvnili followed with the candle. They entered one of the empty rooms, and Tarag took the coil of rope from his shoulder, rolled cook onto her stomach, and began tying her wrists behind her. "Take her apron off," he commanded, "and stuff it into her mouth, so she can't cry out." Zhenuvnili set the candlestick on the floor and did as she had been instructed. In seconds cook was thoroughly trussed.

From the passageway came voices. Tarag and Zhenuvnili glanced at one another, alarmed, and she swiftly blew out the candle. They crouched in the dark and watched through the half-open door as the bobbing flicker of a candle came closer. "I just can't think where I put it," a man was saying in Vli. "It's not the sort of thing one uses every day."

"Well, we'll find it right enough," his companion said. "It's got to be down here someplace." The light faded; evidently the two had gone into another of the rooms.

Zhenuvnili snatched up the candlestick. They stepped out into the passageway and shut the door softly behind them. A door glowed farther on, and they heard a crash as something was overturned. They went stealthily back to the stairs and ascended. At the top Zhenuvnili peered out cautiously. The kitchen was deserted. "Wait here," she whispered. "I won't be long."

Tarag hoped she was right. If the men below didn't find what they were searching for, they might easily look for it elsewhere and stumble upon cook. He stilled his breath to listen to the voices, but they remained low and intermittent; there was no outcry. Zhenuvnili had crossed the kitchen and disappeared into the hall. After what seemed a very long time she came back leading the nalas. When he saw that one of them was clutching only a statue for baggage, Tarag had to suppress an urge to laugh. Even hooded, she looked forlorn. He stepped back against the pantry shelves to let them pass, lightly touching each at the shoulder to hurry her. The nala carrying the statue shrank back from his touch, but did speed up. The four went down the stairs in single file, and at the bottom Zhenuvnili pointed toward the untenanted wing. But Tarag saw that she had forgotten to light the candle. "Wait," he called softly. He took the candle from her and sprinted back up the stairs three at a time. The kitchen was still empty; the stove was only two quick steps away. Going back down he had to move more slowly, not to let the candle blow out. He cupped his hand around the flame and breathed through his nose. The three hooded figures were still waiting, and now it was his turn to lead the way. Beyond the first turn in the corridor light was spilling from an open door. They halted, and Tarag sidled up to the door, his back pressed against the wall. The two men inside had their backs turned as they rooted in some large packing-crates. Tarag beckoned with his free hand, and one at a time the others slipped noiselessly past the open door. Shielding the candle with his hand so it would not cast light into the room, he followed.

They reached the tunnel without further incident, and Zhenuvnili picked up the pillowcase she had left. "I'll go first," Tarag whispered, "and see that the alley is empty. You two follow as close as you can. And you"—to Zhenuvnili—"blow out the candle before you come. No sense leaving a beacon." He scrabbled up on the dirt slope where it spilled out of the gap in the wall and went forward on elbows and knees. Behind him he heard Zhenuvnili translating his instructions into Vli. One of the nalas began a whining complaint, but a low order silenced her.

The grate stymied him for a minute—he had forgotten the trick to getting it open. Daylight blazed overhead, the sky still glaring white with smoke. At last he tried pushing sideways, and the grate slid a fingersbreadth and allowed itself to be raised. He popped his head out and twisted his neck to look in every direction. Good. He got his elbows up on the rim of the hole and swung torso and legs out, then reached down to lend the first nala a hand. She grasped his forearm strongly and came out of the hole in one fluid motion. But the second twisted away from him, and, burdened by the statue, could not get out of the hole unaided. Tarag very nearly shouted at her in exasperation; only the need for silence stopped him. He beckoned urgently to the other nala, who readily dropped her sack and reached down for the statue. When the transfer had been made, the hooded figure was able to extricate itself, and Zhenuvnili came close behind.

Not bothering to replace the grate, Tarag herded them down the alley toward the rear of the estate. Hair prickled on his shoulders; he was sure a shout would go up. But they reached the end of the wall, turned, and, nearly running, went down a long hill past stable doors and garden gates to where the alley opened out at last on the public street.

There they slowed to a more comfortable pace. "You're sure you want to go through with this?" Tarag asked. "It's not too late to turn back. Remember, my ship may not be there when we reach the harbor, and if she is, we may fail to capture her."

"And we may be blown onto rocks in a storm and drown before we reach home," Zhenuvnili said, "whatever ship we take. I can only choose whether to ship with you or Ranga Strell, and my heart tells me you are a good man."

"Not everybody would agree with you on that. Osher, for one. But I'm honored by your confidence." Tarag inclined his head in a small bow, not slackening his pace. The nalas, not used to exercise, were puffing to keep up. The street was still crowded, but some of the madness had abated. In the west, only a few scattered plumes still curled into the sky.

Ahead, the street opened out into a public square. In the center of the square a dozen of Chespid's black-clad guards were stopping traffic at random to poke among the contents of carts and scrutinize passing pedestrians. There was little doubt what they were looking for. Tarag grabbed Zhenuvnili's elbow and guided his charges into the shelter of an awninged fruit stall, most of whose merchandise was spilled and trampled fragrantly underfoot.

"What's the matter?" the lilith asked.

"We're far too odd-looking. You've all got to pull your hoods back. Nobody goes hooded in Falnerescu, unless it's raining. That lot will have been told you were kidnapped, and they'll be looking for you."

Zhenuvnili bared her head, and after a moment's hesitation Ehlanli did likewise. Predictably, Karanli made a fuss. She

twisted away from Zhenuvnili and let go a stream of Vli of
which Tarag understood almost none, except that it seemed to
contain repeated references to shame, death, and foreigners.
The scene was attracting the attention of passersby, who were
stopping to stare curiously into the stall. In a moment the guard
would notice the disturbance and come to investigate. Tarag
put his fists on his hips. "Tell her," he instructed, "that unless
she puts her hood back right now, I'll strip her robe off and
tear it into pieces, and she can run back to Habil Metterner's
stark naked."

Zhenuvnili translated this, adding, for good measure, "And
all the old women in the gutter will pinch you and make bruises.
You must choose. Which is it to be?"

Karanli stood as if stone. The lilith reached out and gently
drew the hood away from the nala's face. Karanli's eyes were
squeezed tight shut, and tears were leaking out. Her lip was
oozing blood where she had bitten it. Zhenuvnili lightly stroked
the nala's forehead and cheeks. "It'll be all right," she promised. "You'll see. I've been all over the city this way, and
nobody looked at me any differently than they look at one
another." Pulling a kerchief from her bag, she dabbed at the
blood on Karanli's mouth. "If you're frightened, just hold my
hand tight and keep walking. Before you know it we'll be safe
aboard Salas Tarag's ship, and we can all have a cuddle."

With a little more urging they got Karanli's feet working
and proceeded out into the square. Ehlanli's jaw was set, her
knuckles white where they clutched the neck of the pillowcase.
Her curling red-blond hair, Tarag thought, was extraordinarily
beautiful. Karanli walked stiffly at Zhenuvnili's side, so close
they bumped hips at every step. She had half wrapped the
statue in the folds of her cloak, determined that it, at least,
should be shielded from desecration. From her expression she
might have been stepping into a cauldron of molten metal.
Tarag hung back a bit to keep the three of them between him
and the guard.

"You! Stop right there!"

Pretending not to hear, Zhenuvnili took a few more steps,

but a burly guard planted himself in their path. "What's in those bags, eh?" he demanded.

"Only a few possessions, kind sir," Zhenuvnili said timidly. "We are women of Khali-Doum, and this"—she indicated Tarag—"is our slave."

"If he's your slave, why isn't he carrying the baggage? Let's have a look what's in there." Zhenuvnili held the mouth of the pillowcase wide, and the guard rooted among the underwear with one hand. He hauled out the vial of perfumed oil, sniffed at it, wrinkled his nose in distaste, and tossed it back. "All right, you can go on. But I'd like a word with your slave."

"He can't speak," Zhenuvnili said with desperate inspiration. "He's mute."

"All the same, I've got orders. All dark-skinned men with fair hair and beards are to be detained till the captain can question them."

"But he cannot answer questions."

"Then he's not the man we want, and he's got nothin' to worry about, has he? When we're done with him, he can rejoin you at your lodgings. Well, go on. Get on with you. You, come with me." He made to grab Tarag's arm.

If he had been alone, Tarag might have played along for a few minutes—at least as long as nobody produced manacles. But he could not afford to be separated from Zhenuvnili and the nalas. They had no idea how to find the Brass Paum. So he jerked his arm away from the guard and, pretending to be the mute the lilith had conjured up, began making inarticulate protests, groaning and mumbling through half-closed lips. Slaves whose tongues had been cut out were far from unknown in Falnerescu, and the imposture might be believed, if only briefly. Gesticulating broadly as he backed away from the guard, he contrived to motion to the lilith to flee. Nodding understanding, she took one nala by each sleeve and drew them swiftly away toward the far side of the square. The guard clamped a heavy hand on Tarag's collar and propelled him roughly in the direction of the main body of helmets. He dragged his heels, not enough to antagonize the guard but enough to gain Zhenuvnili precious seconds. He waited until the last possible moment, and twisted sideways suddenly while dropping his full weight. His shirt tore, but the guard was expecting the trick, and grabbed for his arm to twist it behind his back. There was no time left for subtlety. Tarag rolled with the arm-twisting so he was nearly facing the guard and drove his knee into the man's inadequately protected testicles. The guard howled in pain, and Tarag broke free and ran in a stumbling lope in the direction Zhenuvnili had gone. With luck, he would still look like a mute slave terrified at being separated from his mistress. But the guard who had been told he was mute had been rendered incapable of imparting such complex information to his superiors. Somebody else cried, "After him! There he goes! Don't let him get away!" Tarag abandoned the lope and sprinted. "Run!" he bellowed to Zhenuvnili.

The Vli were not used to running, but they had a long head start. Tarag pounded after them, dodging through the throng of people and vehicles. Behind him he heard hard breathing and the clank of light armor—two or three men from the sound, but he had no time to look back. Ahead Karanli stumbled, forcing the others to come back for her. Zhenuvnili was limping as well, her injured ankle giving way under the strain. Tarag saw he could not hope to escape the guard burdened with such as these. He murmured a prayer to Amera. If ever he had needed Her aid, it was now.

He was rapidly closing the gap between himself and the Vli, and the guards were close on his stern. From a side street just ahead of him rumbled an enormous wagon drawn by two hefty paum. The high sides of the wagon, built of thin slats, barely restrained a mountain of loose brasswork. Evidently the driver was an artisan who had loaded his wares in a great hurry, not bothering to pack them, and was now returning to his shop. Rather than dodge around the wagon, Tarag went straight up its side, using the slats as a ladder. The wagon swayed dangerously under his weight. Before he reached the top, the point of a pike slammed into a slat beside his hand. Throwing his knee over the top rail and standing up, he turned on the jumbled pile of brass candlesticks and serving dishes and goblets, and kicked outward against the vertical support that held the slats.

At the second kick the rail splintered, and Tarag pedaled backward on jagged metal, scraping both ankles and the heel of one hand in the process as the mountain spilled outward on top of the guards, both of whom fell beneath it. The driver, shouting, jumped down from his seat and began berating the guards, belaboring them about the shoulders with his whip, pointing at Tarag, and shouting blasphemies. Tarag crawled up onto the wagon seat and let himself down on the far side. Zhenuvnili and the nalas were far ahead again, and he raced after them. He saw them turn down an alley, and chose a nearer one that he happened to know intersected the other a few tadigs on. Thus he was able, puffing and limping, to come upon them from the front as they hurried between the close-pressing houses. "I think we've shaken them," he said gratefully. "Best we take a few more turnings before we stop to rest."

"What's happened to your feet?" Zhenuvnili asked. Tarag was walking squishily because of the blood running down into his sandals. He leaned against a wall and held up first one ankle and then the other while she inspected them. "The cuts aren't deep," she said, "but they should be attended to."

"When we get where we're going."

Ehlanli said something, and Tarag asked the lilith to translate. "She says you're a brave man, to be injured to save us."

Tarag smiled. "Tell her I would suffer far worse for anybody with such beautiful hair."

Told, Ehlanli blushed and averted her face.

Chapter 19

*A*t this hour of the day the common room of the Brass Paum was only sparsely populated. In one corner a pair of grizzled oar were slamming dice repeatedly into the table while keeping up a stream of supplication to the cubes that was religious in its intensity. Among half a dozen solitary diners, incongruously, a prosperously dressed dowager and three small children of equally grave demeanor were spooning up stew. And at a bench near the wall and not too far from the door a nondescript Eloian in a nondescript gray tunic was sipping occasionally at a mug of ale, between sips turning over and over in his hands a small, intricately carved block of some whitish substance that might have been stone, or tooth, or bone.

The front door swung open and Salas Tarag came in. He crossed to the bar, spoke to the barmaid in a low voice, and passed her a coin for a mug. Slipping in across from Pye, he took a deep draught that left foam on his mustache, set the mug down, wiped the mustache, and waited for several seconds while Pye continued to examine the loops and whorls of the carved white block. Pye looked up at last, and without any perceptible change in the expressionlessness of his face said, "What happened to you? You look as if you've been crawling in dirt."

"So I have. Speaking of which, you had to have known that

283

tunnel led straight from the cellar room up to the alley. You crawled back far enough to see daylight. Why didn't you speak of it?"

Pye shrugged. "Does a thief speak of a secret way into a house when the master of the house is at his elbow?"

"I suppose not. Any word on the ship?"

"She's safe at anchor. The word was that a band of slaves did try to commandeer her, and were driven off by Chespid's men."

"I can thank them for it. Graio and Jutie would only have been tossed overboard. Have we got accommodations here?"

"The two front rooms upstairs."

"Good. We've got company."

"Oh?"

"I've been chartered to take the lilith back to Vli Holm."

For the first time Pye showed surprise—his eyebrows went up. "I don't know how you do it. But I'm fairly certain it wasn't Metterner chartered you. Where is she now?"

"Outside, with her two attendants. I wasn't sure but what we might be walking into a trap, and left them out of sight. I'll get them."

Pye rose more slowly. After a last look at the white block he tucked it into a pouch at his belt, gave the drawstring an extra hitch that thieves know, and sauntered in the direction of the door. It opened again and Tarag came in ushering three people in long robes. One of them was very nervous, one was blond and defiant, and the one he knew was simply open, receiving the impressions of where she was. Pye had seldom seen this depth of quiescent receptivity. He found it intriguing.

"It's the jeweler!" Ehlanli said in surprise.

"I don't think he's really a jeweler," Zhenuvnili told her.

"What is he, then?"

"I'm not sure."

From the kitchen came Jervoe the tavernkeeper, in his leather apron. He was a middling stout man whose black hair fringed an ascendant bald spot. His babyish mouth contrasted with the keen intelligence in his eyes. Fists on hips, he faced Pye. "And who might these be, then?"

"There's been a change in plan."

"Two more gold, then."

Pye fished in his purse and drew out two gold pieces. "You're a pirate," he said without rancor.

"And your mother scrapes the barnacles off me hull," Jervoe said amiably, tucking the money away.

"Remember," Pye said. "If anybody asks, we're not here. You've never heard of us."

"I've heard of this one, right enough," Jervoe said, jerking a thumb at Tarag. "Everybody has, by now. But as to having seen him, I'm a blind man in a cave. When you want supper, tell Dameena. She'll bring a tray up." The tavernkeeper turned and was gone.

The room, when Pye swung the door wide before them, was large and airy, and the furnishings, though crude, were clean. A large square pallet, stuffed with straw no more than three days ago, was the bed, and a roughly adzed three-tiered shelf stood against one wall. On a table were a pair of pewter candlesticks with half-burned white candles. Pye held back the curtain that hung over the doorway to the inner room, and Tarag stepped through. There he saw another pallet, a smaller window, and a table and chairs but no shelves. Against one wall sat the twin chests of gold. Tarag nodded satisfaction. For a moment he thought of opening one of the chests to check its contents, but of course that would be a deadly insult to Pye.

"Jervoe and I brought it up ourselves," Pye said. "He wanted to have two stable-boys do it, but I convinced him that we were the men for the job. You might caution the lilith not to mention her price to her young friends, if she hasn't yet. They look a pair of chatterboxes."

"No fear. They don't speak Olmalin, only Vli. I'll let her know it's here, all the same." Tarag led the way back into the main room, where the baggage was deposited against one wall.

"How long must we stay here?" Zhenuvnili asked.

"Till after nightfall," Tarag told her. "Perhaps till dawn. Perhaps another day or two. I'll have to go down to the dock and have a look at the ship before I decide on a plan for retaking her. While you're waiting, it would be safest for you not to leave the room, nor even stand at the window. If you were seen, the wrong people might start asking the wrong questions. Do you know how to use a dagger?"

"I don't think I could. Li will protect us."

"Li can do as She likes. I'd feel better if you had a dagger."

"No."

"Oh, all right. We haven't got one, anyway. That's the first necessity—" He pressed the tip of one finger hard against his forehead. "Get a dagger. Now, what else?"

"The first necessity," she said, "is to get those cuts on your ankles bathed and bandaged. You can worry about getting a dagger afterward."

So a basin was fetched, and some clean cloths, and Tarag consented to sit at the table in the inner room while the lilith attended to his wounds. Pye brought paper, inkpot, and a reed-nibbed pen, and in a large flowing hand, which jerked occasionally when Zhenuvnili's ministrations stung, Tarag wrote out the names of those he wanted for crew. "We can find a couple of boys to carry word to these," he said, "and they'll bring others. I'll have to be square with them about the risk. They're looking at a charge of piracy. But there's no use even sending word till we can get Graio and Jutie freed. There'll be no voyage without them. I'll not repay their loyalty so."

"As to that," Pye said, "I remembered you speaking of an old man who'd benched under you and is now a jailer in the fortress. I took the liberty of sending him a message asking him to come here as soon as he could. I spoke not of you, only of an advantage for him. And I sent two silver olmins with the lad who carried the word, and a third for him for his trouble."

"Good. Excellent. Ouch. My name might have been better bait, but equally it might have brought the guard down on us. Best you be downstairs when he comes, and bring him up. Don't speak my name unless he balks."

"I'll not let him get away."

"While we're casting money on the waves, we ought to send some gold—anonymously, of course—to Bim the jeweler, to repay him for the cache of trinkets we borrowed and neglected to return. Fifty, do you think?"

Pye cast his mind back over the tray of jewelry. "Sixty, I make it. I'll see to it."

Zhenuvnili finished wrapping the bandages and, carrying the basin, withdrew. Tarag scribbled a few more names.

"Shall we tell them it's your summons?" Pye asked. "If any of them run to Chespid, the guard will be on this place like flies on dung."

"They won't run to Chespid. These are oar."

"Don't forget the reward."

"We'll have to chance it. There's not a lad would come if he didn't know what captain had sent the word." He finished the list and blotted it. "You haven't said what you plan to do with your portion of the gold. You've enough there to set up in business and become a respectable citizen."

"I'd sooner take up residence in Chespid's dankest cell. Truth to tell, I haven't yet begun considering how to spend it. I'm still reflecting on something it's taught me."

"And what might that be?"

"Having too much gold changes you in ways you hadn't foreseen. Look at me: I've no need anymore to lighten purses, which leaves my fingers—" He held them out; they were long and slim, the flesh aristocratically soft, though blistered from pulling the cart. "—with nothing to occupy them. I fear they'll begin to twitch. And what good are twitching fingers to a thief?" He sat down on one of the chests. "I wouldn't have missed the game for that, though. This is the high water mark of my career. I came to Falnerescu with naught but a shirt and trousers. And I've done well. I've never been hungry, and I've never slept under the stars but when I chose to. But now Falnerescu has come to seem a fruit that's already been picked. I suspect it would seem so even if I weren't sitting on a pile of coin. The savor has gone out of life here. I wouldn't feel it so strongly if I hadn't fallen in with you. You've a rare gift for finding what's savory, no matter how high a branch you've got to reach. No, there's nothing more for me in Falnerescu. I'm wondering whether there might be a bench on the *Smiles* for an Eloian oar. I know my hands would serve us both ill till they're toughened up—"

"Hold! Stay! I'll have no talk of benching. There are men and women in plenty can bend oar. But few enough are any use to me on land. I've need of a man can plumb for shoals and read the currents in the streets of a city. You could pay your passage, for that matter, being rich, but I'd be gladder than I can say to see you sign on as first mate."

"I know nothing of the sea," Pye objected.

"Nor do I," Tarag said. "What little I know is nothing when set beside all I'm ignorant of. It's the man who assures you he knows the sea who'll sink your ship. Anything he doesn't know, he's blind to. Say you'll do it. You'll be paid."

"I've never been paid for anything," Pye said doubtfully. "I dislike sullying a blank page. But if you'll have me in return for food and passage to wherever I may disembark, you've struck a deal."

"Aye, then!" They embraced. "Send for that barmaid, and we'll drink a toast."

Zhenuvnili lifted the curtain aside to look at them. "Why the shouting? Is something wrong?"

"Wrong? No, it's as right as can be," Tarag told her. "Pye is coming with us."

Her smile was quiet, but it lit the room. "This is good, I think."

"Very good. But perhaps we'd better postpone the toast. We've messages to send, if we're to have the oar here by midnight."

The first oar arrived even before the last of the messages had been sent—the first oar being, of course, Seve. The grizzled old man stumped into the Brass Paum and demanded of Jervoe where he might find a fellow named Fauxnaster. Jervoe jerked his head at the table near the wall and not far from the door, where Pye was again engrossed in staring into the depths of his little carven cube. Seve slid onto the bench opposite, coughed wetly, and spat on the floor. "Now, you tell me," he began, "what you mean sendin' me a message wi' money tied

to it. I'm a proper sarvant of Lord Chespid, and not needin'
nor wantin' to take money from nobody else, for nothin'."

"I've no doubt. How would you like to right a wrong, reunite
three old friends, and take home a couple of gold pieces into
the bargain?"

"I be listenin'."

"Would you be willing to listen to my friend upstairs? He's
the one should make the offer, not I."

The old man worried his teeth with his tongue, considering
the proposal. "If it's a wrong, it's a wrong," he declared, "and
I'd be pleased to right it. And it never hurts to have a bit o'
gold put by. But best we understand one another." He tapped
Pye's chest with a stiff finger. "I'll not be bribed to let no
ruffians or cutthroats out o' the lockup. You can kill me—I'm
too old to fight, or even run. And I'll let you, before I'll do
anythin' that Amera would not smile upon. If you understand
that, then take me upstairs to meet your friend."

Zhenuvnili had allowed Karanli to set the statue of Li upright
against one wall, where the light from the window shone down
on it. For a few minutes she did her best to ignore this makeshift
altar. It was Karanli's folly, no more, to burden them thus with
a fragile and cumbersome artifact. They would suffer privations
enough in the chetnes to come—not even a bath-sponge! But
after sitting on the pallet for some time, arms wrapped around
her knees, listening to the small noises of the tavern below and
the street, she began to see that the seed of her irritation had
sprouted because she had turned away from Li. The statue was
an intrusion because she no longer felt Li in her heart. How
had she turned away from Li, and when? That was a thorny
question. Was it in running from Ranga Strell? He was of her
flesh; she had no right to turn from him. That was the hour,
in his madness, when he most needed love, and she had denied
him it. There was still time to return to the Metterner house
and the fulfillment of her duty. If the danger to the nalas was
so great, she could send them home with Tarag. But no—
Karanli would never agree to such an arrangement. How ironic
that the danger came not from the foreigners Karanli so feared

but from one of her own people! Karanli's weakness was the same, in its roots, as Strell's; only the flowering differed. Perhaps it was the weakness of all their people. And perhaps, Zhenuvnili reflected, that was what she had been sent to discover. To see something clearly, one must stand outside of it. What would happen to the Vli if they were conquered by these foreigners and had no choice but to live among them? They must find a way—oh, Goddess, the treaty! In the urgency of her need to get away from Strell she had completely forgotten the treaty! That was why she was here, not for her foolish heart's teaching. She started to stand up, but saw the pointlessness of it and sank back onto the pallet. Without Qob Qobba there would be no treaty. By himself Strell was capable of negotiating nothing. And Zhenuvnili had neither the knowledge nor the skill to deal with the Berkenders directly. All she knew how to do, it seemed, was get people into desperate trouble, or get them killed. Her heart contracted in anguish. She must pray—for guidance, forgiveness, anything. She crawled across to the painted statue, touched herself thrice, and tucked her legs beneath her to sit. Li smiled at her. After a few minutes the nalas knelt beside her, one on each side, and touched themselves and sat. She put her arms around them, and the three huddled together on the floor of the bare little room.

Her heart had begun to ease, a little of the warmth of love returning, by the time the knock came at the door. She looked over her shoulder at the door; it failed to open. She touched herself again and rose. The nalas remained seated. She lifted the wooden latch. Standing in the hallway were Pye and a somewhat disreputable-looking old man. Without speaking, she opened a palm to wave them across to the inner doorway. The nalas kept their faces averted, but they had not raised their hoods. The moment was painful for them—a lilith might remain bare-faced among men and women in private, even strangers, but a nala would never do so.

Pye pulled the curtain aside and let Seve precede him into the inner room. The old man stumped to the center of the room, turned, and saw Salas Tarag sitting at the writing table. "I thought it'd be you," he said disgustedly.

Tarag remained seated, but he opened his arms expansively. "Seve, I must apologize for treating you so badly the other day."

"Oh, I don't mind that. I was happy to see the dongie get away, and you too. I took a bit o' ribbin' about losin' me keys, but nothin' I couldn't give back double. Now I take it you'll be wantin' yer two mates out."

"Something of the sort, aye. Are they well?"

"As well as anybody in that hole. The little one's worried his pet will die. The big one's only worn a trough in the floor pacin' up and down."

"I'm glad to hear it. I know it's asking a great deal, but could you see your way clear to helping free them? And can you do it?"

Seve rubbed the stubble on his chin, and nodded. "I reckon."

"What can we do to help?"

"A few gold to grease the wheels might not go amiss, if you've got it."

"I'm not entirely destitute at the moment. How much?"

"Ten, fifteen."

"Done." Tarag had prepared his purse for just that contingency—no need to dazzle Seve by displaying the contents of the chests. He extracted a handful of gold and counted out ten, set them in a neat stack on the table, and counted out five more. "You're sure that will be enough?"

Seve counted on his fingers, laboriously, moving his lips. At length he spoke. "Three more. Garvin's wife is abed sick. He'll stand lookout if I give him enough for an Olmalinese physician."

Tarag added to the shorter stack. "You realize we're depending on you," he said. "Quite a lot rides on your getting Graio and Jutie down here—by midnight tonight, if you can manage it."

"I'll not fail ye." Seve wiped his nose on the back of his hand, and sniffed. "Cap'n, if I might speak? I take it you're of a mind to bend oar before dawn, and I was wonderin'—might I come with ye? I've naught to keep me here, and I'm still stout enough to pull me own weight." He tapped himself proudly on the chest, then, with a stricken look, paused to cough, strenuously and wetly. They helped him to a chair.

"Do you know," said Tarag gently, "I can get oar in plenty. But they're green wood. If I had a man aboard could tell them the ways of the sea and the secrets of shipcraft, the *Amera Smiles* would be a ship blest. Would you consider it? You could mend the odd net as well, and have cakes and a berth for as long as you choose."

"I might teach 'em a thing or two," the old man allowed. Putting hands on his knees, he levered himself to his feet and scooped the gold off the table. "I'll be back wi' yer two scoundrels by midnight or not long after, never fear."

"Strange," Pye said when Seve had gone. "An hour ago you cared nothing for knowledge of the sea."

"Whether a wind is fair or foul," Tarag told him, "depends almost entirely on what port you're making for."

At sunset Jervoe sent up a steaming pot of meat and vegetables, and nutbread still warm from the oven, and a bowl of plump red oba, whose juice squirted down their chins when they bit into them. The meal was the best Tarag had had in days. Afterward he wanted nothing more than to curl up and take a good long nap, but that would have to wait. He tarried only until the last light had faded from the window; no sense letting himself be seen on the street. Then he gathered up the supper dishes. "I'm going to have a look at the ship. Get some sleep if you can. We'll be up the last half of the night." Downstairs, he sought out Jervoe in the kitchen. "Tonight at closing, ring the bell as usual," he instructed, "but don't chase out the stragglers, unless they're drunks. Pye will have a list, and he'll tell you when to bolt the door."

The tavernkeeper nodded. "I don't know that I ought to let the Paum be used for this," he declared. "It could mean my license, or worse."

Tarag slipped two more gold coins into the man's palm. "I'll swear you knew nothing of it."

It was late when he returned, but not so late that the crowd in the common room had begun to thin. Here and there among the roisterers were faces he recognized, but if they saw him at the door, a bulky parcel under his arm, they gave no sign. Only one pair of eyes sought his—Jaima, at her drums on the platform with her fellow musicians. He jerked his head to beckon to her and stepped back out of sight. The tune wrapped itself in a somewhat ragged cadence, and a moment later Jaima was beside him, sweat beaded on her forehead, brass armbands glinting against her tawny skin. "What are you doing here?" she began. "Don't you know every—"

"Ssh. There's too much traffic here." Indeed, a couple of drunks on their way to the door had paused to goggle blearily at Jaima's exotic stage costume. "Let's go upstairs." Tarag led the way up the narrow flight to the upper floor. In the hallway there only one candle burned, so their faces were half in shadow. "You said before that there were questions you'd like to ask the lilith. You also said you'd give her leave to answer or not, as she chose. Does that still stand?"

"You know where she is?"

"Don't raise your voice. I can take you to her, but I must have your word that you won't reveal her whereabouts to anybody. If you're careless, I can be just as careless with what I know of you."

"All right. You have my word. But I can't get away till closing time."

"You won't need to." He stepped past her and tapped on a door. It opened a handsbreadth and Pye peered out, then swung it wide. The nalas were lying curled together on the pallet. When Karanli heard the newcomers her eyes popped open and she watched them from across the room like a frightened animal. Ehlanli only mumbled sleepily and rolled over on her stomach, draping one arm across Karanli and bearing her head back down onto the pillow.

Zhenuvnili was sitting cross-legged in the center of the floor. "Who is this?" she asked Tarag.

"A friend. I promised her that if we found you, she'd have the chance to ask you some questions."

"Questions? There are few enough questions I know the answers to, but she is welcome to ask. What is your name?"

"Jaima."

"You dress like one of us, Jaima." The lilith's finger traced in the air the line of the thigh-high slit in the woman's skirt. "I shall have to remember this manner of dress, and teach it to my Nest-mates."

"I'm not here to talk about clothing," Jaima said impatiently. "We haven't much time. What I would like to know, first, is whether you and your kind are free or enslaved, and if the latter, what kind of help you need to free yourselves."

Zhenuvnili cocked her head to one side. "That's not a question that has a simple answer. The liliths are not slaves, no, but neither are we free. I think perhaps what's true of us is true of men and women as well, in every land. We're free to do or not do certain things as we choose, and under compulsion to do or refrain from doing certain other things."

Jaima frowned. "You know what I mean."

"Yes—but I wonder if you know what I mean. May I ask why you're so concerned to know?"

"Have you ever heard of the Brown Hand?"

"No. I'm sorry."

"Not surprising. We've never managed to make any inroads in Vli Holm. Well, no matter. All you need to know is that the Hand works to bring an end to slavery. We fight, when we must. And we may be able to offer you some help."

"What sort of help?"

"How can I say, without knowing the situation? Sometimes we're able to provide weapons. Sometimes false papers. Perhaps we could provide a ship in which hundreds of liliths at a time could escape to some other island where you could be free."

Zhenuvnili smiled sadly. "You'd wait a long time for your first passenger. What you're proposing is sacrilege, you see. Also highly impractical. None of us knows anything at all about farming, or crafts. Without our people to see to our every need, we'd quickly starve. The slaves you free are bound only by chains; there are other bonds far stronger. But there are compensations. Tell me—if a slave is truly happy enslaved, and would die if freed, do you still work to free her?"

"I've never met a slave who was happy enslaved," Jaima said bleakly.

"You've never been to Vli Holm."

"We will be someday," Jaima vowed.

"For your sake, I hope not. The penalty for being a foreigner is beheading."

"Then your people must learn to fight for their own freedom. Will you carry the word to them? Will you tell them they have brothers and sisters across the Island Sea who will rise up and fight beside them when the day is come?"

"If I tell them this, there is a question they will ask of me. So let me ask it of you, and take your answer back to them. The question is this: Which is the greater blessing—freedom, or love?"

"The two are inseparable," Jaima said. "Without freedom, real love can't exist, only the shadow of love."

"Is that your answer? Are you quite sure?"

"Quite sure."

"Then you are far wiser than I. And being wiser, you can have no need of my foolish answers to your questions. I would only lead you into error."

"But there's so much more I need to ask," Jaima protested. "We need to know who controls the shipping in the Western Sea, and how large their fleets are, and whether there are islands where—"

"I'm sorry. I thought once that I knew a little of such matters, but the more I see of the world the better I understand that what I called knowledge was only a reflection of my own ignorance. There is nothing I can tell you. I'm sorry." She closed her eyes, and it was as if she had left the room. Her face was placid, radiant, remote. Her hands rested in her lap palms upward, fingers slightly curled, and Tarag saw that her posture was identical to that of the statue behind her.

He tapped Jaima's shoulder, and she turned. "She refuses to fight beside us?" Jaima said.

"She has fought beside you already, in more ways than you know. She killed Ashubeleth yesterday. Now you'd better go. You know how to keep silent."

"When there's a reason."

"You think she has no reason. Yet you know nothing of the ways of her people."

"I know the value of freedom," Jaima said.

"When you know the pain of freedom, you'll be ready to liberate the Vli."

Zhenuvnili, who was not asleep but merely sitting with her eyes closed, heard what Tarag said, and wondered whether even knowing the pain would be of any use.

"You've seen the ship?" Pye said when Jaima had gone.

"Aye. There look to be only three or four of Chespid's guards aboard, but there could be more below. Still, with the help of a few stout lads Graio and I should be able to retake her."

"You'll have my help if you want it. What's in the package?"

"Ah, this." Tarag patted the parcel, which was wrapped in canvas and tied with string. "A few things we may need, and a few more we might find amusing. You'll have time enough to look them over after we've reached the ship. For now, you'd best be downstairs seeing to it we've no uninvited guests."

"Aye. Or should I say, 'Aye, aye, sir'?"

"You've not signed on yet. When you have, a simple 'aye, Captain' will do when we're around the oar. In private you can call me what you like."

"Aye, Captain." Pye unlatched the door and slipped out.

After glancing at the lilith, who was still seated in her posture of meditation, and the nalas asleep on the pallet, Tarag went into the inner room, taking the parcel with him. In a little while they heard him muttering and pacing up and down. Karanli woke, and began to whimper, and Zhenuvnili went to smooth her brow. Ignoring the music that had begun again in the tavern, she sang Karanli a lullaby, a silly little song that always seemed to soothe nalas to sleep. Zhenuvnili was not much of a singer, but the gentleness in her voice was heartfelt. She herself had no intention of sleeping. When at last the hubbub subsided below, and Tarag emerged from the inner room to cross to the door, he found her waiting, sitting as she had been before but with her eyes open. He stopped and looked at her. "I thought

I told you to get some sleep," he said. "You're worried, aren't you?"

"Yes."

He came and sat before her on the floor, so that their knees were not quite touching. At his belt, where none had been before, was a long dagger. "You've a right to be. I won't lie to you. Any of a dozen things might yet go wrong. The folk I've summoned are tolerably honest, most of them, and loyal when it counts. But they're a hard lot. The life they live, they have to be. All it takes is one to run to Chespid. And if any come here tonight to hear me out but refuse to sign on, I dare not detain them."

"You've broken the law to take the gold, but you would not break it again to save us all? I don't understand."

"The law I broke was the law of the land, and these lads don't care overmuch for that. The law of the sea is another matter. Once they've signed on, I may order them for the duration of the voyage, and they'll obey or be flogged. Not that I flog, unless I'm left no choice. But until they sign on, they and I are equals, and neither may command the other. If I broke that law, I'd lose the good will of those who *did* sign on. And without the good will of the oar, no ship can remain long afloat. So when I speak to them I must convince them, one and all, to bench with us, or we're lost. I've been rehearsing what to say."

"I'm sure you know how to be persuasive. And you must have spoken to reluctant oar before."

"Oh, aye." He smiled. "I recall a time—well, I'll tell you of it someday. The crew wanted to make me soup. That is, they wanted to make soup of me. Nothing this lot can do will be quite that bad, will it?"

"Would it be of help if I were to stand at your side?"

"Aye, it would. I'd not have asked it, but I was hoping you'd offer. Be warned: The danger is greater for you. Once you've been seen, you'll be easier to find if it all goes sour."

She pushed air out through her nose—the adumbration of a laugh. "I've seen so much danger in the past two days, I no longer know what is greater and what is less." She rose and

knelt beside the nalas. "Wake, little ones." Ehlanli rolled over
and looked up, blinking. "I must go help Salas Tarag prepare
for the voyage. Stay here till we return. If Karanli frets, comfort
her."

"Tell her if they hear loud voices, ignore them," Tarag said.
"But if anybody comes that they don't know, they're to—oh,
Bulon, if anybody comes that they don't know, they can dance
a Skavish dance or jump out the window for all the good it'll
do. Just tell them to wait."

The lilith translated the relevant portions of what he had
said. Ehlanli nodded sleepily. "You won't go far, will you?"
she asked.

"Just downstairs. We'll wake you when it's time to go to
the ship."

Pye was waiting at the foot of the stairs, Tarag's list of oar
in hand. "All here?" Tarag asked.

"Five or six extra, by my count."

"As long as they're oar, not spies or stragglers. Watch them
from one side as I talk, and if you see anything untoward,
pounce on it. You," he told the lilith, "wait with him. I'll call
you forward when the moment comes." He smoothed his hair
and beard with his hands.

The lilith brushed imaginary lint from his chest. "I know
you'll do well," she said.

"Amera willing." Squaring his shoulders, he stepped into
the common room. The air was foully smoky. He stood waiting
at the rear until heads began turning toward him and the roar
of conversation began to subside, then strode forward between
the benches. A few of the oar called out greetings as he passed,
and he nodded to them and smiled. Stepping up on the platform
the musicians had occupied, he turned to face the room. Within
seconds the only sounds were shuffling and a cough or two.
Sixty-odd faces were turned toward him. Most he knew, some
better than others. He let the silence stretch out as he tried to
read the mood of the oar from their faces. He saw some curiosity, some wariness, but no overt hostility as yet—the best
he could hope for.

"For coming here tonight, many thanks," he began. "The

hour is late, and I know you'd rather be abed. As would I. But circumstances leave me no choice. My friends, I am in dire need of a crew. I must be off on the dawn tide. If I tarry in Falnerescu, Nule Chespid will have my head on a pike, and that's the plain truth. So I made a list of the stoutest oar I know—you, and those you see around you. I'm hoping you'll sign on, one and all. If you decline, it will mean not only my death but the death of another, a person of gentleness and kindness who has stumbled into a net of terror from which she has no other hope of escape. I'll explain the circumstances, and when I'm finished you may ask all the questions you like. Let me begin, though, by saying that those who ship with me will be well paid—five gold before we leave the harbor, and another five when we reach our destination." A murmur of approval swept the room—that was nearly twice the usual rate. "But you'll earn your pay. The risk is great. I would not ask you to take it if I had any alternative. The risk is that if it becomes known you've shipped with me, you'll be branded pirate." The murmur grew louder, and less friendly. He held up a hand for silence. "I do not mean to *turn* pirate. This is to be an honest voyage. But I've run afoul of both Chespid and the Berkenders. My name, and that of the *Amera Smiles*, will go out by their swiftest ships—though as long as the weather holds, we'll stay ahead of them. As to you, no one will know the names of those who ship with me unless you let slip the word yourselves. So unless the ship be captured, your risk will be less than mine. If it still seems too great, you can disembark at the next port with my blessing, and ship home with half-pay in your pocket. But I would not have you sign on not knowing what's at stake. Most of you know me. You know I'll not play you false. And you know the *Amera Smiles*. She's fast, and she's a tight ship in any weather. I hope to stand on her deck before sunrise, and all of you with me. If you're not with me, I have no hope." He stopped and looked around the room. The oar, unconvinced, were waiting to hear more.

A heavyset woman in the front row spoke up. "We heard you set the fire."

That was the tricky part—to acknowledge responsibility and

claim inadvertence, without looking weak or foolish. "How many of you have heard that—that I set the fire?" There were many nods and raised hands. "It's true. I set the fire. But before you judge me" he added quickly, raising his hands, "hear me out. I'd like to tell you how it happened."

Extending an arm, he beckoned to Zhenuvnili. She came forward slowly, the long gray robe brushing the floor, her chin raised proudly. She took his hand to step up on the platform and stood beside him.

"Is there anybody in this room," Tarag went on, "who has never benched with an oar of another race, an oar with unfamiliar customs, perhaps another language?"

"What's that got to do with the fire?"

"Patience. Is there anybody in this room who has never benched with a foreigner?" He got no takers. "Then you all know how various are the folk on the Island Sea. Doubtless, what folk you haven't met you've heard tales of. Am I right? Tales, perhaps, of the wogglies. But if you've shipped with me, you know Jutie. You've eaten his cakes. And you know he doesn't have hair on the palms of his hands, as the tale has it. But some of the tales are true. If you were here in this room three nights ago, at that table down there, you heard us speak of the Vli. You heard it said how among them there are not two sexes, as among us, but three. And there was some disbelief, I seem to recall. But this person beside me came to Falnerescu from Vli Holm. It was she who occasioned our conversation. And she is not a man, nor a woman either, but a lilith."

That announcement caused a good deal of conversation, which he made no effort to quell. Somebody called, "You've won it, then!" and he called back, "You can pay me later." When he could be heard, he went on. "Her name is Zhenuvnili. She is the one I spoke of as being in danger. We voyage to Vli Holm, to return her safe to her people. Why and how she came to Falnerescu are subjects too complex to speak of now. If you ship with us, you may learn something of them. What matters now is that through no fault of her own, she fell into the hands of Ashubeleth the slaver. It fell to my lot to rescue her. And in rescuing her I set the fire.

"Probably none of you has ever counted a Vli as a close friend. Their reputation for standoffishness is well earned. I ask only that you extend to Zhenuvnili the same courtesy you would to any foreign bench-mate, and not pass judgment on her without knowing her ways. I have spoken with her, and I can tell you she is as stout of heart as any oar in this room. But I didn't know that when I set the fire. When I set the fire I had only seen her for a moment, and not yet heard her voice. Yet I set the fire to save her, as well as to save myself, for I would not see her sold into slavery in a foreign city, any more than I would stand by and let such a fate befall any member of my crew. Ashubeleth meant to kill me. I don't know whether he meant to kill Zhenuvnili or only sell her. But we were unarmed, and Ashubeleth's men had swords. In trying to keep from being skewered, I tossed a torch into a bed of straw. I meant only to distract them so that we could escape. In the end we did escape—it was Ashubeleth who died. Many another died in the fire as well, I'm certain. It's a thing I bitterly regret. But it was Ashubeleth's treachery that caused the fire, not mine." Neatly put, he congratulated himself. He was far too honest to stand there and deny he had intended treachery against Ashubeleth. But it was true enough that his own treachery by itself would never have caused the fire.

Zhenuvnili, unbidden, spoke. "What he has said is true," she said in a ringing voice. "My name is Zhenuvnili, and I am a lilith. It was in rescuing me from the slaver that he set the fire. And his heartache over the suffering it has caused is not half mine. But still we are both sought by cruel men who mean us deadly ill. I have asked Salas Tarag to take me back to my homeland. He has agreed. But he cannot row a galley by himself. So now I must ask you, for it is your arms that will convey me home, if ever I am to see my home again. This has been a more perilous voyage by far than I imagined when I left Vli Holm, and the peril is as great at this moment as it has ever been. If there are any among you who have been in peril in a foreign port, and in desperate need of friends and a stout ship, I pray you will stand now, and stand with us."

The room was hushed. Tarag had time to reflect how good a speech the lilith had made, and to wonder whether after all it would do the trick. Then a short, muscular man in the second row straightened his shoulders and stood up.

A tall bony man two benches away did likewise.

A man and two women in the back, so alike in appearance they could only have been brother and sisters, stood up in a body. After that, everybody was standing at once. When the scrape of benches and stamping of feet subsided, only half a dozen holdouts remained seated. One of those, a scrawny specimen with squashed features and big ears, was none other than Omur, the skeptical southerner. Omur glared right and left, arms folded stubbornly across his chest.

"You remain unconvinced, friend Omur," Tarag said.

"What I want to know," Omur said in a high, creaky voice, "is how you mean to get us a ship to bench. This talk's all very well, but I was out in a dinghy afore dark and saw the *Smiles* with Chespid's men sittin' on her like carrion durlies." Durlies were a species of dark, sharp-faced avians.

"A fair question," Tarag said. "How can we get the *Amera Smiles* away from the guard? I say we board her now, under cover of dark. The guards are few, and by now they'll be asleep. I'll be first up the side, and with me four or five stout men. The rest of you can wait in boats under cover of the docks. If we're victorious, we'll raise a flag. If you see no flag by sunrise, you're free to go back to your homes—and I hope you'll pray for me, for I'll be dead."

But Omur was not finished. "Who might these stout men be," he persisted, "that you're so sure can stand against the guard with their pikes and armor?"

From the door, where none of them had been looking, a deep bass voice bellowed, "I, for one!"

Tarag looked up and saw Graio towering above the heads of the oar, and his heart leaped for joy. Graio strode forward on his massive legs and stood before the crowd scowling at them. "I only just got here," he declared. "I only heard Cap'n

Tarag call for stout men. But I've been locked in the dungeon in the fortress these two days past, and this night Cap'n Tarag got me out, without Nule Chespid hearin' a whisper. If the cap'n calls for stout men to dive down and cut out Bulon's heart, I'm here to do it. I'll do it alone, if I've got to. Are there any of you brave enough to stand beside me?"

The room roared with a chorus of volunteers. Down among them came little Jutie, hobbling on his bowed legs, the green lump at his shoulder intact, and beside him old Seve. Zhenuvnili had paled a little when Graio appeared. His people were her people's enemies. But she pressed her lips together and stood her ground. Tarag raised both arms high to quell the cheering. When quiet had been restored he looked at Omur, who was still seated, arms crossed. "What of it now, friend Omur? The Ship's Articles are here." From his vest Tarag drew a stiff parchment, which he unfolded and spread smooth. "Taverner," he called to Jervoe, who was standing in the back. "A pen, if you will." He turned again to Omur. "Will you be the first to sign?"

Omur stood up and glared around the room, as if defying anybody to challenge his judgment. "I'll be the second," he said. "After the Potheqi."

Chapter 20

hile the oar were lining up to put their name or mark on the Ship's Articles, Zhenuvnili slipped away upstairs to see to the nalas. She found them sitting bolt upright in bed, clinging to one another. "You're all right!" Ehlanli cried. "We were afraid you'd been murdered. What was that terrible noise?"

"No cause for alarm, dear heart. The oar were cheering for Captain Tarag, that was all. The more I see of him, the more convinced I become that we've chosen wisely. If anybody can get us home safe, it's he."

"And you like him a little too," Ehlanli said with a mischievous twinkle.

"Hush, now," Zhenuvnili said, not really displeased. "He's a foreigner, remember? Make sure everything we brought is packed again. We must be ready to leave in a few minutes." Rummaging in her own bag, she brought out a hairbrush, sat on the edge of the pallet, and began brushing her lustrous dark curls in long strokes. It seemed important in some obscure way to prepare herself thus for the impending departure. After a minute she felt Karanli's fingers on hers, and let go of the brush. The nala took over the labor, and Zhenuvnili let her head hang back, let all the tension of the past days flow out and down through her hair as Karanli stroked it, and away.

"I'm sorry Qob Qobba's dead," Karanli said. "I liked him."

"So did I. Very much."

After a few more strokes Karanli spoke again. "I haven't been a very good nala, have I?"

Zhenuvnili turned and wrapped her arms around Karanli and held her close. "Don't fret. It's all right. I love you. I only wish I could have made things easier for you."

"No, it's I who should have made things easier for you! I've been nothing but a burden."

"Each of us is a burden that others must bear, dear one. You're a burden to me at times, yes—though not so often as you fear. And I'm a burden to Salas Tarag, and he's a burden to the Berkenders, and they're a burden to the whole Island Sea. You see? It's all right to be a burden. Li doesn't mind. She carries us all in Her heart, and it burdens Her no more than a pin, or a grain of sand."

"I'll try to be better," Karanli said, wiping her eyes. "I'll try not to cause any more trouble. I wish I could be brave, like you."

"I'm not brave. I'm as frightened as you, sometimes."

"But you don't *act* frightened."

"That's because I know there are certain things I've just got to do, if I'm to get my dear Kari home safe to her nice warm Nest."

"I wish I could do something for you," Karanli said, "even if it's not anything so brave. Would you let me brush your hair every night, to remind me that I'm here to care for you?"

"That's a lovely idea. Every night, I promise. You have no idea how nice it feels."

"Can I brush it for a little while longer now?"

"I think so. Captain Tarag will let us know when it's time to leave."

Downstairs, the first groups of oar were departing for the docks. Tarag stood just inside the front door seeing them off. He had cautioned them to travel in threes and fours, and to go by different routes. As each group left he touched shoulders and clasped hands. "Remember," he said. "Stay out of sight till you see the flag." If the guard noticed any unusual activity, the whole enterprise would be in danger. Jutie and Seve had led the first group, bound not for the docks but to wake the proprietor of the nearest chandlery. They took six oar, to speed the loading of the wagon. Tarag had entrusted the fat purse to Seve. Jutie knew exactly what was needed to replenish the ship's stores, but he had never mastered the intricacies of coinage.

Pye came across the common room from the rear of the tavern. "The roaty's hitched," he told Tarag.

"Good." Tarag turned to Graio. "Feel up to lifting another chest or two, my friend? Or did your muscles waste away during your stay under the hill?"

Graio flexed his brawny shoulders. "I reckon I c'd lift anything," he declared. "What is it this time? Do you and master Pye mean not to be seen on the street?"

Tarag laughed. "No, I'll not try that trick again soon. You haven't heard, have you? The Berkenders made us a little present. They'd like it back, but we don't mean to give it to them." From his purse he drew out a gold coin, which glinted softly in the candlelight. "We've more of these. Rather a lot more."

Graio showed his wide stumps of teeth in a grin. "I might of known. Cap'n Tarag has a way of sniffin' out money when it's needed. Gettin' it from the Berks, though—that's a new one. Where is it?"

"Upstairs. I'd best come with you. Pye, stay here and see that these lads don't all rush off in a body." The stairs creaked under Graio's weight. "Be careful coming down," Tarag added. "You'll be heavier still." He tapped on the door and poked his head in. Zhenuvnili and the nalas were sitting on the pallet. "Graio is with me," he said. "The Potheqi. Should they be told before they see him?"

Zhenuvnili nodded, and explained the situation in Vli. Ehlanli feigned indifference. Karanli swallowed hard, but she neither moved nor spoke. Graio followed Tarag through to the inner room. "Are those the ones I saw the other morning?"

"Aye. They'll be coming with us."

Graio snorted a chuckle. "Next time the talk turns to strange cargos, you'll have a new one to tell."

"If I choose to speak of it. Can you lift one of these by yourself, or shall I lend a hand?"

Graio put one meaty hand under each end of the nearest chest and stood up with it cradled in his arms. "It's a sackful of straw," he boasted. "Want me to carry 'em both at once?"

"No, we can make two trips. Come on." Tarag picked up his own precious parcel from the table, and held the curtain aside for the giant.

The cart that had traveled with them from the garrison was standing in the stable-yard, a skittish little roaty hitched between the traces. When Graio thumped the chest into the cart, the animal shied, so Tarag stood stroking its narrow, bony head while Graio went back upstairs alone. The Vli would find the Potheqi underfoot often enough on the voyage—they might as well start getting used to him. In short order he was back with the second chest, and stood guard in turn while Tarag went inside. The common room was empty but for the group of oar he had selected to board the ship with him, and Jervoe the tavernkeeper hovering discreetly in the background. Bek and Med Lavorien were twin brothers; both had dark curly hair and beards, and they were shaped like small barrels, but Tarag had seen them fight, and knew they were quick on their feet. Wiry Omur, as loyal now as he had been reticent, had unstrapped from his kit a short recurved bow and a quiver of arrows, weaponry not often seen in the islands. "Will we be needin' this?" he asked.

"Aye. I'm hoping there'll be no blood shed, but we must be ready for anything. The rest of you should be armed as well." Tarag patted the dagger he had bought earlier in the evening. The hilt was wrapped in black leather that matched the tooled sheath. The blade was as long as his forearm, the edge freshly honed.

Med Lavorien rummaged in his seabag and drew out a wooden cudgel, which he tied by a thong to his belt. "Never ship out without this," he said. His brother had produced a knife nearly as long as Tarag's.

"What about you, friend Pye? I seem to remember last night you were in a tight spot, and wishing you were armed."

"Words spoken in a moment of weakness. Wits are the best weapons."

"Then mind you don't get hit on the head. Graio's out back. Wait with him. I'll be along shortly." He took the stairs two at a time and threw the door open without knocking. "We're ready," he announced. Zhenuvnili and Ehlanli picked up their pillowcases, Karanli the statue of Li, and they blew out the candles and followed.

Though the streets were far from deserted even at this late hour, the trip was uneventful. Pye led the roaty, Graio pacing beside him, and the Lavorien brothers brought up the rear. Zhenuvnili was limping again, and Tarag insisted that she ride in the cart. Here and there they passed beggars picking over the odds and ends dropped in the mass panic, though anything of value must long since have been scavenged. What guards had night duty must be in the western quarter, keeping more ambitious looters away from the still-smoldering ruins. Only once was the party forced to halt, huddling in an alley while a pack of kelg trotted noisily past. Zhenuvnili shivered, thinking again how she had lured the mnoerri to their deaths, and stared up at the silent stars. "I wish Li's Promise were stretched out above us," she said softly when the cart was creaking onward again. "The sky seems empty without it."

"You mean the Moons Road?" Tarag said. "It's up there. The world's shadow is cast on it just now, that's all."

"What do you mean? The shadows of our misdeeds?"

"No, just an ordinary shadow. It's eclipsed the way the moons are, when the sun passes behind the world. But because it's an unbroken ring, it's eclipsed every night." He wondered a little at the naivete of her question; on nights when Cheth and Gavril were near full the faint streak of the Moons Road could be seen clearly in reflected moonlight, stretching from east to west. But of course a lilith must spend most nights indoors.

Light was spilling from the little shack far out on the public pier. Leaving the others out of sight, Tarag walked out on the pier alone. At that time of night there was no traffic, and the watchman would feel it in the boards beneath his feet if a large group approached. Making no attempt at stealth, Tarag went up to the shack and poked his head in at the open top half of the door. "Evening," he said.

The watchman, a pimpled youth, stood up in the cluttered little shelter. "Evenin' to you, sar."

"Any excitement out here tonight?"

"Quiet as breath, sar."

"Good. Let's hope it stays that way. I'm returning to my ship late. The rest of the crew went before me, and took the boat. Is there another below I can have the use of?"

"Aye. Two pennies."

Tarag put the money on the counter. "Can you show me which one?"

"She's a broad-beamed dinghy with a triple notch cut in the port rail just aft of the prow. Can't miss her."

"Can you come point her out to me? I'd hate to take the wrong boat in the dark."

The lad's expression said clearly what he thought of somebody who could not locate a dinghy with a triple notch for identification, but he opened the lower half of the door and went across to the rail, where he leaned out and pointed to one of a dozen small craft moored and rocking on the swell. Foam glimmered faintly in the light of Nardis, nearing full in the west, and a crescent Gavril, attended by the near-invisible sliver of Aptar, which had just risen. "She's the fourth in from the—" Tarag brought the edge of his hand down hard on the base of the lad's skull, and caught him under the arms as he collapsed. Leave him in the shack? No, somebody might come. He dragged the body to the stairs and down out of sight. The cart came rumbling forward. He went back to the shack and rummaged until he found rope. By the time he got back to the top of the stairs, Graio was carrying the second chest down to the waterline, and Pye was leading the roaty back to land to unhitch it. On the stairs, Bek Lavorien was kneeling beside the watchman, whose eyes were wide with alarm. Bek's dagger was pressed against his neck. "What'll we do with this one?" Bek wanted to know.

"You." Tarag brandished a forefinger. "You'll not be hurt if you stay silent. Cry out, and you're dead. Understand?" The lad nodded rapidly. Tarag rolled him over, and bound and gagged him, and with Bek's help carried the trussed form down the rest of the stairs and well back on a platform that extended back between the pilings beneath the pier. The platform was crusted with dried weed, but the tide would not rise so high again for days. Graio had put the gold in the largest of the available craft, and was standing in its bottom looking up at the others. Tarag beckoned to the lilith. "You'll have to wait here," he told her. "It'll be safer."

"Must we wait alone? I've seen what manner of creatures prowl your city at night."

"There are only six of us. We've none to spare. Unless perhaps..." From the platform, he recalled, he had seen the prow of a boat back among the pilings, where no boat ought to be. He whistled twice, and in a moment oars dipped and the boat swung toward him. In it were five of his oar. He leaned over the rail toward them. "I'll need you to stand guard with our passengers," he called softly. The woman in the prow saluted, and her four companions navigated expertly among the pilings to where Zhenuvnili and the others were waiting. Already the tiny craft rode low in the water, and Tarag did not need to ask whether three more could board safely. "Two of you come up here," he said, "and wait with them under the pier. The others get back out of sight. There's a lad tied up here; if he makes a fuss, hit him on the head. And if we fail to gain the ship, I'll charge you as your final duty to see these three safe to wherever in the city they choose to go."

"Aye, Cap'n."

Briefly he debated leaving the gold behind as well. In a fight, the boat might capsize and send it to the bottom of the harbor. But the oar might find such a sum too tempting; better to trust Amera with the gold than jeopardize the safety of the lilith. His men had boarded the boat Graio had chosen, the Potheqi alone on the forward bench with an oar in each hand, the Lavorien brothers side by side on the aft bench. Tarag unhitched the mooring-rope and tossed it to Omur, who was crouched in the bow, then stepped carefully into the boat and made his way back to the stern, where he sat beside Pye. "Got my package, have we?"

"Aye, Captain." Pye nudged the parcel with a toe.

"Then pull." With a creak of oarlocks and a gurgle of water along blade, the craft nosed out into the harbor.

They headed not directly for the *Amera Smiles* but out past her into the anchorage. If a lookout were posted on deck, he would be alert for vessels approaching from shore, but might have his back to the open side of the bay. There was enough moonlight that Tarag could make out the graceful lines of his beloved ship as she hove up on the starboard. There seemed to be nobody on deck, but from such a low angle it was impossible to be sure.

"What say we tie up behind another ship," Bek Lavorien suggested, "and swim for it? They'd be less likely to spot us."

"I'd considered that. But we can't leave our cargo, and we can't spare a man to guard it. I'd also thought of swimming over alone to see if it's safe to bring a boat near. But if I stumbled and raised an alarm, you'd be too far off to come to my aid. We'll have to go in as we are now. We'll round the *Five Stars* there—" he indicated a shorter, higher-sided galley beyond the *Smiles* "—and come at her from the stern. I'm assuming they've shipped the ladder, but we can climb the steering-oar. The last open stretch we'll pull the oars and paddle. Less noise."

When they were safe on the far side of the other galley, they slid the oars from the oarlocks, careful not to knock them against the side, and those who had been rowing turned around on the benches to face forward. Graio could handle only one oar in this arrangement, and Pye went forward to sit beside him. Graio watched to see that his new bench-mate had the shaft gripped properly before he set the tempo of the stroke. They rounded the bow of the *Five Stars* and struck out across the moonlit open water on the *Amera Smiles'* starboard quarter, clearly visible if anybody had been looking in their direction.

The dip of paddles was no louder than the chuckle of the swell among the steering-oars of the ships nearby or the gurgle of nightfish breaking the surface to feed on water-stalkers. The last two dozen tadigs they paddled as little as they could, drifting slowly after each stroke and watching the stern of the ship loom up gradually above them. The windows in the stern-castle were dark.

"Oars inboard," Tarag whispered, and the oars were shipped and set down very carefully in the bottom. Graio, Med Lavo-rien, and Pye fended off the side of the ship with their bare hands, bringing the boat to a halt not quite touching her, just forward of the great blade of the steering-oar where it hung in its outboard mounting blocks. They could not moor the boat as close as they would have normally, because they could not afford to have it knocking against the side. Omur passed the rope back to the stern and Tarag drew a loop around the steering-oar, leaving plenty of slack for the boat to drift free. Better to have to swim to retrieve it than have it sound the alarm. Then he tested his weight on the steering-oar itself. It creaked in its mounting, but it was designed to withstand gale-force seas— one man's weight was nothing. Reaching up, he gripped the massive wood block of the main bracket in both hands and stepped out of the boat into the air. He lifted himself slowly by his arms until the bracket was at chest level. He was still too low to see over the rail, because the tiller end of the steering-oar extended out across the afterdeck, which formed the roof of the sterncastle. He got his arms wrapped around the shaft of the oar and drew himself up so that his knees rested on the bracket. The ship was rocking uneasily under his exertions, and he stopped and waited for the motion to smooth out. Had he been aboard and someone else trying to board her, he would have noticed the change in motion, perhaps even in his sleep. But no landlubber was likely to be so sensitive. Below him Graio gripped the bracket while two of the others pushed against the top edge of the steering-oar to keep the boat from capsizing under the giant's off-center weight. One of the chests of gold slid a little, with a scraping noise. Tarag winced, and waited for a shout to go up, but still there was no sound from the deck. Could the ship be deserted?

At last he got his head above the rail and surveyed the afterdeck. It was empty. Moving very cautiously, he levered one leg and then the other over the rail and set his feet with exquisite gentleness on the deck. Graio's head appeared beside him. Graio flipped one hand palm up in a gesture that meant "Where are they?" Tarag shrugged. Testing each plank before he put weight on it—for the guards were most likely asleep in his own cabin, directly below—he crossed to the fore rail and, crouching down so as not to silhouette himself against the stars, peered out across the main deck. The idol of Amera, at the foot of the mast, smiled up at him. He crossed his hands momentarily on his chest. That was all the greeting She would get until this was over. He unpegged the loop that held his dagger in its sheath and drew the weapon, saying a swift prayer for those he was about to kill.

Standing at the port rail gazing across the harbor at the lights of the city was one of Chespid's pikemen. He was at least six tadigs off, across open deck. They could rush him, but he would have time to cry out and waken whoever was below.

The boat bumped gently against the side of the ship. A moment later it bumped again. Tarag cursed silently in every language he knew, and one or two he did not. The pikeman raised his head to listen. Tarag and Graio had already ducked below the line of the rail. Their forms might still be visible, for the inboard rail was built of arm-thick poles, not solid board. But the man failed to look in their direction. He crossed the deck aft of the mast, heading for the point where the starboard rail abutted the wall of the sterncastle. In a moment he would be looking out over the side. Tarag glanced behind him. Bek and Med Lavorien had gained the deck—which meant that Pye and Omur were still clinging to the steering-oar.

Tarag stood up and in a single motion vaulted the afterdeck rail, landing with both feet square on the pikeman's shoulders. The man twisted as he fell, and for a moment Tarag teetered in the air, afraid he was about to be pitched overboard. He brushed the rail and fell back on the deck, landing on his side with a jarring shock that drove the breath out of him. Half stunned, he rolled onto his back and saw that the guard had picked up his fallen pike with one hand—the other arm hung limp from the shoulder, evidently dislocated or broken—and was swinging the cumbersome weapon around to bring the point into line with his assailant's throat. This was no time for half-measures. Without rising, Tarag forced his torso up from the hips and drove one heel into the man's chin, snapping the head back. The guard slumped against the rail, and the pike clunked on the deck. Tarag saw where his dagger had fallen, picked it up, and got to his feet, breathing hard. The encounter had taken only moments, and the ship was still strangely silent. Graio was coming down the ladder, the Lavorien brothers not far behind.

The cabin door swung open and another guard, helmetless and weaponless, peered out sleepily. "What in Bulon's name is going on out here?" he demanded.

Pretending to be the fallen guard, Tarag moaned inarticulately. As he had hoped, the new guard took another step forward. "Pekka?" he called. "Are you all right?"

Graio was pressed flat against the wall beside the door. He reached out, seized the man by the throat, and dragged him back against his massive chest in a crushing hug. The guard drove a heel into Graio's instep, and in retaliation Graio jammed a thumb into the line of his jaw. Tarag stepped forward. "How many more inside?" he hissed.

The guard's face was a mask of defiance. He said nothing. Graio's fingers pressed tighter into his windpipe. "How many?" Tarag repeated.

"Three," the guard rasped.

"Liar. How many?"

Another guard stumbled out the door, struggling to pull his helmet on. Med Lavorien swung his cudgel at the man's ear, pulping both the ear and three fingers that were caught between the cudgel and the helmet. The guard turned and tried to bring his pike up, but a second blow sent him sprawling to the deck.

The ship was quiet again except for the gasping breath of the guard in Graio's grip. The door stood open, and nobody else came out. Whoever was still inside was unquestionably awake now, and armed. From the captain's cabin they might easily go belowdecks and emerge from the main hatch just forward of the mast, or even make their way forward to the forecastle. And if they gained the deck with time to spare, they would use their whistles to call for help. Omur took up position on the afterdeck and unlimbered his bow. At night the shooting would be poor, but it might save them if all else failed. The Lavoriens, who knew the layout of the ship, were already moving forward to guard the hatches. Pye went past them at a run and clambered up the foredeck ladder far enough to see that nobody was lying in wait at the bow.

"Listen, you," Tarag said to the captured guard. "We have no wish to harm you. We only want the ship. Tell your friends below to lay down their arms, and you'll be let ashore safely before we bend oar. If they fight, they'll end up as those two have."

The guard glared. "That's a coward's trick. You scum are no match for trained fighting men." Graio tightened his fingers. The guard goggled, and his face purpled.

"You're in a fine spot to boast. Have you ever fought a Potheqi before? Now swear by Amera and Tha together that you'll do our bidding, or you'll never draw breath again."

Graio let a little air down the man's throat. After coughing and gagging, he managed to say, "All right, I swear. What is it you want me to do?"

"First, tell me how many are—"

Tarag never finished the sentence. Behind him a guard sprang from the main hatch, and with a shout Med Lavorien engaged him. The cudgel whirled and struck the shaft of the pike, and the shock of the blow stung both men's hands so that the weapons clattered to the deck. Roaring, Med grappled with the man. They were shoulder to shoulder, shoving, feet slipping on the deck. Med pummeled the guard's sides, but the leather body armor broke the force of the attack. A fist to his cheek cost him his footing. He went backward onto the deck, and the guard leaped on him. At the same moment three more pikemen appeared, two rushing from the forecabin door and a third clambering up out of the main hatch, whistle already at his lips.

An arrow spitted him through the neck. Arms windmilling, he fell back into the hold.

Pye, poised above the forecabin door, dropped onto the second guard who emerged there and bore him down from behind. The first of the two faced Bek Lavorien. Bek feinted left and then moved right, but the guard was too slow-witted for the trick, and merely drove his pike straight forward. The point sank into Bek's abdomen. Bek looked down at himself in surprise, clutched the pike in both hands, and sagged sideways. The point came free with a soft sucking sound.

A second arrow flew, but wide of the mark. It thunked into the forecabin wall.

The guard who had dealt with Bek turned to attack Pye from behind, but Tarag was pounding across the deck, dagger gripped ferociously, and got between them. Dancing aside from the point of the weapon, he slashed at the guard's hand on the shaft, and missed. The swing left him off-balance, and before he could get his footing the guard brought the butt of the pike around and slammed it into his side, throwing him to the deck. Momentarily everything receded. There was no pain—his hands and feet had simply gone somewhere else. He knew only that he must keep moving or die. Pushing a heel and an elbow against the deck, he rolled. As it happened, he rolled toward his attacker, which was not what the man was expecting. The point of the pike, still slick with blood, smashed into the deck a handsbreadth from Tarag's head, and before his opponent could raise the heavy weapon again Tarag had rolled in and up and driven the blade of his dagger into the flesh of the man's lower leg below the back of the knee with such force that the tip came out again through the front. He wrenched the blade downward with all his weight, and the guard toppled forward across him. Drawing his knees up, the guard groped for the injured leg with both hands and screamed a raw, high-pitched scream. Tarag crawled on his elbows toward the guard's face. The guard took a breath and began another scream. Tarag drew back his fist and drove it into the narrow gap between the chin-piece and the nose-piece of the helmet. The guard's eyes rolled up and his hands went slack, allowing the leg to loll free. Blood spurted from the horrid wound in a widening pool, black against the boards.

Rubbing his knuckle, which he had cut on the nose-piece of the helmet, Tarag got to his knees and looked around. Pye had his opponent pinned to the deck on his stomach with a knee in the small of his back, an elbow crooked around his neck, and one hand trapped in a finger-lock. The guard was trying hard not to move or make any noise, so as not to lose any fingers. Omur was standing on the afterdeck, another arrow nocked, and Graio was still clutching his captive. Bek Lavorien lay sprawled on his back, one hand pressed against the wound in his gut. Only Med and his opponent, both weaponless, were still fighting, and as Tarag watched Med got the man's arm twisted behind him, grabbed his collar, and ran him forward so that his helmet bonged against the sterncastle wall. The guard's weight sagged, but Med was not finished. He backed up and repeated the run. The guard's legs went to putty, and there was no running with him, but Med pounded the helmet twice more against the wall before letting him fall. Perhaps that was not strictly necessary, but Med had seen his brother lying gored.

Tarag got laboriously to his feet. His side was beginning to throb below the ribs, where he had been hit. He pressed two fingers to the spot. It was tender, but there was no lancing pain. He hoped nothing important had been ruptured. Nobody else popped out of the hatches. The ship was as peaceful as it had been an hour before, except for the bodies littering the deck. And looking around at the ships anchored nearby, he saw that nobody had come out on deck to see what the commotion was about. That the hideous scream had gone unheard was impossible, of course. The ships were not that far apart. Even the sounds of the fight would have carried perfectly across the water. But not a lantern had been lit. The explanation, Tarag realized, was simple: The folk who used the anchorage had little use for Chespid's taxes, or his men. They must know whose ship had been confiscated, and their sympathies would be entirely with her captain. One and all, they had rolled over in their bunks and gone back to sleep.

Ignoring, for the moment, the four fallen guards, Tarag knelt beside Bek Lavorien. Med knelt on the other side, muttering, "Oh, no, please, no." Bek's breath was fast and shallow, his face very pale. They had to pry his fingers away from the wound in order to pull back his clothing to examine it. Blood was flowing freely, but not flooding. Mercifully, the pike had gone in and come out straight, without tearing, but the triangular point made a hole far more dangerous than the clean slash of a flat blade. Med pressed his hands over the wound and kept them there as Tarag got his arms under Bek and struggled to his feet. "Want help, Cap'n?" Graio asked.

"No, I've got him." Together Tarag and Med moved toward the sterncastle. "Get the manacles from the forecabin and chain those two to the foredeck rail," Tarag told Graio. "Take their whistles if they've got them. If they start shouting, knock their heads together. Put a tourniquet around that one's leg. When you've done that, search the ship. And be careful. There may be more hiding below. Don't give them a chance to jump you."

"You'll regret this," the guard Graio was holding said nastily.

"I regret it already," Tarag said.

The door to the cabin was narrow, and they had to go sideways to get Bek through. Tarag listened in the dark for wrong noises and, hearing none, led the way to the bunk, where he laid Bek down. Med stayed beside his brother while Tarag opened the cupboard and groped on the shelf for matches. He struck one against the wall, and it flared and dropped sparks. By its light he found a candle and lit it, and from the first candle lit another, and another. The hatchway to the hold yawned black, and he shut and bolted it. He had had enough surprises for one night. From a lower shelf in the cupboard he drew out a small pottery container whose lid was secured by an iron clasp. He slid the clasp aside and removed the lid. The fragrance of the salve within cut sweetly through the bitter smoke left by the match. Though he was holding the jar quite still, the salve began pulsing and rocking from side to side as it felt the

fresh air, and deep within the thick green ointment phospho-
rescence shimmered. The substance was compounded of a rare
type of tree-blood, not quite alive but not entirely dead either.
The jar was less than half-full; perhaps on the way to Vli Holm
he would make a detour to see if the old woman who had given
it to him was still alive. Leaving the jar open on the cupboard
to breathe, he drew water from the cask into a basin, got a
clean soft cloth from the footlocker, and leaned over the bunk
to wash Bek's wound. The skin around the edges was hot, but
the blood flow was slowing. "Tear your shirt into strips," he
instructed Med. "We'll have to bind it shut."

He dipped a finger into the jar, and the salve wrapped itself
around him, tingling warm and cold at the same time. When
he daubed it on the wound, it flowed obediently, spreading
itself evenly and leaving almost no residue on his finger. He
repeated the application again and again. He had seen the salve
work on lesser wounds, closing them to a tight scar-line in
days. What limit its power might have he hoped not to discover
now. Med lifted his brother's torso far enough to slide the strips
of cloth under him so they could be tied above. Tarag made
another rag into a compress and let a little more of the salve
flow onto it, and Med tied careful knots to hold the compress
firmly but not too tightly. Tarag put the lid back on the jar and
put it back on the shelf. He had done as much as he could;
Amera would have to do the rest.

On deck, all was quiet. The two unharmed guards were
standing at the forecastle, arms raised above their shoulders,
wrists chained to the foredeck rail. They glared sullenly at
Tarag as he went to retrieve his bloody dagger. The other four
lay where they had fallen. Tarag went into the forecabin, which
was empty, and down the interior hatch to the hold. In the
gloom candles flickered, casting huge shadows. Flanked by
Pye and Omur, Graio was searching among the benches and
oars. Pye had furnished himself with a pike, and Omur kept
an arrow nocked, but there was no need. The only other occu-
pant of the hold was the guard lying dead at the foot of the
main hatch ladder. His sightless eyes stared up at the heavy
beams supporting the deck. Graio knelt and closed the eyes.

They wrestled the body up the ladder and laid it out on the deck, and Tarag went to look at the other casualties. The first guard, whom he had kicked in the chin, was dead of a broken neck. The one whose leg had been knifed had lost a great deal of blood, and would probably die before long. The one whose head Med had slammed against the wall was sleeping peacefully. And the one who had been cudgeled before he could get his helmet on was sitting up now, whimpering softly as he cradled the pulped remains of his hand.

"Two dead," Tarag said wearily. "Possibly three or four by morning. We should have tried to buy her."

"Perhaps," Pye said. "And perhaps if you had he'd have doubled the guard, and more would have died."

"I'm remembering what you said before about possessions causing unhappiness. For better or worse, she's *my* ship. But the unhappiness falls to others as well." He trudged across to the foot of the mast, where Amera was waiting. Crossing his hands on his breast, he bowed his head in prayer. *Thank you, Goddess, for returning this ship safe to me. I pray that I will prove worthy of Your kindness. I pray that You will keep Your hand upon me, that I may steer her wisely.* When he raised his head, She was smiling down at him—only a painted statue, true, but in the uncertain moonlight the face seemed as soft as a living woman's. Stepping back, he called to the others. "You've not come aboard yet!" Graio and Omur stepped to the mast, and Pye followed, watching closely to see what the ritual required. Tarag went to the starboard rail and leaned out. The boat was still drifting on its line. He waited until Graio had finished his obeisance. "Get the cargo aboard. Omur can swim for it while you get the hoist. Put it in my cabin. And mind the small parcel doesn't get wet."

"Aye, Cap'n." Graio tromped off to the forecabin to fetch the turn-block and the hoist cradle.

Tarag went back to his own cabin, where Med Lavorien was sitting gripping his brother's hand. He touched Med's shoulder. "You've got to come aboard," he said gently. "You can do it for him too. She'll understand." When Med looked down at his brother doubtfully, Tarag said, "I'll stay with him.

He'll be all right. The worst is over." Med stood up and moved away, trying to hide his tears. Tarag sat beside the bunk. Bek's face was pasty and damp with sweat. Tarag put his palm on the man's forehead and said a brief prayer. Looking around the cabin, he was pleased to see that his precious books were where he had left them. Most were rolled parchment scrolls, though a few were cut into flat sheets and stitched into bindings. There was Gidelon's treatise on the motion of astronomical bodies, and next to it a somewhat fanciful illustrated account of animal and plant life in the southern islands. So little was known of the world that even speculation was a treasure. Med came back, and Tarag went to the locker to fetch the white flag. He caught a glimpse of himself in the mirror and was shocked to see how much older he looked. Had it been only three days? Doubtless the haggardness of the reflection was only a trick of the light. He took the flag out on deck and tied it to the fore-point-reef line as high overhead as he could reach. Scanning the shore, he saw no immediate sign of activity. He waved an arm back and forth slowly several times. In a few more seconds small boats appeared at three separate points along the docks, heading in his direction.

The boat in which the guard had arrived was tied amidships on the port side. He uncoiled a rope ladder, draped it over the side, and tugged hard on its lashings to test them. Those land-lubbers might have done any sort of mischief with the lines. Then he returned to Amera to take a hasty leave, and went over the side.

About halfway back across the water, alone in the moonlight in an open boat, he felt suddenly and with great force how utterly tranquil and beautiful the harbor was. The moment was crystalline in its purity. The well-worn wood of the oars was weightless in his hands. His shoulders bunched and flexed, and his side ached dully, and breath came and went quietly in his nostrils, laden with the odors of fish, and sewage, and his own cooling sweat. Before him as he sat facing backward ships rode at anchor, dark avians whose wings were furled in sleep. And somehow it was all so completely right that to have been any-where else at that moment would have been impossible. He was suspended motionless between starry sky and foamy sea, and had always been, and would always be. From behind him at left and right came boats moving almost silently, bearing his oar toward the ship. They waved, and he waved, and both rowed on, he this last time toward the shore they had already quit.

Chapter 21

O*f all that he was leaving behind in Falnerescu, only* one thing was cause for regret—that he should be parted on bad terms from Vod Penna Osher. Osher lived by a different code, but Tarag had counted him a friend, and to bend oar betrayed by and having betrayed a friend, without speaking of it, saddened him. So when he pulled in beside the pier and saw the stiff figure of a Berkender officer, helmet tucked beneath arm, standing on the stair, his heart was glad. But a moment later he was wary. Was this a trap? Where were the lilith and the others? Instead of rowing straight up to the pier and making the boat fast, he back-oared and stood off a little in the water. Osher descended the last few steps to the platform and came forward to the edge. "Toss the rope," he said. "I'll secure it."

Tarag sat where he was. "You're not who I was expecting to see."

"Who were you expecting?"

"Some friends," Tarag said.

They let that lie between them for a moment.

"I take it you've managed to steal your ship from Chespid," Osher said.

"Is it stealing when you take back what belongs to you?"

"I'm not here to talk philosophy. I came to warn you. I don't know why I should—you're nothing but a liar and a

323

scoundrel. But perhaps if just once you listen to reason, it'll save more innocent blood being spilled."

"I'm listening."

"Shuma's not dead. She escaped your trap, just as I did."

"*My* trap? You mean when somebody threw fire from the roof?"

"I see you know about it. I expected better of you, Tarag."

"I had the word from one of your men before he died," Tarag said, exasperated. "You'd already run off. We could have used your help against Ashubeleth. He did his best to kill us all. It was his trap you were caught in, not mine."

"You're grasping at straws. Ashubeleth didn't know my men would be there. You did."

"He must have learned of it somehow. He knew who I was, when we went in with the gold, though I'd given him a false name. Where could he have gotten that sort of information? You don't suppose he was in league with Chespid, do you? Throwing fire—that'd be like Chespid."

"But that's an act of war," Osher protested.

"Not unless you can lay it at his feet. And you can't. All you can think to do is lay it at mine. You've got no evidence. You're only accusing me because you're upset at me. You can call me a scoundrel and a liar, and I'll say aye and aye. But to say I deliberately engineered the deaths of sixteen men just for the sake of a little gold—I'm hurt. I'm really hurt that you think me capable of such a thing."

"If you're as innocent as you claim, why haven't you brought the gold back? No, don't tell me. I'm sick of your lies."

"We didn't bring the gold back because we couldn't, after you made so much noise about my setting the fire. Borando would have turned me over to Chespid for trial. You know he would."

"Amnesty could have been arranged. I'm your friend, you know. I would have seen to it you weren't punished."

"Just as you saw to it I wasn't imprisoned for kidnapping."

"Well, perhaps I've not been blameless," Osher said testily. "But you're trying to make it sound as if I forced the gold on you against your will."

"You did present a temptation that was difficult to resist. Let's just say we collaborated, you and I, and should share the blame. You said something about a warning."

"Oh, that. I came to tell you your situation's hopeless. You've no hope of getting out of the harbor. Shuma has guessed that you'll try to get away. She's given the watch on the tower a description of your ship. There are two galleys standing by to intercept you when they get the signal. You'll be rammed and sunk."

"That remains to be seen. Is that all the warning, or is there more?"

"Gods, isn't that enough? You can't outmaneuver a pair of war-galleys in that little tub!"

"I wasn't planning to." Tarag smiled enigmatically.

"Then you'll stay."

"On the contrary. I've tarried too long already. It's a pity you're so perturbed at me. I was going to offer to let you come with us. I'm afraid I've more or less ruined your career, and I was hoping to make it up to you. There are some islands out there I know you'd enjoy seeing. You'd have to sleep on deck, of course—the forecabin is already spoken for. But I think we could safely say that your passage has been paid in full."

Osher gaped. "Paid in full? Why, you unconscionable—"

"I imagine Shuma will have figured out a way to shift the blame for the theft onto you. Will you be sent to prison, do you suppose, or only demoted and shipped off to some outlying garrison?"

"Why should my fate be any concern of yours?"

"Because I like you. I'm not sure why, but I do. I could ask you the same question. You didn't have to come down here to warn me, but you did."

"It's not you I'm concerned about, you ungrateful fool; it's your oar. I'm sure you've convinced them there's no danger. Have you ever seen a ship rammed?"

"Only once. Once was enough."

"Then you see how idiotic you're being. Oh, all right, I'll admit it." Osher lowered himself to sit on the edge of the platform, set his helmet beside him, and let his legs dangle over the water. "I'm concerned for you too. I don't want to see you killed needlessly. I've enjoyed conversing with you, even when we don't see eye to eye. Perhaps especially then."

"Yet you'd rather stay here than come with us."

"Oh, I won't be staying here. You're right about Shuma. If she thinks of it, she'll claim there never was a lilith, that I fabricated the whole story to get my hands on the gold. The woman's mad, Tarag. Half her hair was singed off, and it hasn't improved her humor."

"And this is whom you'd have me beg for amnesty?"

"The very best I can expect is to be sent home in disgrace."

"That doesn't sound so awful."

"You wouldn't say that if you knew my mother. She'll disown me. She can't afford to be embarrassed before the other families at Court. But first she'll spend days vilifying and belittling me, purely for her own pleasure. She's always hated me. The labor was—painful for her. She's never stopped reminding me of it. And she had too many sons already. It was a stroke of luck for us both that she was able to get me a commission. She wouldn't have done it if the Minister of the Navy hadn't promised I'd be sent overseas. Without her support I'll be summarily discharged. I'll have to take up a trade, Tarag. How will I live? I'm no good at anything."

"I'm sorry. If I'd known, I might have acted differently. But would it have been a kindness to you, to leave you dangling on that line? As it is, you're free to live your own life. Why not come with us, and see a little of the world? Somewhere out there you might find a trade that suits you, or an island you'd like to call home. And you need be in no hurry to settle on one. You can call the *Smiles* home for as long as you like."

"I wish I could. I wish it were possible. But you're forgetting—your ship is going straight to the bottom!"

"You know," Tarag said conversationally, "your great failing is that you've never learned to trust people. Especially me. You persist in telling me that I'm wrong, that I can't possibly do what I say I mean to do. And when I've gone ahead and done it, do you learn from your mistake? No. You come straight back and tell me I can't possibly do something else. Am I

right? Three days ago you were telling me in no uncertain terms
that I could never, under any circumstances, hope to come face
to face with the lilith. You recall the occasion?"

"Yes, of course. But what's that got to do with your ship
being rammed?"

Instead of answering, Tarag beckoned at a spot past Osher's
shoulder. Zhenuvnili and the nalas came forward across the
platform, carrying their baggage, followed by the two oar who
had been left to guard them. Tarag guided the boat in to the
edge and steadied it while his passengers, one by one, embarked.

Osher's perplexity mutated by stages into astonishment.
"You're not—This can't be—How did—Why haven't—"

"I told you the forecabin was already spoken for. Some
people, you see, are capable of acting on trust. Are you coming,
or not? Do you know, I've just realized I haven't yet told you
my idea about why there are so many legends of our having
been sent down from an ancestral kingdom in the sky. I was
examining some human bones not long ago, and I thought to
compare them to animal bones. I found that there are some
quite distinct—"

"Bones? What have bones got to do with legends?"

"Would you like to find out? Or would you rather go back
and face your mother? What's it to be?"

"Then you really do know how to get past Shuma's galleys?"

"Do you trust me, or don't you?"

"Oh, sink it, all right." Osher slid off the edge of the platform into the boat, which rocked precariously.

"Sit down, before you drown us all."

"Wait just a minute. Hand me an oar." Osher's helmet was
still sitting on the dock, its sightless eyeholes staring reproach-
fully at him. He gripped the oar like a bat and, after taking
careful aim, swung the blade at the helmet with all his strength.
The helmet clanged beautifully and flew off in a flat arc that
ended in a clean splash. With great dignity he handed back the
oar and sat down beside Tarag in the stern. "Row on," he said.

By that time the sea around the *Amera Smiles* was cluttered
with a considerable number of small boats. Three teams of oar
were moving among them, tying them bow to stern to tow them

back to land. Tarag's craft wove a course through the maze. "You know our customs?" Tarag asked Osher. "You know how to come aboard?"

"I'm not sure."

"Cross your hands on your chest like this, the right hand to the inside above the heart, the left hand over it. The Goddess is at the foot of the mast. You go straight to Her and bow your head before Her like this before you do *anything* else on the ship, understand? You don't stop to wipe your nose. If you're pious, you don't even breathe. I'll go first. Watch me, and do as I do." He turned to the lilith. "They know what to do, don't they?"

"Yes, of course."

"They're not going to make trouble? Amera isn't Li."

Zhenuvnili smiled at him. "Don't be silly," she said. "Of course Amera is Li."

For once in his life, Salas Tarag could think of nothing whatever to say.

The deck was a hive of activity. Sacks and barrels of provisions, stacked by the hatch, were being carried below and stowed in accordance with Jutie's babbled stream of instructions. "Careful, careful!" the little man cried, hopping from one foot to the other. "Casks of ale, yes, yes!" Another team had gone aloft to inspect the rigging. When the new arrivals had boarded properly, Tarag climbed the ladder to the afterdeck, where Graio was standing, hands on hips, keeping an eye on everything in the captain's absence.

"How are we doing?" Tarag asked.

"The cargo's stowed in your cabin," Graio reported. "All the oar are aboard, except for those that are gettin' the boats clear. Two or three were for slittin' the throats of the guard and pitchin' 'em overboard, but I persuaded 'em you'd not look kindly on it. A couple of others have asked whether we might haul anchor and bend for it now, while it's still dark. If the Berkenders see us comin', they'll have time to blockade the channel."

"It's worse than that, I'm afraid. They mean to ram us. But I'd rather chance that than try to run the ship through a crowded anchorage in the dark. We'd lose half our oars, if we weren't stove in. We'll have to wait for first light. It won't be long." In the east, the red tip of the Moons Road was already rising.

"I've seen you this calm before," Graio said. "You've got a plan."

"Let's say I'm hoping for a little help from a friend. In the meantime, best not talk of ramming. We don't want a mutiny. I'll caution Osher to be silent as well."

"I was wonderin' what he's doin' aboard."

"He's decided to give up his military career and throw in with us."

Graio snorted. "That wooden shirt? I see the plan. He's a hostage. You're plannin' to lash him to the prow."

"That's a possibility I hadn't considered," Tarag said slowly. "If all else fails . . . Oh, I nearly forgot. How's Bek Lavorien?"

"Feverish. His brother's with him. Your cabin'll be a mite crowded until he gets better."

"Oh, I don't mind. I'll sleep on deck. But our passengers can't. I've got to show them their accommodations." Zhenuv-nili and the nalas were still standing on the main deck, looking a little lost. Tarag went down the ladder to join them. "You'll have to forgive my ignoring you."

"I'm sure you have many things to attend to."

"We'll have our hands full for the next hour, yes. Let me show you to your cabin. I'm sure you'd like to rest and unpack. When we get underway, I'd be honored to have you join me on the afterdeck."

"You're sure it wouldn't be better for me to stay out of sight?"

"Positive."

"And I won't be in the way? Very well, then. I think I'd like that."

The forecabin was smaller than the one they had shared on the voyage out. The sloping sides of the prow pressed close, and there were four narrow bunks. A good deal of gear was stowed here as well, including a chest of Graio's belongings that he had had no time to remove. "You'll have to try to make it homey," Tarag apologized, lighting a candle. "There were

more furnishings until lately. I ran short of cash. At the next
port we'll pick up a table and some chairs."

Zhenuvnili looked around at the bare wood beams and the
clutter. "Actually, this is very nice," she said. "We'll manage."
As Tarag shut the door, she was already showing Karanli a
niche the right size for the statue of Li.

The deck was quieter now. Most of the supplies had been
stowed, and many of the oar had gone below to wrangle over
who would bench with whom. Old Seve was on the afterdeck
sharing a word with the sturdy young seaman who would man
the helm. Osher and Pye were standing over Chespid's guards,
who sat or lay in the lee of the port rail. Those who were alive
were bound and gagged; the other two lay sprawled. Tarag
looked down at the man whose leg he had ripped open. Somebody had wrapped the leg, and dark blood had soaked through
the bandage.

"You haven't spoken to anyone of Shuma's plans?" Tarag
said to Osher.

"No, but I'm not—"

"Good. Then don't. We don't want a panic."

"I'm not sure but what I ought to swim for it."

"There's the rail. I only wish I could be there to hear you
explain what happened to your helmet."

One by one four men and a woman came over the rail at
the head of the rope ladder and padded across barefoot to the
idol. A second woman, an impish wench he had seen that night
for the first time, stopped on the ladder with her head above
the rail. Seeing Tarag, she flashed her teeth in a grin. "Boats
away, Cap'n. Shall I kick this last one free?"

He returned her grin. It never hurt to be on good terms with
the crew. "No, you can come aboard. We've a use for it yet.
You can give us a hand, if you will." She extended her hand,
and he grasped it—it was warm and dry, broad and calloused—
and hauled her inboard. Her hips swayed as she crossed to the
mast, and she cast a swift glance back over her shoulder and
wrinkled her nose coquettishly when she saw him watching
her. Tarag stroked his beard and savored a lustful impulse. One

way or another, the voyage should prove pleasant. "Time to get this lot into the boat," he said when she returned.

"Should they take their leave of the Goddess," Pye asked, "or should we just heave them over the side?"

"I don't suppose they came aboard proper, so there'd be no harm if they left the same way. But maybe we've taught them manners. You." He nudged one of the uninjured guards with his toe. "If we untie your arms, will you bow before Amera, or will you make trouble?"

The guard mumbled through his gag. By the look in his eyes, he was saying something obscene.

"All right. Have it your way." Tarag turned to Pye and Osher. "You two climb down into the boat. The lass and I will lower them to you."

Osher started straight for the rope ladder, but Pye collared him. Embarrassed, Osher went through the ritual. "Seems a lot of trouble to go through every time you want to step ashore for a bit," he said as his feet thumped in the bottom of the boat.

"It's a lot of trouble to drop your pants when nature calls," Pye replied. "But you get used to doing it, if you want to keep your friends."

At the rail above them, Tarag and the young woman appeared with the first of the guards. A rope was looped beneath his armpits, and they lowered him over the side like a sack. Between them Pye and Osher got him into the boat, though they nearly swamped it in the process. They untied the rope and laid the unconscious form in the bottom. With that inert weight to stabilize the craft, the second arrival went easier, the third easier still. Up above, Tarag was ushering each of the living guards before Amera and forcibly bowing the man's head before hustling him to the rail. The dead he saved for last, and those he did not take to the mast. It would be no reverence to the Goddess to present Her with corpses. They had already taken their leave.

When the dead and the living lay pressed together in the bottom of the boat, Tarag leaned over the rail. "One of you has got to stay down there," he called. "We'll be lifting anchor at first light, and somebody's got to row the boat free before we unship oar, so we won't smash it."

Osher and Pye looked at one another. Osher saw that he was being given a chance to back out gracefully. He could simply row the boat back to shore. Given the temptation, he probably would. "Do you mind?" he asked Pye. "It may sound odd coming from a military man, but dead people make me quite ill."

"That's all right," Pye said. "I'll take care of it." So it was Osher who climbed the ladder.

Tarag went aft to join Seve and the helmsman. From here he could see all the great bowl of sky. Nardis was westering, Gavril and Aptar high in the east. The Moons Road was a silver streak arching nearly to the zenith, and at its base the sky was pale. Although he knew the answer, Tarag asked Seve, "How's the tide running?"

"Just at crest, Cap'n. Ebbing til midmorning."

"We'll have to bring her about. She's headed the wrong way."

"Aye, sir. We've enough room to starboard back-oar, and once we're about there's a clear channel, as long as the lads are ready to pull inboard at the call."

"How did you ever come to take up life on land?" Tarag asked. "You're born to this."

"Me daughter," Seve explained. "She says I'm too old." He stopped to cough, then spat over the side. "Made me get a job in that stinkin' hole, so she could 'care for me,' she says. The air down there were worse than her care could salve."

"Well, it's a blessing you let her have her way, else I'd never have gotten out. You can thank the Goddess for showing you a bit of what you missed by living a life at sea, eh?"

"Aye. Aye that."

Osher came up the ladder to the afterdeck, where he stood feeling ill at ease, an intruder in Tarag's domain. He wandered about in the somewhat restricted area, looking up at the lines to the yard and peering over the side at the shaft of the steering-oar. "We're bound for Vli Holm, are we?" he said at last.

"Aye. I'm wondering whether the day has come for a foreign

ship to make port there. I'll have to sound our passenger out
to see if she's got the influence to protect us. Something's
bothering you, is it?"

"Well, yes. If I'm to live on the sea—and it seems I am—
I'd like to understand the business with the statue. I'd heard
of it, but I'd never imagined anybody took it so seriously. What
does it mean? Why do you do it?"

"Now, there's a question. I knew I was going to be glad to
have you along. Why do seafolk bow to their idols?" He squinted
at the eastern horizon, and raised his nose to sniff the air. "Most
would say it's that the Goddess protects us from the dangers
of the sea. Not just Amera, either. I've seen many a deity at
the mast, including some who are no longer worshipped anywhere on land, if they ever were. But if that's not enough
explanation for you, consider this: Coming aboard proper
reminds you that it's a ship you're on. A ship is not like a
house, though you can live in either, and they're both made
of wood. A house you can let fall down around you, and the
roof will still keep off most of the rain. But a ship has got to
be kept up. If the lines are tangled, the sail won't reef in a
squall, and you may lose your mast. If the hull is matted with
weed, you can pull all day and make no headway. If the fresh
water goes bad, you'll have nothing to drink. So coming aboard
proper is a reminder that here everything has got to be done
proper. It means your life."

"It's like military discipline," Osher said, "but you impose
it on yourselves."

"Didn't I tell you the common oar has more wit than you
give him credit for? I'm also of a mind of the time, though
perhaps now is not the best moment to speak of it, when a ship
I was benching was driven onto a rock in a storm, and broke
up. We all had to swim for it. And all the time I was in the
water, thrashing about trying to keep my head up for air, I was
mindful that I hadn't taken proper leave of the ship. It seemed
the Goddess Herself was there with me in the water, holding
me afloat in Her hand, because She wanted Her respects paid.
In order to take my leave proper, I *had* to get back to land.
You see?"

"Not really. Or perhaps I do. I'm not sure."

"Then don't worry about it. Just do it. All you need concern yourself with is that if you're disrespectful of the Goddess, the crew will cheerfully throw you overboard, no matter if we're clean out of sight of land, and there'll be precious little I can do to stop them."

Tarag's head jerked to the left. On the public pier two lanterns had flared alight. As those on the ship watched in apprehensive silence, the lanterns bobbed down the stairs toward the platform where the hapless watchman was still lying bound. The yellow sparks flickered among the pilings, and a moment later the shrill whistles of the guard echoed across the water.

The ships that lay to either side were now dark bulks against the gray of approaching day—enough light to steer by. "Get down there," Tarag snapped to Osher, "and tell Pye to untie that boat and kick it as wide as he can." Osher jumped for the main deck. "Weigh anchor," Tarag called. At the winch at the bow, four oar leaned into the handles, and turn by turn lifted the thick rope dripping from the sea.

Osher leaned over the rail. "Kick her free!" But there was no boat below him, and he stared confused at the empty water.

Pye had anticipated the order. On hearing the whistles he had jerked the mooring-line free, unlimbered oar, and begun rowing in the direction of the docks. After half a dozen quick strokes, he dropped the oar and gave the boat an extra kick as he dived overboard. The bottom of the rope ladder seemed a very long way off; for all his accomplishments, Pye was not a good swimmer. But at last he grasped it and pulled himself up far enough to cling, spitting and gasping.

Seeing the wet head at the waterline, Osher lifted his arm and waved to Tarag. "Oar outboard," Tarag called. "Unship those broomsticks, Graio, and make it quick!" Belowdecks, Graio repeated the order, and thirty oars, fifteen starboard and fifteen port, rattled out the oarlocks and dipped, more or less in unison, into the sea.

"Starboard back-oar, port forward. Bring her about!"

Again Graio relayed the word. As the oar reached backstroke, he struck the great drum. The port oar pulled and the starboard oar pushed, and with a creak of beams and a lapping of water the ship began ponderously to rotate, bow swinging away from the city in the direction of the northern marsh. Another drum-stroke and she came about further, rocking from side to side. Pye, still clinging to the rope ladder, got his head ducked. He came up spluttering and began to climb. On either side of him the great shafts of the oars were thumping and groaning on their pins. He climbed between two of them and got one arm over the rail, just in time to see the high arc of the Moons Road come around the bow, standing silver in the golden flush of dawn. Below him the oars reversed direction, vantage, the majestic power of the galley was palpable. He felt back-oar to steady the ship in the water. port starboard pulled together, and the the rush of movement as the sea gurgled along the hull. He climbed the rail and made wet footprints past Osher to the idol, where he crossed hands on chest and bowed reverently. In Eloia they preferred their gods invisible, but he had left Eloia a long time ago.

Zhenuvnili came out of the forecabin onto the deck. The sky overhead was gray, but still a few stars glimmered faintly in the west; Nardis was setting. On the afterdeck Salas Tarag, standing between the helmsman and the old man she had seen at the tavern, shone with the light of dawn on his face. She went to join him.

On their starboard quarter a guard cutter was heading out from a pier near where the alarm had gone up, cutting a smart wake. Tarag noted its presence, but it was no more than a nuisance. The real danger lay ahead. He leaned on the fore-rail of the afterdeck, gripping it hard. Ahead, as they slid past the last ships in the anchorage, lay the channel, and off to the right of the channel stood the tall watchtower of the Berkender garrison, the beautiful open latticework of its wooden structure belying its sinister function. He did not see the signal being passed down from the tower, but suddenly the prows of two huge war-galleys appeared at the end of the breakwater, moving steadily outward, and across the water rolled the ominous beat of two new drums.

Any other captain would have called down for double-stroke. But Tarag knew double-stroke would not save him. The Berkenders could reach the channel before him no matter what he did. Better to save the lads' strength: Either they would be rowing all day, or they would need it to swim.

Zhenuvnili mounted the ladder to stand beside him, Pye and Osher at her heels. "They've seen us," she said unnecessarily.

"Aye." Tarag was looking hard at the glare-shimmering surface of the bay.

"Can we outrun them?"

"No."

"C—er falling behind, sir," Seve said. "S——"

"I know." Tarag d—— ——

The day was brightening with every stroke of the drum, the ships sliding toward one another along the glassy swell. But a galley is slow at its fleetest, and the harbor was large. They all continued on their courses for some time, until at last the Berkenders came about, one on each side of the channel, in a well-drilled maneuver. Seve was staring terrified at the warships' sharp rams jutting forward at the waterline, cutting their own wake. "Maybe we ought to back-oar, Cap'n," he ventured. "They'll be on us in another dozen strokes."

Tarag said nothing, only stood watching the water. There, and there. Yes.

"This is madness," Osher said. He turned as if to run for the rail.

Tarag put out a hand to restrain him. "Watch," he said.

The nearer of the Berkender ships began its ramming run. Two layers of oars dipped and rose in terrifying precision, and the ram cut the water so it bled white foam.

But before the ship could gain ramming speed, the well-drilled stroke faltered. Oars dipped and rose crookedly, waved wildly high in the air, crashed and tangled among one another, and slid outward into the water, where they bobbed and rolled. "Starboard helm," Tarag ordered, and the *Amera Smiles* angled past the now-helpless galley. Its deck was too high for them to be certain, but there seemed to be nobody at the helm.

The second warship began its run. And the same thing happened. The oar lost their stroke, a seaman's nightmare, and the oars dropped and dragged so the ship lost headway and wallowed in the swell. Tarag did not need to call a course correction; Graio's drum continued its pulse, and they glided up along the silent vessel, passing it so close they could have hit it with a thrown rock. After gawking, Osher turned to stare at Tarag, and one by one the others did the same. Tarag smiled, pleased, and the first rays of the rising sun cut through the rope to bathe his face. Without saying a word, he strode to the starboard rail and looked out over the water. In the low chop astern the Berkender ship, half a dozen round green heads were bobbing. A green arm with webbed fingers was raised in greeting. Tarag waved back. "I thank you, my friend," he shouted.

ing, frowning in irritation. "I you've got some perfectly reasonable

They all could just happened."

friends in low places," Tarag said. "It occurred to last night that Shuma might not be eager to see our stern, so in the course of running a few errands I went down to the water and made some arrangements of my own."

"But those were duongnué!"

"Bravely was quite excited when I'd gotten him to understand this new tactic," Tarag said. "Now that it's worked so well, I fancy your navy will hear of it again. That's no longer any concern of yours, of course."

"Except for the men who may die."

"Except for the men who may die," Tarag agreed.

Zhenuvnili was gazing at the sunrise. Her lip still burned where the kelg had struck her, her shoulder and hip and ankle were bruised, and she had left behind one whom she had loved, who was dead. But somehow the sweetness of the morning air made the hurt a little easier. She would be glad to get home.

In her pocket her fingers brushed the brooch she had taken from the dressing-table the day before. She drew it out. Li sat

Jim Aikin

serene in the amber oval. After pressing the brooch between her palms for a moment, she held it out to Tarag. "This was the sign I brought for you," she said.

He met her eyes, and saw in them some expression he could not quite fathom. Gratitude? Or a promise? He pressed her hand and the brooch between both of his; the moment stretched out, tingling and uncertain. He drew the brooch gently from her. "I've got something for you too. Wait here. I'll be right back."

Bounding down the ladder, he burst into his cabin. In candlelight outspoken by the blue glow of impending day, Med Lavorien was sitting with his brother. Treading more softly, Tarag went to the bunk and rested his hand on Med's shoulder. Bek was awake, his eyes milky with pain but alert. His lips moved, and though there was no sound he said to him,
"I'll be all right."

Tarag sought the man's hand and squeezed.

The parcel was where Graio had promised it would be. He scooped it up and strode back out on deck. Up the ladder and fumbling at the twine in his eagerness, he spread the canvas wide on the afterdeck and rummaged among the treasures. New books he had had an eye on for aptarnes, but had lacked the money to buy. A little wooden box glinting with dozens of assorted lenses—a street-vendor's entire store. Tarag had not forgotten the idea of making a distance-glass out of two reading glasses. A new pair of sandals for himself, to replace the pair he had left at the bottom of the watery passage under the fortress. And a thick, soft scarf, dyed in swirling violets and indigoes, that billowed large as a blanket in the breeze when he unfolded it and let it flutter across the deck.

"It's very beautiful," Zhenuvnili said.

He gathered up the scarf and held it out to her, and when she made no move to take it but only bowed her head, he lifted it, a bit awkwardly, and draped it across her shoulders as a shawl.

She met his eyes again—hers were dark, and said everything and nothing. "I shall count it among my dearest treasures," she said. But of course that might only be a phrase liliths always used when anybody gave them anything. Turning, she descended the ladder with regal grace and crossed the deck. Pausing at the idol, she touched herself briefly, forehead, heart, groin, and then went slowly on toward her cabin, limping just perceptibly, not looking back. They all watched her go, Tarag and Seve and the helmsman and Osher and Pye.

"Remarkable," Pye said.

Tarag raised his nose to sample the air. The wind was southerly, and steady, and spiced with greenwood spores, which promised fair skies. Good. They could raise sail and run north around the island, the short way west. And by the color of the deeps, they would have all the fish they could eat for days. The pickled stores could stay sealed.

He wrapped the parcel again, tied it, and tucked it under his arm. Standing, he saw a small avian spiraling down out of the blue sky, wings outspread in a controlled glide. With a ——————— back-oared and dropped neatly to wrap its ——————— it was a baby mnoerri, a voracious little bundle not much more intelligent than a roaty. But someday, if it lived long enough, it would find an island to settle on, and learn to speak and fashion crude implements, and come together in a circle with its kind under a quadruple moon.

The mnoerri shifted its footing on the yard and opened its toothy mouth in a satisfied "raaaakkkhh." Tarag frowned at it. Why did avians have to croak like that? Shouldn't they warble, or chirp, or something?

The mnoerri spread its wings wide and waved them forward and back languidly. Tarag watched the motion, fascinated. The jointed bones were traced as clearly under the translucent skin flaps as little sticks of wood. He scratched his beard. One ought to be able to build a machine out of wood, jointed like that and covered with light canvas brailed with twine. If the joints were hinged properly with leather hinges to a pair of oarhandles, one could sit on a little seat in the middle and work the oars and make the wings move. What an extraordinary idea! "Jutie!" he called. "Ho, Jutie! Bring me some little sticks of wood, handfuls of them, and some bits of scrap twine!" A model, first, to see how it fit together. And if the model worked, perhaps they would rig up a full-sized flying-machine on the deck of the *Amera Smiles*, and one day Salas Tarag would row away into the sky.

About the Author

Born in Decatur, Illinois, in 1948, Jim Aikin has lived in the San Francisco Bay area since 1960. He attended Reed College and, later, the University of California at Berkeley, where he learned how to take the English language apart and put it back together again in a muddy trench in the dark. After a brief and spotty career playing bass guitar in several long-forgotten bands, he was hired as an assistant editor at *Keyboard* magazine, where for the last ten years he has been doing feature-length interviews with musicians like Keith Jarrett, Brian Eno, and Glenn Gould, reviewing records and electronic music equipment, transcribing recorded jazz piano solos into sheet music form, and proofing a never-ending stream of galleys. He lives alone in an apartment full of books and electronic music equipment. *Walk the Moons Road* is his first novel.

THE HEECHEE SAGA

an epic galactic trilogy
by
FREDERICK POHL

Available at your bookstore or use this coupon.

____**GATEWAY**   31859   2.95
The HUGO and NEBULA award-winner! Rich man or dead man—those were the choices
that Gateway offered, and Robinette Broadhead happily took his chances.

____**BEYOND THE BLUE EVENT HORIZON**   27535   2.50
In the critically acclaimed sequel to GATEWAY, Pohl unlocks the mystery of who the
Heechee are, and what they want from Man.

____**HEECHEE RENDEZVOUS**   30055   3.50
In the suspense-filled conclusion to THE HEECHEE SAGA, Broadhead is forced to make
one last voyage into space—where the Heechee are waiting.

 BALLANTINE MAIL SALES
Dept. TA, 201 E. 50th St., New York, N.Y. 10022

Please send me the BALLANTINE or DEL REY BOOKS I have checked
above. I am enclosing $.................(add 50¢ per copy to cover postage and
handling). Send check or money order—no cash or C.O.D.'s please. Prices
and numbers are subject to change without notice. Valid in U.S. only. All
orders are subject to availability of books.

Name_____

Address_____

City_____State_____Zip Code_____

08   Allow at least 4 weeks for delivery.   TA-91